Praise for Isabel Ashdown's Writing

'Fiendishly clever' – *Red*, Best Crime & Thriller Novels Autumn 2019

'So atmospheric' – *Crime Monthly*

'Had me gripped throughout, with a heroine worth rooting for' – Ian Rankin, author

'Beautifully crafted and satisfying' – Mari Hannah, author

'Satisfying on every level' – Elly Griffiths, author

'Tense, edgy and nerve-wracking. I loved it!' – Helen Fields, author

'Beautifully written . . . original and compelling' – Howard Linskey, author

'A dark, unrelenting psychological thrill ride' – *Publishers Weekly*

'A gripping read' – *Sunday Independent* (Ireland)

'A heart in your mouth read' – *Red*

'A taut thriller' – Nina Pottell for *Prima*

'It's a̶ ̶ ̶ ̶ ̶ ̶ ̶ ̶ ̶ ̶ ̶ ̶ *he Sun*

33 Women

ISABEL ASHDOWN

Isabel Ashdown was born in London and grew up on the south coast of England. Since her award-winning debut *Glasshopper* was released in 2009, she has written a further seven novels, with two of her dark family thrillers shortlisted in the prestigious Dead Good Reader Awards. She is a full-time novelist, a Royal Literary Fund associate, and a regular creative writing host at the Theakston Old Peculier Crime Writing Festival in Harrogate. *33 Women* is her eighth novel, set in historic Arundel, not far from where she lives.

For news, previews and book prizes, join Isabel's newsletter at
www.isabelashdown.com

You can also find Isabel on:
🐦 @IsabelAshdown
📷 @isabelashdown_writer
🇫 IsabelAshdownBooks

#33Women

By Isabel Ashdown

Glasshopper
Hurry Up and Wait
Summer of '76
Flight
Little Sister
Beautiful Liars
Lake Child

33 Women

ISABEL ASHDOWN

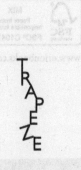

First published in Great Britain in 2020 by Trapeze
an imprint of The Orion Publishing Group Ltd
Carmelite House, 50 Victoria Embankment
London EC4Y 0DZ

An Hachette UK Company

1 3 5 7 9 10 8 6 4 2

A CIP catalogue record for this book is
available from the British Library.

ISBN (Mass Market Paperback) 978 1409 17895 8
ISBN (eBook) 978 1409 17896 5

Printed and bound in Great Britain by A.

For all the good women I've known, and all the good men

AUTHOR'S NOTE

When I wrote this novel back in 2019, the world was a very different place.

33 Women is a story about families separated by circumstance, set, in part, in an isolated community. It is a secretive place; an unusual way of life. But, beyond the walls of the commune, the day-to-day goes on. Shops and cafés are open for trade. Rush-hour train carriages offer standing room only. Old friends embrace in public places. Lovers meet in secret rendezvous. The normal stuff of normal life – or, I reflect now, life as we once knew it.

The story takes place in May 2020, which (as I write this) is the present day, and it is clear that the backdrop I imagined a year ago bears little resemblance to society as we recognise it now. In *33 Women*, there is no pandemic, no social distancing and no lockdown. My characters move about unrestricted, free of face coverings, absent of the caution we have all lately been forced to adopt.

And so, I ask you to suspend what you know about this strangest of times and read on as though this dreadful virus had never visited at all. I hope you enjoy reading *33 Women* as much as I enjoyed writing it.

Isabel Ashdown
May 2020

'I ask no favors for my sex. I surrender not our claim to equality. All I ask of our brethren is, that they will take their feet from off our necks, and permit us to stand upright on that ground which God designed us to occupy.'

— Sarah Moore Grimké, 1837

THE SISTERS OF TWO CROSS FARM:
CODE OF CONDUCT

1. *Come as yourself, sister, whoever that may be.*
2. *No man shall enter through the gates of our community.*
3. *In all things, sisters are equal.*
4. *Trust is implicit, loyalty a given.*
5. *33 will be the number at our table.*
6. *6 will be the number of our Founding Sisters, the caretakers of our community.*
7. *All who dwell here must first shed their limpets, who or whatever they may be.*
8. *Come for a day or stay forever, but all must come in the spirit of sisterhood.*
9. *Every sister will be afforded a week to weep and a lifetime to grow.*
10. *Each sister will rise with the sun and rest with the moon.*
11. *She will labour six days out of seven for her weekly shelter.*
12. *Banishment is final.*

* * *

THE SISTERS OF TWO CROSS FARM

CODE OF CONDUCT

1. VANESSA

There is a moment in which pain and fear slips into acceptance.

I am there now, and all around me is still, a midnight hush of shock and awe. No more can I feel the weight of fists slamming into my jaw, or the snap of my ribs, or even the gasping pressure of fingers closing around my throat. In fact, I barely feel a thing, just the frost-damp grass beneath my palms and the cool white whisper of my breath as it slips through my broken lips. Above me, the stars are out, the indigo sky quite lit up by them, and, as white wings soar by, it occurs to me that they are silent witnesses to my passing. I wonder if I should feel afraid.

But then I am sixteen again; I see Celine and Pip shrouded in sunlight at the kitchen table, laying out bread for cheese on toast, and Celine is cutting the crusts off Pip's because she won't eat them, and drizzling Worcester sauce on mine because that's how I like it. And I'm standing there in the doorway in my school uniform, biting down on my lip because I love these two so much – I'm feeling *too* much – and it's chaos inside my

3

head; and now we're sitting on the back steps, arranged like pot plants, one-two-three, eating our toast and looking out across the courtyard, naïvely planning summer day trips and meal rotas, and Celine is saying 'Delilah who?' and the light is radiating through Pip's scruffy blonde hair and she's sticking two fingers in the air, blowing raspberries and we're laughing, all three of us through tears, and we have each other and we'll cling to that, and we'll never walk away . . .

A sound, a *thud* like iron against hard earth, brings me back to this starry night, and even through my inertia fresh panic grips me. How will they know how to find me? How will my sisters know where to look?

The night sky is obscured as women gather over me, their faces lined with age, eyes moving closer, closer, closer still, testing me for life. Whether they see it or not, I wish them only love in this final breath, before their eyes, like the stars, fade to nothing.

2. CELINE

Present day, May 2020

From behind dark shades, Celine's eyes skate over the shimmering harbour as she hurtles along the motorway, briefly glimpsing the jaunty sway of yachts and dinghies on the water. It's a fleeting scene that appears entirely unreal to her, like a frame from a movie. She takes a deep, conscious breath and tries to anchor herself in the present, all the while sensing herself as though viewed from afar: glossy-curled, thirty-something, crisp white sleeves rolled back, her businesslike appearance strangely at odds with the 1970s camper van she drives.

As the harbour gives way to industrial units, Celine feels time both slowing and speeding up, but the sensation is not unpleasant and there is no real panic attached, just a sort of low-level sadness or regret. *Derealisation*, a therapist once described it to her, this feeling of detachment, but Celine's not convinced. She doesn't go in for labels, and her time with the therapist came to an end after just two or three sessions, the experience leaving her feeling worse than when she'd started. She prefers to think of herself as just very slightly fucked-up, a diagnosis which is far less complicated, being one which requires no particular treatment. It isn't that she *doesn't* feel things, more that she doesn't always allow herself to react to them or let her feelings be seen. She's found life to be easier that way, and it's not a big deal.

Now, she squints against the sunlight and concentrates on the fast-moving traffic ahead. She's on her way to her mother Delilah's place in Arundel, and she swallows the reality of it like a stone, masochistically forcing herself to recall the last time they met, in a café in Tarrant Street ten years earlier, on a warm May day not unlike this one. On that day, despite a two-year gap since they'd last seen each other, Delilah had skirted around difficult topics like her abrupt departure from Celine's life, or Vanessa's death, instead making polite conversation across artfully mismatched teacups and a pretty tower of scones. At one point Celine had tried to broach the subject of the police investigation, to find out if her mother had heard anything more about her sister's now cold case, but Delilah had waved the unpleasant subject away, her fixed poise never once giving any clue to the inner workings of her mind. If anyone looked through the window and saw us now, Celine had thought at the time, they would view us unmistakably as mother and daughter, so alike with our dark eyes and curls; and they would think, *how lovely*. Just as that thought had landed, there'd been a rap on the glass beside them and there really *had been* someone looking in at them – a man in a smart coat and hat – and it was as though Celine had conjured him up by her thoughts alone. 'Oh, darling, time to go,' her mother had sighed, breathlessly grazing Celine's cheek with hers, the mere scent of her Shalimar perfume flattening any objection Celine might have made. 'Let's do this again, shall we?' she'd said, and, just like that, she'd vanished. But for the twenty-pound note lying crumpled on the lace tablecloth, she might never have been there at all.

Desperate to get out of that café, Celine had left without waiting for her change and navigated her way down to the river, where she'd sat on a bench overlooking the pleasure boats and wept. These would be the last tears she ever shed for Delilah, she had sworn, the woman she'd once called Mum.

At some point along this interminable stretch of road, a sign welcomes Celine from Hampshire into West Sussex, and a glance at her phone's satnav confirms she has just thirty-four minutes until she arrives – just half an hour to get her emotions in line and work out what she's meant to feel. It's at times like these that she wishes she were more like her younger sister, Pip. Pip, who will be waiting for her at the end of this journey, neither judging nor feeling judged, just being who she really is, feeling what she really feels. Right now, Celine feels close to nothing, and yet, physically, she is acutely aware of *every* sensation: the sharp, blinding glare of the sun's rays; the stretch of her jeans over aching knees; the irritable prickle of rosacea across her cheekbones as her skin responds to the unseasonal heat of the van. More than anything, there's the thud of her heart, which seems to grow in volume and momentum as the miles tick away.

She skirts past the market town of Chichester, rumbling along the A27 in her van, passing signs for Sussex hamlets and villages with mouthful names like Crockerhill and Walberton. Where the roads begin to narrow, the signposts become more local in theme – the arboretum, the trout farm, the castle and lido – and when the satnav directs her off the main road, down a secluded country lane, she knows she must be close. She knew the place was out of town, but she hadn't anticipated this. The lane quickly becomes an unmade track, and she finds herself driving at a snail's pace to protect the camper van's suspension, her stomach clenching at every pothole, lurching at every bump. When she reaches a large gated property, she lets the engine idle a while, wondering if this is the place, as she takes in the impressive façade of the red brick building, its carved wooden bargeboards painted a deep forest green, the door to match. Spotting activity beyond the house and front gardens, she lifts her sunglasses as her gaze lands on a group of women tending the flower borders at the rear. One of them turns in her direction. Pale, scarf-headed and tall, the woman strikes an imposing figure as she plants her hands on her hips like a challenge, and Celine feels immediately caught out, a voyeur. She quickly turns away, and drives on, another mile down the lane, until she finally arrives at the tree-shrouded entrance to another grand property that can only be her mother's. Yes, the name plate on the gatepost confirms it: 'Belle France'. Only Delilah would name a house so ostentatiously, a reference to her French grandparents, the fragrance tycoons responsible for her comfortable lifestyle. Celine wonders how those hard-working pioneers would have viewed Delilah's choices: the houses, the holidays, the jewellery, the endless stream of men. The desertion. And then, with shame, she wonders what those same ancestors would make of *her*, if they could hear her harsh thoughts now, at a time like this.

Turning in through lion-and-unicorn-topped pillars, Celine takes the long tree-lined drive towards the house, knowing her mother will hate the fact that she hasn't upgraded her vehicle from this 'abominable monstrosity' in all these years. *Would*, she corrects herself with a shake of her head. She *would* have hated it. As she skirts the final tree, a large house comes into clear view, a red-brick statement standing tall against the river-side backdrop and manicured gardens. Celine doesn't know what she was expecting, and the scene is so entirely unfamiliar to her that it seems impossible to imagine that Delilah, the woman who was never without a man on her arm, had been living here all alone.

That she died here all alone.

3. BRAMBLE

1976, Two Cross Farm

It was late, a still, muggy full-mooned night, and in my forty years on this planet I'd never felt more alive.

In the living room at the back of the house, all the ground-floor windows were flung wide, and in the absence of furniture Fern had covered the parquet floor with throws and scarves and cushions, on which we now sat in a circle so that all five of us might view each other and connect.

'The eyes are everything,' Fern explained, her soft American accent lingering over the last word. Drawing her dark hair into a long rope coil, she dropped it carelessly over one shoulder and opened up her hands. She was wearing a tiny crocheted bikini top and bell-bottomed flares that hugged her lean thighs and frayed around her bare, conker-brown feet. 'I once took a series of photographs of a blind man I met in Calcutta. He had the most generous of hearts, the deepest wisdom, and yet I never got over the profound sadness I felt at not being able to look inside him, to see through his eyes.' She studied us each in turn now, intensely, and I could swear I felt the shudder of my spirit as she did so, as though it knew it was being scrutinised and decoded. 'The eyes are *everything*,' she repeated. 'Do you understand what I mean by this? Susan?'

Alert, young Susan sat a little more upright, leaned a fraction further forward over her crossed legs. 'You mean like how, if you look into someone's eyes, you can see what they're feeling? What they really mean?'

'Yes!' Fern clapped her hands together. 'Yes! You see, we live in a warped kinda society where we're taught to not always say what we feel – but the eyes can't lie, can they? They don't know how to – not like our lying mouths and minds and hands and bodies! Because the eyes are connected to the soul.'

'Like your photographs,' Kathy said, earnestly pushing her glasses up her nose. At thirty-five she was only a few years older than Fern, but she had a frazzled quality about her, her hair a greying blonde frizz, her brow already deeply lined. '33 *Women*. That's what I really felt your exhibition was about. Truth.'

She was talking about Fern's show in London, where we'd met for the first time on that night when I'd been invited to join in this most marvellous of ventures. Where, for the first time in my life, with no one to direct me otherwise, I'd allowed myself to be reckless and abandoned, and simply said yes.

'We were looking at thirty-three naked women,' Kathy continued, 'stripped back to their true form. But it wasn't the bodies I was drawn to, it was the eyes. How do you do that? Whenever my husband takes a picture of me, my eyes aren't my own.' She frowned a little, gazing off beyond the group into the darkness outside. 'It's like I'm not even there.'

Fern placed a hand over her own heart, and was silent for a while. It had been this stillness and certainty that had drawn me to stay back and talk with her at the gallery that day, and, when she'd invited me to join her and the others for after-show drinks, I'd been captivated by their talk of *equality* and *patriarchy* and *emancipation* and *release*. I was the oldest in the group by a good few years, but somehow it didn't matter. I had something to offer, and, like the rest of them, I had something to escape. *My* tormentor was now dead, but I couldn't go on living the way I was, holed up in the prison of my family home, alone and decaying. I was certain this chance meeting had great significance; after all, I'd only stepped inside the gallery for a few minutes' respite from the scorching afternoon sun, and there she had been to welcome me – Fern, offering up a glass of cool wine and a smile. It had to be fate at work.

'I make a commitment to you all now,' Fern said. 'This place will be a shelter from oppression, a place women can enter, free of their chains of enslavement, where they may never fear the raised hand of violence again. I will photograph every sister who passes through our home, so that, wherever they go next, they'll know a real image of them exists in the world – a true representation of themselves, one which cannot be altered by the will of others. Others – partners, children, parents, siblings, so-called friends – they reduce us, whether they mean to or not. Essentially, they are limpets, clinging to us, covering our truth, obscuring our eyes. This is what you're seeing in those old photographs of yourself, Kathy: it's the lesser-you, the half-you. But the other half is still there, you understand; it's just drowning beneath the surface, crying to break free.'

All focus was on Fern, so it wasn't until she stopped talking that we realised Kathy was silently weeping, nodding almost imperceptibly, her gaze firm on our new leader. Fern gestured to Regine and Susan on either side of Kathy, and they each took a hand; when I joined, the circle was complete, and there wasn't a dry eye in the room.

After several long minutes of conscious contemplation, Fern broke away to fetch paper and a pen, and returned to her place with a rolled joint and a half-empty bottle of American whiskey. 'We will never forget tonight,' she told us, as she passed the joint one way, the bottle the other. 'But we need to have our wits about us, so this will be our last night of indulgence, of intoxication. We have a job to do, and stimulants will only dull our resolve. Enjoy this last taste, sisters.'

We each took a swig, and a drag – my first and last ever experience of marijuana – and waited for Fern's instruction.

Setting the empty bottle aside and extinguishing the stub on the floor between us, she spoke. 'This will be a place of sanctuary, for thirty-three women. All in this room will be considered Founding Sisters, but it is my aim that we will be six in number. Do you know the significance of the number six?' She waited for a response, but none came. 'Six,' she said, with great ceremony, 'is a multiple of three. Three is the Holy Trinity, a divine perfection.'

I felt a pang of validation; perhaps all my years of half-hearted church attendance with Father had not been wasted, for was not the Bible itself littered with references to trinity and divinity?

'I've been studying numerology for some time now,' Fern continued. 'And you would not believe the power of it, my friends. The more I've looked into it, the more enlightened I've become, and, sisters, it has blown my mind. Why d'you think my exhibition was called *33 Women*? Thirty-three is the highest of the master numbers; whether you follow organised religion or not, it shows up in all of them throughout history – it was the age of Jesus at his death, the number of prayer beads commonly strung. It appears in Buddhism, Judaism, Christianity, the Occult.'

'*Call to me and I will answer you and tell you great and unsearchable things you do not know,*' I said, the line coming to me without thought. '*Jeremiah 33:3.*'

13

Fern brought her hands together beneath her chin, and I felt the full force of her approval wash over me like heat.

'Those women-deniers the Freemasons hold it in reverence,' she continued. 'Thirty-three is a dominant number of goodness *and* of chaos, of life-giving *and* destruction. I myself was born in Solano Beach, California, directly in the path of the circle of latitude known as the 33rd parallel. This is the same latitudinal path on which the Kennedy boys were assassinated in Texas and LA, the very same path where those UFOs landed in Roswell.' Fern's voice was rising, her hands dancing expressively as she grew ever more animated. 'You women each have thirty-three vertebrae making up your spines. Thirty-three is the point at which water boils on the Newton Scale of measure. And 33rpm is the number of turns your record player makes each minute when you turn on and tune into your favourite album.'

There was laughter, a moment of lightness in our dawning understanding of this woman's great vision.

'Sisters, thirty-three is associated with love and harmony and creativity – everything we women have striven for since the dawning of time; and yet, somehow, this "master" number has been appropriated by the patriarchy of every society, every religion, every mythology, and so often used in the disservice of women.'

We were rapt.

'Tonight, my beloveds, if you are with me, we *five* will write a Code of Conduct for a new community of women, a sanctuary for thirty-three sisters, a new way of life. And when that is written, in the name of balance, the search for our sixth Founding Sister will begin. Are you with me?'

I looked around, at these brave women, my past flashing before me like a great grey disappointment of oppression and abuse, and I knew I had found my place. 'Yes,' I said, with true conviction, my voice falling in with the chant of assent. 'Yes!'

Eyes gleaming, Fern slapped her flat palms against her knees. 'So! I will kick off with an important code: *Every woman must first shed her limpets.*'

None of us really knew what Fern meant by this, we just knew we wanted to be part of it. Never before had I smoked cannabis; never before had I taken liquor straight from the bottle. Never before had I mixed with women of different ages and colours and cultures and religions. Never before had I believed I truly possessed power.

'Limpets?' Susan asked, and it was natural that it should be she who raised it. Looking back, I realise how grateful I was for Susan and her youth. At sixteen she was forgiven for her endless questions – questions which, if we were honest, were on the tips of our own tongues. 'How do we shed our "limpets"?'

'A limpet is a passenger who weighs us down,' Fern replied. 'Some of us are free of limpets; others have one or two; some poor creatures carry many, many limpets, and they don't even know it. Kathy, from what you tell me, your husband is a limpet. Does he weigh you down?'

'He does,' Kathy replied with strength.

'And your patients? You're a doctor. You must feel the burden of your patients?'

Kathy nodded, perhaps a little less firmly.

Fern leaned in, her expression intensifying. 'And your children? You have three.'

At this, Kathy, still maintaining eye contact, merely blinked. From where I was sitting, I could see the slow rise and fall of her throat as she swallowed, the long, controlled exhalation of breath.

Fern reached out to lay a hand on her ankle. 'Of course, every woman who comes here must not only shed those things, she must also bring something of value. In Kathy here we have a

15

distinguished medic. You have plans for a medicine garden, am I right?'

Kathy's face brightened again, and I think it was then that I knew exactly what Fern's gift was: she understood people. She knew how to make them believe in their own worth.

'I hope we can,' Kathy said, falteringly, 'as much as is humanly possible, be pharmaceutical-free. We can grow most of what we need right here in the gardens! Garlic, valerian, sage – there are so many real alternatives to conventional medicine. Our bodies don't need all those chemicals. We can heal ourselves.'

Fern nodded, then turned to Regine, her fellow American. 'Meditation is part of that process, isn't it, Regine?'

Regine mirrored Fern's earlier gesture, laying a hand over her heart. She idolised Fern, it was clear in the way she even aped her code of dress, albeit less elegantly, and despite their obvious differences in colour and background they were cut from a similar cloth. They had history, having travelled together via India, and from the outset Regine never missed an opportunity to bring attention to this special bond. I wondered if she was attempting to use their previous connection to position herself as a close aide. 'As you know, Fern,' she said, 'from our experiences together in the East, my teachings in the arts of yoga and meditation are what I have to bring. The healing benefits of these practices can be transformational. And as for limpets,' she continued, in an accent somewhat coarser than Fern's, 'I left them all behind in Long Island.'

Fern pressed her palms together again, a symbol of her approval. 'Susan?' she said, moving along. I felt my hands begin to sweat, knowing that soon the question would fall to me.

Susan's expression was momentarily crestfallen, but then she spoke quickly and eloquently, as though she feared getting it wrong would see her ejected from the chosen few. 'My limpets are my bourgeois parents and their expectations of me. My limpets are the husband they have imagined for me, and the grandchildren they would have me birth for them. But I don't have any skills—' she starts to say, her face crumpling.

Still cross-legged, Fern reached out to embrace her. 'You are young,' Fern said, 'and for these first two years you'll be our apprentice. You'll shadow us in our work. And you'll welcome new sisters and show them the way.'

Susan's relief poured from her, and I thought she looked as charming as a woodland nymph, with her long unbrushed hair and hippy robe, free of make-up or artifice.

'Brenda?' Fern asked finally, and I flinched at the sound of my own name, the conventional consonants of it, its internal rhyme with *tend* and *fend* and *end* and *penned*. Had I been predestined to minister to the needs of others my entire life, by the poetics of my name alone?

'I have no one,' I replied, and for the first time since my father had died the year before I felt no pain in the truth of it. 'I am limpet-free.'

Fern laughed with warmth, and rewarded me with her pressed-together palms. 'Tell me,' she said now, addressing us all, 'what rules, or codes, would you have me write on this piece of paper?'

'May we change our names?' I asked, though I knew it wasn't what she was asking.

She glanced around the group. 'If a woman is prepared to shed her limpets, I don't see why she shouldn't shed her name too.' Her pen hovered over the paper. 'What would you call yourself, Brenda?'

Without conscious thought, my mind's eye conjured up a moment of almost perfect contentedness, of skipping Sunday School to pick blackberries from the churchyard hedgerow with 'that gypsy girl' Annie Jessop. The late autumn sun was warm on the backs of our hands as we reached for the high fruit on tiptoes, pricking our fingers on brambles and rolling our eyes at the divine sweetness of the fruit. I had liked Annie, with her gaudy gold earrings and scuffed patent shoes, but I hadn't been allowed to keep her as my friend.

'Bramble,' I replied. 'I'd like to be called Bramble.'

Fern nodded sagely and bent over her legs to write on the sheet. 'Bramble, you have inspired our first condition. *Number one: Come as yourself, whoever that may be.*' She looked up from the list, and fixed her hard gaze on me. 'And what do you bring, Bramble?'

The intense heat of the night weighed down on me, and for a moment I was light-headed, out of myself as I allowed my gaze to drift over my fellow sisters. They all had so much to offer, and I had . . . what? My parents had restricted and constricted me my entire life, and now they were both dead, and I was forty years old, all alone in the world, with no real talents, with nothing to offer . . .

'I have money . . .' I said, and in the pause which followed I feared this was the wrong thing to say.

'How much?' Fern asked, her expression unchanged.

I looked around the high-ceilinged room, with its grand French doors, rotten and peeling, its walls soft with damp, and my confidence soared. 'Enough to do up this place,' I replied. 'Enough to make it fit for thirty-three women.'

Something flickered across Fern's face, and she lowered her eyes, appearing to study the backs of her hands. When she looked up again, she was smiling, her straight white teeth gleaming in the candlelight. 'That is a fine gift, Bramble,' she said.

And, with that smile, my life, as I know it now, began.

4. CELINE

Present day

For a few moments Celine doesn't move from the driver's seat, unable to avert her gaze from the front door of this house she's never visited – never been invited to.

That awful word plays at the back of her throat, and she realises she hasn't yet managed to say it aloud. *Dead.* Delilah is dead. Still, despite all these years without seeing her mother, it seems barely possible to imagine that she is no longer alive, somewhere in the world.

Una appears in the ivy-draped doorway and on seeing Celine her face breaks wide and warm. Something in that wholehearted smile, in the abnormal scenario – the strange house, the early heat, the sweet scent of jasmine on the breeze – quite knocks the air out of Celine, and emotions rush in. She feels her face collapse as she steps out of the van, hating herself for it as Una sweeps her up in her tough little arms, just as she did when Celine was still that gawky kid who lived in the terraced house next door.

'Hey, baby,' Una says, pulling back to appraise her, running her hand down the contours of her cheek, her touch solid and affectionate. It's not hard to see why Una had made such a successful police officer: she had an ease about her, a manner which suggested that all people were equal, that all would be treated even-handedly. 'Nice to see the old rust-bucket's still on the road,' she says, her eyes wrinkling up as she nudges Celine towards the front steps. 'Wanna see your sister? I'll stick the kettle on.'

Following Una through the imposing front entrance, her eyes adjusting from the bright light of outdoors, Celine finds she's lost for words, assaulted as she is by so much that is unfamiliar. Her mother has lived here for over seventeen years, and yet this is the first time Celine has set foot in the place. The sensation of being here is unreal.

'Pip's out back with the girls,' Una says as they pause at the foot of a sweeping staircase.

It's a small palace, Celine thinks, composing herself with a long, slow breath as she glances at the gallery of original artwork adorning the walls, at the aged Persian rugs and antique sideboard. A trio of silver-framed photographs sits beside the telephone, and, even before she reaches to pick one up, Celine knows that none of them will be of her or her sisters. Indeed, the three pictures are all of Delilah: Delilah as a pretty toddler on the beach in Cornwall, as a show-stopping bathing beauty at the edge of a pool in her twenties, and, in the last one, as a sophisticated forty-something in a cocktail dress on the deck of a Thames riverboat. 'So, this is home,' Celine murmurs to herself.

Una takes the photograph from her and returns it to the sideboard, tilting her head to appraise Celine's expression. 'I don't think any of us knew what to expect, did we?' She holds Celine's gaze.

'I'm *fine*,' Celine says with a decisive nod which tells Una to lead the way.

As they reach the large, light kitchen at the side of the house, Celine lingers in the doorway, taking in the unmistakable smell of Una's Caribbean rum cake.

'You go on, see your sister,' Una urges as she scans the room with a frown, before grabbing up a tea towel and heading for the oven. 'I'm still finding my way around the place.' She smiles warmly.

Celine hesitates, glancing down the hall towards an elegant living room with patio doors opening on to the garden, where the chatter of songbirds drifts along with the distant sound of children's voices. She knows she's stalling, scared perhaps of her younger sister's reaction; scared perhaps of her own. If only Vanessa were here. Things wouldn't feel so entirely broken if Vanessa were still here.

With a puff of heat, Una deftly flips the dark cake on to a cooling rack before filling the kettle. She's so efficient, so warm and homely, and Celine realises she's missed her more than she's missed her own mother. She crosses the kitchen and reaches out a flat hand, hovering it over the cake, savouring the warmth that rises from it. 'It's my favourite.'

'I know. Aunty Una special.'

Celine anchors herself against the worktop, fighting the feelings which threaten to overtake her again.

Frowning, Una's face momentarily owns the years that have passed, before her expression eases back into a smile and she pats down her tight-cropped hair, now more grey than black. She moves closer, to hook an arm through Celine's, lowering her voice confidentially. 'We had the solicitor here this morning, Ceecee. Stuffy old suit, he was. White as a ghost and bald as a coot. He reminded me of one of Delilah's old boyfriends – Johan, the banker. *Yawnhan*, I used to call him – remember?' And now she laughs raucously, the unmistakable bellow of it thawing Celine, forcing her to join in.

'You're so wicked,' Celine says, hating herself for the time she's let slide by without Una. She feels a little pang of jealousy that Pip has remained close to her, still living as she does in their old family home in Kingston, with Una next door. 'I'd forgotten just how bad you are.'

'Ha!' Una laughs again, releasing her arm to pick up the tray and head for the garden. 'Bad cop, that's me. Here, let me take you to your sister.'

The back garden is even more glorious than the front, with a well-tended lawn rolling downhill towards a riverbank carpeted with crocuses and bluebells. A gardener pushes his wheelbarrow along the far perimeter, stooping every now and again to gather small piles of cuttings; in another life, this might be an idyllic scene of British springtime. Celine scans the lawn slowly, trying to imagine Delilah here, before her gaze lands on Pip, who stands waiting for her on the decked veranda, one small hand clamped to her mouth. Una sets down the tray and leaves them alone.

The two sisters stare at each other for long moments, as though silently agreeing there are insufficient words.

It's been months since Celine last saw Pip, but her sister's appearance is almost unchanged; despite being a woman in her early thirties, she's still as slight as she was at sixteen. Her children, on the other hand, have grown and changed again, and Celine watches in awe as they stop in their tracks at the foot of the garden, watchful as deer, before galloping across the lawn to the safety of Mother. Beebee is no longer a babe in arms but a sturdy blonde-haired angel standing on her own two feet, a mangled soft dog hanging by the ear between crossed fingers, a thumb resting loosely at the corner of her mouth. She wraps an

22

arm around Pip's leg, peeping out just enough to blink a single nut-brown eye in Celine's direction. The older girl, Olive, must be, what, four? She has a mischievous twinkle about her and her curls have deepened from their honey shade into a darker brown. An early black and white image of Delilah comes to mind, and Celine finds herself staring at the poor child, almost believing that she's her grandmother, back from the grave.

'Celine?' Pip says, rousing her.

Celine notices the little girl's alarmed expression and she smiles widely to compensate, telling her she was simply mesmerised by how much she's grown. 'She looks like—' Celine starts to say, but Pip interrupts.

'Like you? I know. I can't see a drop of me at all.' Pip reaches out her hands and lets her tears fall, and Celine is glad she hadn't finished her own sentence. 'It's a bloody mystery, sis,' Pip says. 'I stare at these two when they're sleeping – I stare and I stare, and all I can see is you.'

Of course, Pip can't see it, can she? She would hate to think of her children inheriting their looks from Delilah. After all, Pip, with her poker-straight hair and pale complexion, looks nothing like their mother, so why should her kids? Let her believe it is Celine they take after; let her believe their looks come from someone who loves her back.

Olive scowls self-consciously at the attention, before making crab hands at Beebee, opening her eyes wide in mock threat. The pair streak off across the garden, the youngest one screaming as though her life depends on it.

'How's work?' Pip asks, pulling out two seats at the veranda table, and Celine feels some sadness at how quickly they've resorted to small talk.

'It's fine. You know I'm leaving at the end of the year, to set up my own practice? It's a bit risky, giving up my salary like that, but I'll work from home at first, until I get enough clients.' She glances at her sister, and realises how dull she sounds.

Pip smiles. 'Still specialising in "securing settlements for sad divorcees"?' It's an old joke; it was the way Celine always used to describe her work, poking fun at herself, back in the days when she still tried not to think of herself as one of the grown-ups.

'Yup. Living the dream,' she replies. She wants to ask Pip if she's planning to return to *her* work any time soon, but she knows it won't go down well, that she'll only see it as a dig. She suspects straight-laced Stefan prefers Pip to stay at home, rather than returning to the physiotherapy work she spent so many years training for. Better she stays put, playing the pretty wife and mother to his manly provider. *Is it enough for you, Pip?* is what Celine wants to ask, but she won't. 'So, what've you been up to?' is the question she opts for instead.

Pip merely gestures towards the girls on the far side of the lawn, and Celine finds herself chewing the inside of her cheek to stop herself from being mean. For a while, the sisters simply sit, and sigh, and avoid any talk of Delilah, until Una joins them again.

'Shall we get the dirty money stuff out of the way first?' Una suggests, pouring the tea.

Celine shrugs. 'Sure.' She'd been relieved to hear that Delilah had appointed Una as executor, freeing them of the responsibility of raking through their mum's accounts, and she knew Pip would feel the same.

Una cuts two slabs of cake and hands them to Beebee and Olive, who have returned like heat-seeking missiles at the arrival of food. Pip points towards the far end of the garden. 'Picnic,' she says simply, and they're off again, steering clear of the gardener, who Celine senses is actively avoiding looking in their direction.

'Time to find out if Delilah left us anything useful,' Celine says, reaching for the milk.

'What, apart from a bunch of mental health issues?' Pip replies through a mouthful of cake, and they both laugh, rendered teenagers again by the grave nature of their meeting.

'Oh, she's left you something, all right,' Una says. She opens up her reporter's notebook and rests her boots on the chair opposite, sliding her spectacles down and scanning the page. 'The big things first: Pip – the family home in Kingston, River Terrace – that's yours, as you're currently living there. Celine, you're bequeathed an equivalent market-value sum, as you've already got your own place in Bournemouth.'

'So we're not out on the street,' Pip says, wincing as she realises how spoilt she sounds.

'This place,' Una continues, 'is to be cleared and sold, along with all Delilah's stocks and shares. She's left me something too – she wanted to pay off my mortgage . . .' Una glances at the girls, obviously embarrassed.

'Too bloody right!' Pip says, slapping Una's leg. 'You've been more of a support to us than she ever was – it's the least she could do.'

Celine nods her approval, and flaps her hand to make Una continue.

'She's asked that, once those bequests and any outstanding charges and taxes are settled, the remaining funds are to be shared between her daughters – you two.'

A gentle breeze dances over the table, lifting the paper napkins and scattering them across the lawn. At the far end of the garden the children have finished their cake and are now chasing each other with piles of grass cuttings, pilfered from the gardener, who pretends not to notice. Celine recalls her and Vanessa playing that way as tots in Canbury Gardens, and Pip too, later on, when she was big enough. She looks at Pip now, and she knows she's remembering some of the same things, she too feeling the loss

25

of their sister fifteen years ago more keenly today than the recent loss of their mother. Vanessa had been their tether, the middle sister who bridged the gap of their years, and the absence of her name in Mum's final will is heartbreaking.

'I wish Vanessa were here,' Pip says quietly, and all Celine can do is anchor her gaze on those carefree girls at the bottom of the garden.

After an early supper, Pip runs a bath for the kids, and Una takes advantage of the time alone with Celine to persuade her to stay the night and help make a start on the contents of the attic.

'They're not going to release your mum to the undertakers for at least a week or two,' she says, easing down the attic steps on the first-floor landing and heading up, large torch in hand. 'You must be able to take some time off, Celine. It's a bereavement.'

Celine's in no rush to get back to work – in fact her boss has told her to take all the time she needs – but the idea of trawling through the detritus of her mother's recent years fills her with dread. She's got no real idea what Delilah's been doing with herself during these past couple of decades, and this snooping feels like rummaging through the belongings of a dead stranger.

'You said you never had anything of Vanessa's to remember her by,' Una calls down. 'Maybe you'll find something up here – Delilah's bound to have kept something.'

As Celine climbs the aluminium steps, breathing in the musty heat of the confined space, she feels certain she won't find any evidence of Vanessa up there in Mum's things. Her sister had given up on their mother years before her untimely death, so the chances of Delilah's having something of hers is slim.

'You know it's been fifteen years,' Celine says as she fumbles along the attic wall. 'Since Vanessa's death.'

'Fifteen years this March,' Una replies through the gloom, and for Celine there is some comfort in knowing that others are tracking the time too, that Vanessa has not been forgotten by them, even if the same cannot be said for the police.

Celine locates the overhead light switch, and the attic is lit up to reveal a wide, low-beamed space filled to the eaves with boxes and crates of clothes and paintings and pictures and papers. It's suddenly clear that they've got an enormous job ahead of them, and Celine hopes Una and Pip won't expect her to stay on for more than a day or two. She just wants to get this job and the cremation out of the way as quickly as possible so that she can return to her quiet life in Dorset with its far-reaching horizons and wide open sky.

'Urgh, look at these,' Una yelps, bringing Celine back to the present as she holds up a lank old mink coat. 'There's a whole box of them here.'

'Charity shop,' Celine says without hesitation. She remembers the nasty furs – an heirloom – and her mother complaining that the 'right-on brigade' had rendered them virtually unwearable. There was a day in Celine's early teens when Delilah wore one of the minks to the local supermarket, just to be perverse. As she left the shop carrying pink roses and Sancerre, she was roundly egged by a group of dungaree-wearing students, and Celine had thanked God that she hadn't been with her at the time, simultaneously wishing she'd been able to witness it. Twelve-year-old Vanessa had been so taken with the drama at the time that she'd turned vegetarian the very next day, just to add passive-aggressive insult to her mother's injury. Celine smiles at the memory, at the way Vanessa would take everything they couldn't stand about their mother and turn it on its head.

'Definitely charity shop,' Celine says now, 'or incinerator.'

Dedicating one side of the attic to donations, Una and Celine continue to work through boxes of old clothes and handbags, culling Delilah's belongings ruthlessly, the 'keep' pile remaining conspicuously small. When Pip eventually appears at the top step, precariously balancing a bottle of red wine and three glasses, the women gather on upturned crates for a brief pause.

'Hmm, this is good wine,' Celine says, holding hers up to the light.

'You know Mum,' Pip says, chinking glasses with Una. 'Only the best for our Delilah.'

'That bottle probably cost more than my shoes,' Una replies with a nod.

'And the rest,' Pip says, topping up their glasses before they're even halfway empty. 'She really was a bloody nightmare, wasn't she?'

Celine gives a small laugh. 'The worst.'

With her free hand, Una drags a nearby box of papers into the centre, plucking a photograph from the top. 'She was a diva for sure,' she says. 'She was unpredictable, and vain – and she never stuck with anything. But she was also a good friend to me for a time.' She passes the photograph to Celine, in which Delilah appears to be helping out at some local fundraiser. 'People do change, you know?'

Celine raises an eyebrow. 'Delilah?' she says. 'The only thing she ever changed was her hair – or her shoes – or her nail colour.'

Pip laughs. 'Or her home!'

'Or her husband,' Celine adds, Pip's hilarity having a contagious effect.

Una bellows with laughter. 'Or her nose!'

'Oh, my God,' Pip wheezes. 'Yes! She went away for a week with Johnnie and came back with her face in bandages, after a "skiing accident". I don't think they'd even left the country.'

Una is still chuckling as she rummages through the box, casting photographs into one pile, papers and letters into another.

'When the bandage came off it was a completely different nose!' Celine sighs, wiping her eyes on the back of her sleeve. 'Remember she got us a cat that same week, trying to deflect attention from her tiny new nose?'

'She ditched the poor cat too, once it became too much bother,' Pip recalls.

Celine snorts. 'Just like everything else.'

As she puts her glass down, she spots a postcard Una has just dropped on top of the pile. The image is of London Bridge and the Thames, a typical tourist postcard.

'What's that, Una?'

Una turns it over and studies the handwriting on the reverse. She looks up, a deep furrow forming between her brows. 'It's from Vanessa.' She hesitates before speaking again. 'Girls – I thought your mum hadn't seen Vanessa in the year before she died?'

Celine feels her stomach tighten.

'The year she was *murdered*, you mean?' Pip's already drunk, clearly. Her filter's off.

Celine quietens her with a gentle slap to the wrist. 'No, none of us had. After that last phone message she left me the March before, there was no more contact. It was exactly a year.'

Una nods. 'And you're sure she hadn't been here, to visit Delilah?'

'Certain!' Celine replies, making a grab for the postcard, but Una doesn't release it. 'Mum gave a statement to the police, just as all of us did, and she said she hadn't seen her either.'

'*Una?*' Pip says, sounding afraid now. 'What's on the postcard?'

Una hands the card to Celine. It's from Vanessa to Delilah, addressed here at Belle France, and dated April of 2004, soon after she was known to have left her boyfriend and the flat they shared in London.

Dear Mum

I'll be with you on Wednesday afternoon, about teatime
– hope that's still OK? It will only be for a couple of days,
but I'm really looking forward to catching up with you.

> *Love,*
>
> *Vx*

Nobody speaks for a moment or two, as each in turn they inspect the brief message and try to make sense of what they're reading.

'I don't understand,' Pip says. 'This was, what, a couple of weeks after she'd left him?'

Him. *Jem Falmer*. The bastard she'd been running away from; the man who'd isolated her, cut her off from friends and family, and fractured her collarbone when she'd tried to walk away.

'The police thought she'd been staying in a women's refuge for at least some of that year, didn't they?' Una says.

'Yes, that's what she said in the voice message. That a place had come up and she was on her way there. I tried to call her back as soon as I picked the message up, but it was too late, she'd changed her number.'

Una pulls at her earlobe, her detective instincts clearly at work. 'Maybe she stopped in to see your mother on her way to the refuge. Maybe she needed to borrow some money or something?'

'Why would she have gone to Mum, though?' Pip asks, hurt radiating from her. 'Why? When she had us? Celine was still living at home in River Terrace back then – she could have come to us. We would have helped her. If she'd just told us about Jem, we could've done something to stop him!'

'No, Pip,' Una says firmly. 'Don't do this to yourself again.'

Celine reaches an arm around her sister and pulls her to her chest, allowing her tears to soak into the fabric of her shirt. 'We couldn't have stopped him,' she says. 'Jem Falmer was a monster, and he would have found Vanessa wherever she hid. And he did find her, didn't he? He found her, when even we couldn't.'

A sob escapes Pip. 'I can't stand to think of her alone like that – just dumped on the boardwalk. Like she was nothing – like she was *rubbish*!'

Celine holds Pip tight, wishing she could somehow take the nightmare away from her. But she can't; she lives with it too, and she knows it can't be escaped. And it never gets easier to live with. The media's unflinching descriptions of her twenty-year-old sister's corpse, laid out on the boards of Brighton pier, will be etched in her imagination forever. *Beaten and strangled*; those were the words they printed. *Beaten and strangled to death*. Celine swallows hard, trying to keep it together.

'But why would Mum say she hadn't seen Vanessa, if she had?' Pip demands, pulling away. 'I really don't think she would have lied to the police.'

Una shakes her head. 'God only knows. But this postcard tells us Vanessa was heading here just before she went off the radar altogether. If she was stopping off to see Delilah on her way to some refuge, maybe the refuge was somewhere nearby?'

Pip takes a long slow sip of her wine. 'But she was found in Brighton.'

'That's only twenty miles away,' Una says. 'You know, one of the biggest problems the investigation team had was in the fact that no one knew where she'd been in that year before her death. And of course, Jem Falmer had disappeared from their London home without a trace—'

31

Pip slams her glass down. 'I'd kill him,' she says, her face shifting from tears to steel. 'If I could get hold of him, honestly, I'd happily do time in prison, just to wipe him off the face of the earth. I mean it. I'd do life if I had to.'

'I know,' Celine murmurs. 'I know you would, Pip. Me too.'

Una nods sadly. 'Anyway, Falmer wasn't around to be questioned, and none of Vanessa's friends had heard from her at all.'

'Only because he'd scared them all off,' Celine murmurs.

'I know they made enquiries at all the refuges in the Greater London area, and Brighton where she was found, with no joy, but this—' Una waves the postcard between them, growing quietly animated '—this small detail could change *everything*. If we could work out exactly where Vanessa was between April 2004 when she visited your mum here and March 2005 when she was found in Brighton, maybe—'

'You think we can track down Jem Falmer, Una?' Pip clutches at her sister's shirt sleeve. 'You think we can finally put him away?'

Celine feels woozy with wine and allows her eyelids to close, conjuring up the memory of Vanessa's face, now somewhat faded with the passing of time. They'd tried to put all this behind them long ago, and the thought of opening up these wounds again fills her with dread. Would she go there, back to those dark places, if it meant bringing that man, that lowlife, to justice?

When she opens her eyes, Pip and Una are staring at her with an intensity that frightens her.

'It's got to be worth another look, Celine,' Pip says. 'This could be our one chance to prove Jem murdered our sister.'

Celine feels the fury building up inside her again. The discovery has fanned the flames of her long-held rage. 'OK,' she says, simply.

Una gathers up the glasses and slides the postcard into her back pocket, indicating that they should head back downstairs.

'Don't get your hopes up, girls, OK? But I'll make a call to an old mate of mine tomorrow,' she says calmly. 'I'll see what I can find out. And we'll take it from there. Agreed?'

As Pip follows Una down the steps, Celine pauses to cast her gaze around the inconsequential objects of her mother's life. Picking up the photograph of Delilah, she follows them down and closes the trap hatch, wondering how it might feel to turn back the hands of time.

5. BRAMBLE

1976, Two Cross Farm

Once the funds of my legacy had transferred to my bank account, Two Cross Farm became a centre of activity as we worked tirelessly to prepare our home for its first new residents.

The four of us – Regine, Kathy, Susan and I – soon fell into a pattern of hard work, labouring from dawn until dusk each day, clearing the neglected house and sprawling gardens, breathing new life into the place, while Fern visited her contacts in London as she tried, and failed, to find a suitable sixth Founding Sister.

'So many of them have the skills we need,' she told us over supper on her return from another week away. We were sitting in the freshly painted dining room, around the vast ecclesiastical table Regine had haggled for at the local auctions, getting it at a knockdown price because of its unwieldy dimensions. 'But none of the women I meet are right,' Fern continued wearily, passing the bread basket to me. 'Too many are overprivileged, or uncommitted or unfocused. It's vital that our sixth Founding Sister has need of our sanctuary, *and* is a good fit.'

We all agreed; it *was* vital. Since that first day here, the group had bonded, and despite our obvious differences there was a cohesive atmosphere of trust and purpose – none of us wanted to put that at risk. Only today, as we painted together in the upper bedrooms, young Susan had confided in me about the physical abuse she'd suffered at the hands of her mother – the one woman who should have been trusted to protect her. It provoked in me such a strong maternal response that, in the spirit of openness, I did something I'd never done before, and confessed the sins of my own father against me. Afterwards, that young girl and I laid down our paintbrushes and clung to one another, me a forty-year-old spinster, her a sixteen-year-old girl.

'Anyway, I'm beat,' Fern said now, looking pale and shadow-eyed as she poured herself another glass of water. 'And I'm not going away again for the foreseeable future. Number Six will present herself to us in good time – I can feel it. Now, sisters, tell me about the building works!'

We were all keen to share news of our progress, and Regine went first, proud as she was of our emerging garden. 'Kathy and I have cleared the entire plot of weeds and overgrowth,' she said. 'Though the chance of anything actually *growing* seems slim to me.'

Kathy smiled wryly, holding up her fingertips, dark-stained after endless backbreaking hours turning the arid soil, attempting to outwit the heatwave we'd been experiencing that summer. She leaned back in her chair to look out through the cloudy glass towards the lawn. 'It's like the Serengeti out there. Completely dry. Still, we can plan out the planting schedule, and prepare the ground. Do we have funds for a greenhouse?'

Fern nodded.

'Good,' Regine said, purposely not looking in my direction. Although she never said as much, I sensed resentment at the fact it was my money we were spending. 'And I'm gonna get one

35

of the guys to build some raised beds before we kick 'em out. Might as well make the most of the muscle while they're here.'

Despite our idealistic vision to transform this place ourselves, much of the renovation work required was skilled, and there was a notable absence of female builders in this quiet corner of England. We'd had to accept that, for the short term, men would be admitted. In the past two months, stud walls had been erected, damp courses treated, plaster lathed and roof tiles replaced. Gradually the place was starting to take shape, and it gave me quiet gratification to know that my money – my father's money – had funded it.

'Ted and Barry finished plastering in the kitchen today,' Susan updated us. 'And they've given the basement a thorough inspection now – if we get the damp course and ventilation sorted, they can't see any reason we shouldn't have the laundry room down there.'

As well as helping with the painting, Susan had been put in charge of meals and refreshments for the workforce; being so young, she had an easy, guileless way of chatting to the men, of getting the best from them. It didn't escape my notice, the way their eyes followed her as she fetched them their tea, and there were times when I wanted to march over and point out that the girl was young enough to be their daughter. But I knew that had never stopped a man before, and I let it slide, instead quietly anticipating the day we would close our doors to those men altogether.

'So that's the upstairs, the dining room and kitchen done,' Susan concluded. 'Just the hall to plaster now and they'll be off in a day or two.'

'Excellent,' Fern replied.

'I picked up a second-hand sewing machine and some plain fabrics in town yesterday,' I offered, pointing to two large bolts of furnishing material leaning against the door frame. 'This time next week, we'll have curtains in all the windows.'

'Wonderful,' Fern said, and it struck me that she'd started to grow distracted. She lifted a napkin to her forehead and blotted away the perspiration there, dropping it on her half-finished meal and pushing her plate away.

'The wood store's going up tomorrow,' Regine added, 'so we can prepare ourselves for the winter ahead.'

Abruptly, Fern stood, pushing her chair back with a scrape.

'Are you all right, honey?' Regine asked, making to get up too.

'I'm fine!' Fern barked. It took us all by surprise, and in apology she raised a hand, making it clear she didn't want a fuss. All the colour had drained from her skin, and despite her deep tan she looked quite unwell. 'Continue supper without me,' she murmured, exiting the room. 'I'm tired from my journey, that's all.'

For long minutes after she'd gone, we sat in silence, wondering whether to eat or not, hands folded on the scored wooden surface of the table, four women at a table fit for thirty-three. When Kathy started to serve up, Regine swore under her breath, and headed out through the French doors to the end of the garden and on to the river path beyond.

'Shall I go to Fern?' Susan asked brightly, as always looking for ways to put herself at our leader's side. She worshipped Fern like a disciple.

Kathy shook her head. 'She said she wanted to be left alone, Susan. But she didn't look good, did she? I wonder if I should take her a cup of tea?' With this, she got up and headed for the kitchen to put water on the stove.

I glanced at Susan across the table from me, seeing the helplessness in her expression.

'Would you clear the table, Susan, there's a dear?' I said, keen to set her a distraction. 'If you wash, I'll be along to help dry up in a few minutes.'

37

I watched her leave before I too left the dining room, to head along the hall to Fern's room, the only bedroom currently inhabiting the ground floor. For long moments, I hesitated outside her door, worried she might think me intrusive.

'Fern?' I called eventually, resting a soft hand on the sanded wooden door. 'Fern, can I come in?'

When she hadn't answered after several seconds, I eased the door slowly open and found her curled up on the single bed, sallow-skinned and, to my great concern, with a face wet with tears. It would be the one and only time I would ever see her cry, or ever see her anything less than resolute and strong. I perched at the edge of the mattress and put my fingers to her forehead.

'You're cold,' I said, taking in the waxy sheen of her shoulders, the tremble of her lean body. I couldn't stand to see her like this, so altered, so fragile. So very reduced. 'Are you unwell?'

With the slightest tilt of her head on the pillow, she rolled a dark eye towards me. 'Bramble, I've had a vision,' she replied.

Against the leaded glass of her window, a branch of the willow tapped gently, though there was little breeze on that muggy summer night.

'Is that what's making you ill?' I rose then and moistened a face cloth at the small corner basin, returning to place it over her forehead.

'This isn't illness,' she said, now easing herself to a sitting position, bringing her bare feet to the floorboards. With shaking hands she ran the damp cloth over her face and neck, pushing her hair away, gathering herself. 'This is epiphany.'

'What was the vision?' I asked her as I pulled an upright chair closer, so that our faces were level.

'I have the answer to our sixth sister.' She stared at me intently as I waited for her to continue. 'I failed to locate a grown woman suitable to join us as a Founding Sister, and I began to wonder if such a woman does not yet exist.'

I nodded.

'And then I came to realise that no woman I met was without flaws – every one of them damaged in some way by her time in the world, as we all are – and I knew, we must have one sister without blemish or taint. We need an innocent.'

It was hard for me to take in what Fern was saying, for a small part of my mind had made the leap. All that remained was for her to say the words. I gazed at her expectantly, noticing how the vibrant shine of her eyes was miraculously restored, as though the very essence of her was nourished by this epiphany she spoke of.

'An innocent?' I murmured.

She reached out her hand to grasp mine, and I felt the jolt of her energy as it passed through me.

'*Yes*. The sixth Founding Sister must be a child.'

6. CELINE

Present day

The local police turn up early, just as Celine is helping Una and Pip load the camper van with bags to take to the charity shop.

'That was quick, Una,' Pip murmurs, shielding her eyes against the morning light as she watches the squad car approaching on the long driveway. 'I thought you were going to call your guy after lunch.'

'I am,' Una replies. 'This has nothing to do with me. I've no idea what this lot want.'

Minutes later, they are assembled in the living room at the back of the house, and once again Celine is feeling that disquieting sense of events being taken out of her control.

'We're making routine enquiries in the area,' the more senior of the two uniformed officers says, lifting his backside off the sofa to reach across the coffee table for sugar. He heaps two spoonfuls into his mug and sits again, stirring his tea in an infuriatingly unhurried manner. On the doorstep he'd announced himself as Sergeant Edwards, putting unnecessary emphasis on the 'sergeant', while the constable at his side muttered his own name uncertainly. They look completely out of place against Delilah's William Morris scatter cushions, and Celine wonders if she's imagining their discomfort or whether it's real.

She sits down on the facing sofa beside Pip and sips her own tea, hoping her silence will speed them along a bit. She hadn't *actually* expected them to say yes when she'd offered them a drink. They're waiting for Una to return from the kitchen, after she'd volunteered to settle Olive and Beebee with colouring pens and paper.

Now, with a clap of her hands, she's back, pulling up a high-backed chair and setting herself slightly apart, where she can see them all, feet planted wide. 'What's this about, sergeant?'

She's smart, Celine thinks to herself. In those few seconds – in that confident gesture, those words, Una has established herself as superior. They don't know it yet, but she is: she outranks them both. When the officer frowns at her use of his title, Una disarms him with a winning smile. 'Ex-force,' she explains.

The younger officer looks even more nervous now, and Celine figures he must be new to the job, because he fidgets, picking invisible lint off his trousers, waiting for his sergeant to speak first. God, they're drawing this out.

'Well, it's fairly unpleasant,' Sergeant Edwards eventually says, 'and I can only divulge limited information – but a woman's body was found yesterday afternoon, about a mile down the river from here.' He passes a small studio photograph across the table, in which a young woman in her twenties poses with a baby.

Pip puts her mug on the glass-topped table with a clatter. 'Oh, God, that's horrible. She was a mother?'

The sergeant nods his head. 'We found the photograph in her wallet, along with documents identifying her as a Robyn Siegle. Do you recognise the name? Perhaps you've seen her around the area lately?'

Celine shakes her head. 'Do her family know?'

41

'Yes, the victim's relatives have been informed.'

'Victim?' Pip says.

The sergeant takes the photograph back without acknowledging her question.

'Was it not an accident?' Una asks. 'A drowning?'

'We're not sure,' the officer replies cautiously, at exactly the same moment the younger one says, 'Probably not.'

'O-kay,' Una says, urging the sergeant to elaborate. 'I take it you're treating her death as suspicious, then?'

In the pause which follows, Celine feels the tremor of her pulse quickening.

The sergeant scowls at his younger colleague, saying, '*Thank you*, constable.' Silence follows for a few uncomfortable seconds, as he narrows his eyes, appraising Una and the sisters.

Celine looks at her watch. 'I'm really sorry, officers, we're expecting my mother's solicitors to arrive any minute—' It's a lie of course, but she finds she suddenly just wants to get them out of the house, not to think about this dead young woman at the water's edge. She makes a move to stand up, but the sergeant raises a halting palm.

He addresses Una. 'As you're ex-force, I suppose I *can* be more straight-talking, Ms—'

'Call me Una,' she says, nodding encouragingly. She leans forward, resting her elbows on her knees, and the sergeant seems happy that clear lines have been drawn, whatever her past – she's now a civilian, and he's establishment.

'We can't be sure until further tests have been carried out, but because of the circumstances – the way the deceased was found, carefully arranged – we've good reason to think she may have been murdered.'

Pip is silent, pale, and Celine doesn't think she's imagining the tension radiating from her. Is Pip thinking what she's thinking?

42

'Do you get much of this kind of thing around here?' Celine asks, her confident tone belying her inner turmoil. 'Arundel seems so sleepy – so peaceful.'

The sergeant shakes his head. 'No. It's almost unheard of, to be honest. It's going to shake the community, that's for sure. Now, I don't want you ladies worrying yourselves – but I do need to ask you if you've seen or heard anything unusual of late. Any strangers about the place? Any unfamiliar vehicles – or noises at night?'

'What do you mean, "carefully arranged"?' Pip interjects, her voice wavering at the end.

Celine reaches out a hand, rests it on her sister's knee, applies reassuring pressure to silence her. *Carefully arranged.* Those were the exact words the police had used to describe how their sister's body was found all those years ago. 'We only arrived a couple of days ago, officer,' she says. 'We're just visiting.'

'Oh, how's that?'

'This place belonged to our mother.' She gestures to herself and Pip. 'We're only here to sort the house out and arrange the funeral.'

Sergeant Edwards nods, offers his condolences, and asks each of them if he can take their full names and addresses, which the constable jots down in his notepad.

'I notice you have direct access to the river path via your property,' he says, standing to gesture through the large windows, out across the rolling lawn. 'You haven't seen anyone hanging around down there at all, at the perimeter?'

'No one,' Celine answers.

'Just the gardener,' Una says. 'You spoke to him yesterday, didn't you, Pip?'

Pip nods. 'His name's Harry. But he's not a stranger – I mean, he's been tending Mum's garden for years. He comes twice a week.'

'Which days does he come?' the constable asks, finally finding his voice.

'Mondays, usually – and I'm not sure which other days.'

'We'll need to speak with him too – PC Whitman, can you follow that up? Does Harry have a surname?'

Pip shrugs, looks to Una and Celine, who do the same. 'Sorry. There's a noticeboard in the kitchen. We can check to see if his details are there before you go?'

The constable makes another note. 'That would be great.'

'So, no unusual activity, no strangers spotted,' the sergeant summarises. 'And I don't suppose you have security cameras here?'

'Nothing so high-tech, I'm afraid,' Una replies.

'You said she was "arranged",' Pip persists.

The sergeant nods slowly, his expression shifting as he works out how much he's happy to reveal. 'She was discovered by a dog walker a good mile down river from here. She didn't appear to have been in the water, and yes, it seems she was laid out with some degree of care.'

'On the river bank?' Una asks.

'There's a little wooden pontoon, and, well, she was there. Laid out on the boards. It's all rather—'

He halts as Pip expels an unexpected sob, dropping her face into her hands. 'I'm sorry,' she murmurs. 'It's just . . .'

As she tries and fails to gather herself, Una leaps into action, gently taking her hand and drawing her out of the room.

'Sorry,' Celine says, now finding herself alone with the officers. Her mind is racing at a hundred miles an hour. 'We're all a bit jittery at the moment—'

'No, no,' the sergeant interrupts, clearly regretting his candour. He jerks his chin towards the constable and they both rise, hurriedly making their way into the hallway and towards the front door. 'I'm sorry,' he continues. 'I can see this is a very difficult time for you all, and I should have judged it better. And of course, it's very upsetting to think of someone coming to this kind of harm so nearby.'

Celine opens the front door, the sight of the wheelbarrow on the far verge a reminder of the gardener. 'Oh, shall I see if I can find that name for you?'

Sergeant Edwards is already on the gravel, heading towards the squad car. 'Oh, yes. PC Whitman?'

As his superior starts the engine, the constable waits on the doorstep while Celine checks the kitchen board for any details of Harry the gardener. Pip is now sitting at the table, doodling with the kids; Celine winks at her, a reassurance, and when she finds nothing on the board she returns to PC Whitman on the doorstep, where he's now chatting with Una.

'Sorry, there don't seem to be any details for the gardener,' Celine says. 'But we'll be sure to nab him next time he's here, get him to give you a call.'

Una runs a hand over Celine's back. 'The PC was just telling me about the property down the road – the big gated one,' she says. 'You'll never guess what?'

Celine shakes her head.

Una looks back at the young man. 'He tells me it's a women's commune.'

Celine thinks of the women she spotted through the gate as she paused there the other day, remembering the uneasy sense she'd had as she drove away along the woodland path. The way they were dressed, so out of kilter with the grand setting of the house and grounds, had led her to assume they were workers – gardeners or landscapers – not residents.

'A commune?' she repeats, the word 'cult' popping into her head as she says it.

'It's called Two Cross Farm,' PC Whitman says. 'They're a bit of a funny bunch by all accounts. We're just off there to try again now. No one answered when we called before, and we're very keen to speak to the women there.'

'You think they know something?'

Whitman looks over his shoulder, towards the idling police vehicle. 'I shouldn't really—'

'It won't go any further,' Una says, leaning in conspiratorially. 'Did I mention I was a detective at Scotland Yard before I retired?'

'The Met?' His face lights up. After a moment's hesitation, he goes on. 'Well, we think there's a chance the dead woman was a resident there.'

Una's face remains impassive, but Celine can almost feel the vibrations of her mind whirring. 'What makes you think that?'

'Tattoos,' he says, lowering his voice.

'Tattoos?' Celine frowns.

'Forensics told us she has tattoos, and it all adds up. Two black crosses.' When neither Una nor Celine are able to form an answer, he elaborates. 'Like the name of the commune, you see? Two Cross Farm? We think it could be connected.'

'Oh,' Celine manages as she takes in the relevance of what he's saying. 'Of course.'

'Anyway,' he says, handing Una a contact card and starting to turn away, 'if you hear anything, you'll let us know?'

'These tattoos . . .' Una says casually, halting him in his tracks.

Celine is aware of Pip's presence in the entrance to the kitchen behind her, but she can't turn away from the officer, from the question she knows Una is about to ask.

'Whereabouts on the body were they?'

Once again, the constable glances towards the police car and back at Una and Celine. 'I shouldn't,' he says, but then, quite

46

unexpectedly, he raises his two index fingers and subtly taps his lower abdomen. Then he lifts a farewell hand, and he's gone.

Over her shoulder Celine hears Pip's sharp intake of breath, mirroring her own internal lurch of horror.

Softly, Una closes the door, and turns. They can hear the children's voices from the kitchen, squabbling over some small thing, and the distant rumble of the police car retreating across the driveway. Spring sunshine cuts shards through the decorative glass panel above the door, slicing bright crescents over the polished floorboards at Celine's feet, and she feels sick at the idea of what they're about to say.

'It's probably just—' Celine murmurs, but Pip turns fierce eyes on her, shaking her head in disbelief.

'Don't you dare say it's a coincidence!' she cries out.

They both turn to Una, looking to her as the voice of reason, the deciding vote.

'You heard what they said about the way she was laid out? *Carefully*. On wooden boards?' Pip is visibly trembling. 'And – and – these tattoos, for Christ's sake, Celine!'

Celine's mind can't keep up, and she's desperate to think of reasons for this *not* to be related, *not* to be connected to their sister. 'But Vanessa was found in Brighton.'

'You said it yourself, Una, Brighton's only twenty miles away!' Pip blinks at Una and Celine, waiting for them to answer. 'We can't ignore the tattoos. I always said there was something strange about it – Vanessa was the last person you'd ever expect to get one done, and now, here we are hearing about another dead woman, with identical tattoos. *Celine!* Say something!'

Celine presses her back against the cool wall, anchoring herself.

'Vanessa went to a refuge, not a commune,' Una says, but it's clear she's just thinking aloud, the gears of her mind working it through.

'We don't actually know that,' Pip insists.

'She's right, isn't she, Una?' Celine gulps a hard lump down, feeling light-headed; feeling *too much*. 'There *are* too many similarities. In that phone message, Vanessa only told us she was safe – away from Jem – that she had somewhere safe to go. But did she ever actually *say* it was a refuge? Or did we just jump to that conclusion? I can't remember, can you?'

Una runs the heel of her hand over her forehead. 'I don't know.'

'And now, with that postcard we found in the attic, we *do* know that Vanessa came to see Mum in the year before she died,' Pip says. 'It makes sense – she came to see Mum, not because she was desperate to see her, but because she was on her way to this women's commune – just down the road!' For a few seconds, the three stand in silence.

Una stares back at the sisters, her eyes moving between them, calculating.

'Mummy?' Olive calls from the kitchen. 'Mummy! Beebee won't let me have the yellow!'

'Just a minute, sweetheart!' Pip calls out, her gaze fixed resolutely on Una.

Celine's heart feels as though it's about to beat right out through her ribcage. 'Una?' she whispers. 'What are you thinking?'

'I'm thinking,' Una replies, with a deep, sorrowful sigh, 'that these deaths might be fifteen years apart, but from where I'm standing there are far too many coincidences for my liking.'

For a few seconds, no one speaks.

Pip is the one who breaks the silence. 'Una, is this enough to persuade the police to reopen the case?'

'I don't know,' Una replies. 'They're gonna need something fairly concrete to persuade them,' she says, her focus on some faraway thought as she runs a hand along her jawline.

'Please, Una—' Pip begins to plead, but she doesn't get to finish her sentence, because all at once Una is striding out towards the back garden, mobile phone in hand.

'Give me a bit of space, girls,' she calls over her shoulder. 'I need to make that call.'

7. BRAMBLE

1977, Two Cross Farm

By the time the child arrived at Two Cross Farm on a cold afternoon in darkest February, our number had swelled to sixteen, just under half of the desired thirty-three sisters laid out in our manifesto. Seed brought the number up to seventeen.

In less than six months, Fern had gathered a community workforce of two cooks, two gardeners, three housekeepers, two on building and decorating, two running the art studio, one physiotherapist, one yoga teacher, one treasurer – me – and in Kathy, an experienced doctor.

Not only was Kathy a GP, she was also a mother of three, and so that afternoon, when Fern summoned the rest of us to join them to meet the long-awaited infant, I assumed it was to tell us that Kathy would take a lead role in caring for the child. As Susan, Regine and I cautiously entered the bedroom, we found the room lit only by candlelight, and Fern sitting at the edge of her bed, staring intently at the baby cradled in Kathy's arms.

'How was your journey?' Regine asked, still, I think, smarting at Kathy's having been chosen over her to accompany Fern. On more than one occasion in recent weeks, Regine had tried to engage me in gossip about the possible paternity of the child, but I wouldn't bite, and I was certain she knew as little as the rest of us. We Founding Sisters knew who the mother was, but of the father we knew nothing whatsoever.

Fern and Kathy were shadow-eyed with exhaustion, that much we all could see, even in the low candlelight of the room. The run-up to this point had not been without its tests, but now the child was here, and Fern's relief was writ large.

'The journey was what it was,' she replied, with a long at-peace sigh, 'but now the struggle is over.'

Kathy shifted on the edge of the bed, silently rearranging the baby in her arms. I wondered what was going on inside her head – whether the child's presence resurrected memories of her own children, the three she'd left behind.

'Meet our sixth Founding Sister,' Fern whispered in a low voice, indicating for us to find seats where we could. 'Her name is Seed, and she's travelled a hard path to get here.'

In turn, we each laid a hand on the child, and inwardly I marvelled at the soft crown of her head, at the perfect innocence of her. She was mesmerising, and for long minutes we sat there, all five of us simply gazing on this sixth member of our group, the child we would raise as a sister. I felt as though I was witnessing some historic event, a world-altering moment which would change all of our lives forever. Beyond the bedroom a door banged shut, and at the noise the baby arched her back, stiffening as though in pain, her face creasing into a red grimace.

'May I?' I asked, reaching out to take the small bundle from Kathy. I held her against me in the same way she had, supporting the child's head in my palm, feeling the light rise and fall of her breath against my body as she struggled weakly. Gradually, the little one's face relaxed, and her body eased into a contented dense weight, and I looked at the others to share in my joy.

'Oh, Fern,' young Susan whispered, hooking her little finger under the child's curled hand. She cast about the room in awe. 'Don't you all just adore her? She couldn't be more perfect.'

There was a strange pause, as Kathy's eyes briefly flew to Fern's, before returning to the child. Discreetly, she wiped away a tear, smiling now and patting Fern's leg reassuringly. 'You're right, Susan,' Kathy agreed. 'She's beautiful.'

It was a harshly cold night, but warm in Fern's musky den of a bedroom, and the body temperature of the baby in my embrace felt so much like my own that for a moment I wondered if she and I had fused to become one. I was gripped by a sudden, irrational fear that I'd soon have to give her up, and when I looked up to see Fern watching so intently I wondered what it could mean. As our eyes met, and she nodded very slightly, the whole room, and everyone in it, seemed to drop away.

'Bramble, you have never mothered before,' she said. 'This, I am guessing, is your one great regret.'

All at once I was exposed: Fern truly saw me, stripped bare, and now they all could see it. My motherlessness; my worthlessness. I had nothing to offer the community, except money.

'And so this is my gift to you. Bramble, *you* will mother the child, and Kathy, you will see to her health and development. It is my vision that Seed will one day be my successor, and so, when she comes of age, I will take over her tutelage, to lead her towards the helm.'

Regine remained silent.

'And me?' Susan asked, her expression hopeful.

'You and Regine will be her sisters and her friends,' Fern replied. 'And she will learn great things from you.' After a pause, she indicated that I should hand Seed back to Kathy. 'Kathy, I believe no one here has changed a baby's diaper before. Take them to Bramble's room to show them how it's done, and explain to them about the child's complications.'

'Complications?' Regine asked.

'Shush,' Fern replied, lying back against her pillow with a yawn. 'It's nothing of great concern,' she murmured sleepily. 'Kathy will explain everything, and tomorrow, when I am rested, I will answer any further questions.'

And, with that, she closed her eyes.

Regine and Susan left the room before me, and I paused to look at Kathy as she stood and redistributed the child's weight in her arms. Earlier, I'd seen sadness in her expression, and regret. But now, as she looked up and her eyes met mine, I saw something else altogether.

It was fear.

8. CELINE

Present day

Una's police contact is away on a day's leave when she first tries to phone, and the long hours until the next day have been agonising for Celine and Pip. Is it possible that the truth behind Vanessa's death is more complicated than any of them had dared to think?

This morning, with the kids getting restless back at Delilah's place, Una had pressed some cash into Pip's hand and persuaded the sisters to take a trip to the medieval castle at the top of the town.

'There's nothing you can do here,' Una had bossed them. 'You might as well make the most of the good weather, and give the girls a nice time. They don't want to sit around looking at your long faces all morning, do they? Neither do I, for that matter.'

As they left for the castle, Una was already pulling on her walking boots, planning to set off along the river to see if she could get a good view of the women's commune from the rear, to kill time while she waited for a call back from her DI pal, Dave Aston.

Now, as the sisters meander through the castle's manicured grounds, Olive and Beebee run ahead, battling with tiny wooden swords bought in the gift shop with Auntie Una's pocket money. Everything feels surreal to Celine: Delilah's sudden death, her big lonely house, and now this – this resurrection of Vanessa's tragedy.

'I can't believe Mum lived here all this time,' Pip says, breaking her thoughts. 'With no sign of a man, not recently anyway by the looks of it. Could you ever have imagined that?'

Celine shakes her head. 'Never. Does Stefan mind you being away with the kids?' she asks, pausing to stuff the girls' soft toys to the bottom of her bag. Somehow she's become the official guardian of Lady-Dog and Spider-Boo, their most treasured possessions.

'Not at all,' Pip replies rather too quickly, and there's no denying the defensive tone in her voice. She must notice it herself, because she sounds more jovial when she adds, 'He's probably having a lovely break without us there, making a racket. Olive can be a bit full-on at times, and he finds it really hard to concentrate at work if she's woken us in the night.'

'So, he's good at helping with the girls, then?'

'Huh?'

'He gets up and deals with Olive in the night?'

'Oh, well, no, I do that. But, you know, it still takes its toll on him.'

If Celine is truthful with herself, she'll admit she's never taken to Stefan, but she knows she would sound like a cow if she were to voice her reservations. He's *too* nice, too charming and attentive by far. But how could she ever say that aloud, when their other sister almost certainly died at the hands of a partner who was at the opposite end of the charm spectrum, who wasn't nice at all? 'Well, you know what they say,' she says instead. 'Absence makes the heart grow fonder.'

Pip makes a little scoffing sound, and they drop the subject. 'Did you sleep much last night?' she asks Celine as they pass through the apple arches, the branches almost in full flower.

'Barely a wink,' Celine admits. 'You?'

'I kept drifting off, but then my mind would conjure up that dead woman they've just found, and I'd imagine her lying there on the pontoon by the river at the bottom of our garden. In my dream, it was night-time, and I knew she was there, but I couldn't stop myself from running across the garden, down to the river, because somehow I *had* to check the riverside to be sure she hadn't moved.' She puffs air through pursed lips, and when she speaks again her voice trembles. 'Every time I reached the decking and looked down at her face—'

'You saw Vanessa.' Celine finishes her sentence, knowing exactly what Pip saw, because she's seen it too, played it over and over again in her mind's eye. Just as she had fifteen years ago, when Vanessa was found dead.

Pip halts on the path and grasps Celine's wrist. 'We're not being hysterical, are we? I mean, after all this time, it *is* completely mad to think the two deaths are connected – Una has said as much – but, I mean, the details are just too close, aren't they? And, God, those *tattoos*. They sound identical – what are the chances of that? I always said Ness was the last person you'd expect to get a tattoo, but no one took me seriously. What if someone *made* her have them, Celine? You hear of it, don't you, killers leaving their mark on a body, a signature of sorts. What if that's what those tattoos are?'

'It's *very* hard to accurately tattoo someone against their will, Pip,' Celine says, recalling the scorching pain of the tiny gavel she'd had inked on her ankle in a moment of post-exam madness ten years back. 'And the police would have said if the tattoos had been done post – you know, *after* death.' A wave of panic rushes over her, to hear herself talking so reasonably about something so dreadful. Why does she always have to be the calm one? She didn't ask for the job. Right now, what she really feels like doing is crumpling into a ball and screaming until her lungs give out.

Forcing a smile, she raises a hand to return a wave to Olive, who is now standing on the arm of a wooden bench at the far side of the courtyard, calling her name. The little girl has her fingers jammed into her mouth, and she's trying to whistle in the way Auntie Ceecee can. Circling her finger and thumb between her own lips, Celine sends a piercing whistle across the courtyard, causing Olive to throw down her arms in frustration.

Pip sighs heavily beside her. 'Do you think it could be Jem again?' she asks. 'Do you think he could have killed them both?'

'Why would it be Jem?' Celine replies, letting her irritation show. 'Jem's got nothing to do with this new girl.'

'You don't know that.'

'No one's even *seen* him for fifteen years, Pip! He's long gone! I'd like to see the bastard swing for Vanessa's death as much as you would, but the police are never gonna listen to us if you start throwing mad ideas into the mix. The best we can hope for from this is that they get to interview those women at Two Cross Farm, and find out more about Vanessa's last movements. We're not looking for a serial killer, you know. We're looking for *Vanessa's* killer.'

'What's so mad about the idea that Jem *is* a serial killer? If he did murder Vanessa, he's capable of murdering other people, isn't he? What if that's why he disappeared in the first place – because he's keeping a low profile and killing other women?'

Celine takes a deep breath. 'Why here?' she asks, throwing an arm out, gesturing around. 'Why target Two Cross Farm?'

'Maybe he just hates women. There are plenty of them there,' Pip replies, starting to walk again, sounding less certain.

'But why *here*, in Arundel?' Celine's frustration is getting the better of her.

Pip throws up her hands, matching Celine's tone. 'Maybe he moved back to the area.'

There's a two- or three-second delay while Celine takes in what Pip just said. She spins her sister round to face her. 'What do you mean, "back"?'

Pip's forehead crinkles. 'Back to Sussex.'

'I don't understand,' Celine says, her heart accelerating.

'He grew up in Littlehampton,' Pip says. 'You know that – the papers printed it at the time. It's only down the road from here.'

All at once, Celine remembers this small detail of Jem's life, the name of the town he grew up in. She'd never made any connections before, because there had been none to be made. 'Where exactly is Littlehampton?' she asks now.

'It's four miles away,' Pip replies. 'In the direction of Brighton.'

'Jeez, Pip. *Brighton*.' Where Vanessa was found, a small voice murmurs inside her head. Is this relevant? Does this make a difference, or will it be just like all those other leads they've explored in the past that end up meaning absolutely nothing?

'Yes! He's *local*, Celine.' When Celine doesn't reply, Pip tries to call Una, but finds her phone engaged. 'She must be speaking to her DI pal,' she says, tapping out a text message instead. 'Una will listen to me,' she adds, angrily, 'even if you won't.'

As the possible implications of this new connection sink in, the sisters walk in silence for a while, until Olive and Beebee start to squabble around their legs and Pip diverts them with a visit to the café for hot chocolate.

'You go on your own,' Celine tells them, feeling in desperate need of some space. 'I'll make my way up to the Keep. Come and find me there when you're done?'

'Ollee bopped my nose,' she hears Beebee complaining as they set off in the opposite direction.

'Off with her head!' Olive replies, and she darts along the path on sturdy legs, dark curls flying, a tiny wooden sword held aloft. Celine wonders if she and her sisters were ever as untroubled as those two little girls. She thinks about Vanessa's wicked sense of humour, and it occurs to her that Olive is very like their sister; she hopes Pip can see it too, that perhaps the knowledge of it brings her some comfort.

The footbridge to the Keep is completely empty of visitors, and Celine is glad of the solitude, of the momentary quiet in which to think. She follows the stone path, leading her inside the bowels of the round tower, up sets of narrow and winding steps until she reaches the top of the fortress with its peep holes and open-air viewing gallery, where she pauses to check her phone. No update from Una yet. As Celine walks around the railed battlements she can see as far as the coast on one side, and across miles of field and country all around. Which direction is Littlehampton? Which way points to the childhood home of that monster Jem Falmer? Across the landscape, little clusters of hamlets and individual dwellings are dotted around, and after some searching she is able to calculate where the River Arun runs along to Delilah's house, past the women's community and beyond. Both properties are hidden from view, each entirely shielded by the dense canopy of trees and surrounding woodland. If you didn't know better, you'd never guess they were there at all.

For a moment she allows herself to remember what really brought them here in the first place: their mother. She wonders what motivated Delilah to buy Belle France, and to live there alone. It has all the usual Delilah Murphy hallmarks – it's big and grand, comfortable and stylish – but it's so far removed from her previous life in Kingston, located as they were on the edge of 'what's happening'. There, Delilah was never without company, some man or other calling to drive her into town for a show or a meal. But at the end of her days it seems she had no one. If it hadn't been for the mobile pharmacy making his fortnightly call to Delilah's that morning, she might have lain there for weeks, or months, undiscovered, dead in her bed.

What a waste, Celine thinks now, not for her mother, but for the relationships Delilah might have had with her daughters, if she'd wanted them badly enough. If she'd wanted Celine and her sisters more than she'd wanted the company of men. Had the girls minded all those men at the time, traipsing through their lives? Celine thinks not; all the time Delilah had her adoring audience, Delilah was happy. Happy to stay and play mother. Had she been following some man when she'd left her teenage girls to fend for themselves all those years ago? It had always been the most likely explanation, more palatable to imagine that she was running *to* something rather than *away from* them. She'd certainly had a boyfriend back in 2010 when she'd met Celine for tea. And yet there's no sign of anyone in her life in recent times: no clues around her home, or among the possessions they've raked through. Perhaps, finally, Delilah had learnt to live independently, without the constant reassurance and approval she'd seemed only to find in the company of men.

In the distance, beyond the walls of the Keep, Olive comes into view, springing through the gardens below, followed by Beebee and Pip. 'Woo-woo!' Olive shouts, delightedly, and Pip breaks into a run, chasing them with arms outstretched, playing the ogre. As they rush past the jasmine, tiny petals rise up in their wake, and Pip catches her children, one under each arm. She draws them close, kissing their heads in turn, dozens of little pecks, and Celine can see that she's lost to it, entirely consumed by her love for them.

A crashing sense of hopelessness weighs down on Celine, as she watches unseen through the gap in the turret. It's not just about *being* loved, is it? It's about *having* someone to love. Pip has her children; *she* has someone to love, and even if her husband *is* an arse, even if he were to leave her tomorrow – or her him – she'd still have those children. How did Pip learn to love like that? For *their* mother, Delilah, the children had never been enough.

A lurching sob rises up in Celine's chest, and she grinds her teeth against it, forcing it back down. She shouldn't be here, opening up the past like this. It makes her weak. They need to get on with the funeral, and with the task of clearing the house and tying up the legal details of Delilah's will. What the hell are they thinking, dragging up the horror of Vanessa's death all over again? The more she thinks about it, the more certain she is that Una's DI pal is going to say these connections are too tenuous to link the deaths – far too many years apart. The officer who'd visited yesterday said Robyn Siegle's injuries weren't immediately evident, that they'd need a post-mortem to determine how she'd died. Vanessa's injuries were entirely different, and they couldn't have been more evident. She was beaten and strangled in a frenzied attack. Surely that disparity alone is enough to make the police dismiss whatever it is Una is putting to them, tell them to drop it, get over it and get on with their lives. Embarrassment creeps through Celine's nerves, a feeling of deep shame that she's let her usual guardedness slip. They've got themselves carried away with this insane idea about finding Vanessa's killer – a fantasy at best – and Celine needs to stop it before they go any further.

Turning to make her way down, she resolves to pack her bags as soon as they arrive back at the house, for Pip's sake as much as her own. First thing tomorrow morning, she'll return to her life and work in Bournemouth, and try to forget all about this place. Forget all about Vanessa and Jem Falmer and that poor dead stranger left at the riverside.

She almost doesn't hear her mobile phone ringing as a party of foreign students passes her on the narrow stairwell, and when she manages to retrieve the handset from her pocket it's Una's name displayed on the screen.

'Una? Hello? Listen, I've been thinking—'

'Hang on a sec, Celine.' There's a moment's hesitation on the other end of the line, of footsteps on dry earth and the distant sound of flowing water. Celine imagines Una sitting on the bench beyond the garden of Belle France, her steady dark eyes gazing out over the river.

When Una at last speaks, her tone is buoyant. 'Celine, you know I said we were gonna need something more concrete to link the two cases?'

'Ye-es,' Celine replies cautiously, her focus locked on Pip and the girls making their way through the courtyard below.

'Well,' Una says, 'I think I've found it.'

9. BRAMBLE

1979, Two Cross Farm

'She doesn't meet any of the criteria, Fern,' Kathy complained. 'We want another cook, or someone with carpentry skills. Another pair of hands in the laundry room. Not a tattooist!'

The Founding Sisters were sitting around Fern's desk, in her newly refurbished office, preparing to interview a prospective resident. The first-floor window overlooked the front drive, from where Fern could see anyone who came to the gate as she worked, and she could get the peace she needed for the running of this place. Right now, outside was a landscape of white, snow having fallen heavily in the night, and little Seed was balanced on my knee, quietly gazing out through the window, mesmerised by the strangeness of the scene.

'I like the look of her resumé,' Fern said, pushing Sandy's letter of application towards us where we sat on the other side of her desk. 'She won't be *employed* as a tattooist, Kathy, that's just an additional skill. Look – she's travelled extensively, worked in bars, on plantations – picking potatoes, scrubbing toilets, washing dishes. She's a grafter. *That's* what we need at Two Cross Farm.'

Sandy, the young woman in question, was currently waiting to be interviewed in the front reception room, having trudged two miles from the train station in the snow with her life's belongings strapped to her back.

Kathy allowed her eyes to flit over the letter, before nudging it away with a short-clipped fingernail. 'I still think someone with a skilled trade would be more use to us.'

'You're forgetting dynamics, Kathy,' Fern replied persuasively. 'We always talked about achieving the right balance of skill and temperament, of age and experience, *and* newness. This girl, Sandy – she's young, but she's seen a bit of the world, and she's clearly a team player. She doesn't seem to have any family to speak of, so she's alone. And she *does* have a trade, whether you approve of it or not.'

'I don't *not* approve of it,' Kathy argued. 'I just really don't see the use for it here.'

Fern spread her hands. 'Well, as ever, it'll come down to the vote – fifty per cent or more of us in favour and she stays; less and she goes. Tell the others we're ready, and let's get her in. Susan?'

Susan left the room and by the time she returned with Sandy, the prospective new sister, we had arranged ourselves in a cross-legged circle on the Indian rug at the centre of the room. A space had been left for Susan to complete the circle beside Fern, and with a silent gesture Sandy was invited to sit on the cushion in the middle. Little Seed sat nestled in the hollow of my lap, quietly plaiting a friendship bracelet, her demeanour and dexterity already advanced for her years.

'You'll be nice and quiet and listen to the new lady?' I whispered in her ear.

'*Woman*,' Fern reminded me in a low voice, having overheard. 'We say "woman" here, Bramble.'

I felt suitably chastened; it wasn't the first time I'd made the mistake. *Women are warriors*, Fern was always telling the group. *Ladies are lily-livered.* 'Be nice and quiet for the new woman, OK?' I told Seed.

The little girl turned her face up towards mine and nodded earnestly, placing a small finger to her pursed lips, and Fern smiled at me approvingly, before turning the full light of her attention on our new visitor, now sitting at the centre of the circle, facing Fern. Sandy really was young, and she wore a long paisley dress with gathered cuffs, her tangled hair pinned high on her head. But she was no innocent; she had a hungry look, a lean-nosed, deprived aura.

'Hello, Sandy,' Fern said. She was holding a soft ball now, which she rotated between the tips of her index fingers in a rhythmic motion. 'Thank you for travelling to us through the snow. I think your trip was cold, no?' She smiled, nodding towards Sandy's ruddy bare feet, and gently threw the ball into the young woman's waiting hands.

'It was fackin' freezing,' she said, her estuary accent hard and surprisingly out of kilter with her beatnik appearance.

The room burst into laughter, and Sandy threw the ball to Susan, shifting slightly to face her.

'How old are you?' Susan asked, clearly pleased at the prospect of someone close to her own age joining us.

Sandy caught the ball. 'Nineteen, nearly twenty.' She threw the ball to Regine.

'Where were you before this?'

'Indonesia.' To me, and another shift on the cushion.

'Are you a runaway?' I asked, for many of the younger women were.

Sandy pulled a face, as though the question was ridiculous, but then she seemed to think better of it, and I believed the answer she gave was the truth. 'I left home when I was fourteen. My family, well, they're not good people. My mum died the year before, and my dad and brothers, they all thought I'd join the family business soon as I left school, but I didn't want a bar of it. So I made my own way.'

'Was your father violent?' Regine asked.

She nodded, and passed the ball to Kathy.

'What can you offer us, Sandy?' Kathy asked, pushing her spectacles up her nose in her customary way. 'What skills do you bring?'

'I'm strong. Artistic. And I ain't scared of muckin' in and makin' friends.'

Before Sandy could rid herself of the ball again, Kathy held up a hand. 'Yes. That's very good, but I asked you what *skills* you have. Specifically.'

The girl looked around the circle, and with her large heavy-lashed eyes she reminded me in some strange way of a cow at the boundary of a field, assessing approaching humans for signs of danger. She rolled up her sleeves and pulled back her skirts to reveal limbs so entirely tattooed that, apart from her hands and feet, not an inch of skin was visible. She threw the ball to me.

'I – I—' I stuttered, because truly, I was completely stumped at the sight of her. Only on sailors and ex-cons had I ever seen such comprehensive inking, and even then only in photographs. 'I wonder how this might benefit the group?' I asked, returning the ball to her.

'I've brought my kit with me,' she replied, one corner of her mouth turning upwards. 'You know the ancient Egyptians used to tattoo their high priestesses, to signify their importance? They've found them – mummified – from thousands of years ago.

66

Tattoos mean all kinds of things. They can mean a journey, or a challenge, or achievement, or love. They can mean belonging too, membership of a special group.' She hesitated a moment, checking she still had our full attention. 'How would you describe this place? Is it a brainwashing cult, like people say? Or is it a safe place for women?' When no one answered, she shifted and threw the ball to Fern.

Fern was radiating her best self, her happiest, most fulfilled self, because she knew she'd chosen well, and the girl was saying everything she wanted to hear. 'It's the latter. And I couldn't have put it better myself. Sandy, tell me, how do you think your skills could enhance this community and our atmosphere of belonging?'

Sandy caught the ball. 'Well, I'll work at anything you set me to, I said that, didn't I? Cooking, cleaning, gardening – whatever wants doing.'

Fern nods.

'Aaa-nd,' Sandy says, drawing her skirts back down to cover her legs, 'If you wanted, I could create a tattoo just for you. For the group. To be gifted to only the most dedicated women; to be earned, if you like?'

'Like a Brownie badge?' Susan said, clamping a hand to her mouth when she realised she wasn't in possession of the ball. Swiftly, Sandy threw it to her.

'Ball!' Seed exclaimed as Susan caught it with a surprised squeal. I wrapped my arms across her small warm body, and kissed her on the head. 'That's right,' I whispered, and she fell to her plaiting work again.

'What kind of tattoo?' Susan asked, sparkle-eyed as she returned the ball to Sandy.

'I dunno – you could all help to design it, couldn't you?'

The ball went to Fern.

'It would be two crosses. Two black crosses. Here,' Fern said indicating first to one side of her pelvis and then the other. 'And here. Representing our strength; our refusal to bear the fruit of the men who would seek to govern us.'

'Two black crosses it is.' Sandy nodded confidently.

Fern set the ball down outside of the circle. 'Women,' she said, 'this is Sandy who wishes to join our number. All those in favour, raise your hand high.'

Susan's was the first hand to join Fern's, followed by Regine, by me and little Seed, and when Kathy's hand joined ours, however reluctantly, the vote was unanimous.

'Welcome, Sister Sandy!' Fern cried, rising to embrace the young woman with fervour, and Seed and I went directly to prepare her room.

10. CELINE

Present day

Back at the house, there is an atmosphere of urgency as Pip distracts the girls with a plate of snacks and children's TV while Una sets up the laptop at the kitchen table.

Celine makes the coffee, knowing better than to interrogate Una until they're all assembled, and they move about the room in heavy silence until the three of them are seated around the screen. She brings up a BBC News article, reporting on the recent discovery of twenty-four-year-old American chef Robyn Siegle, who had arrived in the UK a year earlier after her marriage broke down.

Una reads aloud from the screen: '*Police investigating the as yet unexplained death confirm that mother-of-one Ms Siegle had, until very recently, been a resident at Two Cross Farm, an all-women community located in the Arundel area of West Sussex.*'

She pauses, allowing the confirmation to sink in for a moment, before continuing: '*Archie Chowdhury, the victim's estranged husband, is being sought by Sussex police, who say they would like to eliminate him from their enquiries. US-born Chowdhury is thought to be currently living in London, where he also works as a chef.'*

Pip drums the table with her fingernails, her expression confused. 'So, they think the ex-husband did it?' She glances between Celine and Una, crestfallen. 'If it was the husband, it can't have anything to do with Jem Falmer – or Vanessa – can it?'

'Exactly,' Celine replies, stopping just short of *I told you so*. The very fact that Robyn's ex is in the frame is surely enough to establish that this is a one-off, and not related to Vanessa at all. 'Una,' she says, 'when you called earlier you made it sound as though you'd had a breakthrough. All this article does is show us how *un*related the two cases are.'

'I agree,' Una replies, rising from her seat to cross the kitchen and pick up a small framed print. 'But that got me thinking. What if Jem Falmer and Archie Chowdhury were only part of the story? What if the police's knowledge of the victim's bad relationships – the violence in Vanessa's case, the separation in Robyn's – was stopping them from looking in other places, from considering everything?'

'Lazy policing, you mean?' Celine asks.

Una shrugs. 'It's not unheard of for senior officers to get an idea in their head and refuse to be diverted from it. That's how the Yorkshire Ripper got away with it for so long – one senior officer decided it was a man with a Geordie accent, and the rest of the team stopped considering anyone who didn't fit that description.'

'What's that you've got?' Pip asks, gesturing towards the upturned picture.

'You know I took a stroll along the riverside this morning, while I was waiting for Dave Aston to call? I walked all the way down to the footbridge and back, passing Two Cross Farm en route. Of course, it's not a farm these days – don't think it has been for a very long time, if at all.'

'Could you see it from the path?' Celine asks.

Una opens the photos app on her phone and scrolls through. 'They've purposely grown the hedges high at the back, just like around the rest of the property. It's properly fenced, with leylandii almost entirely obliterating the view. But the good thing about leylandii is that it stops the residents seeing out as much as it stops others looking in, and I found a little break in the hedge to spy through.'

There are a few still photos, but most interesting is the short video clip Una has captured, giving a slow panorama of the grounds, panning over lawns and greenhouses, vegetable plots and compost heaps. In the further distance there's a driveway, not unlike Delilah's, and, close to the hedge, a well-stocked wood store and shed. A brick footpath meanders across the lawn, coming to a stop outside French doors to the back of the house, through which two women emerge, carrying laundry baskets. Both are wearing hemp-coloured tunics; one has her hair cut short, the other wears hers long and loose. They begin pegging bright white sheets along a washing line which stretches the full length of the garden. It's almost hypnotic viewing.

'It's like something out of a movie,' Pip murmurs.

'But did you learn anything new?' Celine asks.

'I did,' Una says, not reacting to Celine's abrupt tone as she presses pause on the video. 'Do you see that, on the right-hand-side of the screen?' She points to a miniature windmill at the edge of the drive, maybe five feet high, a traditional white stone construction, with a black cap and working sails.

The sisters nod.

'There was something so familiar about that image, something I couldn't put my finger on. Anyway, my phone rang at this point, which is why the video ends here. I didn't want those women catching me stuck in their hedge, so I got moving sharpish.'

'Was it your police friend?'

'Dave Aston, yes. I actually had two conversations with him, one then, and another when I got home and found this.' With a cryptic smile, she taps the back of the picture.

'Oh, for God's sake, Una,' Celine barks, flipping the frame over.

Pip lets out a hoot, laughing at her sister, but when they see the image behind the glass they fall silent again. It's postcard-sized, a black and white linocut of a windmill. That very same windmill. Along the foot of the image are the words: *Handprinted at Two Cross Farm*.

'Where did you find this?' Celine asks.

'Hanging in the spare bedroom,' Una replies, raising one eyebrow. 'The minute I got through the door after my walk, I remembered – I've been waking up to this image every morning since I got here. It was on the wall beside the reading lamp.' She turns it over and unpins the casing, removing the original print and sliding it across the table to Pip. 'Read it,' she says.

Pip reads the message aloud. '*Dear Mum, I'm sorry I missed you when I visited. Just want you to know I love you and forgive you, Vx.*'

'Is it dated?' Celine asks.

Una nods. 'Three months before Vanessa's death.'

'So, Vanessa was *definitely* a resident there – just like Robyn?'

'I think this confirms it,' Una replies, 'though there's no way of telling from this exactly when she got there or how long she stayed. It also suggests she never actually got to see Delilah when she came – so your mum was telling the truth when she told the police she hadn't seen her in the previous year.' She pauses for a moment, thinking. 'Either way, this would certainly explain the tattoos. Like that young PC suggested – two crosses for Two Cross Farm.'

Celine puts her head in her hands; it's all too much. She thinks about her plan to pack up and go home, but she knows this latest

72

discovery puts paid to that. How can she leave now? And it's not as though she's got anything pressing to rush back for in Bournemouth; there's no partner waiting on the doorstep with open arms, no cat wanting to be fed, no children missing their mummy. Even her boss has made it clear they can do without her, since she'll be leaving soon anyway. 'God, Una,' she says, 'I don't think I'm any clearer than I was this morning. What can we do with this information?'

'That's where DI Aston comes into it.' Una opens a new tab and starts to dial up a number on FaceTime. 'I filled him in on Vanessa's situation and he said he'd go away and do a bit of digging. He's expecting a call back from me about now.'

Pip and Celine exchange a concerned glance. 'Do you want us to leave the room?' Celine asks. 'As it's police talk.'

'No, no, he said he might have a few questions for you.'

The line connects and the steady-eyed face of a man in his late forties fills the screen. 'Hello, Una – are we connected?'

Una adjusts the laptop so all three of them are visible in the small screen reader. 'Yup. Hello, Dave. I'd like to introduce you to Celine and Pip Murphy – sisters of the young woman I told you about earlier, Vanessa.'

He bobs his head. 'Good to meet you both, though I'm sorry it's under these circumstances. And I understand you're dealing with another bereavement at the moment – my condolences to you both.'

Celine likes him, *trusts* him, instantly. 'Thank you,' she says.

'So, what did you find out, Dave?' Una asks.

Celine's not sure what the dynamics of their working relationship are, but it's instantly clear that these two know and respect each other, sharing an easy shorthand which does away with superfluous pleasantries. This comes as a great relief to Celine, who just wants to hear it straight.

'Well – and this is privileged information so it stays within this group – I can tell you that I've had Robyn Siegle's father on the phone from the US this afternoon, who was able to tell me that, since leaving for England a year ago, Robyn had embarked on an intense correspondence with a woman here, at a place called Two Cross Farm.'

'She told her dad all this?' Una asks.

'Yes. Seems father and daughter were close – spoke on the phone at least once a fortnight, and she'd been fairly open with him, up until three months ago, when she jacked in her job and moved away from her London flat.'

'Was he worried when she lost contact?' Celine asks.

'Not too much, because she was still dropping him the odd postcard or letter, and her messages were very positive, telling him how she'd settled into the women's community, and how happy she was. In these letters, she spoke very warmly about this woman called Seed.'

'Seed?' Pip says. 'What kind of name is that?'

'A cultish one,' mutters Celine, and Una nudges her to behave.

Dave riffles through some papers, before looking up again. 'Seed – no surname that we can yet establish – is the leader at Two Cross Farm.'

Beebee wanders into the kitchen and pulls on her mother's sleeve, causing the image to blur momentarily. 'Hungry,' she murmurs.

Pip closes her eyes and sighs heavily.

Without a thought, Celine jumps up and leads the little tot to the fridge, where together they find a new block of cheese. She chops a chunk into tiny squares and sends Beebee toddling off again, balancing the bowl between pudgy hands and promising to share with her sister. *Thank you*, Pip mouths as Celine closes the fridge door.

'Robyn was having a relationship with this Seed woman?' Celine asks as she returns to her seat.

'Platonic, or something more?' Una adds.

'We couldn't say,' Dave Aston replies. 'We've spoken to Seed via telephone – thankfully, they do *actually* have a landline – and she maintains Robyn was just another resident, that there was no special relationship, but still, she sounded very edgy.'

'Well, one of her women *has* just been murdered,' Una says, ever the voice of balance.

Dave nods his agreement.

Celine leans in closer. 'Dave, do you think Vanessa's murder might be related to Robyn's in some way?'

'It's impossible to say right now, Celine. But with the tattoos, the waterside locations and now Una's new evidence suggesting Vanessa stayed at Two Cross Farm – my boss reckons if the post-mortem confirms Robyn was definitely murdered, there's a good argument for revisiting Vanessa's case while we're at it.'

Pip's expression brightens. 'Really? You really think they might reopen her murder case?'

Celine can barely speak. In the fifteen years since Vanessa's death, and the decade since the police officially scaled back the investigation, they hadn't dared to allow themselves to think new evidence might turn up like this. 'I can't believe this is really happening,' she says finally.

'Anything you want to ask the girls, Dave?' Una suggests.

'Yes. I'd like to know if you think Vanessa would have told anyone else exactly where she was heading after she'd left Jem Falmer. Do you think there's anyone, other than you, who she might have confided in?'

'No one,' Pip replies. 'She would've told Celine over anyone else – before me or Mum or any of her friends. They were close.'

75

Were we? Celine thinks. *How can that be true, when Vanessa just went off like that, with barely a goodbye?*

'And can you think of any other connections she might have in the area, apart from your mother? Schoolfriends, ex-boyfriends, work colleagues?'

'No one at all,' Celine says. 'Jem was her first real boyfriend, and all her schoolfriends are in the Kingston area. The only reason I'd even heard of Arundel is because Delilah – our mother – moved here.'

There's a pause while Dave makes a note. 'What happens next?' Celine asks, biting down on her thumbnail.

Beside her, Una reaches out and takes her hand away from her mouth. It's a small gesture, but one Celine suddenly recalls from her teenage years, when Una helped her to kick her nail-biting habit once and for all. 'Is there anything you want from us, Dave?' she asks.

'Not for now,' he replies. 'I just need to remind you that this is strictly off the record, and I know it's going to be hard, but for now you're just going to have to sit tight. I won't even consider making an official proposal about Vanessa's case until the forensic results come back for Robyn Siegle.'

'How long will that take?' Celine demands. 'Surely the police need to talk to those women at Two Cross Farm as soon as possible? You need to get in there and ask about Vanessa's stay back in 2005.'

'Dave's already made some preliminary enquiries—' Una starts to protest.

'I have,' DI Aston agrees. 'But it's not straightforward. Already this Seed character is proving tricky, refusing to grant us access to the property without a warrant. And because the victim wasn't found *there*, and CCTV in the town places her elsewhere on the night she died, there's no real grounds for a search warrant. Yet.'

76

'So, we just wait,' Pip says, wearily.

'Well—'

'While this Seed woman hides away in her bloody commune, keeping a lid on God knows what information about Vanessa and Robyn!' Celine throws her hands up as her frustration spills over.

'Let the man speak!' Una says, slapping Celine's leg under the table. 'Tell them about tomorrow, Dave.'

'What's happening tomorrow?' Pip asks.

'Tomorrow,' he says, 'Seed, the leader of Two Cross Farm, is giving an independent press conference, just down the road from you. There'll be a police presence, of course, but I've asked Una – unofficially – to come along to assess the situation too. Merely as an interested bystander, you understand. And if you two wanted to tag along, there'd be nothing to stop you. It's a public meeting, after all.'

Celine's eyes meet Pip's. Good old Una. Thank God for her and her police contacts.

'We're gonna be there, girls,' Una says as she cuts the connection to Dave Aston and closes her laptop. 'And we'll be right in the front row if I've got anything to do with it.'

11. BRAMBLE

1982, Two Cross Farm

My love for Seed was so complete, I often found myself wondering what kind of a mother I would have made, if things had worked out differently for me. If I'd ever married. If I'd left home. If I'd had children of my own.

By the time Seed was five, Two Cross Farm was at full capacity, with thirty-three women, including the Founding Six. Little Seed was beloved by all, wise beyond her years, funny and playful, hard-working and kind. Already she was showing glimpses of the great leader she would become, and, while this was something which was rarely discussed openly, there was an inherent understanding that this would be her path.

On the morning that Sandy was banished, Seed had awoken before the dawn bell, as she so often did, dropping down from her own bed and plodding across the small space to mine, to clamber beneath the covers and curl up beside me. As we nestled together like a nut inside its shell, I wished for the bell never to ring, so that we might stay in our warm cocoon for precious moments longer.

By 6am that wishful thought was a distant memory, and, as was our daily routine, we were seated at the table with our fellow sisters, breaking bread and discussing the day's plans.

'How are the beehives doing?' Fern asked Nancy and Buttercup, two recent arrivals who had brought this new skill to the group.

'We should be harvesting first-flow honey in the next few weeks,' Nancy told her, and Fern continued around the table in this fashion, checking on community progress in all our areas of work.

'How about the gooseberries? Are they ready for jam yet? And the courgettes? Have we got enough wood in, ahead of the autumn months? And what have we got coming out of the art studio, Sandy? Any new greetings cards to add to the market stall?'

Sandy, the young woman with all those exotic tattoos, had taken over the running of the art studio in the three years since she'd joined us, and her linoprint cards had proved popular at the local market stall Fern ran with Regine each Saturday.

'I'm hoping to run out some new ones today,' Sandy replied. 'Of the castle. Thought they might go down well with the tourists.'

'Very good!' Fern replied. 'And Seed's rota says that she's helping you this morning?'

Sandy nodded, giving a thumbs-up across the table to Seed, who was sitting to my right dipping toast soldiers into a soft-boiled egg.

The child's early schooling was based around a schedule of activities which included reading and writing, basic arithmetic, cooking, gardening, art and meditation. Play was naturally woven into all of these things, as each teacher was as delighted as the next to welcome her into their sphere of work, setting her to tasks which they knew would both inform and delight. So many women came here having left their own children behind, and, while Seed might be a sore representation of what they had given up, her status as 'child of all' meant that everyone benefited from her sunlight.

On this particular morning, after cleaning her teeth and changing into a fresh tunic, Seed ran along to join Sandy in the art studio, a large purpose-built shed at the end of the garden where the light was good. I waved to her as she disappeared through the studio doors and set to my own task of planting out sunflowers in the borders, something Seed had suggested at our last monthly around-the-table ideas meeting. 'Sunflowers,' she'd replied simply when she was asked, as every sister was, if she had any ideas for the improvement of the community. Everyone had laughed and smiled at the time, and it was added to the list. Together, we'd been growing the seedlings ever since.

I decided to start at the far end of the garden, where the flowers would be most appreciated, around the wood store and bordering the greenhouses where many of the women worked. New window boxes had been installed outside the art studio, and after I'd planted out the borders I decided to place some dwarf varieties there, so that our residents could look out and see the sunny plants from the art trestles as they worked. Waving at Seed and Sandy through the window, I pulled up my step stool and began to fill the boxes with compost. Inside, Sandy was laying out card along the workbench, getting Seed to fetch the blocks and inks required as they prepared to print. She was lucky to have such a teacher, I thought, because Sandy had blossomed into a quite exceptional artist. She had attracted a few complaints for her argumentative nature, but she'd proven herself to be someone with something valuable to contribute.

She'd even spent time training me to use the tattoo gun, a new skill I'd perfected over recent months, practising on fruit in the evenings to the point at which Sandy said I was ready to take on a real 'victim'.

Smiling to myself at this wonderfully absurd thought – *me*, a tattooist – I dropped the seedling plugs into the holes I'd thumbed and glanced up to see Seed uncapping a bottle of indigo printing ink. But, distracted by the sight of me through the window, she let the bottle slide on the tabletop, and it up-ended, instantly drenching her yellow tunic and pouring across the floor. Sandy shrieked in alarm, throwing old rags over the blue puddle on the ground and whipping the ruined tunic over Seed's head to plunge it beneath running water. Unsteadily, I stepped down from my stool and hurried round to the front of the studio, stumbling on the damp path in my rush to help.

'NO!' I could hear Seed shouting, her tone uncommonly defiant.

Righting myself, I reached the studio door to see Seed, stark naked beside the workbench, head down, her little fingers gripped around her blue-stained knickers as she engaged in a tug-of-war with Sandy.

'I have to rinse them!' Sandy insisted, rolling her eyes at me. 'That ink will never come out if we leave it!'

Heart in my throat, I snatched up an apron, hoping to cover Seed's modesty, but I was too late because, as Seed's complaints turned into hysterical screams, Sandy released her hold on the knickers, and Seed fell backwards, sprawling across the floor like an upturned beetle. I threw the apron over her poor exposed little body, my heart breaking as she covered her face with her hands, sobs racking through her.

'What were you thinking?' I shouted, causing Sandy to start. 'You don't just strip a child down like that!'

Sandy's face was set in an expression of shock. She pointed towards the child. 'But Seed – she spilt the ink – she—'

'I don't care what she did! Are you her guardian?'

She shook her head.

'No, you're not.' Gently, I helped Seed to her feet, wrapping the large apron around her like a sari, pulling her close to my leg where she stood, face lowered in shame. 'I want you to apologise, Sandy. You should never humiliate another human like that.'

'But I – how was I meant to know? She—'

I simply shook my head in reply, desperately trying to quell my own anger.

For a few seconds we stood like that, and I watched as Sandy's remorse shifted into something else: outrage.

'Fuck you, Bramble!' she yelled when I stood my ground, her accent emerging rough and hard-edged. 'Fuck you and your freaky little cult baby! You all think you're so special – but you're just warped.' She stared at Seed. 'That poor fackin' kid. Jesus.'

I was so staggered by this outpouring of fury that it was as much as I could do to stand back and watch her march across the lawns towards the main house, still ranting. Beside me, Seed shivered and sniffled, and I wondered how much she understood of what Sandy had just said.

'I'm not a baby,' she murmured sadly.

I knelt down and took her chin between my thumb and forefinger and I gave her face a firm little shake. 'Seed, you are beautiful. You are strong. You are special.'

She nodded sadly, as her tongue darted out to lick at a tear.

I stood and held out my hand for her to take it. 'I don't think we should let Sandy live here any more, do you?'

Cautiously, Seed shook her head. And then, hand in hand, we too marched across the lawns, and up the stairs to Fern's office, where I presented our half-naked, blue-stained child and explained the events that had just played out.

Fern's steady gaze travelled over Seed's body, and I felt the little girl shrinking at my side. After a few moments in which she turned away and gazed through her window to the gated entrance beyond, Fern unlocked her desk drawer and counted out several notes. 'Help Sandy to pack her bags and give her this for her train fare. Tell her we're keeping the tattoo kit – there's an extra hundred there to compensate her. And then see her off the property, would you, Bramble?'

From the distance of her desk, she turned her attention fully on our daughter. 'Well done, Seed,' she said as though she were talking to any adult one of us. 'Sandy's been growing more and more restless and quarrelsome of late. We don't need that kind of cancer at Two Cross Farm, sisters. Now, leave me while I look through our waiting list. We have a vacancy to fill.'

That evening, Seed refused to leave our room to join the sisters for supper, instead curling up beneath her bedcovers and pretending to sleep.

'You'll feel fine tomorrow,' I told her, but I didn't really believe it. I could see it in her scared little face.

She was five years old, and already the doubts were starting to creep in.

12. CELINE

Present day

The 6pm press conference has been set up on the large grass verge at the front of Two Cross Farm, with the imposing iron security gates separating the world from the house and gardens of the commune beyond.

By the time they have walked the woodland mile from Delilah's place, the narrow lane is buzzing with news crews, police officers and general gawkers. The sun is low in the sky, throwing long shadows through the iron railings and painting a radiant hue over the faces of the assembled.

'Jeez, there must be a hundred people here,' Pip says, taking up Olive and Beebee's hands and looking around the crowd distractedly. 'Listen, we'll hang back if you don't mind. It looks like a bit of a bunfight at the front and I don't want these two getting trampled.'

Celine and Una push through the crowd until they're close enough to get a good view, as a tall woman dressed in a full-length claret tunic and leaf-print headscarf ascends the makeshift platform, while a younger woman stoops behind the wooden lectern, running leads out towards two huge speakers. The former can only be Seed. From this distance, it seems as though her face is slightly out of focus, and it gradually dawns on Celine that the woman's skin is discoloured in some way, by a birthmark perhaps, the tone of her chin and neck appearing more pink in tone than the upper half of her pale face. Celine watches as Seed waits, passive-faced, arms relaxed at her sides, while the other woman checks over the microphone and gives it a solid tap. 'Can everyone hear me? Put your hands up at the back, please? Good, thank you.' She gives the thumbs-up sign and descends the steps, leaving Seed standing behind the lectern, alone.

As Seed looks out over the throng, her gaze on some distant point, Celine has the strangest feeling, somewhere between *déjà vu* and foreboding. Seed hasn't moved an inch. She's elegantly built, quiet and still, and under her calm gaze Celine is aware of the crowd gradually falling to silence. It feels like a set piece, something rehearsed, and Celine is certain that Seed has choreographed every element of this display, from the audience's first sight of her to the tiniest pause or glance; from the slight tilt of her head to the rich tangerine backdrop of sky which now shrouds her.

From somewhere inside the gardens, there is the sounding of a hand bell, rung six times, perhaps to signify the hour of the day. Seed raises her palms now, messiah-like, and speaks into the microphone, her amplified voice low and lyrical.

'Thank you for coming, all of you. My name is Seed, and I am the custodian of Two Cross Farm women's community.' She pauses long enough for her audience to grow uncomfortable, and there is some shifting of feet and clearing of throats before she continues. 'Looking around now, I sense some degree of mistrust, misunderstanding perhaps, as to what we do here and *what we are.*'

85

She smiles at this, inviting a ripple of amused agreement.

'Well, let me tell you. This community first opened its doors to women in 1976, at a time when ordinary women and girls were really starting to fight for something of their own. Our Founding Sisters came from a variety of backgrounds. Some had money; others had nothing. Some were educated; others had been kept ignorant. One or two were unhappily married or tethered to family, while others had been cut loose, set adrift whether they wished for it or not.'

Next to Celine, a news reporter tuts and checks her watch, as a pair of wood pigeons breaks through the canopy overhead, casting their shadows as they pass the crowd. Celine feels like slapping the journalist, and she's shocked by her own strength of feeling.

'While these first women were different and varied, they had one thing in common: they wanted more for themselves. They wanted more, but on their terms – as individuals – as *women* without *men*. And so it was that Two Cross Farm was conceived, as a place where women were welcome to come and stay in safety, to work and learn and contribute, and in many cases to escape and start again. It was to be a place where women could reinvent themselves in their own image; a place where the voiceless could choose their own names.'

'Why the history lesson?' A male voice cuts across Seed, and she turns her head slowly, effortlessly locating the source.

'Because, despite our successful forty-four-year existence, there are – sadly – still those among you who doubt the need for a women-only community like ours. Those who are suspicious of our intentions and seek to undermine the peace we have created here.' She smiles her captivating smile again, and raises a balletic arm. 'If you'll indulge me, I'd like a show of hands, please,' she says. 'Would you lift your hand if you have ever heard us called, or thought us to be, a CULT?'

The strength she puts behind this last word is so powerful that a number of people close to Una and Celine gasp a little. Celine raises her hand, as does Una, as do dozens and dozens more.

Seed nods serenely. 'Young man,' she says, now singling out that earlier heckler. '*This* is "why the history lesson".'

From behind Seed, through the iron railings separating the press crowd from the gardens of Two Cross Farm, a line of women snakes out through the front door of the property, in a vibrant array of coloured tunics: women of different ages, colours, shapes and postures. One by one, they line up on the far side of the gate, looking out, facing the crowd. There is strength in their number, in their shared expression of peace and solidarity.

'God help us,' the journalist next to Celine whispers to the guy filming at her side. 'If I didn't think they were a cult before, I certainly do now.'

'There are thirty-three of us at full capacity,' Seed says, raising her voice to subdue the crowd. She gestures to the assembled women behind her. 'We are currently three down. Two of them departed a month ago, with our blessing, to return to their native New Zealand. And one of them left us less than a week ago, to meet up with a man she had known some years earlier – her ex-husband. That woman's name was Robyn Siegle, and to our great sadness it is a name you will all be familiar with, and the reason you are gathered here this afternoon.'

To a barrage of questions and the frenzied jostle of cameras, Seed holds a framed photograph aloft, a black and white portrait of Robyn. It is designed to gain their attention, but something has shifted in the crowd and Celine suspects Seed is losing them. They're growing impatient.

Una nudges her, animated. 'I've just spotted Dave Aston on the far side,' she says. 'We'll grab him at the end, introduce you properly.'

Seed taps the microphone, sending a sharp squeal through the speakers. 'I *will* answer your questions in a moment. But first, I must make this firm statement in relation to Robyn's time here.'

She's got them back, Celine thinks, *just like that.*

'Robyn's body was found a mile down the river from Two Cross Farm. We – the women of this community – are *devastated. I* am devastated. Robyn was our friend. She was a beautiful soul, a gifted, kind, warm person, and the world is a poorer place without her.' For the first time, Seed shows signs of struggle as her voice falters. Long seconds pass while she composes herself, her eyes downcast. But when she looks up again there is fire in them. 'However, our mourning at the loss of a sister will *not* divert us from the heart of our work. Like many others, the police are made nervous by matriarchal communities, and they are now, once again, harassing us to open our doors to them. They say they want to inspect Robyn's old quarters. For what? She took everything with her. They say they want to search the property for evidence. Why? Robyn wasn't killed here. Nor was she found at Two Cross Farm. They say they want to interview the women. To what end? *I* have answered all their questions, sat behind that desk at the local police station for eight hours or more, volunteering my fingerprints, co-operating without reserve.' A pause, a slow-sweeping assessment of the audience. 'Furthermore, the police have confirmed, to me personally, that the women of Two Cross Farm are *not* suspects, and it is for this reason that I have forbidden them access.' She gestures towards a woman in the front row with her arm in the air. 'I'd like to invite your questions now.'

The noise is deafening as reporters shout out, waving notebooks and microphones in a bid to gain Seed's attention. Celine scans the crowd, surprised to catch a glimpse of Harry the gardener over on the far side, next to Pip and the kids. He leans in and says something to Pip and she breaks into a smile, nodding, holding out her hand to shake his. After this brief exchange they both turn their attention back to the stage. Perhaps Harry was on his way to their place but couldn't get past this lot, she thinks, making a mental note to catch him before he leaves, so she can ask him what he's owed. She turns back towards the podium as Seed's voice takes command of the crowd once more.

'Please,' she says, 'if you could repeat the question so everyone can hear?'

The woman raises her voice, and her question lifts on the evening air. 'You say the police are harassing you, but surely if you let them in to look around they'll find nothing, and they *will* leave you alone?'

Seed's expression is calm, yet steely. 'We take the peace and safety of Two Cross Farm very seriously. Imagine, if you will—' Seed addresses this directly to the young woman asking the question '—that you have taken refuge here, perhaps afraid for your life or freedom in some way. Perhaps escaping violence or oppression. Imagine the overwhelming sense of relief you might experience when you realise that all you fear is safely locked outside of this gate here, and that you are now surrounded by sisters whose only concern is to harbour and support you. It's a nice vision, isn't it?' she asks with that customary smile. 'And then, I want you to imagine that vision blown asunder, destroyed, as police – *male* police for the most part – trample through the place, opening cupboards, turning out drawers, raking through your personal possessions, uninvited. Shattering your peace of mind.' She leans in so that her lips touch the microphone and her low voice transmits loud and crystal-sharp from those huge speakers. '*Raping* your peace of mind.'

There's a collective shock of silence, like an electric current undulating through the crowd.

Seed raises those palms again, her tone gentle. 'The women here have appointed me their custodian, their gatekeeper if you like. This is my duty. The police have no reason to enter and destabilise the sanctity of our community without due cause – without a search warrant. And of course, they have no grounds for a warrant.'

Another question: 'The deceased might not have been found here, but how can the public be sure Robyn's killer is not being harboured inside your community?'

Seed is impassive as she turns her attention to the uniformed officers closest to the stage. 'Have the police actually *confirmed* Robyn was murdered?'

There is no reply, and the officers look away, made awkward.

'At any rate,' Seed adds, 'no man has set foot inside Two Cross Farm in forty-four years, so, if there is a killer to be sought, he's not here.'

'You assume it's a man?' the journalist beside Celine calls out.

'Isn't it always?' Seed counters.

'She's got a point,' Celine mutters, her irritation at this jumped-up girl starting to get the better of her.

'And if the police *do* obtain a search warrant?' the same journalist demands.

Seed obviously doesn't like her either; she's asked more questions than anyone else here, and her tone has been the most challenging. She narrows her eyes, zoning in on the woman. 'If the police impose a warrant on us, so be it – so long as the investigators are female. But if they try to impose a *man* on us, rest assured we will exercise our own power with the full might of the law. We have a lawyer within our community. We understand our human rights – *to the letter* – and we will, without hesitation, employ them.'

A murmur erupts, followed by more questions, but it seems Seed is finished. 'I'd like to take the opportunity to thank you all for coming and hearing what we have to say. We wish the police every success in bringing Robyn's case to a satisfactory conclusion, and now I ask you to join us in a minute's silence, in memory of our lost sister.'

Behind her, the bell sounds out a single ring, and Seed bows her head. The crowd falls silent too, many lowering their faces as they follow her lead. When the bell rings again at the end of the minute, Seed is gone, already safely secured on the other side of the gate, her claret form drifting across the lawn towards the grand house, before disappearing behind the front door. Beyond the gates, the women remain motionless until she is gone from view, at which point they form their single-file line again, and retreat through the back of the property.

The crowd breaks apart, many of the news crew sprinting straight to their vehicles to get on the road, to start editing and broadcasting their updates in the Robyn Siegle case. As the lane opens up a little, Una tells Celine she's going to grab DI Aston before he leaves, and she heads off towards the stage, where he's being interviewed by a member of the press. The sunset beyond the house is spectacular now, the sky a deep fuchsia pink, and as Celine searches the crowd for her sister there is a sense of dystopia about the place, the image of that moving line of brightly tunic-clad women still sharp in her mind.

'Auntie Ceecee!' Olive cries out, colliding with her legs in a running bear hug, winding her momentarily.

'Ollie-Ollie,' she replies, quite taken aback by this unexpected show of affection. It dawns on Celine that she hasn't known these children at all; that she *should* know these children by now.

When Pip catches up, Celine hugs her. 'I'm sorry I've been such a crap sister,' she finds herself saying, and she reaches down for Beebee, to run a hand over her silky little head. She's close to tears, and she doesn't know what's wrong with her. This isn't what she's like.

Pip scowls, perplexed or worried, it's hard to tell. 'God, Celine – you've been anything but crap. Will you just stop it? Celine?'

'Ignore me,' she says with conviction, and Pip rubs her arm and points in the direction of the stage, where Una is now deep in conversation with the detective. They head over, turning a blind eye to Olive and Beebee who immediately clamber over the empty stage, running up and down the steps and stomping across the boards like pygmy goats.

'Ah, here they are,' Una says, extending an arm. 'My surrogate nieces, Celine and Pip. DI Dave Aston of Sussex Police – this time in the flesh.'

He is stocky, not much taller than Celine, with a strong handshake, his steady blue-eyed gaze more arresting in real life than it was on screen. 'Are you local?' he asks.

'Celine lives in Bournemouth now,' Una says, answering for them, 'and Pip's still my next-door neighbour in Kingston.'

'Lucky you.' Dave Aston smiles. Then he inclines his head towards the empty stage and asks, 'So tell me, what did you make of that?'

'I'm guessing for many it was a media dream,' Celine replies. 'There's nothing more likely to whet the news-makers' appetites than talk of cults and murder.'

Dave nods. 'Remind me: you arrived on Monday afternoon, Celine, and my officers visited you all on Tuesday?'

'Yes, they came the morning after the body was found.' There's something about that phrase that so saddens Celine, that so echoes with the namelessness that Seed alluded to just minutes earlier, that she immediately corrects herself. 'After Robyn Siegle was found.'

'Horrible timing. Particularly given your recent . . .' Dave Aston struggles for words. 'Once again, my sympathies.'

92

Celine and Pip smile, closed-mouthed, still unaccustomed to speaking about their mother's death outside of their tight unit. *My sympathies.* The expression is unbearable, so inadequate.

'What do you think our chances are of reopening Vanessa's case?' Celine asks, jumping at the opportunity to ask him straight.

'I don't know, Celine. What I'd really like is to track down some of her friends from that time. Can you have another think about it, both of you, see if you can't come up with a few names for me? At the moment, we're working with very little information, and if I'm going to put together a proposal I need something more.'

'Thanks,' she says, exchanging a nod of agreement with Pip.

Una clears her throat, deftly shifting direction. 'I only discovered you'd been transferred to Sussex when I called the Yard, Dave. Congratulations on your promotion, mate, well deserved.' She turns to the sisters. 'Dave was one of my first juniors when I was made up at Scotland Yard. A long time back. As you can tell, he's a bigger cheese now.'

'I learnt a lot from Una here,' he smiles. 'To be honest, I learnt more from Una in five years than I had in the ten years previous. She was the one who put me forward for my first big promotion.'

'Dave was just telling me a little bit about Two Cross Farm,' Una says. 'Apparently this lot aren't all that popular around here.'

'It's the "cult" thing,' he replies. 'She's right, Seed is – people *are* suspicious, and I get it, but I also understand the women's desire for privacy.' Now he lowers his voice and leans in a little. 'To be honest, Una, we're desperate to get in there to interview the other women and take a look around, but Seed's running rings around us. You know she's got it covered in-house? As she said, one of the women in the community is a hotshot lawyer.

They might look like members of a hippy commune but they're as sharp as tacks, and I know she's not bluffing when she says she'll sue.'

Beebee jumps from the platform and lands badly. 'Ah-fuck-it!' she curses, grabbing at her ankle and rolling around with her knee up by her ear.

'Beebee said *fuckit*!' Olive shouts from the stage, before clamping a hand to her mouth, wide-eyed.

Pip starts to protest – 'I can't believe she just – they never normally—' but gives up when she sees the others stifling their laughter. 'I think it's time I got these potty-mouths back home, don't you, Celine? They'll be getting hungry.' She scoops up Beebee, as Celine gives Olive a hand down. 'You coming, Una?'

'I was thinking of asking DI Aston here if he's got time for a quick pint,' she says, thrusting her hands into her jacket pocket, looking every bit the boss.

Aston checks his watch and nods, clearly needing no persuasion. 'The lads can finish up here. The Eagle?'

'Sounds good to me. Save me some supper!' Una calls over her shoulder, already striding towards Dave's car.

Leaving Two Cross Farm behind them, the sisters turn towards home.

'So, I saw you and Harry the gardener getting chummy earlier,' Celine teases her sister. 'Not bad-looking, is he?'

Pip elbows her and swears under her breath. 'Not every man is a potential conquest, you know!'

'Ha! As if I've ever conquered any!' Celine replies, laughing, and Pip can't disagree.

As they walk, Celine is playing over the image of those women behind the railings of the security gate. They appeared so tranquil and compliant, devoted to Seed, yet entirely self-contained and confident.

'There's something not right about that woman,' Pip says, breaking her sister's thoughts. '*Seed*.'

'Like what?' Celine replies. 'I mean, I know the tunics and bell-ringing was all a bit odd, but she seemed pretty genuine to me.'

'I dunno. There's something off, aside from how strange she looked in all those robes and scarves. And what was that discoloration on her face? Looked like burns to me.' After a pause, she continues. 'Maybe she's just *too* convincing? Too calm and assured? Shouldn't she be in a complete panic right now, after one of her women has just been found dead on the riverbank? If I were her, I'd be worried for the safety of the others, wouldn't you? She's a bit of a robot, if you ask me.'

Celine's been called the same in the past. 'I don't agree. She's good at talking, that's for sure, and she's good at holding it all together, but that doesn't make her a robot. You saw how upset she seemed when she first mentioned Robyn's name.'

Pip kicks a stone along the path, the way Celine remembers her doing as a sulky child. 'Do you reckon she was the leader when Vanessa stayed there?'

'*Custodian*,' Celine corrects her. 'I don't know, Pip. It's a long time ago. I'd guess Seed isn't all that much older than me, so it's unlikely.'

'It took everything in my power to stop from calling her out on it. To ask her if she remembers Vanessa.'

'Thank God you didn't, Pip. If Seed does know anything about Vanessa, the last thing we need is you giving her the heads-up on it before the police are ready to reopen the case. You heard the DI yesterday – our best bet right now is to keep a low profile, and wait for Robyn Siegle's post-mortem results to come in. And you never know what Una's going to come back with after her meeting with Dave.'

The entrance to Belle France comes into view and the girls sprint on ahead, disappearing up the drive. They seem entirely at home here and it strikes Celine how sad it is that they never knew Delilah, never got to enjoy this place as beloved grand-children, because they were never invited.

As they step on to the gravel, Pip halts, holding Celine back. 'I'm telling you, Celine, that place has to have something to do with Vanessa's death. If only we could get inside and talk to some of those women . . . I know the police always believed it was Jem Falmer who killed Vanessa – as have we – but there's a bigger story here, I'm certain. I know it's a massive coincidence us being here when this happened to Robyn Siegle, but some-times the stars align – fate or chance or whatever you want to call it – sometimes we're in the places we're meant to be for a good reason.'

Celine blinks back at her little sister, seeing her as a real grown-up for perhaps the first time in her life. 'And what is that reason, Pip?'

'We're going to find out what happened to Vanessa, sis. Now that Mum's not around, there's nothing stopping us from opening up that old box of hurt, is there? I'm up for it. I'm tough enough, whatever pain it brings. Are you?'

For a moment, Celine cannot answer. She turns towards the house, so similar to Two Cross Farm in its layout and aspect. The pink glow of the sky has deepened to an inky crimson, making bold silhouettes of Olive and Beebee as they chase each other across the far lawn. Celine is transported back in time; she could be looking at Vanessa and Pip, so familiar are their movements.

'Celine?' Pip urges.

'Of course I'm up for it,' she replies, turning resolute eyes on her sister. 'And you're right, Pip. One way or another, we've got to get inside that place.'

13. BRAMBLE

1991, Two Cross Farm

The teenage years are difficult, so they say, and for Seed, with her various complications, it was a particularly turbulent time.

There were changes she was going through that she couldn't understand, even despised, and by her early teens, plagued by adolescent acne and growing like a weed, she had started to disappear inside herself. Where we had once been so close, she began to reject my affection, to resent my concern and to bristle at the very sound of my voice. She toiled as diligently as ever, but there was a new detachment to her which unsettled the other women, and, instead of looking forward to the rota days when they would be paired with Seed for work, they came to dread her sullen darkness.

One winter night, soon after Seed had passed her fourteenth birthday, we lay in the single beds of our little twin room, separated by just a small side table and lamp, following an afternoon in which she'd walked out on Fern as she'd tutored her in the art of numerology. While I knew Seed's rage wasn't restricted to me,

I was the one who felt the most direct force of it, being in such close proximity to her, the one who had raised her as a mother might. Across the room, I could hear her shallow breathing in the darkness, and I yearned to look inside her heart, to try to understand what I could do to take away her pain.

'Seed?' I whispered, trying again to open up the conversation with her. 'Are you all right?'

The pattern of her breathing altered, but her silence did not.

'It's just that, well, I want you to know you can always talk to me,' I said. 'You do know that, don't you? Seed?'

She shifted in her bed, and I could tell she'd turned her back to me.

'How are your sessions with Sister Kathy going?' I hated to probe like this, but I was increasingly scared that I was losing her. Her weekly sessions in Dr Kathy's clinic room had begun just after her thirteenth birthday – *talking therapy*, Fern called it – and I was starting to wonder if Seed's growing distance from me was in some way related to the time she spent there. 'Are you finding it useful talking to her? Maybe you could tell me some of the things you tell her? What did you talk about today?'

'I'm different,' Seed said quietly.

'Of course you're not, my darling! Oh, you know it's normal for teenagers to feel this way – we've all felt like outsiders at some time in our lives. I know my own teenage years were terrible,' I said, although, of course, my own troubles couldn't have been more different from Seed's.

'It's not the same. You didn't grow up in here. You're not me,' she growled, turning to face me in the darkness so that her voice grew clearer. 'You don't know what goes on inside my head. I'm nothing like the rest of you. I've never been outside of here, never met another person my own age. Never been alone.'

I didn't know how to answer her, because she was right. I didn't know what went on inside her head. And she *was* different from the rest of us, that much was becoming increasingly obvious, with each passing day and each new battle.

'Is there anything I can do to make you happy?' I whispered.

For long seconds, we lay in the darkness, neither of us speaking, as all the while I felt like a woman standing on the precipice of a great mountain, looking down.

'My own room,' she finally replied, her voice cracking. 'I'd like my own room.'

Of course! With relief, and, I admit, some sadness, I inwardly berated myself for my naïve stupidity. It was only natural, wasn't it? She needed her own space more than anyone in this community. Everyone else who came here had experienced the privilege of privacy at some point in their lives before Two Cross Farm, but Seed had known nothing but company. The child needed some space. She didn't want to be sharing a room with dusty old Bramble, did she?

The following day the request was put to the Founding Sisters, but, after a short but heated debate which led to a 3-2 result, it was rejected on the grounds that all women were equal. Fern wouldn't hear of a sister taking a room of her own, no matter who or what the circumstances. When Seed was called back to the office and received the verdict, she remained silent, her unblinking stare betraying her fury. With a chop-chop clap of Fern's hands we were dismissed to go about our work, and Seed silently complied, going down ahead of us to return outside to continue helping Francine with the task of clearing the autumn leaves and branch-fall.

Anxious at Seed's lack of response, I watched the activity in the garden from the top window, where the views stretched across the lawns, out to the greenhouses, to the wood store and art studio, and further, past the high hedge to the river and wetlands beyond. It was an icy morning, and the sisters were going about their various tasks swaddled in heavy coats and hats, gloves protecting their fingers from frostbite. There'd been a storm some days earlier and as Francine stoked the bonfire, built high with broken branches and garden debris, Seed did the rounds of the work groups, collecting up natural fodder to add to the pile. From my window, I followed her movements as she swept out the wood store, casting log dust and rat droppings on to the pyre. I saw her talking with Rose and Goldie at the potato plot, before collecting up an armful of rotten canes and dried husks, and I watched as she crossed between the largest raised beds and dropped the bundle on to the burning stack.

And then, I bore witness as she turned her face to me at my high window, and raised one arm in a wide cheerful wave, before she plunged herself into the fire, and was consumed by its flames.

14. CELINE

Present day

When Celine and Pip get home from the press conference at Two Cross Farm, they sit down together to draw up a list of Vanessa's friends, in a bid to provide something more for Dave Aston to work on.

The list, they discover, is pitifully poor.

'Surely she had more friends than that?' Pip says, searching through the kitchen cupboards for ingredients to make a pasta bake. 'She was really popular at school.'

Celine has a sudden inexplicable urge for a cigarette, something she hasn't felt in the ten years since she gave up. 'She pretty much dropped everyone once she took up with Jem, didn't she? Including us.' She stares at the three names on the scrap of paper in her hands. 'And to be honest, Pip, two of these are girls I know for certain she hadn't seen since she left sixth form. Which just leaves Georgie.'

Pip is weighing out dried pasta, frowning hard. 'They couldn't get hold of Georgie before, when it happened. The police – do you remember? I think she'd gone off travelling or something. Do you want to see if you can track her down and give her a call, or shall I? You knew her better.'

Celine wonders what she will say if she locates Georgie, Vanessa's oldest friend. Will she even want to talk to her – will she even remember who Celine is?

When morning comes round, as much as she dreads the conversation she's about to have, Celine picks up her phone and dials the number she traced online last night: a City firm in London where Georgie is listed as working.

While she waits for the receptionist to put her through, she wanders out into the waking garden, down towards the river path to gaze over the water beyond.

'Hello?'

Even after all these years, Celine recognises Georgie's tone, having regularly sat beside her and Vanessa on the bus, back in their school days.

'Georgie, it's Celine here. Celine Murphy? Vanessa's sister.'

There's a long pause at the end of the line before Georgie speaks again. 'God, Celine! Hi. Um, how are you?'

Hearing the warmth in Georgie's voice, Celine feels relief seeping through her veins. 'I'm, you know, good, thanks.'

'And Pip – and your mum?' she asks.

Celine is surprised that she even remembers her younger sister's name. 'They're – well, Mum died actually. Just recently. Me and Pip are at her house in Sussex, sorting stuff out.'

'Oh, I'm really sorry to hear that. Your mum, she was – she was—'

'A flippin' nightmare,' Celine finishes, and she's grateful when Georgie laughs and the tension is broken. 'Listen,' she says. 'It's about Vanessa's murder case. There's a possibility the police

102

might reopen it, and I wondered if you'd consider meeting me for a chat. No pressure at all, just a few questions to help us understand what was going on with her and Jem Falmer back then.'

'When were you thinking?' Georgie asks without hesitation.

'Is today too soon?' she asks. 'I could get a train up . . .'

Celine waits, while Georgie flips through some papers. 'Sure – I'm out this evening but lunchtime is clear? Where shall we meet?'

Celine waits for Georgie at a window seat in The Yacht restaurant overlooking the Thames, not far from where Vanessa once shared a flat with Jem Falmer. She's early and her mind is working double-time, torturing her with thoughts of missed opportunities and what-ifs. Even now, she struggles to believe that her sister had lived this other life, quite separate from her and Pip, a life they were never invited to be part of. What the hell had Vanessa been doing in the first place even getting together with Falmer, a man ten years her senior, but never her equal in moral fibre or worth? Celine hadn't actually met him, but everything she's heard since tells her he was a violent thug, and she shudders to imagine what lies and manipulation Falmer had used to reel her beautiful sister in. Was he charming at first, persuasive, reassuring? Did he promise the world? What was it that he could offer Vanessa that she didn't have with Celine and Pip? Independence, perhaps? A chance to reinvent herself; to separate herself from her dysfunctional family and the pain of the past? Maybe she was just looking for someone to show her a bit of attention in her own right. God knows, all three of them had been crying out for that in the years since Delilah had left them, and it wouldn't take a particularly sharp psychologist to recognise they were all desperately seeking security and approval of one sort or another. Celine had found it in hard work and professional success, Pip, later, in her marriage and children. Maybe Vanessa thought she'd found it with Jem Falmer, before he'd moved her in and turned violent on her.

Celine's gaze falls on the sparkling water of the Thames and that nightmarish image comes to her again, a picture conjured up from the words of the police officers who broke the news; from the media reports she pored over and over in the weeks that followed Vanessa's death. Fifteen years have passed now, but still Celine asks herself daily, can it really be true? Her beloved sister, beaten and strangled to death, laid out on the boardwalk of Brighton pier. It never gets any easier to think about, to imagine.

When Georgie walks through the door, Celine recognises her instantly, and they embrace warmly before ordering glasses of wine and self-consciously browsing the menu.

'I've always meant to try this place,' Georgie says. 'Thanks for choosing somewhere so close to my work.'

Celine *had* made a point of choosing somewhere close to the City, but also somewhere nice, by way of an unspoken apology for dragging Georgie into this. 'No problem – I'm grateful you could make the time.'

Georgie orders a light bite from the vegetarian menu, and Celine says she'll have the same, opening up her file of papers the moment the waiter has taken their order. 'So – Jem Falmer.'

The startled expression on Georgie's face tells Celine that she's moving too fast, as ever, not reading the cues. 'Sorry,' she says, closing the file again. 'Vanessa always used to tell me I was too impatient – I think she was probably right.'

'She did used to moan about that,' Georgie says, smiling. 'But she also used to say she didn't know how she and Pip would have survived without you holding the family together after your mum left.'

104

'She said that?' Celine and Vanessa had never really got round to talking about that time in their lives. They were so busy just getting on with it all, trying to keep themselves away from the notice of social services, that they never actually gave voice to their struggles.

'*So*, OK, Jem Falmer,' Georgie says, picking up her wine glass. 'What do you want to know?'

Celine flicks through the papers she's gathered with Una's help, locating a printed list of Falmer's non-custodial convictions. 'Did you have much to do with him?'

Georgie sighs. 'To be honest, he's the reason Vanessa and I drifted apart. I don't know if you remember, but Ness and I were talking about getting a flat together, before she started her job at Waterways and met Jem. We hadn't begun looking at places yet, but once she started seeing him she lost interest in the idea anyway. Everything moved pretty quickly with the two of them.'

'I know: they moved in together after only a couple of months.' Celine remembers her feeling of disquiet at the time – she'd never even met this new boyfriend – but Vanessa had been adamant that it was what she wanted to do, said that they'd all meet up soon enough. But of course, that never happened.

'Anyway,' Georgie says, 'after that I didn't really see much of her.'

'Did you meet him?'

'Just the once.'

'And?'

'I hated him. It was at some bar in Soho – I can't even remember the name – but Vanessa had invited me along because she wanted Jem to meet me. By the time I got there they'd obviously had a few drinks, and he was full of it, wanting to let me know he was in charge.'

'What do you mean?'

The waiter places a jug of water on the table between them and makes room for their plates.

'I mean, he kept putting Vanessa down in front of me, saying crude things about her not being "up for it" as much as he'd like, asking her why she couldn't wear low-cut tops like some girl he'd spotted further along the bar. And then suddenly his mood shifted, and it was like he was flirting with me to hurt Vanessa, kind of daring her to complain, while at the same time challenging me to step in. It was fucking horrible, if I'm honest.'

'And did she complain?'

Georgie shakes her head. 'No. She just took it. I was boiling up inside; I couldn't bear to see her so downtrodden, and when she went off to the loo I asked him what his game was.'

'I bet he didn't like that?'

'He wanted to know what I meant, and I told him I didn't like the way he was treating my friend. I told him he should have more respect. And then I got up to follow her, to check if she was OK, but he came after me, cornered me in the passageway to the toilets. There was no one else around, and it only took a second. He slammed me against the wall and grabbed my breast, *really* hard – left bruises. He hissed – and I'll never forget this – "Are you dyke bitches at it behind my back?" Someone came round the corner then and he let me go.'

'Did you tell Vanessa what had happened?'

'I tried to, but she wasn't listening. She wanted to put it all down to the drink, but I could tell she didn't believe that. Anyway, I left the bar on my own that night, and even though we kept in touch a bit – the odd phone call and one awkward lunch – we never talked about Jem again, and our friendship fizzled out.'

'The police tried really hard to contact you,' Celine says, giving the waiter a nod when he asks if they'd like another drink.

'I didn't even *know* about Vanessa until over a year after it had happened. I was out of the country. Two or three months after the last time I saw her, I got a job offer in Greece, and I didn't come home for nearly two years.'

'Didn't you think to check up on her, to see if she was OK?' Celine can't help herself as the accusation seeps through her tone.

'I didn't think I needed to,' Georgie replies. 'As far as I was concerned, Vanessa and Jem had gone their separate ways.'

'Why would you think that?'

'Well, I got a postcard from her just before I left. Must've been around May time – let me think: May 2004, it would have been, and I left in the June. It was an apology, I guess – saying sorry that she'd let Jem get between us, and that she was safe and away from him. I had the sense that she was getting her life back on track, putting right some wrongs.'

'Do you know where she was writing from?'

'I can't remember – this was years ago, and the card probably got thrown away when I was packing up for Greece. It was some kind of farm, I think. There was a windmill on the card, I remember that much.'

Celine opens up her photo app and shows Georgie a picture of the postcard Una found just two days earlier. 'Could it have been this place – Two Cross Farm?'

Georgie studies the image, and nods firmly. 'Yup, that's it. It's the same postcard. I wrote back to her eventually, once I'd got settled in Greece – sent her a little present I'd picked up – and she wrote back to thank me a couple of months later. Actually, it was around December, because I remember she wished me a happy Christmas. It was the same card design again, so I assume she was still there.'

Celine counts the months off on her fingers. 'That means she was in the same place for seven or eight months at least. I guess now we just need to find out what happened in the last three months before she was killed.' She looks out over the water again, trying to subdue her anger at the ease with which she's just gathered this vital piece of information about her sister's movements – information the police should easily have uncovered at the time.

She turns back to Georgie. 'What was the gift you sent her?'

'It was one of those little blue glass pendants you see all over Greece. Just a cheap thing, strung on a leather thong. They call them "evil eyes" because they're meant to . . .' She smiles sadly. 'They're meant to ward off misfortune and evil.'

Celine returns her smile. 'It's just the kind of thing Vanessa would've loved. And, talking of evil, Jem Falmer – did you ever hear about him again?'

'Only what I read online after I got home: that he was the police's prime suspect. He was thought to have fled abroad, wasn't he? As I say, Vanessa had been dead over a year by the time I came back home. I was distraught when my mum told me, and I called the police to see if I could help, but they weren't that interested as I didn't have anything new for them. To be honest, I got the impression they'd run out of steam.'

Celine runs her finger down Falmer's list of offences. 'He'd been arrested on twelve separate occasions prior to meeting Vanessa.'

Georgie takes a sharp breath.

'Affray; breaking and entry; possession; and four counts of assault against women.'

'But he'd never done time in prison?'

'Some of the convictions were when he was a minor. Some were suspended sentences. And all but one of the women involved in the assault cases dropped their charges before it went to court.'

108

Georgie pinches the bridge of her nose, appearing suddenly exhausted. 'So, no rehabilitation, no repercussions for Jem Falmer. Is it any wonder these men reoffend – they can basically get away with just about anything, can't they?'

And it's no wonder some women want to shut themselves away in Two Cross Farm, Celine thinks to herself. She'd put her money on Seed protecting her women in there, but she's not so sure she can say the same about the police in the outside world.

'Did you know that Falmer grew up in West Sussex?' she asks.

Georgie shakes her head. 'I'm not even sure Vanessa knew that much about him.'

'My notes say he'd trained as an apprentice shipwright in his home town of Littlehampton, before getting a job boat-building in London, where he met Vanessa.'

'Do you think that's relevant?' Georgie asks.

'Well, only in that the commune where she was staying, Two Cross Farm, is in Arundel, just four miles from Littlehampton. Falmer had gone missing a few days before Vanessa's body turned up in Brighton, so it's possible he'd worked out where she was, and headed down there to get her back. He knew the area well enough.'

Georgie looks thoughtful. 'Arundel. Wasn't a woman found dead there just this week?'

Celine pulls out a recent news report. 'Robyn Siegle. There are strong similarities.'

Even as she says the words, Celine doubts herself. Is it conceivable that Falmer's back in the Sussex area – and also responsible for Robyn, fifteen years later?

'He'd be mid-forties now,' Georgie says. 'Do you think it's him?'

Celine shrugs. 'I don't know – Pip thinks Two Cross Farm could be involved somehow. I guess we're just trying to think of all the possibilities. It sounds far-fetched, but what if he's been abroad all this time, and he's only just returned to the UK – he'd probably head back to his family home, wouldn't he? He's a proven misogynist; his conviction list tells us that much. Maybe he still holds a grudge against the women's community for keeping Vanessa from him back then?'

'I don't know.' Georgie sighs. 'All I do know is, he scared the hell out of me when I met him.'

'But do you think he was capable of murder?' Celine asks.

Georgie glances at the wall clock and starts to pull on her jacket. 'In my opinion, Celine? Without a shadow of a doubt.'

Afterwards, as Celine waits on the platform at London Blackfriars looking out of the glass across the Thames, a delayed text pings on to her mobile from Una.

Just spoke to Falmer's ma – she hasn't seen him since before Vanessa's death. I believe her. Says rest of family are certain he went abroad – apparently always talked about boat-building jobs in the Caribbean. Could be anywhere by now.

Celine's heart sinks. After meeting with Georgie today, she'd really started to hope that Falmer might also be responsible for Robyn. At least that made some kind of sense; at least that narrowed the field of possibilities. She feels a deep weariness wash over her. If it weren't for Pip, pressuring her to stay, to keep digging, would she carry on with this?

As the train pulls in, Celine boards, finds her seat, and is just about to plug her phone in to charge when Una calls.

'I've just been with Georgie,' Celine plunges in, not waiting for a hello. 'She told me that Vanessa wrote to her from Two Cross Farm – and confirmed that Falmer was just as violent as his criminal record would suggest. But I'm not sure what use any of that is to us, if the police can't even track him down.'

'Yeah, it's too bad we're no closer to locating Falmer,' Una says. 'But, on the flip side, there's good news too.'

'There is?' Celine squints against the sunlight as the train leaves the station and picks up speed.

'There is,' Una replies. 'I've just heard back from Dave Aston and he wants us to meet him at HQ in Lewes on Monday.'

'So he's got an update for us?'

'Yup. Robyn Siegle's post-mortem is in – and foul play is strongly suspected. His boss is sufficiently convinced of the similarities between Vanessa and Robyn's cases—'

There's silence for a second or two as the train passes through a bad signal patch.

'What does that mean? Una? Are you still there? What does it mean?'

Una's voice returns to the line, and Celine can hear she's smiling. 'It means Vanessa's case is on the table again, baby. We've got another real shot at solving her murder.'

15. BRAMBLE

1995, Two Cross Farm

Four years had passed since Seed's terrible accident, which, while leaving her face and neck irreparably scarred, did not, as she'd hoped at the time, kill her.

Thanks to Susan's swift response in pulling her from the flames, Seed had been saved, and, following many weeks of bed rest and Kathy's homeopathic compresses, she'd slowly recovered. Although we knew her burns would never heal entirely, the pain of them gradually subsided and the livid colour began to fade. It was a time of quiet contemplation for the Founding Sisters, all of whom had been as upset and disturbed as me at this sudden and traumatic turn of events. None of us really knew what had triggered Seed's desperate actions that day, and her refusal to speak on the subject was respected by all. But, deep down, I think we each suspected what was going on: Seed felt trapped. Trapped inside this community of ageing women, with no one to relate to. No one like her at all.

During her recovery, Seed's request for a single bedroom was reconsidered, and by way of a compromise it was decided that she could move from my room and into Susan's, so that she might share with someone closer in age. Of course, even Susan was seventeen years her senior, but her arrival at Two Cross Farm at so young an age had rendered her perpetually childlike and she was as delighted as Seed at the prospect. With the help of a little medical intervention arranged discreetly by Dr Kathy, by the time Seed reached her late teens she had, thank God, settled back into being the warm, level-headed girl we all loved.

Traditionally, birthdays at Two Cross Farm were a low-key affair, and so on the day of Seed's eighteenth it came as a surprise when Fern called us all to the art studio after Seed and Susan had left for market.

'The past few years have been far from easy for Seed,' she reminded us. 'For one so young, she has encountered more trials than most, but this, we can be sure, will ultimately make her a stronger, wiser and more insightful sister. She is an example to us all. Today, we will mark her official entry into adulthood, so let us show her the importance of her role within the community.'

The applause was unanimous.

For the remainder of the morning, the entire community downed tools to turn their labours to decking out the art studio, and to the production of rare treats and entertainment. There were cakes to be baked, bunting to be hung, winter flowers to be picked and arranged. Had this been a special party for any other one of us, perhaps jealousies would have reared up, but this was Seed, and a growing atmosphere of celebration vibrated through the house and gardens. Fern dashed about in the sleety rain, calling out orders, and inwardly I smiled to see her among the group, so animated, so full of vim.

'Bramble! Do you think someone could make a branch wreath for the door?' she called to me from the path as I entered the studio carrying armfuls of winter flowers. 'I've put a few more sisters on baking,' she added distractedly. 'And Kathy's putting together a short harmony to welcome her when she arrives.' She gave me a thumbs-up sign and disappeared inside the house, leaving a sprinkling of her energy in the damp February air.

In some ways, I reflected, at almost fifty now, the years had barely changed Fern, cocooned as she was inside our safe walls, but at nearly sixty I hadn't fared so well with the passing of time. How was it that some women grew more vibrant with age, while others would fade and wilt? It was clear that Seed possessed that same timeless quality, her radiant intelligence growing deeper and brighter with every passing year, and I wondered if it was a result of the increasing time she spent with our leader these days, or pure genetics. As the rain made music on the tin roof of the art studio, I set to work on a bay leaf wreath, and said a quiet prayer of thanks that Seed was still in our lives, that she was happy and healthy – and alive.

When Susan and Seed returned after lunch, still shivering from hours spent on the damp market stall, they were ushered directly to the art studio at the rear of the house, where Seed was met by a rousing rendition of 'Ave Maria' and a roar of whooping cheers.

For long seconds, the poor girl hid behind her hands. The other women swooped around, hugging her, foisting cake into her hands, kissing her head, helping her out of her winter coat and wrappings as Fern looked on with pride. Normally so poised and unshakeable, Seed was quite overcome, and from my distance I felt, as I increasingly did those days, shut out of her sphere, physically unable to reach through the wall of affection that surrounded her. Susan too was pushed aside, and I waved to her across the room, noticing how tired she looked, how dark the circles were beneath her eyes. As she returned my wave, her face broke into a smile and I felt grateful for the friendship she shared with Seed, for the difference she'd made to all our lives.

'Sisters!' Fern climbed up on a chair at the far end of the central workbench, raising her voice over the rain that lashed against the roof and windows of the studio. 'Sisters! Let the poor child go now!'

She waited while the women dropped back. All was quiet inside the studio, and with the rain now pelting harder against the glass, obscuring the world beyond, I had the strangest sensation that we might be the last remaining women alive.

'Sisters, this is an important day,' Fern said, one hand clenching the fabric of her tunic, making a fist at her heart. 'Not just for Seed, who is now grown, but for every one of us and for the future of Two Cross Farm. As you are all aware, Seed has been here from the outset, from the very conception of Two Cross Farm. She is our youngest Founding Sister.'

Seed stood at the far end of the large bench, the space around her intensifying the effect of her uncertainty. Nervously, her hand went to the scarred side of her face, cupping her cheek in a habitual soothing motion.

'Sisters, we are none of us immortal, and one day I will need to hand the role of custodian to someone deserving and right. When that time comes, your new custodian will be Seed.'

There was raucous applause, before one woman, Judy, a resident of less than a year's standing, called out delightedly, 'When?' and was rewarded with a fierce glare from Regine on the opposite side of the room. It was one thing to be pleased with the news; quite another to sound so impatient for the change.

Fern gave a slow bow of her head, her eyes seeking out the other Founding Sisters: Kathy, Regine, Susan and me. 'What is our number, sisters?' she asked.

'Thirty-three,' the entire group replied, in unison.

'When Seed is thirty-three years old, she will take over. And in the intervening years you are instructed to treat her as my second-in-command, as custodian-in-training. Anything you would bring to me, you can take to Seed. You will afford her the respect that she deserves, and consider her your second leader in all but name. She will be my shadow.'

When the room fell silent, Fern raised her palms and broke out that wide, charming smile which poured light and warmth over its recipients. 'To Seed!' she called out, loudly, joyfully.

'To Seed!'

As we filed from the art room to return to our duties, I glanced back at our youngest sister, now in a huddle with Susan, Kathy and Fern, surprise writ large across her sweet damaged face, and I felt myself fading away. Who was I now? What was I? I had once believed *I* was Fern's second-in-command, I thought with some degree of detachment. But her plan for Seed was the right one, the one we always knew was to come. So, what was it I was struggling with? What was it that wounded me so deeply?

Then it hit me, as I took one last look at Seed across the room. She no longer needed me, no longer came to *me* first to share in her celebrations. She had her room-mate Susan now, for companionship, and she had the support of the entire community for everything else. I had nothing unique to offer.

Catching me watching, Fern gave me a solemn nod, and I fell into line with the other women, gently directing them back to their labours.

As I walked alone across the garden path, I wondered how happy our women would be about their future if they knew what we Founding Sisters knew. If they'd seen the things we'd witnessed together, harboured the secrets we'd shared, perhaps they wouldn't have applauded quite so fervently.

16. CELINE

Present day

When Celine arrives back at Belle France after her meeting with Georgie on Friday afternoon, she catches the tail end of a conversation Pip's in the middle of, and can't help but eavesdrop as her sister's voice carries from the room where she's taking the phone call.

'No,' she says, resolutely. 'I'm not giving it to you . . . Because you'll only come down here and make trouble.'

This has to be Stefan, Celine thinks. Other than *her*, Stefan's the only other person she can imagine Pip speaking to so bluntly.

'*Of course* they're fine. I don't know why you'd suggest they'd be anything else! They're always fine! It's me who's not fine, Stefan . . . Why? Because I haven't been fine for years! Because you – you – I can't even—'

Celine feels dishonest, lurking in the hallway in silence, not announcing herself. As she proceeds towards the living room to make herself known, Pip's voice rises in pitch.

'If you do, Stefan, I swear to God I'll call the police.' There's an icy quality in Pip that Celine has never heard before, and a quiet, terrifying tone of dread. As she ends the call, Pip spins to face her sister, alerted to the sound of her presence in the room.

'Where are the girls?' Celine asks, casually dropping her rucksack, not wanting Pip to know her call was overheard.

In a second, Pip's expression shifts from startled to serene. 'They're upstairs! I found them a nasty plastic racing track in the charity shop this afternoon and they're trying to put it together in the spare room.'

Celine fetches a new bottle of wine from the rack. 'Who was that on the phone?'

'Oh, just Stefan,' Pip replies breezily, accepting the glass Celine hands out to her. 'Wanting me to kiss the girls goodnight for him. Anyway, tell me all about *your* day!' And just like that the conversation is diverted, brushed beneath the carpet, as Celine updates Pip on Una's news that the reopening of Vanessa's case has been officially approved.

By late evening, leaden skies open in a torrential downpour, and with Una back home in Kingston for a couple of days the sisters spend a strangely idyllic housebound weekend with the girls, baking and watching TV, and even managing to rustle up a half-decent Sunday roast. There are echoes of their teen years, when Celine suddenly found herself guardian to her two younger sisters, but it's not in a bad way. She's starting to remember some of the good things about that time too: those lazy days spent together on the sofa, rain lashing against the high sash windows, the world beyond them shut safely outside. Late nights eating cobbled-together meals and last-minute school uniform panics; hours spent styling each other's hair or painting their bedroom walls in garish and ill-advised colours. It really hadn't been all bad, had it?

Now, with Vanessa's case finally starting to move forward and a fresh week ahead of her, Celine stands in the doorway of the living room, watching her sister and the girls curled up on the sofa in front of *Jungle Book*, and thinks that she feels something near to peace. It's good to be close to Pip again, and the intense affection she has for her nieces grows by the day. Perhaps, if they can solve the mystery of Vanessa's death once and for all, she'll be able to sort herself out and get on with her life, but this time with Pip in it.

On Monday morning, as Celine meets Una and signs in at Lewes police headquarters, her mind is still on Pip, who has stayed behind, planning a trip on the pleasure boats with Olive and Beebee.

'Did you update your sister?' Una asks now as they sit in reception waiting to be shown up to DI Aston's office.

'Yes, but I played it down a bit, to be honest,' Celine answers. 'I guess I don't want to raise her hopes too high if we only have to dash them again after this meeting. I think she's got a lot on her plate at the moment.'

'Stefan?' Una asks.

Celine shifts in her seat, returning a quizzical look.

'Well, there's something going on, isn't there?' Una says. 'He's been phoning her mobile at all hours, and I've heard her hang up on him at least twice. You must have noticed.'

Celine could kick herself. She *has* heard Pip's phone ringing frequently too, but she didn't think to question it when Pip told her she's been plagued by bogus sales calls lately.

'She was in the middle of an argument with him when I got home on Friday night.'

'Did you ask her about it?'

'No.' Celine is ashamed as she says it. 'You know she'd only tell me to butt out if I did.'

Una nods. 'I've asked her about it a few times, but she clammed up, told me to take off my detective hat and leave her alone. But things haven't been good between them for a while. You notice things when you live next door—'

'Una!' Dave Aston appears in the doorway, beckoning them through.

They pass through the security barriers and along the halls and stairwells to his office, where he gestures them inside and closes the door.

'Those your kids, Dave?' Una asks, indicating towards a framed photograph of two handsome young men.

'Huge, aren't they? Nineteen and twenty-one. University's costing me a fortune,' he says. 'Why do they all have to go to bloody uni these days? Not like us, eh, Una?'

'Barely knew what uni was when I was nineteen,' she replies, and she pulls out a chair and indicates for Celine to sit beside her as Dave takes the seat at his desk.

'So,' Celine says, impatient to get going. 'What's this all about?'

Una gives Dave a smile that suggests Celine's brusque manner is par for the course. 'Well, I explained to you that Dave was on my team for a while, a few years back,' she says. 'And I don't like to say he owes me a few favours, but—'

Dave laughs. 'All true,' he says, 'which is why I know I can trust Una with privileged information relating to these murder investigations, and why we'll be approaching things a bit differently when it comes to gathering information from the women's community at Two Cross Farm.'

Celine turns to Una. 'I'm not sure I understand.'

'Dave, maybe we can start with Robyn's case?' Una pats Celine's leg, reassuringly.

'Yes, apologies, I'm running ahead. Celine, Una told you that we've had the post-mortem back for Robyn Siegle? It tells us she suffered a broken neck, and revealed fingertip bruising on her upper arms, which suggests a struggle. I'm fairly confident we're looking at murder, or manslaughter at the very least.'

This is more information than Celine has previously heard from Una, and the stark reality of it is more shocking than she'd anticipated. A broken neck.

When Celine doesn't answer, Una sits forward in her seat. 'I've explained to Celine that the powers-that-be are now in agreement that the cases could be related – and that you're officially connecting the two crimes.'

Dave drags a file of papers across his desk, and places Vanessa's postcard on the surface, with its windmill picture from Two Cross Farm. 'This recent evidence you discovered at your mother's home – suggesting Vanessa was a resident at the commune – is certainly cause for our interest. It's a strong link.'

'And the tattoos,' Celine adds.

'That's right,' Dave agrees, flipping through his papers. 'At the time of her death, Vanessa's tattoos weren't considered to be relevant to the case – in fact, I think we can be sure they weren't given any consideration whatsoever.'

Celine catches a glimpse of a photograph in Aston's pile. It's a close-up of a tattoo against pale skin: solid, black, like a mark against a wrong answer. Please God, let that be Robyn, not Vanessa. Celine couldn't bear to see that . . .

Bringing herself back to the present, she swallows hard, remembering Pip's upset over those tattoos back then, how she'd insisted they were completely out of character for their sister. The police hadn't been interested at the time. 'Why weren't they considered?' she asks now.

'Well, a lot of people get tattoos these days. It's not the least bit unusual – even fifteen years ago. Their presence would simply have been recorded on the post-mortem as a feature of the—'

Celine braces herself for the word 'body', but Dave corrects himself just in time.

'Of the victim,' he says instead. 'However, I've studied Robyn Siegle's tattoos and they *are* identical to Vanessa's: a pair of two-inch symmetrical black crosses on the lower abdomen, each adjacent to the hip bone. Then there's the fact that they both met a violent death; both laid out with care near water – albeit twenty miles apart; and finally that prior to their deaths they had both been residents at Two Cross Farm.'

'How is the Robyn Siegle case progressing, Dave?' Una asks. 'Can you tell us the basic facts?'

He thumbs through his papers. 'Well, we know that Robyn had had sexual intercourse shortly before her death, but there were no signs of violence in relation to that. Decent semen samples were recovered, but there's no match on the database. We picked up a partial fingerprint on her clothing, but it's not clear enough to record – so I've asked forensics to go back over her garments again, to ensure they haven't missed any others. We're in contact with Robyn's father, Adam Siegle, and he has told us that Robyn had apparently been staying at Two Cross Farm doing research into her family history.'

'Really?' Una says. 'Doing her family tree?'

'I think so. Adam Siegle said Robyn believed her mother might have stayed at Two Cross Farm at some point in the 1990s, but he wasn't sure whether that was true or not. Anyway, at the moment the main man in the frame is the ex-husband, Archie Chowdhury. Seed claims that Robyn had formally left the community very recently – the last anyone at Two Cross Farm saw of her, apparently, was when she departed for the train station in Arundel a few days earlier, to join Chowdhury in London.'

'Have you spoken to this ex yet?' Celine asks.

'Not yet. We're having trouble locating him. CCTV *does* show Robyn and Archie Chowdhury together at Arundel station forty-eight hours before her body was found, and Seed claims they didn't see her at all in those two days that followed. Like Robyn, Chowdhury is a US citizen, but he works as a chef in London – it's thought he moved out here a couple of months after Robyn, but quite independently of her. The details about their recent reconciliation are all a bit sketchy, so we're hoping someone inside Two Cross Farm will be able to fill in some of the gaps for us.'

'Are the Two Cross women under suspicion?' Una asks. 'I realise you've got Chowdhury in the frame for Robyn, and Falmer for Vanessa, but we – you – can't let that stop you from considering other suspects, Dave. Right now, that community is your biggest common link between Robyn and Vanessa.'

'I know the drill, Una. I learnt from the best,' he replies, and with a smile she raises her hands in surrender. 'Strictly speaking, no, they're *not* under suspicion. *Yet.* We do, however, want to know more about Robyn's living arrangements there, and her movements before she left the community.'

Celine reaches for the postcard, turning it over in her hands. 'And Vanessa's case?'

'There's no doubt we'll be up against it, with the age of the crime,' Dave replies. 'It's never easy going back over old evidence, and often the vital piece is something we've not yet found, something outside of the case files. I've actually asked one of our journo contacts to leak the fact that we're looking into Vanessa's 2005 case again, to see if it throws up anything new.'

'Like what?' Celine asks. 'I've been in contact with Vanessa's best friend, if that's any help? She confirmed that Falmer was violent – and she got a postcard from Vanessa, too . . .'

'Thanks, we'll certainly follow that up, but what I'm really hoping for is that the publicity will bring someone forward who knows where Jem Falmer's been all these years. Witnesses who are resistant when a crime is first being investigated sometimes have a change of heart with the passing of time. Again, we're hoping the Two Cross residents will remember her and tell us more about the months leading up to Vanessa's death.'

'So why aren't you in there now, gathering evidence – interviewing that Seed woman?' Celine demands.

Dave clasps his hands together on the table, fixing Celine with his steady gaze. 'After her initial voluntary interview at the station, Seed is now refusing to co-operate with the police at all. She's threatening to sue us for breach of human rights if we even suggest sending a man near the place. And it's not as simple as sending in a female officer, because she, and the entire community by the sound of it, are completely anti-establishment.'

Celine rubs her eyes with the heels of her hands. 'This is unbelievable. She does know a woman died, right?'

Dave continues. 'The other thing is, between you and me, the entire force is under instruction from the Commissioner to tread carefully when it comes to women's groups at the moment, since a recent enquiry opened in the Midlands relating to police conduct at a number of women's refuges there. We have to avoid any suggestion of heavy-handedness.'

'So basically, you're telling me your hands are tied,' Celine says, bringing her palm down on the edge of the desk. 'For God's sake, it's possible those women hold *all* the answers—'

'Hang on a sec,' Una says. 'This is kind of where I come in.'

Dave smiles. 'Una here has agreed to act as a civilian consultant – as a kind of liaison between the community and the police force. We think her past experience, her proximity and the fact that she's, well, a woman, will give her an edge when it comes to finding out more about the goings-on at Two Cross

Farm. If Seed understands Una's there merely as a go-between, with no police powers, she may be more forthcoming.'

Celine shifts in her seat, heart racing. 'And she's agreed?'

Dave jerks his chin towards Una, so she can break the news.

'Seed's running it past the other Founding Sisters this morning,' she says, eyes sparkling. 'But we're confident that's just a formality. In theory, it's all set for tomorrow. Celine, I'm going in.'

After Aston escorts them off the premises, Celine and Una walk down to the river where they've parked the car, neither speaking for several minutes as Celine registers the monumental shifts in the case. They stop to lean on the defence wall, looking out across the River Ouse as overhead the sky darkens with heavy clouds.

'You know I'm coming with you, right?' Celine says.

'To Two Cross Farm?' Una replies. 'I hadn't expected anything less, baby.'

17. BRAMBLE

Present day, Two Cross Farm

The Founding Sisters are gathered in Seed's office: Seed, Regine, and me. It still saddens me to note the absence of Kathy and Susan, long gone, and Fern, missing in all but body. I looked in on her on my way up here, to see how she was doing, and the carers told me she'd had another restless night, having woken confused, chattering anxiously and pacing about. She looked small as a child, laid out in her bed, deep in sleep, her lips slightly parted, the skin of her jaw slack. Oh, Fern, I wanted to cry out. Where are you now, you great warrior?

'I've just come off the phone with the police,' Seed tells us now. She's seated behind her desk, her arms folded on the top, resignation in the slope of her shoulders. 'DI Aston tells me they're getting very close to imposing a search warrant on us.'

For a moment no one speaks. Regine shifts uncomfortably in her chair, gripping its arms, bony-knuckled. Over the years, her body seems to have crumpled in on itself, and, although at

126

seventy-three she's over a decade younger than me, the newer residents treat her like a grand old dame.

'Is he a decent fellow, the policeman?' she asks, her once husky voice now grown papery. 'Do you trust him, Seed?'

Seed inclines her head in thought. 'Him specifically? I don't know. The police in general? Not a bit.'

'What happens if they do get a warrant?' I ask. I'm thinking of all the things we don't want the police to know about. I'm thinking of all the things we don't want them to see. 'Can we challenge it?'

'I've talked through our legal position with Anneka, and she says if they get a warrant we'll have no option but to admit them and help with their enquiries. She says the law is only on our side if they try to force access without a warrant, or if their behaviour is excessive once they're inside.'

Regine shakes her head, her expression set grim. 'Is there no other way, Seed? Think of all the women we've promised sanctuary. You know what happened last time a man—'

Seed raises a palm, silencing her, and I'm grateful for her quiet authority. We're all afraid.

'We've reached an impasse,' Seed explains. 'However, DI Aston has made a proposal, which I'd like to put to the group. There is an ex-police officer staying in the area – a woman. She's retired, and therefore has no authority over us. Aston has suggested we admit her to the community as a go-between of sorts.'

'A spy, you mean?' Regine says.

'A spy is only effective if they're unknown to us, Regine. We know where this woman's interests lie, and we will dictate where she can go and what we are prepared to answer. If we say yes to this, we can closely manage the situation – and we can ask her to leave when we've had enough. And, if the police are satisfied with our answers, there's every chance they will back off and normal life can resume.'

For a long while, we sit in silence, disturbed only by the sounds of the spring blackbirds trilling out their mating calls beyond the open windows, the light of the evening shifting in the direction of the river. Seed's focus is on the view too, where only an hour ago a small gaggle of journalists were still loitering with cameras at the ready. There is concern in her expression.

'Aren't you afraid?' I ask, and I sense Regine's attention intensify, perhaps equally anxious to hear her reply.

Slowly, Seed's gaze returns to the room, and she smiles a little sadly.

'I'm terrified,' she admits. 'I – we – all of us – have a lot to lose here. I'm angry and I'm sad and I'm scared in equal measure; but I'm certain enough of the police force's intentions to know our options are limited.'

Regine shuffles stiffly to the edge of her seat and laces her fingers across one knee, the curve of her spine giving her the all-at-odds stance of an eager-pupil. 'Then I say yes, sister. I'm with you: let the bitch in.' Still the mouthy dame, after all these years. That's what Tattooed Sandy used to call her, before she was ejected from the community for good.

'Bramble, do you agree?' Seed asks.

Reluctantly, I nod.

Seed picks up the telephone receiver, and Regine and I rise to leave.

As I reach the door, she calls my name. 'Bramble? Start drawing up a list of things we need to do in preparation, will you? If we're going to do this, we need to be whiter than white by the time this Una woman arrives. She's going to turn over a few rocks when she gets here.' She holds my gaze, unblinking. 'We need to make sure she finds nothing beneath them.'

When the meeting ends, I leave the office and head straight down to the basement, where I instruct the laundry team to have the floors thoroughly bleached again. We've been over them a dozen times or more already, but it would be foolish to leave anything to chance.

18. CELINE

Present day

As they stand waiting outside the iron gates of Two Cross Farm, Celine is suddenly gripped by nerves.

This has all happened so quickly – her mother's death, Robyn Siegle, yesterday's meeting with the police – she's barely had a chance to think about what it means, or whether they're putting themselves at risk. When they'd returned from Lewes last night, Una had read aloud extracts of Dave Aston's file on Two Cross Farm, briefing them on the little that is known about the commune, and it is very little. All they really learned was that the commune was set up in 1976 by a small group of women sharing feminist ideals and describing themselves not as a refuge, but as a lifestyle based on sisterhood. While they know the current leader to be this woman Seed, nothing more is known about her – what her real name might be, where she originally comes from, or how long she's been part of the community. Celine would be lying if she said she wasn't intrigued, keen to dig deeper, but at the same time her stomach is doing backflips.

'Do you think they heard the bell?' she asks Una, her eyes drawn to a flower-filled wooden boat artfully moored at the far end of the lawns, looking as if the wind has swept it in off the river. Behind them, a couple of press vans are parked in the lane, and Una has already warned off two reporters, telling them they're wasting their time if they expect any comment from the community.

She reaches for the bell rope again, giving it another tug, and as ringing echoes out across the otherwise peaceful gardens Celine has a strong sense that they're trespassing, that this isn't a place they should be. Is this a mistake? Should they just forget all about it, and head back home? She focuses on a spot beyond the gate, where a trio of hedge sparrows peck around the verge, picking up insects in the light drizzle.

Just as she opens her mouth to suggest Una phone Aston, Seed appears in the front doorway of the grand house, today wearing a forest-green tunic, an earth-coloured turban concealing her hair. She proceeds down the steps, gracefully crossing the drive in their direction, a ring of keys in one hand, a serene expression on her face.

'Welcome!' she calls as she approaches the gate, releasing the deadlock and sliding the bolt to beckon them in.

For a brief moment, Celine is struck dumb. She nods a closed-mouth smile and hopes that Una will lead the conversation now she finds herself so incapable. How should she behave in this strange woman's company, in this strange place? In the gloom of the dreary morning Seed's facial scars appear more livid, the worst of them confined to her jawline, licking like flames up the right-hand side of her face. Celine tries not to stare, and wonders when she last felt so out of her depth. Not for years; not since those days in River Terrace, after her mother had gone.

'Welcome. You must be Una—' Seed says, clipping the keys to her belt and clasping Una's hand between hers, 'and you must be Celine. Come inside, before you get soaked.'

She turns, thrusts her hands into deep pockets and breaks into a capable jog as the rain opens up at a pelt. Una and Celine sprint behind, heading for the open door of the house, and moments later they're being led through a dark wood-panelled hallway and into a large old-fashioned kitchen filled with the smells of cooking and good-humoured conversation. The five or six women around the room each look up from their various labours, nodding warmly and offering greetings. None of them wears make-up or jewellery; none of them seems senior to the next. Except for Seed. She really does stand out.

'Welcome,' the women all say in greeting – just that one word – and Celine avoids looking at Una for fear that she'll expose her bubbling disquiet. There's something off; everything feels too serene, too *functional* by far.

Seed fetches two towels and hands them over. 'You're wet,' she says. 'We'll do a tour of the house first, introduce you to some more of our women? Before we start, may I ask for your phones? It's one of our rules, I'm afraid – no mobiles. They're a distraction.'

Una takes hers from her jacket pocket, switches it off and hands it to Seed. Masking her reluctance, Celine does the same.

'Good. Remind me to give these back to you when you leave, will you?' She slips the handsets into her deep pockets and brushes her hands off, as though ridding them of invisible dirt. 'I'm hopeful the rain will let up in the next half-hour, and then we'll show you the gardens – our pride and joy.'

'We'd really like that,' Una says, appearing, unlike Celine, instantly at ease. 'I love gardening, though not on your scale, of course.'

Celine remembers the small patch of courtyard at the back of Una's place in River Terrace, filled with geranium pots and herbs and tomatoes that, of course, she must have nurtured and grown herself. She wonders why she's never really thought of Una in this way, as someone whose life goes on beyond the small parts Celine knows about. 'Yes, that would be really nice,' she says, trying to join in, to find her voice.

Seed holds up a hand to attract the attention of the women across the room. 'Sisters, has anyone seen Bramble? I was hoping she'd join us on the tour.'

A petite woman, perhaps in her fifties, dries her hands on a tea towel. 'I think she was seeing to the Elders,' she says in a broad Scottish accent. 'I'll go and take over from her.' She passes through an adjoining swing door, affording Celine the briefest glimpse of an elderly woman reading in an armchair, before the door swings shut again.

'Bramble can catch us up,' Seed says, with a nod. 'Shall we walk and talk? As you know, I've agreed to just two hours for this first meeting – to ensure we're all aligned.'

'Absolutely,' Una agrees. 'And please ask me and Celine anything at all. I'm sure you – quite rightly – feel cautious, knowing we'll be reporting back to the police, but we want you to trust us. It's important that you know we don't mean you any harm.'

Seed leads them back into the hallway, and, as they head towards a large living room at the rear of the property, Celine is struck by the vast size of the place. The layout is similar in design to her mother's but on a much larger scale. They pass several more closed doors, marked 'pantry' and 'clinic' and 'rest room' and 'medic', before reaching the living room, which, as at Belle France, looks out over lawns in the direction of the river. At Belle France you can actually see the river and path; here there is a wall of trees, and a hive of activity around the greenhouses and sheds at the far end.

'Why you?' Seed asks now, gesturing towards two upright armchairs on either side of a large lit fireplace. 'Why did the police ask you, Una?'

'As you know, I'm ex-force,' Una replies as she takes a seat. 'Retired.'

'Detective?' Seed asks.

Una nods. 'They thought I'd be able to ask you the right kinds of questions, without pissing you off too much, I guess.'

Seed laughs, and it is a beautiful sound, low and unchecked. 'Good. That's good.' She gazes at Una for what seems like a long while, thoughts visibly crossing her face. 'How old are you?'

'I'm fifty-seven,' Una replies.

'The police force can't have been an easy place for someone like you to build a career?'

'Someone like me?'

'A woman. A black woman at that.'

Now it's Una's turn to laugh. 'People aren't usually so straight-talking, but no, you're right. I often had to work twice as hard as most of the men I came up through the ranks with, just to get noticed for the right reasons. I couldn't tell you how much of that was down to my gender, or how much down to my colour – but it's a fair assumption that neither helped my case all that much. Still, I had good parents – they never let me use either condition as an excuse, and I've stuck by that.'

'Either condition. That's good.' Seed smiles. 'Very good. Society does see being female as a "condition", doesn't it? As something to be cured or ignored.'

Celine is leaving most of the talking to Una, punctuating their conversation with unobtrusive smiles and small murmurs of assent, while she tries to get a hold on what it is she really feels about this place. She takes in the layout of the room, noticing how two of the walls are covered, floor to ceiling, with framed black and white photographs of women. Some are close portraits, others distant shots; all look professional. A number are nudes. From the little she knows about photography, the pictures all appear to be taken on traditional film, but as most of the women are absent of make-up and dressed in the plain tunics that Seed favours, they are hard to date.

'You're admiring our gallery,' Seed notices, rising to cross the room and lay a hand on one particular picture at her eye level. It's a close profile of a dark-haired woman wearing a gypsy bandana, her eyes obscured by large sunglasses.

'They're incredible,' Celine says. 'How many women are there?'

'Well, everyone who passes through is photographed,' she replies. 'Ever since 1976. Which means there are close to four hundred faces around the house – we long ago ran out of space in this room. There are more upstairs.'

Celine's pulse races as she thinks about the possibility of finding Vanessa here, hidden among the portraits. 'They look as though they're all taken by the same person?' she says, meeting Seed's eye properly for the first time.

It is a steady gaze, and Celine is at once disarmed by the warmth she sees there. *What is this woman hiding?* is Celine's overriding thought. *What does that easy manner conceal?*

'Our founder was an award-winning photographer back in the seventies,' Seed replies. 'Her images of women won prizes in New York, Milan, San Francisco – she gave it all up to come here. We're very lucky to have her.'

'She's still here?' Celine asks. 'At Two Cross Farm?'

'Oh, yes,' Seed replies, allowing her hand to linger on that one image. 'Though she's taken her last picture, we think. She's fading fast.'

Celine glances at Una, feeling frustration at the slow pace of their meeting, at the way in which Una seems to be slavishly following Aston's instructions to 'tread carefully'. Sure, they don't want to lose Seed's co-operation by being too pushy – but still, Una's restraint is maddening to Celine's restless sensibilities.

'Is there a photograph of—' Celine starts, but Una shoots her a look which tells her it's too early. *Vanessa*, was the word she'd wanted to end the sentence with.

Seed nods her head sadly, obviously assuming Celine is asking about Robyn. But, before she can expand, there is a creak as the door from the hallway opens and an elderly woman enters, wearing a navy artist's smock and loose trousers, a smudge of ink marking one of her round pink cheeks.

'Bramble, you're here!' Seed says, extending her hands and drawing her in. 'Una, Celine, this is Bramble. Bramble is one of our Founding Sisters – one of the first six women who set up Two Cross Farm in 1976. She was at the initial meeting when the vision was conceived, when the Code of Conduct was drawn up, before our first residents were welcomed into our arms. She really is the backbone to this place.' Seed pauses to smile at Bramble, and there is real affection there.

'Welcome,' Bramble says, and she is friendly, though less expansive than Seed. 'Seed, it's stopped raining now,' she says. 'I thought our guests might like to see the garden and the workshops?'

Pushing open the French doors, Bramble leads them out on to the garden path, where the sun is now breaking through.

'I'll join you shortly,' Seed says as she heads back towards the heart of the house. 'There's some paperwork I must attend to. Thank you, Bramble.'

Outside, despite the screened rear of the garden, Celine can sense the river just beyond, the sky above it now clearing as the rain clouds drift away. At the end of a brick footpath, a wood store dominates one corner, while greenhouses run the width of the garden, punctuated by two large compost piles heaped like burial mounds, and a patchwork of raised vegetable beds. To the left is the miniature windmill, as featured in Vanessa's postcard to Delilah all those years ago.

'We try to grow as much as possible,' Bramble explains, plucking at a few weeds as they walk. 'At the side of the house we also have a fruit orchard. We make jams, ciders and juices – some of it we keep for the occasional treat and celebration, but most of it goes to the local farmer's market, to bring an additional income.'

'How *do* you make ends meet?' Celine asks. 'It must be hard, with so many of you?'

Bramble is silent for a few seconds, and it seems clear she's trying to decide whether this is a question she's happy to answer. 'There are thirty-three of us in total. We live simply and we work hard. We own the property outright, and over the years we have benefited from a small number of bequests. We get by. It's hand-to-mouth, but, arguably, that's how it should be. Enough for our needs, but no excess.'

'What's that building?' Una asks, pointing to what looks like a summerhouse to the far right-hand side of the garden.

'That's our print workshop. Our art studio.'

'Can we see?' Celine asks, feeling a whole lot more at ease with the older woman than she had with Seed.

'Are you a keen artist?' Bramble replies, her interest piqued.

'Kind of,' Celine lies, her mind on the linoprint postcard sent by her sister fifteen years earlier. 'I love handprinted design – though it's been years since I picked up a paintbrush. I did lino-cutting when I was at school.'

Inside the studio, several women sit at workbenches, bent over watercolours or carvings. Rows of picture rails run around the walls, displaying old print blocks, new paintings and the occasional photograph.

'Do you sell any of your prints?' Una asks.

'Yes,' Bramble says, pulling open a drawer and bringing out a shoebox of postcards. 'These do quite well at the farmer's market. Seed was the one who really developed that side of our business – it's grown considerably over the years.'

'Was that when she first became leader?' Una asks, casually.

'No, no, she'd been doing it long before then. She's only been custodian for the past ten years.' Celine can see Una is desperate to delve further, but she lets the silence roll, as Bramble picks out two or three different postcard images, holding them out to her. 'The most popular ones are of the castle, naturally – but also the river landscapes and the swans. You know there's a wildfowl trust nearby? They take some of our cards, for their tourist centre.'

'This one's nice,' Una says, picking out the windmill from a separate box on the worktop. 'Isn't that the windmill from the garden?'

Bramble picks it up, pleased. 'That's one of mine – I did it years ago. We don't sell many of these. We let the residents help themselves to anything that doesn't sell – lots of them have family elsewhere in the country or around world, so we encourage them to keep in touch. Unless they have reason not to, of course.'

'What kind of reason?' Una asks.

'I don't need to tell you, officer, that some women—' Bramble says.

'Oh, I'm not a serving officer,' Una interrupts swiftly. 'I'm retired – please, it's Una.'

Bramble scrutinises Una carefully, suddenly shrewd; she's sizing them up. Has Seed handed them to Bramble merely to suss them out? 'Of course. I don't need to tell you, *Una*, that some of our women have come to us from very difficult situations.'

'Like domestic abuse?' Una asks.

'Yes. At least two-thirds of our women have experienced some kind of violence or control before coming here. And that's only counting the ones who want to talk about it. I believe the number is probably much higher.'

'Would you describe Two Cross Farm as a refuge?' Celine asks.

'No. Because "refuge" is connected to words like "victim" and "hiding", and we don't want our women to start life here seeing themselves in that way. It's for that reason we encourage the use of "sister" from the outset – it integrates the women instantly, gives them a sense of belonging, of family. They don't have to follow the old rules laid out for them any more. They're independent, while at the same time supported.'

'But you do have rules here, don't you?' Celine says. 'A Code of Conduct. Seed mentioned it earlier.'

Instead of answering, Bramble gestures towards the door and they step out of the workshop into bright sunshine, as a faint rainbow arcs over the roof of the house, vanishing into distant dark clouds. Two women cross the lawn, each pushing a wheelbarrow full of logs. There's something so peaceful about the image that for a moment Celine allows herself to imagine life here, without her laptop or phone, her business suits and haircuts. What must it feel like to arrive here with nothing – to simply move in, and live?

'Will you join us?' Bramble asks when the community bell rings ten o'clock, and for a moment Celine wonders if she's read her mind. 'For tea?' she adds at Celine's startled expression. 'You can meet the other women and ask them about the Code of Conduct yourself?'

She leads them via the orchard, past stone steps down to a basement laundry and in through a different entrance, to a large dining room dominated by a huge oak table. Mugs and plates are being laid out by a young woman, barely out of her teens.

'What are the crosses for?' Celine asks, noticing the plate-sized white crosses painted on the surface of the table.

'They're place settings.' Seed joins them through another internal door, startling Celine with her presence. 'Thirty-three in total, one for each resident.'

As she pushes the door wide, a stream of women enters, chatting amiably while they each take a place at the table. Two much older women are wheeled in and situated at the far end, opposite Seed at the head, and the last woman to arrive brings a hostess trolley carrying five teapots, jugs of milk and three large fruit loaves. Once all are seated, Bramble directs Celine and Una to two of the empty crosses, and, when she herself takes a seat, two more crosses, and two empty seats, remain. One more vacancy than Seed had previously mentioned.

'One of our number is unwell,' Seed explains, gesturing to the space beside one of the older women. All at once, her eyes brim with tears. 'And the one beside me was Robyn's place.'

After tea, the women go back to work and Seed invites Celine and Una to her office on the first floor. It's at the front of the property, looking out towards the iron gates and grass verge where the press conference was held only days ago. Bramble stands with her back to the window, her arms lightly folded beneath her bosom, each hand nestled inside the opposite sleeve.

'I expect you're burning with questions,' Seed says, taking a seat behind the large desk, with Bramble to her rear. In front of her is a national newspaper which she nudges with her index finger, disdain in that tiny movement. 'It seems the rest of the world is, wouldn't you say?'

Una and Celine sit on the other side of the desk, like clients.

'Listen, Seed,' Una replies, 'the police are not the media – and they're not responsible for what the gutter press writes. Why don't I ask you some direct questions now, so I've got something to take back to DI Aston? If the police are satisfied with what I feed back, I'm sure it won't be long before they give a press statement of their own – and the media *will* eventually leave you in peace.'

Seed turns to look up at Bramble, who nods her approval. The dynamic between the two is fascinating: while Seed is clearly in charge here, Bramble seems to be some kind of close aide, a silent advisor of sorts. 'Yes,' Seed says. 'Let's try that.'

'Can I start with some general questions, about the way the community is run?' Una asks, taking a small flip-over notepad from her inside pocket.

A nod.

'You say there are thirty women resident at the moment?'

'That's right. We never exceed thirty-three, which is our optimum number.'

'Can women leave of their own accord?'

There is a moment's delay, before both women laugh. 'Of course!' Bramble replies, a little too brightly.

'Are they paid for their labours?'

'Money has no meaning here,' Seed replies. 'Women work a normal eight-hour day, and in return they receive room and board. No single activity is valued over another, and so everyone is equal. In a way, it's no different from the Poor Clares convent down the road, or any other religious order.'

'Is *this* a religious community?' Celine asks, her attention falling on the word 'cult', emblazoned across the front of the newspaper.

'No, it is not. But it *is* a belief system. Only women who sign up to our particular way of life may stay. That's why we have the Code of Conduct displayed in every room here – it's a mantra, a reminder if you like. If a woman finds she can't abide by the Code, she must leave to make room for another who can.'

'You said you're interviewing for a new resident today,' Una says. 'How do women get admitted? Do they have to stay for a minimum period?'

'We are very selective,' Bramble answers. 'When a vacancy comes up, we only take a woman with something to offer the community, one who has some need, and who we feel will fit with our values.'

'What do you mean by "something to offer"?' Celine asks.

'It's very practical really. We have a doctor and a lawyer,' Seed says. 'We have several gardeners, a carpenter, two carers, a music teacher – all offering something unique and valuable, you see?'

Una chews on the end of her pen. 'What did Robyn Siegle bring?'

Seed appears to study her own hands closely for a moment, long fingers splayed wide on the desk before her, fingertips pressed white as though anchoring her to the room. 'She was a cook.'

'There are no children here,' Celine says, her thoughts drifting to her sister Pip, who has taken the girls home to Kingston for a night, to see their father and pick up some fresh clothes and belongings.

Seed fixes her with a strangely hard gaze. 'No, there are not.'

'Why not?' Una asks.

Bramble puts a hand on Seed's shoulder. 'It was written into the original Code of Conduct. Children are a distraction – and, sadly, often another weapon for men to use against women. Maternal love is our greatest burden; our greatest weakness.'

A *weakness*. A *burden*. Was that how Celine's own mother, Delilah, had viewed motherhood? Was that how she justified so easily abandoning her children? The fallout from that decision still resonates, and Celine fears she might never forgive her mother, even now that she's dead. 'But many of these women will have left children behind, surely? Is it right, keeping women from their children?'

In answer, Seed rises from her seat, so that she's now looking down on Celine and Una, with Bramble to her side. 'I feel as though we've met before?' she says to Celine, and she appears genuinely perplexed. '*Have* we met before?'

Celine can feel a vein in the side of her neck pulsing so hard that she wonders if it's visible to the other women in the room. All at once she's desperate to ask about Vanessa, and she grips the side of the desk just to hold on to something solid. 'No, we haven't,' she says, 'but perhaps you—'

And thank God for Una, who stops her in her tracks. 'I imagine you keep a record of the women who have stayed at Two Cross Farm over the years?'

Seed shakes her head, and turns to Bramble. 'No,' Seed says, quite firmly.

But Bramble reaches out and lays her hand on a thick, leather-bound journal which lies on the desktop. It looks like an ancient bible, aged and broken-spined. 'We have nothing to hide, Seed. Let them see it.'

As Seed reluctantly sits again, Una pulls the book across the desk. 'Does this date back to 1976?' she asks, reverentially opening the journal to the first entry.

Celine leans in too, and at speed she scans the page, fearful that the cautious Seed could change her mind at any moment. In the left-hand column is each woman's 'original name', and for some, in the next column, is a 'chosen name'.

'The women take new names?' she asks, remembering how Seed alluded to this in her speech from the podium. 'Who chooses them?'

'They do,' Seed replies. 'Not all change their names, but those who wish to are supported in their decision. For some, it's important to reinvent themselves when they start afresh here. For others, it's the only way to move forward.'

'You both changed yours?' Celine says, instantly fearing that Una will think she's pushing too hard.

'No,' Seed responds while Bramble remains silent. 'Seed is my birth name. I had nothing to leave behind.'

143

She smiles at Celine now, and it is a peaceful expression, full of warmth, and Celine is disarmed.

'Can you show us Robyn's entry?' Una asks, perhaps sensing the shift in atmosphere and bringing it back to the subject at hand. 'When did she arrive?'

'Three months ago,' Bramble replies, leaning over the ledger and turning to the more recent entries, three quarters of the way through. 'Here she is.'

There, in February, is Robyn Siegle's name and date of arrival. 'She kept her own name,' Celine observes.

Celine notices how Bramble still stands with a hand on Seed's shoulder, unconsciously massaging it with the pad of her thumb, like a mother reassuring a child.

As Una guides the end of her pen along Robyn's line, she pauses at the last column, headed 'Departure Date', but there is none listed for Robyn. It's still blank. She turns to the previous page, running her finger down the list of women, pausing at those where the departure date has been filled in.

'Bramble, all these ones with no departure date – is it safe to assume they're still here?'

The older woman reaches for her reading glasses, secured about her neck on a string. She peers down the list, nodding them off slowly, 'Yes . . . yes . . . yes . . . yes,' until Una turns the page and she reaches the blank departure column for Robyn. 'Oh, dear,' Bramble says.

Obviously perturbed, Seed reaches across and retrieves the journal, spinning it to face her.

'You said Robyn had moved out two days before she was found dead, Seed,' Una says, failing to keep the accusation out of her voice. 'So why, when you are clearly meticulous in your record-keeping, is there no departure date listed for her?'

Neither woman speaks for a second, and all eyes are on

Seed, as she stares at that glaring empty space where Robyn's departure date should be.

'It's my fault,' Bramble says, breaking the silence. 'I told you I'd do it, Seed, and I must have forgotten. I'm getting so old and forgetful these days,' she says, but she's fooling no one. From the little they've seen and heard from Bramble this morning it's clear she's as sharp as anyone forty years her junior, and, as she leans over the desk and writes the date in, it's also clear she's not the one who usually updates this book. The handwriting is different, the swoops of her educated pen-work quite unlike the simple block print of the other entries.

As the bell for eleven o'clock sounds out, it takes every ounce of Celine's willpower to stop herself from launching across the desk and raking through those pages for evidence of Vanessa's stay fifteen years ago. All she can do is pray that they've done enough to earn a follow-up invitation, so that she might get a second chance.

At the front gate, Bramble stands at some distance while Seed hands back their mobile phones and embraces them each in turn. As their shoulders meet, Celine feels the strength of her in the lines of her shoulders. Her physique is lean and unyielding, and yet she is so elegant and so warmly in control.

'I didn't ask you what you do for a living, Celine?' she enquires as she slides the iron gate between them.

'I'm a solicitor,' Celine replies.

Seed flashes that charming smile of hers again. 'Oh, we could do with another of those at the moment, couldn't we, Bramble? There's a vacancy or two, for the right women,' she says, and she winks to show Celine she's joking. On the charm offensive.

Una scribbles her mobile number down and tears the page from her notebook, offering it to Seed through the bars of the closed gate. 'Can we come back again?'

There is silence, and Seed hesitates before taking it.

'If you talk to us,' Una says, 'the police will stay away from you.'

Seed looks at the number, and back at Bramble, who is waiting for her on the path to the house. 'I'll talk it over with the other women and we'll let you know.'

She starts to walk away, back towards Bramble, but Una isn't giving up. 'Now they've confirmed Robyn was murdered, they'll easily get a warrant, you know? You won't be able to stop them. I'm not saying this to frighten you, but I do know how it works, and I also know the police are running out of patience.' When Seed doesn't answer, she adds, 'If they've got a warrant and reason to suspect someone here, Seed, they'll storm the place.'

Seed halts, halfway between them and the house, and then she turns slowly, the wind catching the hem of her green tunic so it flaps like a sail. 'I'd burn the place down first,' she says, and something in her expression tells Celine she's not joking now.

As the two women disappear behind the front door, Una and Celine turn for home beneath the sun-dappled canopy of the woodland track.

'What do you think?' Celine asks.

Una casts a final glance back at the sealed security gates to Two Cross Farm. 'I think they're hiding a great deal more than we could ever discover in one short visit. Let's hope my threats have rattled Seed enough for her to invite us back.'

19. BRAMBLE

Present day, Two Cross Farm

Following our unwanted guests' departure, I feel compelled to check over Robyn's old bedroom again, and I cannot help but replay the time when she joined us, just three months ago in February, when Seed broke all our rules of recruitment in bringing her in.

Everything was odd about Robyn's arrival. There was no discussion between the Founding Sisters, no shortlisting of candidates, and no interview. We didn't vote for this new resident, or prepare her room, or even have forewarning of when she would arrive. Seed alone made the arrangements, casually delivering the announcement over supper: that we would be welcoming a new cook to the community and she would be arriving to join us some time that week. Of course we couldn't question her in an open forum like that, and so, when Seed returned to her office after we'd eaten, Regine and I swiftly followed, closing the door behind us and demanding to know what was going on. Fern was already in the room, sitting in the high-backed armchair to the left of Seed's desk, sifting through her old photographs on a lap tray, oblivious to the argument.

'Is it a problem?' Seed asked, her tone neutral but her meaning defensive. She pulled out her chair and set to rearranging papers on the desk.

'Well, yes, Seed, honey. You know we don't do things like this.' Regine eased herself into the facing armchair, wincing in pain. 'It goes against the Code.'

I wasn't planning to sit. I planted my hands on my hips, an unspoken invitation for Seed to explain herself.

'What's the big fuss?' she said, smiling, raising her palms. 'We have a vacancy. We need an additional cook, don't we? You know we can't keep up with demand on the market stall, and, if we move young Oregon on to overseeing the preserves, Robyn can take over as head cook. She's been working at a top London restaurant – you'll thank me!' She laughs at this, but the nerves are there for all of us to hear.

'We don't know anything about her,' I replied.

'About who?' Fern asked, looking up from her photos with a baffled expression. Her dementia had revealed itself slowly at first, in the tiniest of word confusions and physical hesitations, but just lately its grip had seemed to tighten, taking a little more of her with every waking day. It was clear to us all that we were seeing less and less of the original Fern, of that power force she once had been.

'Oh, nobody really, Fern,' Regine replied, and, satisfied, Fern returned to her pictures.

'OK, then I'll tell you about her,' Seed said, patiently as though she were talking to one of the hard-of-hearing Elders. 'She's American, and she's been in London for the past year, since divorcing from her husband. She's in her mid-twenties, she has an excellent skill to bring – what else?'

'Does she have need of our shelter?' I asked.

'Who doesn't?' Seed replied. 'She's still recovering from the breakdown of her marriage, but she's strong. But if that is not enough for you, the Code of Conduct is clear on this point. If a woman has no pressing need of shelter, they must bring skills to strengthen the group. That, surely, is not up for debate?'

There was a fog of shocked amazement in the room, and for a while no one knew what to say next. Could this really be our Seed, the most even-handed of all leaders, the woman who had time and again sacrificed her own happiness for the stability of the community, talking in this way? Seed, riding roughshod over our forty-year-old way of life?

Regine clapped her hands together in challenge. 'So, no vote? No consensus? You alone have the power, Seed, is that it? That's not the way of Two Cross Farm. That's *not* how we do things.'

'What would Fern say, if she were still in charge?' I asked. I glanced at her frail form, so reduced in her chair. She didn't even respond to the sound of her own name.

At this, Seed stood abruptly, her jaw set hard. 'Fern handed the reins over to me ten years ago, and I, as custodian, have taken this decision. It's not the norm, I know. You're right, there *is* more to this, and in time I will enlighten you. But for now you're just going to have to trust me, sisters. Can you do that? Trust me and it *will* all work out. I give you my word.'

There was nothing more Regine or I could say without undermining Seed's wisdom and authority, and a few days later, in the dead of night, Robyn arrived while the household slept. The first we saw of her was at breakfast the next morning, when we noticed that the seating had been rearranged without warning. One of the newer women had been asked to switch seats to make room for Robyn beside Seed at the top of the table. As I retained my position at the opposite end, my view of them was

149

uninterrupted, and the apparent closeness I witnessed between the two was unsettling.

Robyn was at first shy, smiling when introduced, raising a delicate hand and shrugging in that way young women sometimes did, to indicate how small they were, how little threat they posed. Her hair was a fuzz of dark blonde waves, bound up in a rough bun so that her pale, slender neck disappeared gracefully into the collar of her new teal tunic. Seed's eyes were ablaze, and she chatted and laughed with the wider group like never before, her energy radiating across the room like heat. From time to time, Robyn would turn and laugh at something Seed had said, her expression close to star-struck. I felt nauseous. A glance in Regine's direction confirmed to me that I wasn't alone in my discomfort, and I vowed there and then to watch the relationship closely for fear that Seed might do irreparable damage to her reputation as a just and impartial leader. How long had she been corresponding with this young woman before moving her in so covertly? Surely she didn't believe herself to be in love?

'Shall I make up Elizabeth's old bed in my room?' This from Irma, whom I could have embraced for her straight-talking innocence. Irma's room-mate, Elizabeth, had moved on a couple of weeks back following a six-month stay, having ultimately decided to fight her partner for custody of their children. It occurred to me now that, uncharacteristically, Seed had made almost no effort to dissuade her from leaving. How long had she been planning for Robyn's arrival? Had a sister's departure been just what she, or *they*, had been waiting for?

Seed lowered her eyes, evidently taking her time to find a suitable answer. 'There's no need for that,' she said eventually. 'I've decided she'll take the room next to mine. I'd like her to be on hand if Fern or any of our Elders need help in the night.' She looked along the table, focusing her attention on our dedicated carers Sue and Blossom. 'The Elders sometimes wake in the night, don't they? I remember Blossom mentioning that a cup of cocoa and something to eat often settles them, isn't that right?' She was going into so much detail with her answer; and none of it made sense.

Sue and Blossom nodded obligingly, although their expressions betrayed restrained surprise. That was what *they* were here for, sharing the room adjacent to the Elders, to be available to assist them day and night. They didn't need a *cook* to help them out.

Seed smiled brightly, her shoulder brushing that of shy little Robyn, whose smile mirrored hers with none of the guile. 'The room next to mine is just along the hall from the Elders, so that works out well. Good! Let's give thanks,' she said, and the conversation was closed.

After breakfast, in furtive little huddles all over the house, gossip and speculation spread like wildfire.

Now, I sit on the edge of Robyn's bed, turning over an old press cutting I've just found crumpled at the back of her bedside drawer, feeling profoundly thankful that I'd thought to check the room a second time. Seed says it's possible we may have to invite those two outsiders back in again, if the police press us hard enough – if the only alternative is an official visit. We need to be prepared. I fold the cutting in two and slip it inside my apron pocket. It wouldn't do for anyone to get their hands on this old news story; you never know what wild conclusions they might jump to.

20. CELINE

Present day

Celine wakes in the night, drenched in sweat after a nightmare in which she's small again.

In the dream, she's in the garden of Two Cross Farm, and it's midnight, but the lawn is lit up brightly by stars. Her heart is thumping and sweat is soaking her hair at the nape of her neck, running beneath her summer T-shirt and making it cling to her back. Alone, she searches the garden, barefoot, looking for Pip behind the greenhouses and wood store; in the shadows where a small child might hide. Though she can't see her, she knows Pip is tiny, maybe two or three – like Beebee – and she's lost somewhere in this garden. As her eyes fall on those two great compost mounds, she feels certain that Pip must be buried here, and she drops to her knees, pawing away at the mulch and soil, desperate to claw her way down to her sister below. Overhead, white wings soar, and, as Celine pauses to follow the trail, her attention is caught by the little white windmill on the far side of the lawn. The windmill has changed position so that it directly faces her now, and she sees Pip is at the window of the fairytale building, her tiny face a mask of fear, trapped behind glass.

When she wakes with a strangled cry, Celine's first thought is to pad along the landing on her bare feet, to check on her sister, but then she remembers Pip is not here, she's stayed on another night at River Terrace with the girls, to sort out a few things. The house and all around it is eerily still, something Celine is not used to back home in her beachfront home in Bournemouth. Here, hidden away on this woodland path, there's no traffic passing by, no midnight revellers staggering home from the nightclub, and no rush and sigh of waves crashing against the shingle. Here, there is only silence, and her thoughts, high on post-nightmare adrenaline.

Sort out a few things. What exactly did Pip mean by that? Celine wonders now as she sits up and flips on the side light. Is Stefan being difficult about Pip spending so much time away from home? Is he that kind of man? At the castle earlier in the week, Pip told Celine she plans to stay on in Arundel a while, to make the most of the few months they have left before Olive has to start at school in the autumn – especially as Stefan works such long hours and she's stuck on her own with the kids most of the time. But perhaps her husband is missing having them around, waiting for him when he gets home. Maybe he's feeling shut out of Pip's grief, never having known Delilah, and barely knowing her, Celine. Could that be it? Una's the one person who *does* know Stefan, living just next door – and she's hinted more than once at troubles between the couple, though Celine's been too much of a coward to confront Pip directly.

It's what they do in this family, she realises; it's what they've always done. She's not the only one guilty of it. They all notice the problems, and then they shut them in a safe corner of the

153

mind and hope they'll go away without too much interference or cost to themselves. Isn't that why Vanessa went off and did her own thing in London? Isn't that how she ended up with a violent criminal like Jem Falmer – how she moved in with him so quickly, with no word of caution from her older sister, let alone her absent mother? Would it have made a difference, if Celine had begged her not to, urged her to wait until she was a little older, a little surer? Maybe not. But it's the seed of doubt which so often slays Celine in the dark of the night – the thought that perhaps she could have prevented all this. That she could have saved Vanessa if she'd cared enough.

She reaches for her water glass and drinks, before switching off the light and curling up against the fresh side of her pillow. What if Pip, too, needs Celine's help right now? What if this dream is some kind of message across the miles, and she really is lost in some way, really does need her? Celine pulls the duvet up over her ears, as though shutting out the silence can somehow mute the endless inner monologue of her deepest fears.

The wait for news on a follow-up visit to Two Cross Farm is interminable, and when Una says she'll try phoning DI Dave Aston at midday Celine takes a stroll around the garden, wondering if she should attempt to call Pip again. Her refusal to answer her mobile phone is maddening, but Celine knows she's feeling more jittery about Pip's silence than usual, following that disturbing dream last night.

Across the lawns, the gardener is at work on the flower borders, his back to her as he tends the roses. Harry.

'Hi!' she calls over, and he turns in her direction and raises a cautious hand. Breaking into a light jog, she approaches him, hand outstretched. 'I'm Celine. Sorry, we've been here a while, and I still haven't said a proper hello yet.'

He shakes her hand firmly, and the rough texture of it is a surprise to Celine, at odds with his slender frame and smooth complexion. He's younger than she'd first thought – mid-forties, perhaps. 'I've met your sister,' he replies, and it quickly becomes clear that he's finding it difficult to maintain eye contact.

'Oh, yeah,' she says, smiling to put him at ease. 'She's the chatty one. I'm the bossy one, apparently.'

When Harry doesn't reply, Celine recognises that he is deeply shy, and finds herself overcompensating as she bestows compliments about the beauty of the garden and the well-tended lawns. 'It seems a bit much for one gardener,' she says. 'How do you manage to stay on top of it?'

'I like the work,' he replies. 'It's nice spending time in a garden like this. I love gardening. I'm lucky.'

'I think a lot of people would like a job like this – doing something you love and getting paid for it.' When he barely nods, she remembers the note she'd left out for Pip a couple of days ago, asking her to settle the gardener's bill. 'Oh, God, did Pip remember to pay you? We're all upside down at the moment, you know, with Mum and—'

Now Harry smiles for the first time, and he's rendered instantly attractive, as deep smile lines appear at the edges of his tanned face. 'Your sister covered it,' he interrupts. 'She paid me before she left yesterday.'

'Oh, phew,' Celine replies, glad to have finally broken the awkward atmosphere. 'So, how long have you been working on Mum's garden, Harry?'

'Oh, a few years,' he replies.

'Can I ask you, do you know much about the women's commune down the road?'

He bends to pick up some cuttings, dropping them into his barrow. 'Not much,' he replies. 'Men aren't allowed in, so I've never seen the gardens, apart from years ago, over the back wall, before they planted in all those bloody leylandii.'

Celine smiles. 'You don't approve?'

'What, of leylandii?' He shrugs. 'Big ugly weeds, if you ask me. They suck the light out of a garden.'

'And what about the community itself? Do people talk much about it around here?'

Wheeling on to the next section of border, Harry continues with his work, removing the withered flower heads from a small scented rose bush. 'They used to, back when I was a kid – when it was still quite new, I suppose. Some called it a cult. But I don't know, the women seem harmless enough to me. Some of them run a market stall in the town. They seem all right.'

'I guess you heard about the dead woman last week – the one found down by the river here?'

Harry gives an almost imperceptible jerk of his head. 'Nasty business.'

'Apparently she was a resident there, at Two Cross Farm.'

'That right?' The gardener doesn't even look up to give his answer, so engrossed in his work is he. With small, delicate movements he snips, removes and discards the heads, turning away from her more with each action.

Celine senses that their conversation has come to end. Feeling self-conscious about standing there watching him work, she checks the time and makes her excuses. 'Right, nice to meet you, Harry. I'd better go and phone my sister while I think of it.'

As she turns and retreats towards the house, she's surprised to hear him call after her.

'Say hello from me.'

'Huh?' Celine asks, halting to look back towards him.

He's standing beside the wheelbarrow, a bunch of rose heads in one hand, a pair of secateurs in the other, and to Celine it appears his lean figure is set towards her in a wide-planted pose of masculine threat. He speaks clearly. 'Your sister. Pip. Will you send her my best?'

For a moment, Celine is light-headed. Is she imagining it, or has Harry's tone abruptly shifted into over-familiarity? Without answering, she raises her arm in a genial wave and returns to the house.

'Una, I've just been talking to—' she begins as she enters the living room, but Una flaps her hand to signify she's on the phone, and points towards the camper van keys on the side.

'Finally, I got through to Dave,' she says once she's hung up. 'He's in Arundel right now, making some enquiries, and he said if we go straight down he'll meet us in The Eagle for half an hour. Says he's got a "significant" update for us.'

Pausing only to grab her rucksack and lock the back doors, Celine is behind the wheel within seconds.

When they arrive at The Eagle in Tarrant Street, Dave Aston is already waiting at the back of the pub and he's ordered three cheese ploughmans, which are being delivered to the table as they take their seats. It's a low table between two leather sofas, and as they're ahead of the lunchtime rush there's not much danger of being overheard while they discuss the case.

'Pint?' Celine offers.

'I'm on duty,' Dave says, 'but don't let that stop you two having a proper drink.'

'Apple juice for me,' Una says, and Celine heads for the bar. While she waits for her change, she watches at this small distance as Una drops her notebook on the table, before sitting back and hooking her arm over the back of the sofa, crossing one leg over the other.

Celine can't help admiring the way Una is with other people. She's businesslike and brisk, without being pushy. How does she do that? People like her instantly, because she's warm, with a laugh that you can't help but smile at, yet it's clear she won't tolerate any crap at all. Her manner borders on brusque, Celine thinks now – not in a thrusting alpha way, but in an unapologetic, never-questioned-it kind of way. I need to be more Una, Celine decides as she carries the drinks over and sits on the sofa facing Aston.

'Cheers,' she says, eyeing his A4 folder. 'So, what d'you know?'

'Actually, I've got something pretty mind-blowing,' he says, reaching for a stick of carrot. 'Well, I've got a few things, actually.'

'Go on,' Una says, with an encouraging nod.

'First off, Robin Siegle's ex-husband Archie walked into his local police station last night and handed himself in for questioning. I've been down there all night, taking a statement and checking out his version of events. Turns out he's been in Paris for the past few days, on some kind of chefs' conference. He says the first he knew about Robyn's death was when he picked up a newspaper as he was leaving the Eurostar in St Pancras yesterday afternoon. Apparently he'd been getting a bit worried because Robyn hadn't returned his calls – they were planning a reconciliation and he thought she'd had a change of heart.'

'How did he seem?'

'He was in a real state. Kept asking if we'd let her father know yet. Seems they were once close. We showed him the CCTV footage of him and Robyn at Arundel station on the night she died, and he tells us they'd spent the afternoon together at a local hotel, and that the video is actually showing us him leaving and her staying.'

'Have you checked?' Una asks.

'Yup. The hotel checks out – the receptionist recognised their photos and confirmed they were there for the afternoon. And we've been over the CCTV again, and yes, the couple arrive together and go off screen as the train pulls in. There's no sign of either of them thereafter, but the platform cameras are situated in such a way that, if Robyn did remain in Arundel, she would have exited the station without being seen. Additionally, we've managed to catch footage of Archie Chowdhury coming off that same train as it arrives at London Victoria. Alone.'

'So, what are you thinking?' Celine asks.

'Well, Archie was adamant that Robyn was heading back to Two Cross Farm that night, to say her goodbyes before joining him in London on his return from Paris. So, either Robyn met her killer on her way back to Two Cross Farm – or Seed is lying about the last time they saw her.'

'What about the DNA samples you took from Robyn?'

'The semen is a match for Archie, and of course he's not disputing that. There were minute skin-scrapings beneath three of her fingernails – arguably those scrapings belong to our killer, and I feel fairly certain the DNA in them is not going to be a match for Archie. Once those tests are back in, he's in the clear.'

Una makes a note in her own pad and taps the page thoughtfully.

'Now, tell me about your visit to Two Cross Farm,' Dave says. 'How was Seed?'

'The visit was good,' Celine replies. 'But I'm not sure if we got anything very useful.'

'You were there, Celine?' Dave asks, surprised. 'Una, that wasn't the deal.'

'No, but I took an executive decision, Dave.'

'But you know—'

'A decision which paid off. Seed likes Celine, and I'm certain we wouldn't have got on quite so well if I'd been there alone. She knows I'm an ex-copper – there's no way she would have opened up so much if it had just been me.'

Dave sighs heavily. 'What's she like, when she's away from the microphone?'

'Seed? She was charming, and she gave a very good impression of being co-operative and open – but I think we both came away feeling that she'd played us. It was a bit like that press conference she gave – the visit was polished, rehearsed.'

'They're definitely hiding something,' Celine adds, her mind drifting back to Seed's comment, about burning the place down rather than letting the police in. On their way here in the car, Una had suggested they omit that detail, for fear that Dave would halt their involvement. 'Although, I think she was starting to trust us towards the end of our visit.'

'What did you find out?' he asks.

'The place feels very relaxed, but it's actually run like clockwork. They live by the bell. They all take their breaks together, so no slacking off in between for a sneaky cuppa or a fag. They eat together, work together, relax together in the evenings. There's a high proportion of women who have left some kind of abuse behind, but they don't consider themselves to be a refuge. Every woman has to contribute to the running of the place in some way, and it sounds as though they live frugally, selling goods at the local market and operating fairly hand-to-mouth.'

'The other stallholders might be useful to talk to,' Dave says. 'I'll follow it up, see if we can track them down.'

Una taps her pen against her notebook. 'To be honest, Dave, we barely scratched the surface, but if we can get Seed to invite us back we might be able to establish some more specific facts about Robyn's time there. One thing's for certain – at least a handful of those women will have got to know Robyn over the past few months, and someone will be able to confirm if she and Seed were in a relationship – or if there were disagreements between her and any of the other women. If Archie Chowdhury isn't our man, perhaps Robyn's killer really is someone at Two Cross Farm.'

'Or Jem Falmer,' Celine says.

'We haven't ruled him out, Celine,' Dave replies. 'His relatives all claim they haven't seen him over the past fifteen years, but there's no denying it feels somewhat significant that his childhood home is only a few miles from the scene of this recent crime. In the end, people on the run get lonely – and they'll often return to the places they know.'

'But what would Falmer's motive be?' Una asks. 'I get why he'd kill his own partner – men do it all the time, out of jealousy, anger, paranoia – but why Robyn?'

'Maybe he still holds a grudge against the community for sheltering Vanessa from him. Maybe he hates women. Maybe he's just a psycho,' Celine adds, the old feelings of powerless rage rearing up in her, as strong today as they were fifteen years ago.

'As I say, Celine,' Dave says patiently, 'we haven't ruled him out.'

'But as Una said,' she quickly replies, anxious to show Aston how balanced she is, 'it could be someone from inside the commune – or someone outside. Have you interviewed our gardener yet – Harry?'

Una frowns, a question.

'I was chatting to him in the garden when you were on the phone earlier, Una. He's quite strange, I think. And he's been working for Mum for a few years. He might be worth a look, Dave.'

He nods. 'I do need to follow that up. I'll get one of my guys to pop by and see him.'

'We did find one important thing you'll be interested in, Dave,' Una says. 'Before we left, we managed to get a look at the residents' ledger, which keeps a record of all the women arriving and leaving. It was immaculately kept, all the way back to 1976 – every entry handwritten.'

'Go on.'

'We found Robyn's entry, and there was *no* departure date logged. Robyn is not recorded as having left the community eleven days ago when Seed said she had.'

Dave makes a note. 'OK, that's good. Now all we have to do is wait and see if you get that return invitation, Una. That journal could well provide confirmation for this other bit of info I've just uncovered.'

There's a moment's pause while a group of suited men loiters beside them, waiting to get to the bar. As soon as they move on, Una leans in and asks, 'Is this the "mind-blowing" bit of news you mentioned, Dave?'

Dave smiles, looking pleased with himself.

Celine sits forward, placing her glass down on the table. 'Well?'

'As you know,' he says, 'I'm fairly new around here, so as far as the history of this region is concerned I have to rely on my junior officers, who only go back so far. This info relates to an old case, one which pre-dates anyone I know who's still working for Sussex Police.' He pauses, flips open a different file and closes it again, as though trying to work out how to tell this story. 'To cut a long story short—'

'I wish you would,' Una says. She snatches up her plate and sits back again with an encouraging nod.

'Turns out,' he continues, 'that one of my elderly neighbours is a retired copper, and, when he heard about the circumstances of Robyn Siegle's death on last night's six o'clock news, he came straight over and knocked on my door. I'd barely spoken a dozen words to the man, but before I knew it we were sat around my kitchen table, a bottle of Jack Daniel's between us, as he told me the story of the "lake suicide".'

'The what?' Celine asks.

162

'In December 1995, an unidentified woman was found dead in a boat on Swanbourne Lake near Arundel.' He places a local news article on the table between them. WOMAN FOUND DEAD AT ARUNDEL BEAUTY SPOT, reads the headline.

'That's just down the road from here,' Celine says. 'But what made him think there was a connection between the two?'

'It was the phrase "carefully laid out" that caught his eye. They'd printed something similar in the 1995 case and it just echoed with him.'

Una reads over the cutting with a frown. 'This was twenty-five years ago. Did your neighbour work on the case?'

'No, it had happened a year or two before he transferred here, but he remembered his colleagues talking about it. From what I can gather, the body was discovered by a local man – a junior lake attendant there at the time, and he was initially treated as a suspect for the woman's murder. But, after the coroner's report ruled out foul play, the lad was released.'

'OK, but how does this relate to Vanessa – or Robyn?' Celine asks. Her impatience is getting the better of her, and she makes an effort to pick at her food, to listen.

'A few weeks later, we get *this* headline in the national newspapers.' He places a second cutting in front of them: MISSING SUSAN FOUND DEAD AFTER 20 YEARS. 'They identified the woman on the boat using dental X-ray records taken two decades earlier. The unnamed woman was Susan Green, who, it turns out,' Dave says, bringing the two cuttings together, 'was one of a group of five women who disappeared together back in 1976.'

'You're kidding?' Celine says, turning to look at Una. '1976? The very same year Two Cross Farm opened its doors? You think Susan Green was one of the founders?'

'Exactly,' Dave says, leaning in to tap his middle finger on the later news article. 'This piece provides a recap of the then twenty-year-old case of those missing women, explaining how they had all left letters for their families and loved ones, saying they were safe and didn't want to be found. For the most part, the story died down and the police didn't get involved, despite the fact Susan had been just sixteen when she left.'

Una shakes her head. 'Jeez. Old-school policing. So, did the police interview the Two Cross Women after they'd worked out who Susan was?'

'No,' Dave replies. 'Even after Susan's body was found, they had no idea where she'd been all those years. And at that time they'd have had no reason to think the community was connected in any way to those missing women. Don't forget twenty years had passed by – that old missing persons story would've been all but forgotten by 1995, at least as far as the police and media were concerned. I may well be the first to make the link between Susan and Two Cross Farm – and your residents' journal could be the key to confirming it.'

'Did nobody care enough to try to find out where Susan had been all those years?' asks Celine, still trying to get her head around the idea that they were now looking at a third dead woman.

'There was curiosity, from what my neighbour Arthur says, but with police resources at a stretch it probably didn't get high priority. We're trying to locate the original case notes at the moment, so we can see if there's anything else of interest.'

Una knocks back her apple juice. 'I think I will have that pint after all,' she says, grabbing her purse.

'You might want to wait a minute, Una. I haven't delivered my punchline yet.'

'There's more?'

'Right before he left, old Arthur mentioned something in passing that made my hair stand on end.' He leans in closer, lowers his voice. 'Those tattoos – the ones Robyn and Vanessa both had? That detail has never been made public – in Vanessa's case because it wasn't considered relevant at the time, and in Robyn's case because we've been careful to keep it out of the public domain.'

Celine nods, feeling a cold sweat forming on the palms of her hands.

'Back in 1995 it was still fairly unusual for women to have tattoos – especially women in their thirties or forties. So, this detail about Susan stood out in Arthur's memory, and he volunteered the information with no prompting from me whatsoever.'

'For God's sake, Dave!' Una explodes. 'Just say it!'

'Susan had the same tattoos. Two symmetrical black crosses, one by each hip bone. Susan Green in 1995; Vanessa Murphy in 2005; Robyn Siegle in 2020 – each of them dead near the water, all of them tattooed in the same way. And now,' he says, 'quite possibly—'

'All of them connected to Two Cross Farm,' Celine finishes.

DI Dave Aston nods, pointing a carrot stick in her direction. 'Exactly.'

21. BRAMBLE

Present day, Two Cross Farm

Overnight, Seed has grown more agitated, and this morning I find her long before the bell, standing alone at the French doors to the garden, looking out over the mist-shrouded compost mounds where the bluebells grow. Something in her broken countenance tells me she is thinking back on those final days with Robyn. As I lead her from the window and settle her at the kitchen table, I too find my mind picking away at that troubled time, as though the answers to our current situation might be found there. Hard to believe Robyn left us less than a fortnight ago; so much has passed in that time. Our world has altered.

There was one afternoon, shortly before Robyn left us, when I'd noticed her and Seed absent from the evening walk – the hour-long riverside circuit the women took at least once a week to stretch their legs and 'get outside'. Seed had always been diligent in attending on most evenings, as a means of making herself available to our sisters in a more casual setting. Her absence on this bright spring evening seemed to be yet another

166

example of her putting Robyn before everyone else, and I was inwardly fuming at her foolishness. Irritably, I returned to the house to check off the rota on the kitchen wall, as Regine passed through, leaning heavily on her walking cane, saying she was heading in to sit with Fern for a while.

'She's been asking for the baby again,' Regine said, pausing this side of the adjoining swing door. She half-turned to look at me, and, as an image of the feisty young Regine returned to me, I felt a profound sadness that we were, one by one, falling victim to age. *We Founding Sisters can't go on like this forever,* I thought, *slowly decaying, weighted down by our secrets.*

Regine pushed the door open with her shoulder, revealing three of our Elders, sitting sedately in their armchairs, each with a reading companion and a cup of tea at their side.

'I'm looking for Seed,' I called after her, and she halted stiffly, holding the door ajar. 'She wasn't with the walking group when they set off,' I added.

With a slow, knowing nod, Regine replied. 'I saw her by the wood store with that young American.' For a moment it seemed as though her mind drifted to another place, and she looked bereft. 'Seed's not like us, Brenda. She's never known how it feels to live outside of this place. Let her be, yeah? Let her have this one small thing?'

As her crumpled body disappeared beyond the swinging door, I felt my anger rise – at Regine's flippant dismissal of Seed's deviation from the Code; at her barbed use of my old name. The name that tied me to my family, forty years dead to me. To my father and his filthy pawing ways – to my lonely life before I took sanctuary here. Smoothing down the creases of my apron, I walked along the dim corridor, the main artery through which all activity flowed, and headed for the living room at the back. This was the quiet hour, when many of our number were off the grounds, and any remaining sisters had tasks to complete before supper at six. At the hearthside, I found the basket full, and so I removed the logs, one by one, stacking them in a pile beside the grate before exiting through the French doors and striding up the path, the wood store in my sights.

Across the lawns, a few women were finishing work, but no one took much notice of me, old Bramble, off to fetch logs for the fire. When I reached the shed, instead of opening the door to enter, I made my way down the side and pressed my ear against the sun-warmed wood to listen in.

To my horror, I could hear Seed weeping, her voice murmuring low, the words unintelligible.

'Don't cry,' Robyn was pleading. 'Seed, don't cry, please.'

There was the sound of movement, melancholy feet against the wood-chipped floor.

'I'm sorry, Robyn, I'm so sorry,' I heard Seed say. 'It's wrong of me to want you to stay – but I do!'

'But my family has to come first.' Robyn's voice trembled with emotion. 'This could be a second chance for me and Archie. He needs me. My daughter needs me.'

'*I* need you,' Seed said, and I'd never heard her so desperate. 'You can't just start something like this and then turn your back on it! You haven't found what you came looking for yet – you can't just give up and walk away. You even went through with the marking ceremony! That must have meant something?'

I felt a sharp prick of guilt. Seed had begged us to allow Robyn to be marked early, and, while my every instinct had cried out against it, we had given in, and permitted it. I tattooed that girl with my own hand. I should have known better; I should have stood my ground.

'They're just tattoos, Seed. It's not a big deal. I don't really know what you want from me – I didn't promise you anything.'

Robyn's tone grew stronger. 'I came to find out more about my mother, and I'm grateful for everything you've been able to tell me about her. But now, well, there's nothing more here for me.'

Her *mother*? Who was Robyn's mother?

'But *I'm* here, Robyn,' Seed whispered. 'I'm . . .'

Oh, lord, where had we gone so wrong, I thought as I stifled a sob of my own, that Seed should feel so desperate and alone? That I never noticed, never helped her through.

'I'm sorry,' Robyn replied flatly. They both fell silent, and I held my breath, my heart racing, fearing they would catch me eavesdropping. 'I had no idea you'd react so strongly when I told you I was leaving. Is it, I mean – you know I don't like women in that way, don't you?'

'That's not what I want!' Seed cried out as though in some great pain. 'How could you say that? That was never what I wanted!'

'Then what *do* you want?'

All grew still, as Robyn, and I, waited for Seed's answer.

'I just want you in my life, Robyn. Not like a lover. Like a daughter.'

As the door to the wood store creaked open, I pressed myself flat against the wooden panels, praying I might evade detection.

'I'm sorry, Seed,' Robyn said as she stepped out on to the path. 'This is just too weird for me. I can't be your daughter.'

Now, the morning bell rings out, and I usher Seed up to her office before the first sisters descend the stairs.

'The women can have breakfast without us today,' I say, closing the door behind me.

Seed sinks on to her sofa, her eyes puffy through worry and lack of sleep.

'Are you going to let the outsiders back in?' I ask her, pulling out the seat to her desk, our usual roles reversed.

As I await her answer, my eyes drift to the old combination safe in the far corner, where each of the Founding Sisters' Last Will letters lie, along with the cash takings from the market stall and a small stack of legal documents and deeds. 'We might be able to delay them,' I suggest as an idea starts to take form.

'How?' Seed's expression shifts, more alert now. 'Una said if we don't let them return, the police are certain to come. And God knows what they'll do if they get access – who they'll send – what they'll find!'

'I'm sure that's true. And this might not work, but it could buy us some time.'

'Time for what?' she asks.

'Time with Fern,' I say carefully. 'With each other.'

Seed follows the direction of my gaze, comprehension in her knitted brows. She nods her agreement, and I rise, crossing the room to open the safe.

Anything's worth a go, I tell myself, when you've got nothing left to lose.

22. CELINE

Celine and Una arrive home from meeting Dave Aston at The Eagle, and there is mail waiting for them.

Celine pulls the envelope free of the letterbox and finds the note inside is crumpled, a torn strip of A4 paper, looking as though it has been carried about in someone's back pocket for a week, its message written out in careful pale grey letters:

YOU BITCHES STAY OUT OF OUR BUSINESS.

That's all. An offensive order, no signature, and a threat of . . . what?

'Put it down on the sideboard,' Una barks, jumping straight to action as she drops her rucksack on the hallway floor. 'Fingerprints, Celine! Put it down!'

Celine does as Una instructs, and steps away from it, as though it might contaminate her. 'Seed?' she asks, frowning at Una. 'Do you think she's capable of something like this?'

171

Una stares at the note, already getting her phone out to call Dave Aston. 'It doesn't feel like her style, does it? But "our business"? We're talking about more than one person, clearly, and the only business we've been poking our noses into is theirs.'

Celine sighs heavily. 'God, Una, I really thought they were going to invite us back in, you know? It doesn't look very likely, if this is anything to go by.'

'It doesn't,' Una agrees, pressing the dial button.

Seconds later and Dave Aston is on speakerphone, having pulled over at the roadside to take the call. 'Did you both touch it?' he asks.

'No, just Celine,' Una replies. 'If I were you, Dave, I'd be getting handwriting samples from anyone you're vaguely suspicious of in either of the cases. You've got Seed's fingerprints already, haven't you – from her voluntary statement?'

'Yep, we've got them. What about the other women there, Una? Anyone else you think we should be looking at?'

'Well, Bramble is very tight with Seed. I'd certainly be wanting to rule her out too.'

'It could be a man,' Celine suggests. 'The language – it feels like a man, doesn't it? *You bitches.*'

'Don't women use that phrase too?' Dave asks.

'Not so much,' Celine replies, pulling at her lower lip. 'Either way, I can't imagine either Seed or Bramble talking like that, let alone writing it.' She hesitates for a moment, recalling Georgie's words from their meeting in the restaurant last week, when she talked about her experience with Jem Falmer all those years ago. What were his words? *You dyke bitches.* 'If you have access to some of Jem Falmer's handwriting, Dave, I think it would be worth checking. From what Georgie told me, it's exactly the kind of language *he'd* use.'

'OK. Listen, I'll swing back your way and pick up the note now, then I'll see what we've got on Falmer. If there's nothing on file, I'll pay his family a visit in Littlehampton first thing – see if they've hung on to anything with his handwriting on. Well done, Una, good call. See you shortly.'

Exhausted, Una and Celine take a pot of tea out on to the veranda, dissecting all that they've learned today while they wait for Dave to arrive. When Seed's name lights up the phone screen on the table between them, Una puts down her mug without a word, and calmly presses the speaker button.

'Hello?'

'Una Powell?' Seed asks, and Celine notes how smooth and resonant her voice is, how controlled. She could be a newsreader.

'Speaking. Is this Seed?'

'I've given your request a lot of thought,' she says by way of an answer. 'And I put it to a show of hands over supper last night. The women voted twenty-seven *for* and three *against* your return visit.'

Una is expected to respond here, but she lets the silence hang, and Celine marvels at her self-control, not jumping in to fill the gap like she would herself.

'We'd like to invite you back,' Seed explains. 'But there are conditions.'

'I'm listening,' Una replies.

'You hand in your phones at the door.'

'Of course.'

'You stay with us overnight – perhaps for two nights, if all goes well.'

'Not a problem,' Una says, gesturing to Celine for confirmation.

'And you come with open hearts and open minds.'

Another pause.

'That's it?' Una says.

'That's it.'

Celine finds she can't sit still, and she's up, pacing the decking, trying to contemplate all the questions they'll need to ask once they're back inside Two Cross Farm.

'When do you want us?' Una asks.

'Tomorrow morning,' Seed replies, and it's not a question, it's a non-negotiable statement. 'Nine a.m., like before.' She hangs up.

Celine and Una stare at each other, their shock turning to excitement.

'Did that really just happen?' Celine asks, her palm pressed to her forehead.

'Dave's never going to believe this,' Una replies, already up and heading back towards the house in anticipation of his arrival.

As Celine rises to follow her inside, a text message pings on to her phone, and to her relief it's Pip, replying at last, after a delay of over twenty-four hours.

Sorry, sis – meant to reply earlier, but got diverted. All fine here, honest. Stop worrying! The girls have a play date tomorrow afternoon with Sid and Iris from down the road, so planning to come back on the train the next day or maybe Saturday. See you then xxx

Celine re-reads the message, unsettled by the Mary Poppins tone of it, all the while telling herself that she's being paranoid, that there's nothing to worry about at all. Pip's fine, her message says as much, and if she's having a few marital problems with Stefan perhaps it's best not to add to her plate with news of these recent developments. But what of that threatening letter? Shouldn't Pip know about that, at the very least, so she can be on her guard? They'll leave her a note, Celine concludes, warning her not to answer the door if it goes, and explain properly what's going on when they get back from Two Cross Farm. She taps out a reply:

All good here, sis. Nothing much to report. See you and the girls soon.

She looks out over the blossom-strewn lawn, feeling inexplicably guilty as soft pink petals flutter along the borders to collect in shallow drifts. After a second's contemplation, she adds: *Love you x*

The next morning, after surrendering their phones, Celine and Una are put to work in the garden at Two Cross Farm.

Una is paired digging over the compost with a woman called Rita, who barely speaks a word of English, and Celine is put with Thistle, a fifty-two-year-old woman from Birmingham who has been at Two Cross Farm for over five years. Dave Aston has instructed them to focus on finding out more about Robyn – who she shared with, what she was like, whether she spoke with anyone about her plans to get back with her ex-husband – and, more subtly, about those six women from 1976, all of whom are still missing according to police records. Celine knows Una will be seething at having been put with someone who'll be able to tell her precisely nothing, while she's been paired with a woman who barely pauses for breath. The problem is, it seems Thistle is only interested in talking about herself. Within an hour, Celine has learned that Thistle lived with an abusive husband for over twenty years, right up to the point at which the last of their three children left home for university. His name was Pete, and he'd beaten her, on a weekly basis, every Sunday night, for two decades.

'Was that what gave you the strength to leave, seeing the last of your kids flying the nest?' Celine is dibbing holes in neat rows

175

in one of the raised beds, as Thistle follows behind, dropping seeds in and covering them with soil.

'Oh, no,' Thistle replies. 'Pete had a stroke. Just a few days after we'd dropped Craig at university. It left him paralysed down one side, and I was giving him his tea the first night back from hospital, and he couldn't even put the fork to his mouth. He was too weak to feed himself.'

She doesn't look up as she tells this story, just carries on reaching into her tunic pocket with those heavy red hands of hers, pulling out seeds and feeding them into the soil.

'I just looked at him across the table, and my first thought was, oh, my God, he'll never thump me again.'

Celine stops dibbing, so that Thistle has no choice but to look up when she runs out of holes to fill. 'That must have been a relief, after all those years?'

Thistle laughs, betraying her unresolved bitterness, and gestures for Celine to get back to her job. 'Not really,' she replies, standing to ease out her back. ''Cause my second thought was, 'ow can I love a man like that? He was so weak, I couldn't stand it. He was no man at all. At any rate, he went and died a couple of months later, thank God. And so I came here.'

Celine has no reply to this. Thistle's response sounds far from normal, but who is she to judge? She doesn't know what 'normal' is, does she? She certainly doesn't know what a normal family feels like, having seen a steady stream of her mother's boyfriends and lovers and stepdads and 'uncles' passing through her family home over the years, not one of them lasting for longer than a year or two. She has no idea what it feels like to be in a regular family unit, abusive or otherwise. Her own father was a man Delilah met overnight at a youth hostel in Cork while she was solo travelling around southern Ireland in the early '80s. 'He was good-looking,' Delilah once boasted, 'but I couldn't tell you his

176

name, darling – or even his nationality. All I can tell you is, we shared a single bunk that night, made wonderful love together, and you were the delightful result. I was up at the crack of dawn the next morning to catch the Dingle bus, and I never saw him again.' The last time Celine had asked about him, she'd been so angered by Delilah's flippant reply that she'd sworn never to bring it up again. 'You should get tested for AIDS,' she had said, quite calmly, before slamming the door on her mother's tipsy whoop of laughter.

Celine catches Una's attention, and they wave at each other across the lawn, before Una gives a little 'what the hell?' kind of shrug and turns back to her work. When will they get a chance to ask all their questions, if they're stuck out in the garden all day long? On their way here, Una had stressed how important it was that they play along with Seed's plans for the day, to gain her trust before launching in. Of course she's right, but *gardening*? As the morning goes on, the heat of the sun grows ever more intense, and Celine starts to feel her patience being sorely tested by Thistle's endless bragging.

'I could drive a tractor before I turned ten,' she says as they get back to work after morning tea. 'Up at five most mornings too, tending to the beasts and the chooks. Milking, egg-collecting, mucking out – I did it all. Shoulda stuck with that. Shoulda found meself a nice young farmer with a bit of money.' She rams her garden fork into the soil with a conclusive grunt.

Celine thinks perhaps Thistle is a woman who's spent so many years keeping her mouth shut, that she's decided to spend the next forty with it open.

'I'm a solicitor,' Celine offers, but Thistle doesn't bite. 'I'm taking a few weeks off to sort my mother's funeral.'

Thistle's mouth turns down at the corners. 'Sorry t'hear that,' she says, without emotion.

'Hello, Celine.' As though from nowhere, Seed has appeared, and Celine springs back in surprise. 'How are you finding things? Is Thistle helping you to settle in?'

'Yes! Thank you,' she stammers in reply.

Seed narrows her eyes in that deeply interested way she does, scrutinising Celine. Despite the pale, shiny burn scars which mask her high-boned face, she is handsome, her eyes a deep, intelligent blue. What would she look like in regular clothes instead of those shapeless tunics, with her hair loose and the lines of her limbs visible? Celine looks away, light-headed in the heat. She sweeps a lock of hair from her brow, tucks it behind her ear.

'You look hot,' Seed says, after what feels like an age. She reaches out, tenderly pressing the back of her knuckles to Celine's cheek.

Celine blushes, aware that her heart is beating faster, afraid that Seed will feel her discomfort through that touch. Something in the moment takes her back to her teen years, and she thinks of Teddy Mackintosh, who used to get on at the next bus stop after theirs. He was impossibly good-looking but shy, yet he would lock eyes with Celine the moment he boarded the bus, silently daring her to look away. It was like a challenge, and the heady memory of it still makes her stomach flip to this day. Every time it happened, Vanessa, sitting bunched up beside her in her matching school uniform, would nudge her in the ribs and whisper, '*Swoon.*'

'I – huh?' Celine is entirely thrown. What is wrong with her? Seed smiles now. 'I said, you look hot, Celine.'

'I didn't choose the best clothes,' she finally replies. What is it about this woman that makes her so nervy? 'I think I'll change at lunchtime.'

'I'll look you out a tunic, if you like? Seems silly to dirty your own clothes when we've got plenty here. I'll find something for Una too.' With that, she turns and heads purposefully back towards the house, her dandelion-yellow tunic swaying.

Over at the greenhouse, it seems Bramble is checking up on Una in the same way. There's no doubt they're being closely watched.

When the lunch bell rings at one o'clock, everyone stops, regardless of what they're doing, and, just as they did for morning tea, they file into the dining room, each taking their predetermined cross at the table, with Seed at the head. Across the table, Una's partner sits beside her, while Celine has the seat next to Thistle, meaning there's no escape from the woman, even at mealtimes. Thankfully the food provides a welcome change of subject.

'Lily made the quiche,' Thistle tells her, leaning in to be heard over the chatter of the room. She points at one of two wheelchair-bound women at the far end of the table. 'She's seventy next week. She'll tell you, given half a chance. Funny thing is, even though her memory's going, she knows how old she is. There's a few in here who are going that way.'

Celine takes a slice of quiche and passes the platter along. 'Do they have a carer?'

'What, the oldies? Oops, shouldn't say that. Seed prefers "elders". But yeah, a couple of women here are dedicated carers. Rather them than me.'

'How old's Bramble?' Celine asks. 'She must be in her eighties?'

'Must be.' Thistle nods, eyeing up Celine's as-yet untouched bread roll. 'Aren't you gonna eat that?'

Celine pushes it towards her. 'She's one of the original six, isn't she?'

'A *Founding Sister*. And don't she let you know it.' Thistle gives a dramatic roll of her head, and she looks suddenly young, like a sulky teenager. 'She's got her beadies on everything, that one, feeding it back to Seed the minute your back's turned.'

'You don't like her?'

'Don't trust her, more like. She's nice enough to your face, but she's a typical deputy. You know, like those women on the ends of the checkouts in Asda? Give 'em a bunch of keys and a clipboard and they turn into a bloody nightmare.' She polishes off Celine's roll. 'My sister-in-law was one of them women. Snout in everything.'

When lunch is cleared, pots of tea are brought through, and Seed chimes a spoon against her cup, to gather attention.

'In honour of our special guests Una and Celine, we're having a slightly extended lunch today, sisters, hence the tea-and-biscuit treat.'

There are murmurs of approval all around.

'As you know, the police have been hounding us since the loss of our dear sister Robyn.' She appears to gather herself for a second or two before continuing. 'Una is an ex-detective, retired now, and, following negotiations with the local inspector on Robyn's case, we agreed to invite her here to answer some of their questions, in the hope that we might finally be rid of this interminable police and media scrutiny.'

Una holds back, waiting to be invited to speak.

'And Celine. She's . . .?' Seed says, and it's suddenly clear that she thinks they're together, a couple.

'We live together,' Una says, smiling, not correcting her, and avoiding Celine's gaze. The interest in them suddenly ramps up, which was obviously Una's intention, and Celine resists the urge to kick her under the table.

'Good, good,' Seed says, pressing her palms together. 'In the spirit of openness, I would like to invite Celine and Una to ask us any questions they have, before we get back to work for the afternoon? Bramble and I thought it would be least disruptive to our working day, and a good way for us all to get to know each other. Agreed?'

The murmurs grow more lively.

'Una,' Seed says, extending her elegant palm. 'Would you like to start?'

Una thanks her and the rest of the group, and launches in. 'How many of your residents are victims of partner abuse?'

'We don't use the word *victim*,' Seed says, 'though of course a high proportion have been through some kind of trauma at the hands of men.' She gestures to a thin, olive-skinned woman in her twenties.

The young woman speaks. 'I'm Oregon. I came here when I was seventeen, straight from my foster home where one of the teenage sons had started—' here she falters '—being a problem.' She talks quietly, in a cool, detached manner. 'Not all of us are running away from partners.'

'Still, you were driven here to get away from a man,' Una says gently.

A number of women around the table agree, until there's another tiny gesture from Seed and a crop-haired woman to Una's right starts to speak. 'I wasn't abused, but I needed a new start. I'd had enough of the world – out there – the greed, the waste, the constant noise of social media. It was like there was this endless buzz in my head, stopping me from thinking and feeling properly. I came here for the quiet. That was four years ago, and I can't imagine leaving now. I wouldn't care if I never saw another mobile phone in my life.'

'I know what you mean,' Celine says with feeling, and there's a ripple of laughter, and a seductive sense of belonging.

'My husband passed away,' a woman in her sixties volunteers. 'I adored him. He was the best of men, and if I hadn't come here I think I would have died of loneliness. I remembered an old friend had come here in the '80s, and I phoned her at my lowest point. She put me in touch with Seed.'

'Not all men are villains,' Una says, and to Celine's surprise a great number of women around the room nod enthusiastically.

'Just some of them,' Seed agrees. 'The ones who drive women into hiding.'

'Is there a time limit?' Celine asks, aiming the question at Bramble who has been silent throughout lunch. 'For how long you can stay here?'

'There's no limit, so long as women abide by our Code of Conduct and embrace the lifestyle.'

'Some of you have been here since the beginning, haven't you?' Celine presses, still focusing on the older woman.

'Yes, we have,' Bramble replies. Several other women nod and agree, but only a handful are old enough to qualify as Founding Sisters. 'Some of us had no reason to leave.'

'But women do leave, don't they?' Celine says, realising Bramble's not about to reveal who the others are. 'I mean, your residents' journal is huge, and Seed, you said there are close to four hundred portraits around the house. Four hundred – if you go back over forty years, that's around ten new residents a year?'

Bramble places her forearms on the table, and slides her hands inside their opposite sleeves. 'You must remember, Celine, women come for different reasons. Some are genuinely searching for a long-term place to call home, somewhere they can feel empowered and independent. And some are just passing through, looking for a place to rest and recover from the world for a while, before moving on to the next thing. We see value in both, and so, yes, many come and go, but a good number stay too.'

Seed raises a finger, as though testing the air for wind. 'A show of hands if you've been here for over two years?'

More than half the women raise their arms.

'How long was Robyn here?' Una asks.

'Three months,' Bramble replies.

'Is that all?' Celine is shocked; from Seed's emotional response to Robyn's death, she'd assumed she had been a resident for much longer.

'What was she like?' Una asks.

'Funny,' says old Lily from her wheelchair. She's wearing thick-lensed glasses, clutching a handkerchief which she uses frequently to mop her rheumy eyes. 'Some of her ways used to make me laugh, oh, so they did. The way she'd say "jelly" for jam and "cookie" for biscuit and all sorts of other American slang. Reminded me of you, Regine, the way she talked.'

An older woman opposite me gives a distracted nod. She wears her hair in a heavy grey plait and her dark face is deeply lined.

'I used to correct her all the time in the kitchen,' Lily continues. 'But she'd just flick a tea towel at me and call me Lily La-di-dah. She used to make me feel young. Didn't treat me like an old has-been, like most of this lot.'

'Oh, that's nonsense, Lily,' a woman only a few years younger says, tapping her hand lightly.

'No, it's not. They all know I'm seventy next week. They all think I'm past it. Robyn didn't think I was past it.'

Seed laughs. 'You're a spring chicken compared to some, Lily.'

'Tell us about Robyn's ex-husband,' Una says, bringing back order. 'Did Robyn ever talk about him?'

There's a ripple as everyone answers at once, the general consensus being no.

'She didn't talk much about life outside of here,' Seed says. 'Although I probably knew more than most. She confided in me that they'd been meeting up, that they were planning to make another go of their relationship.'

'Why you?' Una asks, and it seems as though all eyes swivel towards Seed in that moment, collective breath held. 'Why did she confide in you specifically?'

Seed's eyes are lowered, and she's trying to gather her words. 'We . . .' she says, and for a second Celine believes she might actually cry. 'We were close,' she says softly.

Una glances at Celine, but before she can ask her next question Bramble is on her feet and the room is a flurry of plate-clearing and chatter and, with no warning, lunch is over.

In the afternoon, Celine and Thistle move on to chicken duties, mucking out the hen house and run, and scrubbing clean the feeding stations.

Once she'd got over the gaggingly bad smell of the dirty coop, Celine found the task strangely meditative, and even Thistle stopped talking for a while as they settled to work. Chickens, which Celine had always treated with some level of suspicion, turn out to be surprisingly likeable, one or two of them taking a particular interest in her and following her about as she works.

'Some of the sisters will volunteer for *anything* over chicken duty,' Thistle says as they clear up at the end of the day. 'But you did all right.'

To Celine's surprise, Thistle wipes her chicken-shitty hand down the side of her apron and offers it in a firm shake.

'You too,' Celine replies, humour in her voice.

Thistle snorts. 'Good thing about chicken duty is that you get the first showers. The bathroom rota is based on how dirty your job is, so we're first.'

She shows Celine to the shower block at the side of the house, a campsite-grade outbuilding housing six showers and sinks, where she provides her with a towel and her own bar of handmade soap.

'Shampoo's in the shower,' Thistle tells her, smirking when Celine asks if there's any conditioner. 'Supper's six o'clock in the dining room.'

Within the hour, Celine has showered, dressed, been shown the upstairs bedroom she'll share with Thistle tonight, and is once again sitting in the busy dining room opposite Una. There's something strangely comforting about the predetermined routines of this place, as though the removal of choice gives the women a sense of *more* freedom, rather than less. They can't choose to take their meal at a different time of day; there's just one sitting, one opportunity to eat. They can't sit at a PC trawling the internet for cheap flights and new shoes; there's work to be done. They can't worry over frizzy hair or eye bags when nobody else does, and nobody else cares.

They dine in relative silence, and when the kitchen team have cleared the table Seed announces it's a reading night, and everyone is sent to bed at eight, to read and catch up on sleep before the dawn bell. After using the bathrooms and selecting a book from the extensive living room library, Una and Celine manage to snatch a brief update on their way up the stairs.

'Find anything out?' Una asks in a whisper.

'Not much,' Celine replies. 'You?'

'From Rita? If I could speak Polish, perhaps – listen, work on your woman, will you? She seems like a right know-it-all. She'll be busting to share a bit of gossip. See if you can find out if Robyn and Seed were an item.'

They say goodnight and part in the hallway, Celine heading into her bedroom with Thistle, Una into hers with Rita a few doors down.

Thistle turns her back to Celine and strips, seemingly unembarrassed by her heavy white body. 'There's a nightshirt on your pillow. In case you didn't pack one.'

Celine did pack pyjamas, but she opts for the nightshirt, like Thistle, turning her back and stripping in layers, so as to expose the least amount of flesh. She climbs into bed with her book and lies back, feeling grateful for the bedside table which separates them.

'Knackered?' Thistle asks.

'A bit,' Celine replies. 'Is this a typical day?'

'Pretty much. Except Sundays. That's just a half-day.' She clears her throat and starts thumbing through the pages of her book, and Celine wonders how to break into conversation about Robyn.

'The food's good,' she says.

'I've had better,' Thistle snorts.

'Was Robyn a good cook?'

In the momentary lull before Thistle answers, Celine is certain the women have been briefed not to say too much. Her roommate sighs heavily, shuts her book and slaps it on the side table.

'Better than most,' she says. 'She was a proper chef, like. Worked in New York and London, fancy restaurants, so she shook things up a bit in the kitchen. Put a few noses out of joint, I can tell you.'

'Because she was a better cook?'

'Ah, they soon got over that. No, cos of her special treatment. When she arrived, instead of putting her in with Irma, where there was a spare bed, Seed kept her downstairs, in the room next to her.'

'Sounds to me like Seed and Robyn wanted to be near each other,' Celine says.

Thistle turns on her side and leans out so she can make eye contact. 'I've been here more than five years, and Seed's never had a favourite like that before. No one, except the Founding Sisters, gets a room of their own. The others said it was unheard of, and some of 'em have been here for years.'

Celine rewards Thistle with her best wide-eyed look of surprise and drops to a whisper. 'I heard they'd been writing to each other for a while beforehand. That there was something going on.'

Thistle's mouth draws up into a self-satisfied little pout, and she nods before flopping back against her pillow with a soft thud. 'You ask me, there was definitely something going on. Apart from anything, I'd never seen Seed so bloody happy in all my time here. She's been a shadow of herself since her special one died.'

'Her "special one"?'

'That's what everyone called Robyn – not to her face – but, you know, people notice things, don't they?' Thistle switches off the bedside light. 'Night, then,' she says.

There's a low whistle as the wind howls along the side of the house. Her 'special one'. Celine feels a horrible sick feeling in her stomach, as she wonders, was Vanessa a 'special one' too?

'Thistle,' Celine whispers into the darkness. 'You said you don't trust Bramble.'

'Uh-huh.'

'Well, what about Seed? What do you make of her?'

Thistle gives another long sigh. 'I'd lay down my life for her,' she replies, and with that she subsides into silence.

The wind gets higher as the night progresses, and, although Celine dozes for an hour or so, by one in the morning she's wide awake, lying in her single bed, listening to Thistle snoring just three feet away. She's not accustomed to being in such close proximity to others, and she wonders how quickly these women get used to communal living. The strange thing is, she's really beginning to understand the attraction of a place like this. There are no bills to pay, no text messages to reply to, no fashions to follow or clients to dress up for. There's no family, or past; even the future seems an impossible thing to imagine in here. There's the present, and it's simple, and it's tranquil and still.

Celine closes her eyes, hoping for a return to sleep, but instead finds herself trying to imagine Vanessa lying in a bed like this, fifteen years earlier. What jobs had *she* been responsible for while she was here; what had *she* brought to the community? In her real life she had been a receptionist, but she was also fiercely practical, so she'd have turned her hand to anything. She'd have blagged her way in one way or another. And when she arrived, who had *she* shared with? What was she feeling? Was she relieved to be here? Or was she still afraid? Celine's mind keeps returning to that big old leather journal on Seed's desk, in the office just along the corridor. She tunes in to the sounds of the house, but all she can hear is the wind howling around the building, and the tap-tap-tapping of a tree branch against the window. She recalls the line in the journal recording Robyn Siegle's stay here, and the blank space where her departure date should have been logged. Is there a departure date logged for Vanessa? And did she keep her own name, or was she eager to reinvent herself, to take a new identity?

Eventually, too wired for sleep, Celine eases her legs from beneath the covers and slips her feet into the slippers she'd found at the end of her bed this evening. Barely breathing for fear of waking her roommate, she pulls a sweater on over the top of her nightshirt and slips from the room, hesitating to check the dimly lit hallway before easing the door shut. To one side are six bedrooms, to the other five more, and at the very end, beyond the landing to the stairs, is Seed's office, its door firmly shut. Celine knows Seed sleeps alone downstairs, with Bramble along the hall, and the three more needy Elders and their carers in the large dorm adjoining the kitchen. They're separated by an entire floor, and any sound Celine makes crossing the floor-boards should surely be disguised by the howling wind. With a resolute intake of breath she makes haste, racing along the hallway, turning the handle and pushing the office door open, switching on the overhead light in one fluid motion – and it's only when she finds the room empty that she realises she had been half-expecting Seed to be sitting there, regally poised behind her desk.

Without delay, Celine makes for the journal, pulling it to the centre of the desk, taking care not to move anything else. Beyond the window she hears a crash, and she glances up to see an empty apple crate tumbling across the lawn in the half-light. Adrenaline pumping, she opens the journal to the front page and runs her finger down the first few names, pausing with a gasp when she finds that, indeed, Susan Green, the mystery woman in the wooden boat, was one of the Founding Sisters.

Flipping forward to 2004, she continues to scan the lines at speed, racing down every name from there up to the end of 2005, searching for her sister's name and finding nothing. She must have missed it in her haste. Celine starts again, back to the start of the year Vanessa left her boyfriend, discounting name after name until again she lands at the end of 2005, several months after Vanessa's death. There has to be some kind of a mistake, she tells herself, as her heart races wildly; she has to be in here.

There's another sound from below, and, just as she's about to close the journal, she instinctively licks a fingertip and rubs the relevant page between forefinger and thumb – and to her astonishment the page separates into two, having become stuck together with the passing of time. All at once Celine stops searching, as she stares at the entry containing her sister's name:

Original Name	Chosen Name	Arrival Date	Departure Date.
Vanessa Murphy	—	2 April 2004	14 March 2005

With a swell of nauseating clarity, Celine realises that Vanessa's official departure was just *one* day before she was found on Brighton pier. She was here, she was really here at Two Cross Farm, right until just before she died. The truth of it is written here in black and white, for anyone to see, had anyone bothered looking.

Although another part of her consciousness hears footsteps in the downstairs hall, on the tread at the bottom of the stairs just beyond this open door, Celine can't tear her eyes from Vanessa's entry.

'Hello?' Bramble's voice carries softly up the stairs, a raised whisper.

Jumping back from the desk, Celine quickly gathers her wits and softly closes the journal to hurry out on to the landing. There, she runs directly into Bramble, whose expression quickly shifts from concern to mistrust.

'Celine?' she says, keeping her voice low to prevent waking the others. 'What on earth can you be doing in Seed's private office at this time of night?'

'Oh, did I wake you?' she replies, rubbing an eye with the heel of her hand, feigning a yawn. 'Thistle showed me where the loo was before bedtime, but—'

'Well, it's not in here, is it?' Bramble replies, resolutely stern.

'I—' Celine stutters, pushing down her rising hackles at being ticked off by this elderly woman. 'I'm really sorry, Bramble – I didn't—' She's not good at lying, but she pulls it out from somewhere. 'I should have mentioned it before. I sometimes sleepwalk when I'm in a strange place – I'm so embarrassed. Sorry.' She looks down, praying her lie is enough.

Quietly, more kindly now, Bramble points her towards the toilet, and stands guard outside until she has finished and returned to her room. As Bramble's footsteps retreat down the stairs, Celine slides back into her little bed and stares into the darkness, thoughts and emotions rushing at her in waves.

She's found her sister. She's really found Vanessa.

23. BRAMBLE

Present day, Two Cross Farm

I barely slept a wink after I'd disturbed that young woman, Celine, poking about in Seed's office last night, and while I gave her the benefit of the doubt, sending her back to her room without further questioning, I'm going to keep a close eye on her.

When I did finally drift off, I was assaulted by images and memories from the past, merging in and out of order to confuse me and knot up my insides with foreboding. Beneath spring sunshine, I felt the tug of a bedsheet between my fingers, me at one corner, Regine at the other, pinning it high on the washing line, the sharp white snap of it tethering us in labour. I watched Fern, years younger, taking long strides across the lush grass, arms thrust high in welcome, and a newcomer: a girl with a broken collarbone and dark hope in her eyes. 'She's three days early!' Regine called over to Seed, who had found her on the woodland path, scooped her up on her way back from market. For a moment the girl's face became Susan's, and from nowhere my father appeared, reciting a nursery rhyme, dandling me on his knee. The smell of fresh laundry was heavy in the air, dense and muggy like the basement, not like a spring day at all. 'My mother said she'd be home,' the girl – *Vanessa* – called over, heaving a large rucksack from her shoulder, 'but she flew to Italy instead.' I thought of the barn owl then, gliding pale as the tails of that airborne sheet, and I wondered what it could mean. As a white-robed Fern spirited the new girl towards the open door of the house, the bedsheet flapped like the sail of a galleon; the girl's hair swirled; and Seed watched on, her loneliness pooling around her like invisible ink.

That April day was over fifteen years ago, I remind myself now, as my waking mind conjures up the memory of Vanessa's sweet young face. How we Founding Sisters have altered in that time, both in body and spirit. And number.

There's a shout. All at once my drowsy thoughts are disturbed by some loud disturbance beyond my bedroom door, and within seconds I am up out of my bed, cursing my slow old carcass as I reach for my tunic to wrestle it over my nightshirt, my heart drumming a frantic beat.

Is this it? Is this the moment of our reckoning?

193

24. CELINE

Celine is woken from a deep sleep by the sound of Thistle's heavy feet hitting the floorboards beside her.

'You hear that?' Thistle says, reaching out a hand to prod Celine's leg. 'Shouting – outside.'

There is some kind of commotion going on, and Celine sits up, instinctively reaching for her jeans as Thistle pulls back the curtains of their small room and pushes open the window. The sound of distant voices and car engines drifts in.

'Can you see anything?'

'Nah. Think it's coming from the front. The morning bell's about to ring anyway – let's go down.'

As they open the bedroom door, they're met by other confused faces, apparently also roused by the disturbance. Celine is relieved to find a fully dressed Una, who grabs her sleeve and leads her along the hallway, where they hang back on the landing as the other women head down the stairs, talking above each other and speculating over the cause of the noise. The morning bell sounds out, and on hearing Bramble and Seed's voices from the office Celine and Una put their heads around the door to see the two women standing at the window, looking out.

'Is everything OK?' Una asks. 'What's all the noise?'

When neither woman answers, they join them at the window to see a dozen or more men and women camped out beyond the gates, setting up cameras and film equipment. Several vans are parked up on the verge, and, even as they watch, more arrive in the lane, the sound of closing car doors and shouted instructions lifting on the morning air. The wind has dropped now, but the driveway is littered with fallen branches and leaf debris, and Celine feels as though they're teetering on the edge of something dangerous, something they shouldn't be a part of.

'I should never have trusted you,' Seed whispers, turning away from the window. 'Is this down to you – down to the police?'

'No!' Una says firmly. She's so much smaller than Seed, and yet, with her peppered hair and lightly creased eyes, she still manages to appear wise and in control. 'I swear, Seed, this has nothing to do with us! If anything, the police have been holding back information from the media – they're desperate to avoid bad press. Why do you think they sent me in? They could have stormed this place at the drop of a hat with the evidence they've collected on Robyn – on Two Cross Farm. But they haven't, have they?' She gestures to the window, where Bramble is still fixed on the view. 'This is the last thing the police want.'

'What evidence?' Bramble asks, turning to scrutinise Una with concern.

'Seed told the police that Robyn left two days before she was found dead, but the CCTV shows her that night, saying goodbye to Archie Chowdhury at Arundel station, before, he claims, she returned to Two Cross Farm with a plan to join him a few days later. He reached London safely, alone, and was then out

195

of the country for several days. They *know* Chowdhury didn't kill Robyn. And they know Robyn was planning to head back here – but they don't know what happened next. Except that someone murdered that poor girl and dumped her at the side of the river.'

'Are *we* under suspicion?' Seed asks, her eyes welling up again at the detail of Robyn's death.

'Everyone's under suspicion,' Una replies. 'Everyone who knew her or came into contact with her that night.'

'We should go down there and face them,' Bramble says, striding across the room. 'We need to prepare a statement.'

'Saying what?' Seed demands, her voice growing deeper in anger. 'We don't even know what's driven them here! Something must have happened last night for them to rush down here like this.'

'Seed,' Celine says, feeling that familiar flip of nerves as Seed turns her steady attention on her. 'If you're prepared to give us our phones, we could look it up. We could check the news to see what this is all about.'

'I can phone DI Aston too,' Una adds. 'He'll know what's going on.'

Moments later, Celine is logging on to her mobile, scrolling through the latest headlines while Una speaks with Dave Aston out on the landing. She can hardly believe what she's seeing, as headline after headline leads with sensational suggestions of grisly goings-on at Two Cross Farm. Bramble has gone downstairs to instruct the group to take breakfast without them, and for all outdoor workers to remain on indoor duties until further notice. Seed hasn't moved from the window, where she watches the number of journalists and camera crew grow as the minutes tick by.

'This isn't good,' Celine says as Bramble and Una return to the room. Una puffs out her cheeks in response, clearly trying to hold in her anger.

'What's going on?' Seed asks, taking a seat behind her desk, spreading her long fingers flat in that habitual way. 'What have you found out?'

Unexpectedly, Bramble snatches the phone from Celine and reads the tabloid headline next to a photograph of Seed from last week's press conference.

'*Commune of Killers?*' she reads aloud, meeting Seed's shocked expression. '*Women's Cult Under Investigation. Dear God. Is UK's Latest Serial Killer Here?*' Bramble thrusts the phone at Celine and goes back to the window, as though viewing the waiting press crowd will give her some of the answers she seeks. 'What the hell is this?' she asks. 'What do these people want with us?'

Una sinks on to the sofa beside Celine. 'Apparently there's been a police leak, and the media have got hold of the fact that they're linking some historical cases to Robyn's murder.'

Bramble turns back from the window, taking a step closer to Seed's shoulder, and Celine is struck by the repeat image from their last visit here, when the two women had first invited them into this room. Neither says a word.

'Bramble,' Una says. 'You told us you were one of the original women here. Do you remember Susan Green?'

Bramble's hand goes to her throat, as though searching for an invisible string of beads, while Seed's head drops a fraction. The movements are tiny; guarded. 'Yes,' Bramble replies.

'Do you know what happened to her, after she left Two Cross Farm?'

She shakes her head. 'We never heard from her again.'

'You didn't know she was dead?' Celine asks, but neither Seed nor Bramble acknowledge she's even asked the question.

'I don't know if you're aware, Seed,' Una continues, 'of an unsolved case from 1976, when a group of women went missing together, apparently of their own accord. While the case was never a big police priority, at the time there was a lot of speculation over where those women went.'

Seed blinks slowly, and Una continues.

'Susan, the youngest of the group, turned up dead in 1995, but as for the rest of them—' She looks pointedly at Bramble.

When Bramble doesn't reply, Celine can't hold back, and she leans out to slap her hand on the side of the desk. 'They came here, didn't they, Bramble?' she demands. 'The missing women were the same women who set up Two Cross Farm. The Founding Sisters? And you and Susan Green were two of them.'

Bramble fixes her jaw defiantly and nods her head. She squeezes Seed's shoulder, anchoring herself.

'The history of this place is no secret to me, or to anyone else who cares to ask directly,' Seed says. 'But what do you think it has to do with Robyn?'

'We don't know,' Una replies. 'But DI Aston wants me to ask you what happened to those other women, the ones who left with Susan in 1976. The press is going crazy out there, speculating that Robyn's and Susan's deaths are connected to this place – and now, with this new piece of information about those missing women, they're all wondering if the whole lot of them are going to turn up dead somewhere.'

Bramble gasps. 'Oh, this is all just getting out of hand!' She brings a palm to her chest with a heavy slap. 'What do you want me to say? Yes, I was one of that group back in 1976, and I can vouch that nothing bad ever happened to those other women! If they want a statement from me to that effect, if that's what it will take to get rid of them, I'm quite prepared to give it.'

'If Bramble is your chosen name, they'll want to know who you really are, or were,' Celine says.

'Fine. I am – I *was* – Brenda Harley. But I've been Bramble for over forty years now.'

Out in the hallway there's a scream. 'Bramble!' a woman calls up the stairs. 'Bramble! They're taking photos through the hedge at the back! You can see their long lenses from the back windows!'

At this, Seed's expression grows steely. 'Bramble, go downstairs and calm the sisters. Una, Celine, I'd like you to pack your bags. It's time you left.' Poised, she rises and leads the way, stepping on to the landing with Una at her rear.

With a rush of adrenaline, Celine takes her chance, grabbing the residents' journal from the desk, opening it up to the very first page. The five women are listed right there on page one, in 1976: Fern Bellamy, Brenda Harley, Kathy Hawks, Regine Porter and Susan Green. Celine glances back towards the door, where Una still stands, blocking the view as a woman at the foot of the stairs gives Seed an update on the intruders.

'I'm phoning the police,' Una says, and there's no resistance from Seed at all.

Celine turns back to the ledger and snaps an image of the page, before flipping forward to take a further image of Vanessa's entry in 2004. She slams the book shut, before swiftly she and Una gather their belongings and follow Seed down the stairs, where she makes them wait in the kitchen as she and Bramble talk in whispers just outside the door. The kitchen is empty, all the women having been asked to gather in the living room, so, when the adjoining door swings open and an elderly woman appears, Celine and Una are startled.

'Hello,' Celine says. She doesn't recognise this woman from their meal gatherings.

'A new one?' the woman asks, casting her eyes about the empty kitchen. She looks confused. 'We need three more. Thirty-three; that's the number.'

'What's your name?' Celine asks.

But another cry at the back of the house sends the scared woman back through the swing doors and out of sight.

'They're coming!' a woman shouts through the hallway. 'We're not safe! Bramble!'

There is chaos in the air, as Celine and Una rush into the hall to follow Bramble to the living room at the back, where she's pulling the drapes across, shutting out the paparazzi photographers' view just too late.

'Out!' Seed commands, marching Celine and Una towards the front door, flinging it open and directing them towards the gate.

The assembled press go crazy, yelling questions and snapping pictures, a deafening clamour in the cool morning air.

'Seed, are you sure you want to—' Una tries to reason with her.

They stop a few hundred yards from the security gate, as Seed unclips the ring of keys from her belt, readying herself to eject them from the property. Celine has the overwhelming desire to beg to stay. She doesn't want to leave this place, and yet she feels an urgency to escape.

'You have to go,' Seed says, calmly, but without her former warmth. 'You've brought this to our door – you're under police instruction, so you're as responsible as they are.'

'That's not true,' Una says. 'We had nothing to do with this.'

It seems suddenly important to Celine that Seed shouldn't think badly of them, that they need to put this straight before they part. 'Seed, we would never do anything to compromise your—' she tries to say, but Seed grabs her by the arm and tries to manoeuvre her away.

'Get off me!' Celine yells, lashing out and wrestling from her fierce grip, her heart sinking as a whoop of interest goes up from the paparazzi and she realises the whole exchange is being filmed.

Seed unlocks the gate, zoning out the yelled questions and the cameras pushed up close to capture her image, and she hurries Una and Celine through a small gap before slamming the gate shut again. Una swiftly retreats through the crowd, but something holds Celine back. She turns to Seed, again feeling that powerful magnetism – for she cannot find another word for it – and she's shocked when Seed reaches through the bars for her hand, gently pulling her close.

'Tell me the truth,' she says, not releasing her hold. 'You can see yourself living here, can't you, Celine? You can imagine turning your back on the outside world; giving yourself up.'

Celine stares back at her, adrift.

'You know what it feels like to lose something – someone – I can see it in your eyes. You know what sorrow is.'

Celine can merely stare back, lost in Seed's gaze.

All around them, journalists bray for a scoop, calling out questions they'll never get a response to.

'If you understand what it is we want to protect, you can help us,' Seed says, her voice low. 'You must divert the world's interest away from this place.'

'I can't do that,' Celine replies, hearing the tremor in her own voice. 'You're keeping secrets that the world needs answers to.'

'Sometimes it is kinder to keep secrets of another's making.' With this, Seed drops Celine's hand, her expression softening as she reaches out to brush away the tears now streaking Celine's face. 'Please don't ever come back here.'

Something inside Celine snaps; she feels as though she's been rejected by a lover, and she knows these feelings are irrational and out of character, and surely borne of grief and confusion, but there it is. Anger rushes from her.

'You knew my sister,' she growls, pushing her face against the bars. 'Vanessa Murphy? Do you remember my sister Vanessa?'

201

Seed's serene expression slips, shifting to upset and anger, and, just as Celine thinks she might answer, she turns away.

'I saw her name!' she calls after her, desperate. 'I saw Vanessa's name in the journal!'

For a second or two, Celine can only watch as Seed glides across the lawn, sky-blue tunic billowing in the breeze, before she disappears inside the building and is gone.

Head down now, Celine storms through the media mob, refusing their barrage of questions as she catches up with Una on the other side. When several journalists and camera crew fall into step with them, they have no choice but to break into a run, and they escape through an unmade track at the side of Two Cross Farm, on to the river path to jog the mile home to Belle France. Breathless, they stumble over the lawn and in through the patio doors at the back.

'Bloody hell, Celine, I'm too old for this,' Una gasps, flopping down on the sofa, and, just as Celine herself is about to breathe a sigh of shattered relief, Pip appears in the living room doorway, a small, sad child at either side of her.

'Oh, baby,' Una says, rising to her feet again, instantly moving towards Pip.

But Celine finds she can only stare, because there is her little sister, desperate-looking and silent, thin arms wrapped across her chest.

And her face is black and blue.

25. BRAMBLE

Present day, Two Cross Farm

Thistle and Blossom are out there now, and they've turned the hoses on those press hacks and their cameras.

From Seed's office window we can hear the shrieks and yells of their objections, as they scuttle away like beetles, cameras no doubt still filming. Those two women have been sent away too, and now Seed is sitting on the sofa behind me, shaking her head, white-faced, the tail end of her turban adrift over one shoulder.

'Tidy yourself up,' I tell her. 'Your scarves are coming loose.'

Without a word, she stands and bends at the waist to unwind the fabric, revealing her close-cropped silver scalp. She was fortunate really, when she threw herself on that fire all those years ago, because, while the flames took off most of her hair in a flash, the burns stopped short of her ears; the main damage was restricted to her neck and jawline, creating a chinstrap of shiny pale pink skin. The hair started to grow back, but by then she had grown so accustomed to covering up with her scarves that the style stuck. I think of the tabloid headlines we saw on Una's phone screen, describing Seed as our 'turban-headed leader', headlines which Celine said were designed to incite cultural hatred. I'm so disconnected from society that I had to ask her what she meant, and she said, 'They're appealing to the nationalists. They're presenting her to the public as though she's some kind of threat, or at the very least, "not like us". It's just the kind of subtle hate-mongering these papers get away with.'

I liked her, if I'm honest. I liked them both.

In the kitchen, I locate Regine, instructing her to meet me in Seed's office so that we might take stock of the morning's drama, and make contingency plans in anticipation of renewed police interest. As I move to follow her up the stairs, I'm halted by the sound of Fern, bellowing my name from the living room, where she's wandered from the Elders' dorm.

'Look at this!' she's hollering, her accent growing stronger with volume.

When I enter the room, she's standing before the wall of photos, as she so often does, but this time she has her sights on a particular image.

'You let her back in, Bramble?' she asks, scowling with disapproval. 'Goes against the Code! Number 12. The Code of – the – the – Banishment?' Her focus glazes over.

'*Banishment is final?*' I've grown used to finishing Fern's sentences. It's as though her thoughts and memories are all there, but the route to them is a fast-burning flame which extinguishes before she reaches the end.

She studies me, confused.

Slowly losing patience, I tap the frame of the photograph she was interested in, high on the wall, and her face lights up again.

'Yeah, *her*! She's back? Why'd you let her back in?'

'Vanessa?' I ask. 'Vanessa wasn't banished, Fern. You remember?'

'Oh, yes—' she says sadly, trailing off again. 'Vanessa's buried in the garden.'

I rub her back, and shake my head with a smile, concealing the clench of horror I feel at her confused words. 'No, she's not, silly. She went away, didn't she? We never saw her again.'

I adjust my spectacles and lean in to inspect the photograph, and as I stare at the image, for a split-second I wonder if I'm going the way of Fern too, because it's suddenly clear that there really is a strong resemblance between Vanessa and our recent visitor.

Unhooking the picture from the wall, I escort Fern back to the Elders' dorm, and return to Seed's office, my mind a-whirr. The atmosphere in the upper room is thick with trepidation, and for a moment I stand in the doorway, taking in the sight of my two fellow Founding Sisters, poised on the brink of what feels like our undoing.

'I don't know quite how to say this,' I announce, at last. Regine and Seed look up expectantly, and I cast a backward glance into the hallway to be sure we're not overheard. 'It's something Fern just said, and you might think it's nonsense . . .' I hold up the picture.

Seed, already pale to the point of translucency, merely nods. 'Celine is her sister. She just told me at the gate. She's Vanessa Murphy's sister.'

Regine reaches out for the photograph, nodding sagely as she too recognises the family resemblance. 'And how much, exactly, does this Celine Murphy know?'

'She located Vanessa's name in the journal,' Seed replies. 'And – and they've worked out that Susan was a Founding Sister.'

Regine shakes her head, as though Seed and I have somehow betrayed this information. 'And the baby? What do they know of the child?'

'Which one?' I ask, and it's a genuine question, but Regine tuts and shakes her head again, as Seed covers her face with her hands, stifling a sob.

'Nothing, as far as I can tell,' I reply, feeling panic rising again at the mention of that child. 'Even if they do work it out, Dr Kathy is dead now – there's not a thing they can do to harm us. We have nothing to fear!'

Regine turns fierce eyes on me. 'Jeez, Brenda, sometimes you can be so dumb. You think we won't be implicated, with everything we've managed to conceal all these years? With the secrets buried in our house and gardens? There is everything to fear!'

Beside me, Seed's hands drop limply to her lap. 'They're closing in, aren't they, Bramble?' she murmurs. 'It's just a matter of time.'

26. CELINE

Present day

'I swear, it was an accident,' Pip insists as Celine passes her a gin and tonic, prepared just the way Delilah would have liked it, served in an expensive cut-glass tumbler with ice and a slice of lemon. 'I can tell by your face that you don't believe me, Celine, but it's the truth.'

They sit on the facing sofas in the afternoon sunlight, the only distant sound that of Harry in the back garden, as he runs the lawnmower across the grass in soothing stripes. Vaguely, Celine wonders if Dave Aston has caught up with him yet – and when they will get any news on that threatening note Dave took away for examination. Pip, of course, is unaware of any of it, and there is no doubt she'll be furious when she discovers she's been kept in the dark. Part of Celine believes the note is just some hollow threat from the women at Two Cross Farm; the smaller, more insistent part tells her it's Jem, back after all these years, to wreak further damage on her and her family.

She stares at her sister, Pip, at her bruised face, and sighs. 'Is it the truth, really?'

Pip takes a sip of her drink, unblinking.

They are alone, Una having taken the children into town for pizza, to give the sisters some space, and despite Pip's protestations Celine's not about to give up interrogating her about her injuries. She's still reeling from the morning's drama, and from the indisputable confirmation that Vanessa was definitely a resident at Two Cross Farm. But she can't dump that on Pip now.

'You know I've never liked him,' Celine says. 'Stefan. I've never trusted him.'

'Well, this is the first I've heard of it,' Pip replies, clenching her jaw. She has a wide, bloody graze above one eyebrow, and a dark green-blue bruise spreading across her cheekbone and blooming into black at the eye socket. 'You told me you thought he was handsome.'

'Bloody hell, Pip. Ted Bundy was handsome. Didn't stop him being a psychopath, did it?'

'Stefan is *not* a psychopath.'

Celine bites down on the inside of her cheek.

'This was not intentional. I told you, I fell down the front steps – Marnie across the road saw the whole thing. I'll phone her if you like!'

'But how did the accident happen, Pip? You said you were on your way out of the house with the kids – that Stefan didn't want you to go.'

Pip takes a long slow sip of her drink, and reaches out to place it on the coffee table, rearranging the coaster so it's symmetrical to the edge. She sighs softly, giving in a little. 'He can sometimes be a bit – I don't know, he likes things a certain way.'

'Like what?'

'He likes us to be there when he gets home. Don't get me wrong, I like it too, but sometimes I need a bit of space. I mean, he's supported me ever since I stopped work to have the children – you know, he pays for everything? All the bills, the food.'

'That's because you're not earning anything – because you're too busy bringing up his children and cooking his meals and cleaning his house! For fuck's sake, Pip, he's not doing you a favour, you know? You're married – you put in your share when you were working, and now you're putting in your share looking after the family. I hope he's not controlling your finances.'

'You're twisting it, Celine. He's never done that – he's just better at managing those things. He always gives me money when I ask.'

Celine's jaw drops. 'You have to *ask* him for money?'

'Well, yes,' Pip says, but her eyes show that she's just lost conviction in her own words, like a person diving from a board, their confidence failing at the last second. 'The bank account's in his name. He's the main earner, after all. There's a separate account for housekeeping, but that gets used up by the end of every month.'

'What about your own account – you must have one too, from when you were earning?'

'Yes, but it's empty now.'

Celine drops her head against the sofa back and breathes deeply. When she looks up again, there are tears streaking down her little sister's face; she hasn't seen her this upset in years.

'He was trying to stop me from leaving,' she says quietly. 'He doesn't really like me spending time with you, and he thinks we've had more than enough time together to sort things out down here.'

'You told him we're waiting for the coroner to release Mum's body? And, anyway, why doesn't he like you spending time with me? I'm your sister. I'm your only family.'

'I don't know. He's just never really, well, encouraged it.'

Things start to fall into place for Celine, and she recalls all those times she'd phoned Pip in the early days of her relationship with Stefan. More often than not he'd tell her Pip was out, or working late, or when she was pregnant, that she was tired or 'resting'. It had gradually become more and more complicated meeting up, and, though they'd catch up on the phone or via text every once in a while, the gap between them had widened to the point at which they were only speaking a few times a year.

'*How* did he try to stop you leaving, Pip?'

'He'd been sulking since the night before, when I'd told him we were going back down to Arundel, and then in the morning he announced that he wasn't going in to work, he wasn't feeling well. He said if I was any kind of a wife I'd stay and look after him, but I knew he wasn't really ill. I told him you and Una still needed my help sorting the funeral and the house. And then he said that if I were a decent mother I wouldn't be dragging our kids along with me – so I suggested that I leave them with him.'

'And?'

'He went ballistic. He picked up my suitcase and threw it down the hall; smashed a great hole in the plasterwork. The girls were screaming for him to stop, and he was punching the doors, threatening to block my access to the housekeeping account so I'd have absolutely no money at all. And then he stopped in his tracks – as if none of that had just happened – and suggested he drive us all down here, that we should kiss and make up and make a little holiday of it.' She studies her hands a moment, before looking up again. 'I couldn't let that happen.'

Celine sits forward in her seat, listening intently. 'Why not? Why not bring him here, Pip?'

Pip's focus is beyond Celine, out through the patio windows to where the gardener is raking up grass cuttings. 'Because,' she says slowly, returning her gaze to Celine's, 'he doesn't know about all this. Mum's money. He doesn't know about it, and I don't want him to find out.'

Celine blinks at her.

'I'd stopped talking to Mum years before I met Stefan, and when we got together he urged me to keep it that way, especially when he heard how she'd left us as teenagers. He knew River Terrace was in Mum's name, but all the time we were able to live there rent-free he never asked any questions. That's Stefan all over. If he likes the way things are, he's no trouble at all. But—'

'But if you challenge his authority, he's a bully.' Celine stares at her sister, until she finally looks up.

'He didn't mean this to happen,' Pip says. 'The taxi driver had texted to say she was along the street waiting, and I had the bags and Olive on the doorstep, but when I tried to take Beebee from Stefan he wouldn't let go. Beebee was howling, and I lost my cool, and I didn't know what else to do, so I slapped him – just to make him give her up. He dropped her all right, but he also made a grab for me and I dodged him. I tripped over the door frame. I fell backwards, down the front steps, and that's how I got this,' she says, cautiously touching her grazed forehead. 'Tripping over my own bloody feet.'

'*No.* You got that because a six-foot-one man tried to assault you, *in front of your children.* Pip, you've got to stop protecting him! You have to phone the police.'

Pip closes her eyes, releasing an exasperated breath. 'You know what, Celine? I don't *have* to do anything. And, right now, I just want to go to bed.'

Celine finds she cannot answer.

'Can you and Una sort the girls out for me? I – I've just had enough of today, OK?' Pip takes a weary slug of her drink, and stomps the glass down on its coaster, so that its unfinished contents slop over the edge. 'I'll be fine,' she says, and she heads upstairs.

Celine is left alone, watching the gardener pack up his mower in the afternoon sun, wondering where she went so wrong. First Vanessa, and now Pip. Maybe Seed and those other women have had the right idea all along. Maybe a life without men *is* the only way forward.

By early evening Una has returned with the girls, and after she's bathed them, and Celine has read *Miffy's House* at least three times, they give in to sleep. When she gets back downstairs, Celine finds Una at the kitchen table, a freshly opened bottle of wine in front of her, and she fetches two glasses and pours their drinks.

'You don't usually drink so much,' Una says, observing the large measures.

'Neither do you,' Celine replies, closing the kitchen door so as not to disturb the others, pulling out the chair opposite. 'These are unusual circumstances.'

'I phoned Dave Aston while I was out with the girls,' Una says. 'No real update yet. The note's being analysed as we speak, and Dave says one of the local officers will be stopping by to have a chat with the gardener tomorrow morning.'

Celine is acutely aware that they're both actively avoiding mentioning Jem Falmer's name, both of them too hopeful that the letter is going to turn out to be from him.

'What did Dave have to say about the press leak?'

'Nothing I can repeat in polite company,' Una says. 'But he was pretty pleased to hear we got confirmation of Vanessa and Susan Green's residency there. That reminds me: will you email him those photos you took of the journal? He wants to cross-check the names with those other missing women from 1976. I think he's also hoping the handwriting might be a match with our letter.'

Celine picks up her phone and forwards the images to Dave Aston's number. When she's finished, she pushes it to one side and takes a weary slug of wine. 'This thing with Pip is a disaster, Una. I'm really worried about her.'

Una nods, and listens as Celine fills her in on the details of Pip's confrontation with Stefan, sharing her fears for her sister's safety.

'We're all so messed up, Una,' she says, pouring a second glass and kicking her shoes off beneath the table. 'You know what Delilah was like: she put men before us every time. If Pip ends up putting Stefan's needs before the girls', I don't think I could ever forgive her.'

Una doesn't disagree.

'It's insane. Here we are all these years after Delilah buggered off, sitting around the kitchen table in her palace of a house, and her legacy lives on. Vanessa chose a man who abused her – maybe even murdered her – and Pip found herself a man who it turns out has been controlling her every move for God knows how long. And me?' She laughs bitterly. 'I'm a thirty-six-year-old professional woman, and I've never had a relationship that's lasted longer than a month or two. You know why? Because, even when I really like a bloke, I don't know how to give him the real stuff inside of me – the soft stuff, the kind stuff. I swear, Una, the minute they even hint at feeling something close to the L-word I turn into a cow – I drive them away. Pip says I'm scared of showing my feelings – but maybe I just know they're going to turn out to be hopeless bastards in the long run, because that's what happened with all Mum's men. So, I bail out early. How screwed-up is that?' Celine realises she's barely stopped for a breath; that her second glass of wine is empty, and her sentences are starting to slur.

'Pretty screwed-up,' Una agrees. 'But, baby, they're not all bad, you do know that, don't you? There are plenty of good men in the world. I should know, I've worked with some of the best. Look at Dave Aston.'

'Oh, God, why didn't I see it?' Celine ploughs on, barely acknowledging Una's words. 'I never had a good feeling about Stefan, right from the outset, and I ignored it – kept my nose out for a quiet life. Just like I did with Ness and that bastard Falmer. It was the same there – I knew things weren't right, and I let her persuade me she was fine, that she was safe. I was too busy building my tiny little empire to get in the car and go and see for myself. I was meant to protect them, wasn't I, Una? That was the one job I had to do. And I failed.'

Una slaps the table and pours herself another drink. 'Stop it, Celine! Stop feeling sorry for yourself. You did everything for those girls when your mother left – everything. You were eighteen, for Christ's sake, trying to keep two teenage siblings on track as well as yourself. And you did an amazing job. You were their sister, *not* their mother. I only wish I'd been able to help you more.'

'You did plenty to help, Una,' Celine replies firmly. 'You did plenty.'

For a moment they sit there like that, letting the years wash over them.

'What d'you make of today, then?' Celine says, steering the conversation back. 'There's something about Seed, isn't there? She kind of freaks me out, but at the same time there's something really – I dunno – almost hypnotic about her.'

Una smiles tiredly. 'You like her, don't you?'

'What d'you mean, "like"?' Celine feels her cheeks flushing hot.

'That you *like* her. I saw the way you were around her; the way she responded to you.'

Celine laughs now, loud and embarrassed. 'Una! I'm into men, not women.'

Una shrugs, takes her drained glass to the sink and rinses it out.

'What about you, then?' Celine asks, by way of retaliation. 'You're what, late fifties? I know you've got plenty of male friends, but I don't think I've ever seen you with a man – you know, a *boyfriend*.'

'That's because I *do* prefer women,' Una replies without hesitation. She shrugs again.

Celine is stumped. She had no idea, even after all these years. Of course, it makes perfect sense; but how could she not have realised? Is she so self-absorbed that she doesn't take notice of all these people she's meant to love?

'Don't look so shocked,' Una says, trudging past and kissing the top of her head.

'I – I'm not,' Celine replies, and she's really not, it's just that right now she's consumed by self-loathing and there's no room for anything else. Her entire world is shifting and nothing is what it used to be.

'I'm off,' Una says with a sozzled smile. 'You should get to bed too, Ceecee. Don't wanna hangover on your birthday, do you?' She heads upstairs, cursing as she stumbles on the bottom step, and once again Celine is left alone with her thoughts.

Against her better judgment, she ventures to the living room and the drinks cabinet, pouring a vodka and tonic, remembering it as the tipple Gordon had enjoyed in the summer months, sitting out in the courtyard sun trap in River Terrace, shaded beneath his straw fedora. Which one was Johnnie? Was he the banker or the art dealer? Either, it didn't matter really. Celine recalls that for a while Pip had fantasised that he might be her father, come to reclaim his rightful place in the bosom of their family, but her hopes were

215

dashed when he, like so many others, moved on. Johnnie was OK, but still, a flash-in-the-pan, a temporary bedfellow to absorb the light of Delilah's attentions for a month or a year.

Celine slumps on to the sofa, feet up, resting her laptop on her stomach as she fires it up. The first alert she sees is from the undertaker, asking if the family have had news from the coroner yet. With everything that's been going on, she'd almost forgotten the reason they're here in the first place, and the fact that Delilah is dead, permanently – that she isn't coming back. *Ever.* Swiftly, Celine types out a reply. *Sorry, no news. I'll follow up with you early next week.* She presses send. Can it really be only a fortnight since her mother died? Less since Celine arrived here and set out on this bewildering trail with Una? She reaches for her tumbler, spilling vodka down her front as she stupidly tries to drink from it in this horizontal position. She knows she's too wired to sleep if she goes to bed now, so instead she opens up a fresh Word document and starts to list all the facts they've gathered on these three cases so far.

Facts:
3 dead women
25-year span: 1995 / 2005 / 2020
ALL connected to Two Cross Farm
ALL dead near the water
ALL with two-cross tattoos
Susan Green: Arundel / suicide? (case notes still missing)
Vanessa Murphy: Brighton / beaten and strangled
Robyn Siegle: Arundel / broken neck, fingerprint bruising

Suspects:
Jem Falmer (missing since 2005)
Seed (or any of the women at Two Cross Farm)

~~Archie Chowdhury~~ – ruled out by police
Harry the gardener?
Who else?

Questions:
Was Susan involved with a man i.e. another potential suspect?
When did Seed arrive at Two Cross Farm i.e. did she know
Vanessa or Susan Green?
Who inked those tattoos? The same tattooist, or not?
Was Robyn having a romantic relationship with Seed?
What are those Two Cross women hiding? Why so secretive?

She conjures up an image of Seed, revisiting the warm sensation of that woman's hands on hers, as she held her back at the gate this morning. Seed had spoken of Celine's sense of loss as though it were a badge of honour, as though only those who have experienced pain have really felt at all. Is that what's behind her rule forbidding children in their community? Is she – are they – warped enough to believe a woman is of greater value if she has experienced some profound level of loss or pain? Fury rises in Celine as she thinks of the way Seed dismisses the fact that so many have abandoned children to be there. And then she thinks about the confusing way Seed makes her feel when she's in her presence, and wonders whether, if she had had children of her own, she could ever have been persuaded to leave them behind.

Seen. She realises that's what the feeling is. Seed makes her feel *seen.* Perhaps, if Seed pressed her to it, Celine *could* be convinced to leave her babies behind; maybe she is just as weak as her mother, destined to let others down. This is why she's never settled with a partner, why she knows she'll never have children. She's safeguarding herself, and them, against behaviour of the same kind. Against loss.

She staggers back to the drinks cabinet and pours another glassful, returning to the sofa and laptop, where she stares, hazy-eyed, at her list of facts. Susan. Vanessa. Robyn. With so many parallels, they feel intrinsically linked, and at the same time so far apart, each woman originating from different times and places altogether. What are she and Una, not to mention the police, missing? She Googles Robyn Siegle and catches up on all the recent news reports, coming across a BBC television interview from yesterday, confirming that Archie Chowdhury has been released without charge. There follows an impassioned plea from Robyn's father in America, a well-dressed fifty-something academic with floppy blond-grey hair, who prays that the British police will do everything in their power to find Robyn's killer. As he speaks, the camera pans to a three-year-old playing in a garden, and Robyn's dad talks of his love for his daughter, and how he will now continue to raise his granddaughter as Robyn would have wished. Celine rights herself on the sofa, balancing the laptop on the coffee table to better focus. They know now that Robyn had been in the UK for a year before she was killed, so that little girl would have been without her mother from the earliest age. She imagines Olive and Beebee sleeping upstairs, the warm, dependent scent of them still on her skin. What drove Robyn Siegle to walk out on *her* daughter? Was she running from something, or simply following her own selfish desires – just to be at Two Cross Farm? She knows from personal experience that such women exist in the world, women who will walk away from their children at the slightest diversion. Women like Delilah.

All at once, Celine is seething, head swimming as she tops up her glass again, swearing steadily to herself. As she passes the dining table she snatches up that photograph of Delilah at the castle, the one they found in the attic. What was she, Celine, doing while Delilah stood there posing for that picture, drink in hand? Celine was with her sisters: three teenage girls, left behind in Kingston, with a generous bank account set up to cover their needs, but not a clue where their mother was, and falling to pieces.

What the hell is wrong with all these women? Unable to work out what to do with her drunken rage, she fires off a text to Una, asleep upstairs.

Robyn's just another selfish mother. Left her child behind in USA to start a new life.

When there's no reply she sends another:

Why should we help someone like her?

She drops her head back and drains her drink in one, realising too late that she's failed to add the tonic, that it's neat. It burns as it goes down, and, as her limbs grow heavier still, a message pings loudly on to her phone, forcing her drooping eyelids open:

Una: *Celine, Robyn is dead. We're not doing it for her.*

Celine: *Then who?*

Una: *For the family. For her parents – her child.*

Celine's argument is at once deflated. Una is right, of course. It's never really about the person who's gone, is it? What was it Delilah used to say, when talking about her various failed relationships? *It's better to be a leaver than a left-behind.* Wow, that woman had a nerve. Always the leaver, never the left. But still, as for Robyn's family, why should it be down to Celine and Una to help? They didn't even know her. There was no one there to help Celine and her sisters when they needed it, was there? When Delilah left her to raise a heartbroken fourteen-year-old and an angry sixteen-year-old – when Celine herself wasn't yet out of her teens? And look at the shit job she made of that. Bashing her shin against a dining chair as she zigzags across the parquet floor, she pours the last of the vodka into her tumbler, feeling simultaneously self-righteous and disgusted at her wallowing self-pity. She throws the drink back and texts Una one last time:

You still awake? I'm going back to Bournemouth in the morning. I've had enough.

When no reply comes from Una, Celine switches off her phone and passes out on the sofa.

27. BRAMBLE

Present day, Two Cross Farm

I watch Regine from the rear corner of the house, as she rounds up the few women who have straggled on to the lawn to gawp at the gathered press mob.

'Everyone inside!' she yells, beckoning fiercely towards Thistle, who has abandoned her hosepipe and is turning off the tap at the wall. Several photographers are retreating from the gates, half-drenched, still brazenly stopping every few feet to turn and snap in our direction. 'I'm calling the police!' Regine adds with hoarse intensity. 'This is private property!'

She's the last through the French doors, stepping in backwards as she scans the hedge at the rear, watchful as an owl. I lock the doors behind her and secure the drapes. When she turns to see so many sisters standing around, anxious, excited in some cases, her face shifts from confusion to anger.

'What the hell are you all doing in here? Breakfast, all of you! Now!'

Almost mute with shock, I glance along the hallway and fetch the bell. Only minutes earlier, I'd left Seed in her upstairs office, keeping watch on the front gate and trying to decide what to do next; I wonder if she'll come down now the trespassers are gone. Standing at the heart of the house, I ring the bell, and in the time it takes for everyone to reach their seats at the dining table Seed has descended the stairs and joined us, her slow, graceful movements studied, careful. In silence, Oregon passes a basket of now hardboiled eggs along the table; Thistle pours tea; Seed takes her place at the head seat, her eyes fixed on the empty spaces where Fern and her carer should be.

'Sisters,' she says, finally. 'This is not the first time our community has come under attack. It is not the first time we have had to face great challenge.'

Around the table, the sisters look relieved to hear her speak.

'Who here remembers Dr Kathy, one of our six Founding Sisters?'

A dozen or so hands rise.

'Then you will recall our grief – our panic even – over the loss of that dear sister on the eve of my custodianship, some ten years ago?'

'We were left without a medic,' Regine agrees. 'It was a terrible time.'

Seed glances around, and all eyes are on her. 'We were heartbroken, but we managed, because Kathy had the foresight to produce a care journal during her time here, detailing her research and natural prescriptions – from which many of you have benefited in the years since.'

There is silence around the room, and I, like many others I suspect, wonder at the purpose of this speech.

'We have had occasion to eject troublemakers from our land, have we not? Errant sisters.'

Nods all round.

'We've also seen trespassers before today's breach. Husbands or partners or parents trying to gain access, to take back their unwilling women! Those situations were trying, but we always overcame our attackers, and won out.' She pauses a moment, taking a deep, steadying breath before continuing. 'What I am trying to say to you, sisters, is that we have conquered adversity before – far worse than this – and we will conquer it again.'

Raising her arthritic hands high, Regine opens a round of applause, and with a sweeping gesture Seed invites the women to eat.

Making my excuses, I leave the table early and head up to the office window, to check on the press crowd, who are now beginning to show signs of dwindling. Despite Seed's rallying speech, I feel sick with worry, and as I turn back towards her desk I see the small stack of Last Will envelopes laid out there like an omen. Mine is sealed, as are Regine's and Fern's. Of course, Susan never had one – in fact, it was her unexpected passing which prompted us to write them in the first place – and so, only Kathy's has been opened in the intervening years, on the occasion of her death. But, as I run my fingers over the envelopes, I am alarmed to see Seed has opened her own, and it lies unfolded on the desk, defaced in a zigzag of deeply scored black pen marks, all but obliterating her original words.

As I gaze, shocked, at that demolished letter, the light from the window picks out a single word she has written in block letters across the top of the scrawl: LIES.

My heart almost stops, and I fear for Seed's sanity; I fear what she might do next.

28. CELINE

Present day

Celine is disorientated when she wakes at midday, having somehow made her way upstairs and into her own bed last night.

She has a faint memory of sitting slumped on the loo, with the door to the landing wide open, vaguely concerned that one of the girls would wake and be alarmed to find her there. As she opens her eyes now, she feels the internal grasp of a cruel hangover, her skin breaking out in a cold, sickly sweat, and her mind flashes up a reminder of what she drank last night.

'Do we need to get your stomach pumped?' Una asks, pushing open the door without knocking.

Celine opens her mouth to reply, and the banging pain at her temples intensifies. Her tongue feels stale and dry, and abject paranoia sloshes about at the back of her consciousness as she vaguely recalls texting Una last night.

Briskly, Una throws back the curtains, letting the morning light flood into the room. 'Come on! Up you get, Celine. I expect you'll want to get packed and on the road as soon as possible.'

Oh. She's angry. This is a side of Una that Celine has rarely ever seen; Una doesn't really do angry.

'Shit. I was a dickhead last night, wasn't I? I'm sorry,' Celine says, gingerly pulling herself up to a half-sitting position. Good God, her head is screaming in pain.

'Sorry?' Una says, standing at the foot of the bed, hands on hips. 'Do me a favour and save that for your sister? I'll be just fine if you decide to bail out now. But then again, I'm not the one who needs you, am I?'

Bail out? Una's throwing Celine's own words back at her. 'I'm not bailing out.'

'Well, what would you call it, then? You said yourself it's your default setting. Here we are on the brink of finding some real answers about your poor sister Vanessa, and you're chucking in the towel. Not to mention the fact that you've got another sister downstairs who needs all the support she can get right now – and suddenly, you're off.' She fixes stern, darkly shadowed eyes on Celine. 'Sounds a lot like bailing out to me. Oh, and by the way, happy birthday.'

With that, she leaves the room, slamming the door as she goes, sending fresh tremors through Celine's fragile frame.

'Fuck it,' Celine mutters, gently easing her feet to the carpet, leaning on to her knees to cradle her pounding head.

Easing her sweater on over her pyjama top and cowering against the throb of her hangover, she creeps along the hall to the bathroom, where she washes her face before heading downstairs.

'Auntie Ceecee!' Olive screams, the pitch of it cutting through her like a skewer. The little girl drops down from her seat at the dining table and wraps her arms around Celine's waist in an exuberant hug.

'Yay, Olive-Roo,' Celine manages weakly, and she ruffles the child's hair with limp fingers, doing the same to Beebee when

225

she stretches out her arms to be picked up. 'Sorry, Bee, Auntie Ceecee is feeling a bit feeble this morning. Later, yeah?'

Pip is at the table eating her lunch. 'Go outside and play for a while, girls. And tell me if you see the gardener, will you, Ollie? I need to pay him for this week.' As they disappear, Pip gives Celine the side-eye, smirking a little, before picking up her second sandwich half and taking a bite. 'Sleep all right?' she asks.

'Like the dead,' Celine replies, brushing the crumbs from Olive's seat and sitting carefully. Pip's tuna sandwich smells vile.

'Well, you look like shit,' Pip says through her mouthful. 'You look every one of your now thirty-seven years. Happy birthday, sis.'

Celine rubs her brow with the heels of her hands and groans. 'Una's got the hump with me.'

'Has she?' Pip looks genuinely surprised. 'She seemed fine to me.'

And then it occurs to Celine that Pip seems fine too – that, despite her horribly bruised face, despite what she's going through, she seems her normal chipper self. She's behaving as though the whole appalling episode with Stefan never happened at all.

'Are *you* OK?' Celine asks her. 'After, you know, the fight with Stefan?'

'Celine! It wasn't a fight as such, and don't you dare say that in front of the girls.' And there it is again, that light and sunny voice, masking the truth of it. 'I wish you wouldn't keep—'

'Oh, for God's sake, Pip!' Celine yells, and she doesn't even care about the piercing stab of pain the volume triggers at the base of her skull. 'You can't spend the rest of your life sticking your head in the sand! When are you going to face up to the fact that you've got to deal with this – you have to admit to yourself how Stefan really makes you feel. You're in complete denial!'

'You can talk,' Una says from the doorway. She's holding two fresh coffees, and, while her words are challenging, her expression is not. She hands one of the cups to Celine and sits down between them, separating the two sisters. 'You've spent most of your life with your head in the sand too, Celine, when it comes to dealing with emotions.'

Pip's jaw drops, and Celine suspects her own expression is probably a mirror. In all the years they've known Una, she's never criticised them like this, never openly judged.

'What's that supposed to mean?' Celine demands.

Una shakes her head. 'Last night you told me how much you regretted not stepping in when your instinct told you to – not interfering in both your sisters' affairs when you should have.'

'I probably said all sorts of bullshit things last night,' Celine retorts. 'I was wasted.'

'Don't you dare put it down to the drink, Celine Murphy! You know better than that. If you leave now, it'll be another thing for you to regret. You've got unfinished business here, and you know it.'

'Like what?' She throws her palms in the air, directing the question at them both. 'I've certainly got unfinished business back at home. You know I've got a practice list to run, don't you? You know I've got clients waiting for me in Bournemouth? I'm not retired on a great big effing police pension like you, Una. I've got *real* work to do.' Her childish tone is ridiculous, and she feels nauseous and hateful and worthless and full of rage.

Pip remains silent. Una looks angry and puffy-eyed and older than usual.

'Go on, then, Una,' Celine goads. 'You said I've got unfinished business. Like what?'

'Like your mother's funeral.'

'I don't need to be here to arrange that. We can do it over the phone. I probably won't even go to the service – it's not as if she'll notice.'

Una sighs heavily. 'OK. Like dealing with the house clearance, then. Like finding out what happened to Vanessa. Like talking your sister here out of returning to that bastard Stefan.'

'Una!' Pip gasps. 'What do you mean, "bastard"?'

'You're as bad as she is,' Una replies, huffing loudly, running her hands over her jeans. There are tiny beads of perspiration breaking out across her forehead, making her skin shine darkly. 'How bad does it have to get before you leave him, Pip? Does he have to actually hit you first? Or maybe one of the kids?'

Pip is speechless.

'I think it's been going on for years, hasn't it?' Celine asks, her voice softening. She takes a sip of coffee; it's good and sweet. 'With your salary, before the kids, you should've been able to come away with me on holiday, those times when I asked – but you always had some excuse. You always pleaded poverty, but we both know that's not true. He's been controlling your money since the start, hasn't he?'

Pip's face is blank. She looks over her shoulder, out through the patio windows to where the girls are playing picnic on the lawn with their soft toys. Celine follows her gaze.

'Has he hurt you before?' Una asks.

There's no reply.

Celine rears up. 'You're a grown woman, Pip! Why do you let him do it?'

'*Let* him?' Pip hisses.

'Yes! You *let* him do it. The whole time you stay and accept the way it is, you're giving him permission.'

'Permission to do what?'

'To control your money, your movements, your job prospects, your children. What would it take for you to leave him?'

228

'I love him,' Pip mumbles. 'He loves me.'

'Love? Wow.' Celine coughs. 'You do know you're spouting every bloody cliché in the book now, don't you?'

Una puts a hand over Pip's. 'I've worked with a lot of victims of abuse in the past, Pip, you know that, right? Well, the stats tell us these women will return to their husbands an average of seven times before they gather the courage to leave for good. Now, I've had you and the girls stay over at mine at least six times in the past year, baby, haven't I? And I've never pressed you for details, but I'm wondering, maybe you've reached your number seven? Maybe you're ready to leave for good.'

Pip glances back at the girls outside, who are now tussling on the lawn. 'I'm not ready,' she says.

Pushing her cup away, Celine rises with a speed which sends nausea racing through her body. 'I've had enough of this,' she says. 'Pip, if you end up dead like Vanessa, that's your look-out. I hope you've got provision in place for the girls.' She sees Pip wince at this, and she knows she's gone too far, but she can't seem to find the brakes. 'I'm going upstairs now, to pack. You two can sort out Mum's funeral – I've had it with you both.'

'Don't you dare!' Pip screams as Celine reaches the door to the hall. 'Don't you dare throw one of your grenades into the room and just leave, Celine! You're always so quick to slate Delilah for running away, but what do you think you're doing now? I might be in denial about Stefan, but I'm here, aren't I? You're just like her, you know that? You're selfish, just like Mum!'

In frustration and anger, Celine slaps a hand against the door frame. 'Then you won't be needing me, will you?'

'Of course we need you, Celine,' Una roars, 'whether you like it or not! Pip needs you – and Vanessa needs you! Those little girls out there need you too!'

Something in Celine snaps. 'What about me? Don't *I* ever need anything? Don't *I* ever need support? Do you think my heart doesn't break every time I think about Vanessa and remember she's never coming back?' With no warning at all, Celine crumples in half, hunching down low and cradling her throbbing head as though struck. Sobs break out from her, uncontrolled and overflowing with grief, as two sets of arms rush to embrace her.

'Celine? Celine, stop it, please? I didn't mean that about Mum, I really didn't. You're nothing like Delilah – *nothing*. I just wanted to get a reaction out of you. Of course you miss Vanessa. Just like I do. You and me – we're the only two people who really understand how that feels, sis. It's just, you're so controlled and careful, I never really know what you're thinking.'

From within the dark space of her huddle, Celine feels something like peace descending. Her sister is right, and, while it's not something she really wants to hear, there is comfort in knowing that there is this one other person walking the earth who knows her, inside and out. 'I'm sorry, Pip,' she says, allowing Una to wrap an arm around her shoulders, to help her to her feet.

'Let your sister get you in the shower,' Una says, holding her firmly. 'I'm going to make myself useful and put the frying pan on.'

By the time Celine returns to the kitchen table, Pip is busy with the girls at the table outside, while Una serves up a late cooked breakfast for the two of them: bacon, eggs, sausages, the works.

'Eat,' Una instructs her, taking a bite herself.

It's good. Exactly what Celine needs for this monstrous hangover. 'How are *you* feeling this morning?' she asks, remembering that Una had put away her own share of alcohol last night.

'Like a camel slept in my mouth,' she replies, and they laugh, and wince, and it feels OK.

Beyond the patio doors, there's a sudden clamour and Pip returns with the girls, who are hopping with glee. Olive thrusts a bunch of fresh garden flowers at Celine and, after prompting, little Beebee hands over the hand-drawn card she's been concealing behind her back. *Auntie Ceecee we love you*, it says on the front in shaky letters. There's a drawing of the five of them: the two girls, one curly and dark, the other tiny and blonde; Una's face coloured with a crayon that's more orange than brown; and Pip and Celine, who have been given skin the tone of prawn cocktail.

'Happy birthday,' Pip says, crushing her sister in an unrestrained hug.

The sunlight flows fully through the glass doors, and Celine's eyes fall on the shadow cast across Delilah's parquet floor. Just like the picture on the girls' card, they're all there, a shadow family and a bunch of flowers.

'I'm sorry I've been such an idiot,' she says, looking to each of them in turn and wiping her nose on the sleeve of her jumper. 'I had a good think while I was in the shower, and I've decided: I'm not going anywhere.'

'You're not?' Una asks, her face lighting up.

'Course not. We've got unfinished business, haven't we?'

'That's just as well, isn't it, Una?' Pip says, releasing her.

'Why's that?' Celine asks, frowning as Una reaches for her mobile phone.

'Because,' Una says, holding the phone out so that Celine can view the screen, 'this message came in from Dave Aston while you were in the shower.'

Celine reads the message.

HANDWRITING ANALYSIS JUST LANDED IN MY INBOX. THE NOTE THROUGH YOUR *DOOR IS A 'HIGH PROBABILITY' MATCH FOR JEM FALMER. LOOKS LIKE HE'S BACK IN THE AREA.*

29. BRAMBLE

Present day, Two Cross Farm

Seed sits at the head of the table, a handsome vision in fuchsia scarves, her expression of serenity masking her inner turbulence.

Her response to threat is so very different from Fern's, and over the past decade none of us have missed Fern's sudden flights of passion or rage, which in hindsight signposted her slow decline into dementia. Thank God we've had Seed at the helm for these past ten years; whatever happens next, we can at least trust her to protect us all – to do the right thing. In the warm glow of early evening, she looks up to take the bread basket from the person to her left, breaking off a piece and passing it over the stark empty cross where Robyn should be, into the hands of the next sister. Her pain pulsates through every one of us; we feel it, and we weep for her in our hearts.

Since the horror of the press intrusion yesterday morning, the police have phoned several times, to question Seed further and to warn her again that they could be arriving within twenty-four hours with a search warrant – giving them full access to Two

Cross Farm. There are certain questions they'd like to ask us, they say, face to face. Questions about Robyn and Susan and Vanessa. Questions about those three good women who passed through our lives and never made it to old age. As though channelling my thoughts, Seed meets my eye across the length of the table, and she brings her fist to rest over her heart. She knows what will come next.

They're closing in on our secrets, and now, all we can do is prepare for the end.

30. CELINE

Present day

'Aston has confirmed we're pretty much off the case,' Una explains as Celine steps up into the camper van and starts the engine.

She glances along the side of the house, to where Pip is engaged in conversation with Harry the gardener, her head thrown back in laughter with no sign of the stress Celine knows her sister is really feeling.

'I know the police have Falmer firmly on their radar since the letter,' she says, indicating towards the pair at the far end of the lawn. 'But I still think that one's a bit strange. And he's definitely got a thing for Pip.'

Una follows her gaze. 'I think he's fine,' she replies. 'Let her enjoy the attention, I say. She's had a shitty time of it lately, and she could do with a confidence boost.'

'Hmm,' Celine murmurs, turning the van around and setting off.

'He said he'd give Pip and the girls a lift into town later,' Una adds, as Celine turns out of the driveway. 'If Harry had anything to do with this, I doubt he'd be making himself so visible. At any rate, Aston's team have interviewed him now, haven't they?'

'Have they? We haven't heard back from Dave to say he's in the clear, have we?'

'He was never in the frame, Celine!' Una laughs. 'Anyway, back to my update with Dave – as expected, Seed says we're not welcome back since the press débâcle on Friday. She's convinced our visit there prompted all this media speculation, and Dave says there's no persuading her otherwise. I updated him on what small details we managed to uncover – that Bramble is Brenda Harley, and that we located the records for the periods when Vanessa and Susan stayed. And those images you took of the residents' log – as expected, the names match those five missing women from 1976, which is a whole other investigation, for sure.'

It hardly seems real, Celine thinks, winding down the window to feel the spring breeze on her skin. 'Did you tell him Vanessa's leaving date is marked down as the day before she was found?'

'I did – also that Seed and Robyn were in next-door bedrooms during her stay. He was particularly interested in that; he thinks if we can prove they were involved in some kind of relationship together, they've got stronger grounds for a warrant. That's partly what today's about.'

The day is warm, the sky a surreal mottled blue over the river as they pull into the car park of the Black Rabbit pub, where they've arranged to meet Robyn Siegle's father, who flew in from the US just last night. They arrive ahead of the Sunday lunchtime rush, and pick a bench overlooking the river and field landscape, just yards from where Robyn's body was discovered on a wooden jetty among the reeds and bulrushes. As Una fetches their drinks, Celine wonders if her mother had ever sat in this spot, looking out over the horizon, with its river and wetlands to one side, castle and hills to the other. When they drove in, she'd noticed the pub had fresh lobster chalked up as a special; it's certainly the sort of place Delilah would have approved of. Refined. Attractive. It's only now that Celine has begun to realise that all her mother's compliments to her three daughters were about these kinds of things – always the external, never the internal. 'You look divine when you make an effort,' she'd say. Or, 'My, what a marvellous long neck you have, darling.' Pip had 'the best legs'. Vanessa enviable eyelashes. Celine a small bosom 'to die for'. She couldn't care less what talents her daughters possessed, so long as they looked good and presented themselves well.

Una emerges from the pub, holding two pints of orange juice and lemonade, since only yesterday they'd both, in varying states of fragility, vowed never to drink again. She's carrying a bag of crisps in her mouth, which she drops on the wooden table with a jerk of her chin.

'Una, how on earth did you and my mother become friends?' Celine asks as Una takes the seat beside her on the bench, overlooking the view. 'I mean, you couldn't be more different.'

Una rips the crisp packet wide, and pushes it towards Celine. 'God knows. We had absolutely nothing in common. I mean *nothing*. She was from a rich landed background; I was a second-generation upwardly mobile immigrant. She had kids; I had a cat. She was all about the glamour. And well, I was a detective constable when we first met, and you know I don't even own a lipstick. I've never been one for making much of myself.'

'Don't talk stupid. You're one of the best women I know, Una. Make-up or not. I reckon that's one of the things Mum most envied about you, now I think about it. You're brave. You don't need to preen and primp to be who you are – the same couldn't be said for Delilah. I don't think I ever saw her not "put together", as she'd call it. She was terrified of being found out.'

'Found out for what?'

'For not being interesting, beneath the veneer.'

'Of course, there was another reason she liked me,' Una says, pulling her cheap sunglasses down over her eyes.

'What's that?'

'I was good with kids.'

'Ha!' Celine smiles. 'Someone had to be.'

'After she left you like that, though . . .' Una says. 'I didn't hear from her directly for, oh, must have been two years. She knew I wouldn't approve of her taking off like that.'

'She left me a list of instructions when she went,' Celine says, recalling aloud. 'A bank card and pin number, and a dashed-out note telling us to knock on your door if we had any problems.' She looks at Una. 'Did she run it past you first?'

Una scoffs. 'Course not. I didn't have a clue where she was until she sent you that first postcard from Italy a few weeks later.'

There'd followed a handful of brief messages from Delilah over those first couple of years, and then, after six months of silence, a final postcard had arrived, breezily announcing her return to England, along with a new address in Arundel. *Hello, girls! Back in the UK (without Gordon). Living in Sussex now. Hope all is well with you, much love, Mummy.* God, how it had sickened Celine, seeing her mother's use of the word *Mummy*. She'd long ago given up that role. By then the sisters had falteringly forged new lives for themselves, without Delilah's help – Celine had been twenty and studying law, Vanessa had just started her first job, and Pip was in the middle of her GCSEs. They had each other; they were fine. And so, by some unspoken agreement, they'd decided that they were doing just fine by themselves; that not one of them needed or wanted Delilah back in their world. It was only after Vanessa's death that Celine had met up with her for lunch, making contact once a year or so thereafter, until that last meeting in the tea shop ten years ago, when she knew she couldn't do it any more.

'It's kind of good to think Vanessa reached out to Mum, after all those years, isn't it?' she says to Una, who nods sadly and pats her hand. 'I think perhaps she was trying to tie up some unfinished business, don't you? She was always more forgiving than me. Maybe she would've done it sooner, if it hadn't been for me and Pip not wanting to.'

'You don't know that,' Una replies with a stern shake of the head. 'None of this is your doing, Celine. It'd do you good to remember that every now and again.'

At the sound of a taxi arriving on the gravel behind them, they turn to see a man they recognise as Adam Siegle getting out of a cab. While he's occupied paying the fare, Celine talks quickly. 'So, if Aston says we're off the case, what are we doing here today?'

'A favour. Dave promised his family a weekend away, but he didn't want Adam Siegle arriving in Arundel without some kind of a welcome. He's insistent about coming down to the river to see where his daughter was found, so I volunteered. I said we'd meet him for lunch, unofficially, reassure him that the police are following up all the leads. Apparently he's been making a lot of noise about the fact the police haven't been inside Two Cross Farm yet—' She stands, raising a hand to wave at Mr Siegle. 'We've just got to smooth the waters really. *Shh*. Hello, Mr Siegle!' She strides towards him, arm extended, straight into copper mode.

'Ms Powell?' he replies, and he offers up his hand to shake hers, before joining them at their bench table. His grief is writ large across his features, in the slump of his posture, in the slack skin around his clean-shaven jaw. He's a lean man, but Celine suspects he's lost pounds in the past fortnight, that he's a man robbed of sleep.

'Are you hungry?' Una asks after the introductions. 'We were going to order some sandwiches.'

'I should eat,' he replies, in a soft New England accent. 'I'll have whatever you two are having.'

When the lad from the bar stops by, they order three cheese and ham sandwiches and a half of local ale for Mr Siegle.

'How's your hotel?' Celine asks.

'It's, um, quaint.' He looks out over the water, surely contemplating his daughter's last moments. 'Actually, I've stayed there before. I taught at the New England College in Ford. It was just down the road from here – closed now.'

'Really?' says Una, clearly surprised. 'DI Aston mentioned that Robyn was doing some research, but I thought it was related to family history?'

'Well, kind of,' he says, taking a slow sip from his half pint. 'Robyn was born here.'

It's obvious to Celine that Una is somewhat thrown by this new revelation, because she offers no more than 'I see,' in response, and so Celine steps in.

'Do you know, Mr Siegle – Adam – why Robyn separated from her husband, Archie?'

'They married too young,' he replies evenly. 'I tried to get them to wait, but they were in love – in a rush to do everything the moment they thought of it.'

'Was he ever violent?' she asks as Una quietly riffles through her papers.

'Good God, no. Have you *met* Archie? He's as nice a fella as you'll ever meet. I loved him – all the family did. When they separated, I think we always held out hope that they'd get back together, but Robyn didn't see it that way.'

239

'How's that?' Una looks up from her papers, interested.

'She – well, she didn't take to parenting in the way we thought she might. She found it hard; really hard. I should have seen the signs, you know? I think it was postnatal depression, but I'm no good at all that – Robyn's mother died when she was only very young. She's missed out on a woman's touch, I suppose.'

'Had you any idea she and Archie were planning a reconciliation?'

'None whatsoever,' Adam replies. He picks up his sandwich, brings it to his mouth and appears to think better of it. 'He hadn't visited Amelia – their daughter – for a few months. You know she lives with me now? I only knew he'd got himself work in London when all this terrible – when . . .' He's struggling.

'When Robyn was discovered?' Una offers.

He nods, takes a controlled bite of his sandwich and uses the few seconds to compose himself. Celine and Una follow his lead, eating their sandwiches, offering him another drink, allowing him to set the pace.

'But you know it wasn't him, don't you?' he says. 'The police let Archie go without charge. Your DI Aston told me as much.'

'That's right,' Una says. 'His alibi is watertight – he couldn't have done it.'

Adam Siegle eyes Una's file of papers. 'You're a civilian consultant, you say? How much access do they give you to the case files?'

'Limited,' she replies. 'I'm an ex-detective, and in this case it was useful for the police to call on me because they wanted a woman who could get inside Two Cross Farm, and I happened to be staying nearby when Robyn was found. We had a family bereavement recently.' She looks at Celine, who nods.

'Oh, you're related?' he says, surprised.

'Yes,' Celine answers, 'though not directly, as you might have guessed.' She nudges Una's hand with hers, so that their contrasting forearms lie side by side, and it breaks the grave atmosphere. Adam rewards them with a smile.

'Jem Falmer is a name I've heard bandied about,' he says. 'I've been reading about another case in London fifteen years ago – very similar, but in that case the boyfriend, Falmer, was the main suspect. He went on the run, so I believe.'

Celine's heart races. She knows the link has been plastered all over the newspapers in the past few days, but it's still a shock to hear someone outside of their circle talking about Vanessa's case. She tries to keep her expression impassive: they'd agreed not to let on that she's related to Vanessa, or that they have any vested interest in this case other than professional.

'Falmer is still the main suspect for Vanessa Murphy's death,' Una confirms.

'Is he a suspect for Robyn too? Aston told me Falmer has some local connections. The similarities between the two deaths can't be ignored, can they?'

'I believe he *is* being treated as a suspect – or at least as someone the police want to speak with. But finding him is another matter.' Una sighs. 'And the fifteen-year gap between the crimes is a problem, Mr Siegle. It's unlikely that someone like Falmer would kill back then, in a very personal way, and then wait fifteen years to kill again so randomly. There's absolutely nothing to suggest Robyn had come into contact with Falmer.'

'What if it's *not* random? What if there isn't actually a fifteen-year gap – if he's been busy killing other women in the meantime? If he's been travelling around, he could have killed any number of women without local authorities making a connection. Have you considered that you might have a serial killer on your hands?'

241

'We really don't think that's the case,' Celine says, though she'd be lying if she said the thought hadn't occurred to her. Feeling Una's weight shift uncomfortably on the bench, she moves the conversation on. 'What we really want to ask you about is Robyn's relationship with Seed, prior to her becoming a resident at Two Cross Farm.'

'You say she'd been in contact with Seed over the months leading up to her stay? By mail?' Una flips over to a fresh page in her notebook.

'Yes, that's right. When she was working in London, we'd talk every couple of weeks, and she was quite excited by the prospect of visiting the place. She had been doing some research into the community there.'

'Did she say anything to suggest Seed was a love interest?' Celine asks.

'For Robyn?' he replies. He turns side-on, so that he can follow the line of the river, deep in thought. 'I don't know. But the exchange *was* full-on, and whenever I spoke to Robyn she talked of little else. Apparently, this Seed woman said she couldn't wait to meet Robyn in person. She told Robyn she knew she was special. Was it romantic? Even if Robyn didn't think of it that way, I did warn her that I thought Seed probably did. She shrugged it off, and then of course she was offered a job as their cook, and the rest is history.'

'Do you think the police should suspect Seed as a potential killer?' Celine asks.

'I think they should suspect everyone who lives there,' Adam replies, draining his drink. 'And everyone who doesn't.'

After lunch Adam says he'd like to walk along the riverbank to see the spot where Robyn was found. The cloud cover has rolled away with the gentle breeze, and as swans and their young glide along the sun-kissed water you could be forgiven for thinking the

242

trio were just a group of friends enjoying a post-lunch Sunday stroll. On the far bank, ramblers are picnicking, and a little further on they pass a mother and her small daughter, who lean out over the wooden rails as the toddler crumbles stale bread between her fingers, dropping it clumsily into the water, to feed a mallard and her ducklings below.

Adam stops momentarily, to gaze at the little girl. 'I would have come sooner, but I had to sort out childcare for Amelia.' He blinks hard. 'At least she died in a beautiful place. Robyn loved nature, you know? I used to bring her here as a child.' He gestures towards the toddler. 'We used to feed the ducks, just like that.'

Una glances at Celine, curious, before stopping at a point where the river narrows and becomes thick with bulrushes and weed. A moorhen bombs out of the foliage, chased by another, as Una indicates towards a dent in the bank where a mooring post stands at the edge of a small pontoon, the cut end of a rope fraying limply from its rusted ring.

'This is the spot,' Una says. She lays a hand on Adam's shoulder, pointing with the other towards a sunlit wooden bench a little further along the path. 'Celine and I will be over there when you're ready.'

They leave Robyn's father at the water's edge, where he stands, stoop-shouldered, his back to them. For a long time, he barely moves, and Celine watches as he reaches into his pocket for a handkerchief, gently mopping his face. So much has happened in these past two weeks, not just in terms of events, but in her own thoughts and emotions. She constantly senses she might cry at the drop of a hat, not just at her own feelings but at the emotional responses of others, something she's previously thought herself immune to. She thinks of herself as a person who lacks empathy, and she's cool at best with most new people. But this past week she experienced such a strong connection with Seed, and such intensity of feeling when it came to Pip's situation with Stefan, that it all seemed to catch up with her when she put Olive and Beebee to bed last night. Una had caught her in the hallway, swiping away her tears, and, when she'd asked what was up, Celine had replied, 'Hormones,' when the truth was simply that little Beebee had just told her, 'I lub you.'

'I had no idea about Robyn's Arundel connection,' Una whispers now, flipping back through her notes. 'And, judging by the file copies I've got, I don't think Dave Aston realises either.'

'Surely that would've come up?' Celine says.

'Not necessarily. Robyn is American, last known address in London, temporarily at a women's retreat in Arundel. Most women at Two Cross Farm are from other places – not local.'

Adam Siegle stuffs his hanky in his pocket and starts towards them.

'You say you lived in Arundel before,' Una says gently as he takes a seat. 'Tell us about that.'

He stretches his legs out before him, crossing his ankles and turning his face to the sun. 'I first came here in the early '90s, when I got a post as a teacher, working alongside my English wife at the New England college nearby. It's closed now – shut down the same year that Robyn came along in '96 – but my wife and I had several happy years working there together. This is such a beautiful part of the world.'

'Happy days?' Celine says.

'Very happy. After the college closed, I was lucky enough to get work at a local primary school. Janey had her hands full with Robyn, and life never felt better. I'd always wanted children, and for a while it looked a little doubtful whether we'd have kids at all, so we felt doubly blessed to have her in our lives. Then . . . well, things changed dramatically in 1998, when Janey found a lump. She went straight to the doctor but it was already too late – she went downhill fast and died within a month of that first appointment.'

'Oh, God, I'm so sorry,' Celine says, blinking away her own tears. 'Robyn was just two or three?'

'Uh-huh. She doesn't really remember much about—' He stops talking, swallows. 'She *didn't* really remember her mother, because she was so small when we lost her. We stayed on for a couple more years, and I did my best, but in 2000 I went back to my home town in Vermont. My family was there – my mother, my sisters – support, you know?'

Una hasn't spoken for a while, but now she runs her pen down a printed document, and clears her throat. 'Adam, you just said Robyn came along in 1996 – but I have her down as born in '95. There's a copy of her passport on file.'

His brow wrinkles a little, and he says, 'Sure – she was *born* in 1995, but we got her in '96.'

Una returns his frown.

'We adopted her. She was an abandoned baby – found on the doorstep of the convent in Crossbush soon after she was born.'

'Crossbush? That's just a mile or two up the road from here . . .'

'That's the one. It felt like a miracle, because we'd been on the adoption waiting list for two years by then, and we were close to giving up. That little mite's misfortune turned out to be our blessing.'

This new information is unexpected and mind-bending. They'd hoped meeting Adam Siegle would shed some light on Robyn's death, make things clearer, but instead the threads of this mystery seem to be knotting tighter and tighter. So when Robyn was looking into her mother's stay at Two Cross Farm it was her *birth* mother, someone she'd never even met. Celine takes the case folder from Una, and thumbs through its pages, looking for a particular document.

'So, that's why she contacted Seed?' she asks.

'Yes. She wanted to find out more about her birth mother, and she suspected the Two Cross community might be able to help,' he replies.

Una leans on to her knees, focusing on the flow of the river, before she turns back to him, her expression shifting. 'Adam, you don't think Seed could be Robyn's mother, do you?'

He shakes his head firmly. 'Definitely not. The adoption agency told us her mother died in childbirth—' He's about to continue when Celine interrupts.

'1995? Robyn's birth date is December 12th.'

'That's right,' he says.

'December 12th, 1995!' Celine repeats, thrusting a news cutting at Una. 'That's just one day before Susan's body was found.' She pauses, momentarily doubting herself and the madness of what she's about to say. 'Adam, I think Susan Green could be Robyn's natural mother.'

Adam Siegle's frown deepens.

'This article talks about "blood loss",' she goes on excitedly, 'but there's no mention of a baby. In the absence of her files, we've been assuming "blood loss" related to a suicide. But perhaps—'

'Hang on, did you say Susan—' Adam tries to say, but Una cuts across him, on automatic pilot.

'I'll call Aston first thing, find out if he's managed to get hold of those files yet – the forensic report will tell us for certain if Susan had had a child before they found her.' Una is animated, but then she looks at Adam and her expression freezes. 'What is it?' she asks.

He has his palm to his forehead as though a great dawning is upon him. 'That's her! Robyn said she thought she'd managed to work out her mother's name – Susan Green – via some old news archives, and that, if she was right, her mother was a homeless or missing woman who died in childbirth nearby. Of course, I couldn't confirm that for her. The adoption agencies don't really tell you much at all during the process.'

'Do you remember this news story at all?' Una asks, passing him the cutting.

He takes it, reads it over, rubs a hand across his mouth. 'I do, naturally, because it was local to us. But – but we would never have made the connection that this woman and Robyn's mother were one and the same. I mean, we didn't get to meet Robyn until a few months after this article was published.' He scans the page, his finger following the lines of type. 'The article doesn't mention a child. Why would they conceal that?'

'The police are very careful about how and when they disseminate information relating to a suspicious death. It's possible the detail of her baby came out in later updates – or not at all, if there was concern about sparing the family. I guess the real answer is, I don't know. We're waiting to get our hands on the official police file.'

What Una doesn't say is that Dave Aston's been trying to obtain Susan's file for days now, it having gone missing in the newly archived Sussex records.

Adam Siegle's face is set in a mask of shocked realisation. 'She was found dead by the water,' he murmurs. 'Just like Robyn.'

Celine looks at Una, recognising the suppressed urgency in her expression. 'So, now we have the strongest of links between Susan and Robyn,' she says, calmly. 'They were mother and daughter.'

31. BRAMBLE

1995, Two Cross Farm

Women were screaming.

It was what woke me in the dead of night, rousing me with the distant and unfettered pitch of it, and I felt afraid for the trouble ahead. As I fumbled for the bedside lamp, the door to my room creaked open and young Seed's ashen face told me all I needed to know.

'Will you come?' she asked, her voice low and mournful. 'Will you come now, Bramble?'

All along the landing and stairwell above us, women were opening bedroom doors, leaning out with anxious faces, asking what the noise was all about. *Has the time come? Should we be worried? Should we prepare to celebrate?* Seed ignored them, forging ahead, pausing only to glance back at me with urgency.

'Get back to your rooms,' I called up as I shuffled by, my legs aching from lack of rest. 'Go to sleep, all of you. If you're needed, we'll ask for you – otherwise, we'll see you at morning call.'

They nodded solemnly, every one, and disappeared behind their bedroom doors, knowing better than to get into an argument at this time of night. As we left the dorms behind, I realised the screaming had ceased, and in my murky waking state I wondered if I'd really heard it at all. I dared to hope that perhaps it had been just voices from the hallway, altered in my dreams, though Seed's grave manner suggested otherwise.

'Where is she?' I asked, reaching out to tug at a sleeve to slow her down.

Seed stopped at the creaky threshold to the dining room and turned to face me. Her head was wrapped in an indigo turban, and she was dressed in the same sky-blue smock I'd seen her wearing earlier, making me wonder if she'd been to bed at all. 'Fern thought she'd be best in the wood store, away from the other women. She made up a bed there.'

'In the wood store? For the love of – why? Isn't it freezing out there?'

Seed shook her head and a large tear plopped to her chest, leaving a single dark stain.

In the darkness, we passed the great oak dining table and reached the French doors at the back of the house, where I could make out lamplight from the shed at the far end, flooding through its small windows, illuminating the frosted pathway.

'Fern said it would be less disruptive. The noise, you know?' Even as she said this, Seed's doubt was written clear on her young face, her breath, even inside the house, making white mist as it left her mouth. 'She thought it would be best to keep things discreet.'

I gestured outside, towards the lights at the top of the garden, my nerves fraying. 'What stage is she at?'

But Seed only shook her head miserably and pushed open the glass door, before sliding her elegant hands deep into her tunic pockets, indicating with the slightest movement of her chin for me to follow her.

Outside all was still, not a breeze in the air, and but for those lit-up windows you'd have been forgiven for thinking the entire world was asleep. I glanced back at the house, where a few curtains were twitched back, and I knew unseen eyes were watching for news, for action, for *something*. On the far side of the garden there was a flash of pale movement swooping close to the sails of the little windmill as our resident barn owl took flight across the lawns and out towards the river beyond, unaware of the drama playing out just yards away. I wondered, not for the first time, how free it might feel to be an unthinking creature, a harmless beast or bird, concerned only with the next meal, with the changing of the seasons.

Seed, several paces ahead of me, opened the door to the wood store, and then I heard it again, that keening, piercing cry, and I knew what kind of cry it was, for it could be only one kind. It was not the joy of new life but a wail of grief, and it belonged to Kathy. I rushed through the entrance, brushing Seed aside in my need to *know*, instantly regretting my haste. Because yes, there was Kathy, kneeling on the floor beside a ground-level bed, no more than a mattress really, with Fern sitting upright at the other end in a faded orange canvas chair, her silver-streaked hair braided to one side. Regine, with her matching grey plait, a mess of tears, huddled, knees up, in the shadows of the woodpile. At the centre of them, curled like a foetus on her makeshift bed, was that darling girl. It occurred to me that the scene resembled some terrible, grotesque re-enactment of the Holy Nativity, and even before I allowed my eyes to fully rest on her I knew she had to be dead. It was the blood. There was so very much of it; so much that the mattress was almost entirely soaked, the poor girl's legs crimson with the stuff. Even her hair was tinged pink, God help us.

Without thinking, I made the sign of the cross, knowing even before my hand dropped to my side that it was a mistake. In a heartbeat, Fern leapt out of her seat, and she roared with fury, dismissing me with the whip-sharp motion of her arm. 'This is no time for God!'

I staggered a little, startled by her outrage, shocked by it all. It had been just a small gesture, a thoughtless, unconscious action, hard-wired from childhood, but an action so at odds with the agnostic philosophy of our community that it could only inflame our custodian's wrath.

'I'm sorry, Fern,' I started to say, and all I could think was: *She was two weeks overdue. She was two weeks overdue, and we did nothing!*

'We've lost one of our number, Bramble. Your God's no use to her now! Do you know what this could mean? For me? For you? For all of these women?'

I glanced around the lamplit space again, breathing in the hot metallic anguish of the room, tinged as it was with death and wood dust and damp and tears. I didn't know what to do with myself, and when I glanced over at Seed it was clear she was lost too; she'd backed herself against the cold wooden walls, a hand to her mouth, her eyes not on that poor husk of our sister but on Kathy. Dr Kathy who hadn't looked up once since I got here, who was still just kneeling there, huddled over herself, as though the pain of loss had cut her spine like a string.

'Kathy,' I said, reaching out to touch her hair lightly with the tips of my fingers.

'I couldn't save them. I couldn't save either of them—'

She looked up then, raising first her face and then her shoulders, peeling slowly back to reveal that she was, in fact, huddled over a dark, wet bundle. Suddenly hopeful, she offered it up to me, like a gift, as though I alone held all the answers, but I couldn't take it, because that would have been just too much to bear. As Kathy's arms began to shake under the dense weight of it, and the blanket flopped away, I saw it really was a child; fully formed, blood-red, unmoving.

'What will we tell the women?' I whispered.

'We'll tell them Susan missed her family,' Fern replied coolly. 'We'll tell them she took the baby back home.'

So when the cries started up again, it took long moments before any of us truly believed what we were hearing. The cries were not from Kathy this time, but from the baby in her arms.

32. CELINE

Present day

DI Dave Aston arrives after lunch, on his way from meeting Adam Siegle at his hotel nearby.

It seems yesterday's revelation about Susan Green has come as a great shock to Dave, and he spends the first few minutes with them berating himself and the wider police organisation for failing to make the connection themselves.

'I'm sorry, Una, I know I said you're off the case, but to be frank I could do with a friendly ear right now. Do you mind if I burden you – pick your brains a bit?'

Una sets to making him a coffee as he joins Celine at the kitchen table.

'If we'd managed to get our hands on Susan Green's paperwork earlier, perhaps some of this balls-up could have been prevented,' he says. 'No offence, Una, but I can't believe it took two civilians to spot the link between Susan Green and Robyn. Mother and daughter? I can't believe it.'

Celine indicates for them to move through to the living room, where they can spread the files out on the coffee table between them.

'So, the Susan Green file finally turned up, then?' Una remarks. 'What does it say?'

Dave hands her the report, summarising as she scans the detail. 'The 1995 post-mortem revealed that indeed Susan Green *had* given birth only hours before death, and that, although it wasn't mentioned in the news report, there was clear evidence of birth trauma. She had certainly lost enough blood to kill her, and, while suicide was briefly considered as a viable cause, particularly with the fact of her having abandoned her baby earlier that evening, the coroner's ruling was misadventure.'

'*Not* suicide?' Celine asks.

Dave shakes his head. 'My old neighbour must have misremembered the detail. That news article does hint that she'd taken her own life, but, when you re-read it, it stops just short of saying so.'

'Poor girl.' Una breathes out. 'So, it looks like a tragic, but clear, case of death in childbirth?'

He nods sadly. 'Looks that way.'

'You know, having that paperwork wouldn't have helped us link Susan and Robyn any sooner, Dave. When an adopted baby is placed with a new family,' Celine says, 'they don't give out personal details, so you wouldn't have found a connection to Robyn in that file. I think we just got lucky. And I think Robyn got lucky too, piecing together local news articles from around the time she was abandoned – and going one step further in guessing that Susan had been a resident at Two Cross Farm. It makes sense, when you consider the proximity to the place and how many years Susan had been missing beforehand.'

Dave pulls a face that suggests she's being generous. 'Huh, well, Robyn – and you two – certainly gave my old colleagues a run for their money in the deduction stakes. And me, for that matter.'

'But God knows how she got Seed to agree to talk about it,' Una says. 'Seed certainly wasn't so keen to volunteer any information about Susan to us. Tell you what I'd like to know: who Robyn's father might be, bearing in mind that her mother had been living in an all-women community for nearly twenty years prior to giving birth.'

Dave writes the word 'FATHER?' in his notebook and circles it. He looks up as Olive and Beebee appear, and he gives them a small wave as they pass through the patio doors. 'Cute kids,' he remarks, before flipping open a notebook just like Una's and scowling at its pages. 'Is your sister still here?' he asks.

'Yes, she's in town meeting someone for lunch,' Una says.

'I didn't realise she was meeting someone,' Celine says, wondering why Pip hadn't mentioned it to her.

'OK,' Dave says, breaking her train of thought, 'let's summarise. We now have two women discovered dead in Arundel, twenty-five years apart, and one of them turns out to be the abandoned daughter of the other. I think we can safely say this is our biggest breakthrough to date.'

'Agreed,' Una says.

'We also now understand why Robyn was staying at Two Cross Farm – in order to find out more about said birth mother.'

Celine is desperate to mention Vanessa, for fear that this new development will overshadow *her* case, *her* murder, but she holds back, waiting for the right moment.

'I'm wondering,' Dave says, 'did Robyn go into that community all gung-ho, asking questions about Susan Green – questions that someone in there didn't want to answer?'

'If she *had* discovered something damning about her mother's death, there's certainly motive for someone wanting to shut her up, isn't there?' Una says.

'So, if you suspect motive, what now?' Celine asks.

'We're going to have to make good on our threat and slap a search warrant on Seed and Two Cross Farm,' Aston says. 'The chief wanted us to avoid that at all costs, but I can't see any other way to move this forward. Seed is hiding something, and, now that you two aren't welcome back there, it's time we made it official. If Seed was having some kind of relationship with Robyn, it makes her a strong potential suspect. We'll apply for the warrant this afternoon.'

'And what about Vanessa?' Celine asks, finally unable to hold it in, unsettled by the news that the police are ramping up their approach. 'Are you still linking her death to these two? It's just, all this talk seems to be entirely focused on Robyn Siegle and Susan Green.'

For a second Dave Aston doesn't reply; she's caught him off-guard. 'Yes, of course we're still looking at Vanessa's case, Celine. It's just that all this latest information happens to be directly related to the other two women. When we carry out that house search we will absolutely be looking for evidence in connection with Vanessa's death – but, that said, I don't want to raise your hopes too high. Fifteen years is a long time – long enough to dispose of incriminating evidence.'

'But what about that note from Jem Falmer? If he's back in the area, alive and kicking, surely he has to be your prime suspect? Shouldn't you be looking at ways he might be linked to those two women too? What if you're diverting all your attention on to Seed and the commune, when you should be rounding him up?'

'It's not that easy, I'm afraid,' Dave replies. 'Yes, the hand-writing expert confirmed the note was written by Falmer, but no one – I mean *no one* – has seen him. His family deny any contact from him, as do his old work colleagues, and he has no real friends to speak of. I've had one of my officers checking CCTV cameras all around Arundel for that day the note was left, on the off-chance that he passed through, but with no hits. Until we work out where he is, we can't move forward. We've got nothing.'

'But do you think he could be responsible for killing Robyn?' she asks.

'Yes, I think it's possible,' Dave replies, firmly. 'Although for what motive is another matter.'

Celine's attention is drawn to the words on Dave's notebook, and she is struck by a sudden thought. 'What if – OK, this might sound crazy – but Jem Falmer would've been twenty when Robyn was born. What if Jem is Robyn's father? What if Jem *is* connected to every one of those three dead women?'

Una and Dave exchange a puzzled look, then their expressions shift: maybe it's not such a crazy idea after all.

'Wow, that is a thought,' Dave replies. 'That threatening note he left you shows that he's clearly still got an axe to grind, as well as suggesting he could have been in the area around the time of Robyn's death.' He pauses, staring at his notepad. 'OK. I'll get a few more officers on to the search for him as a key suspect. But we must be clear: he's not the only suspect, and for now we're going to follow up the strong leads we do have inside Two Cross Farm.'

'Thanks, Dave,' Una says, taking his empty cup and standing.

'I want to reassure you, Celine, the entire force is taking this seriously,' Dave says. 'I'll be taking my team down to Two Cross Farm tomorrow afternoon, with a warrant, and we'll be making a thorough search to gather as many answers as we possibly can. And, if it's appropriate, we'll make arrests. You have my word.'

While Dave sees himself out, Celine slumps on to the sofa, a fresh wave of concern washing over her. 'What if that search warrant jeopardises everything, Una?' she asks.

'How?'

'You saw what Seed was like. She hates the police; she hates men. And, apart from anything else, I can't help feeling it's wrong to go storming in there, when they've managed to protect their female-only status for all these years. If feels like an abuse of their privacy.'

'But Seed is refusing to co-operate, Celine. The police are running out of options.'

'OK, but how many officers does Aston plan to take in there with him? And how many of them will be women? Very few, probably. Those women may be the only ones who know exactly how Jem Falmer is involved. All this is going to do is wind them up, make them join shoulders and clamp their mouths tighter shut.'

'What else do you suggest?' Una asks. 'The police tried the softly-softly approach, sending us in, and that didn't work.'

'Didn't it? It was all going swimmingly until the bloody press turned up! If the police had managed their information better, that would never have happened. Storming in there is not the way to get them talking, Una, and I think you can see that as much as I can. *Shit*. I know Falmer is behind Vanessa's death, I just don't know how, and I'm really worried Aston is going to screw this up for us. For *Vanessa*. If only we could get in there again, wipe the slate clean. The answers are in there, I'm certain; just not in all the obvious places.'

'Well, we had our chance,' Una says with a sigh. 'And now it's down to the police.'

'I could do it.' Pip is standing in the doorway, back from town. She looks thin, vulnerable.

'What?' Celine asks.

'I could go into Two Cross Farm – I could say I need their help. They don't know me; they don't know we're connected in any way.'

Una is shaking her head.

'Look at me!' Pip insists, the idea clearly gaining traction in her mind. 'My face is all messed up – how can they turn me away? I'm exactly the kind of woman who'd go to them for help. I'll tell them my husband hits me, that I've got nowhere to stay. I'll throw myself at that bloody Seed's feet if I have to, beg for sanctuary.'

'No, Pip,' Celine protests. 'The answer's no, and that's an end to it.'

A darkness crosses Pip's face, and she shakes her head angrily, heading towards the garden where the girls are playing. 'When are you going to stop treating me like a child, Celine? You can't keep withholding information from me like you have been – and you can't tell me what to do any more. I care as much about what happened to Vanessa as you two!'

'Leave the police work to Dave Aston,' Una calls after her, but already Pip is storming off across the lawn towards the girls, fists clenched as she tries to hold in her rage.

'She'll calm down soon enough,' Celine says, getting to her feet and pulling on a jacket with a weary sigh. 'We're out of food,' she says. 'Wanna come for a trip to Sainsbury's?'

Una picks up the car keys and they set off, pausing only to call farewell to a stony-faced Pip, who is sitting on the low wall with Olive at the end of the garden.

In the car on the way home from the supermarket, Dave Aston calls Una's mobile.

Celine answers on the second ring and flips it on to speakerphone.

'Blimey, Dave,' Una smiles, 'can't stay away from me for more than five minutes, can you? I'm driving, so make it quick – Celine's with me.'

'I've just come from interviewing your gardener,' Dave says, urgency in his voice. 'There's a new development. Can you pull over?'

'We're almost home,' Una replies, continuing along the main road. 'Keep talking.'

'Hang on,' Celine interrupts. 'I thought one of your officers had already spoken to Harry?'

Dave grunts. 'Don't ask. There's a gastric bug doing the rounds at the station – anyway, the long and the short of it is, that particular interview was missed. I've just been with him now. He was very useful as it turns out. Did you know he'd been out to lunch with your sister Pip earlier today?'

Celine turns to Una, scowling hard when she realises she has known all along. They now bump along the unmade track towards Belle France, slowing down as they pass the iron security gates to Two Cross Farm.

'Apparently so,' Una says. 'Now, are you going to spit out what this new development is, Dave?'

'It's pretty significant,' he replies. 'Significant enough for me to have kept Harry in for further questioning.'

'What?' Una barks. 'On what basis?'

'Well, when I realised he hadn't been questioned, I traced his surname via a Google search of freelance gardeners in the area. It's an unusual surname – it certainly rang some bells – and when I did the background check it threw up something alarming.'

'What?' Celine demands as Una draws to a halt on their driveway.

'His name is Harry Glass, and we're holding him at Littlehampton station right now, for questioning in connection with *all three* deaths.'

'Jeez,' Una wheezes, her hand working over her hair.

Celine releases her seatbelt and leans in to speak. 'Dave, that name sounds familiar—'

'Uh-huh. You remember the news article about the discovery of Susan Green's body in 1995?' Dave continues. 'The young man who found her was a lake attendant at the time, a twenty-year-old local by the name of Harry Glass. Turns out your gardener was the fella who found Susan's body, twenty-five years ago.'

Harry the gardener? The shy, evasive, softly spoken fellow they've watched mowing Delilah's lawn this past fortnight. Harry the gardener, who, it seems, has also been making moves on her sister.

'Is he under arrest?' Una asks.

'Not yet,' Dave replies. 'But I've got a feeling it's only a matter of time. He's never moved away from this area, he tells us. And he's been doing your mother's garden ever since she bought the place seventeen years ago.'

Celine sucks in a long breath, anchoring her eyes on the front door of their house as the cogs of her mind whirr double-time. 'He'd have been Mum's gardener when Vanessa was in the area? In 2004?'

Una blinks at her, the implications of this new information gaining momentum.

'That's correct,' Aston agrees. 'And guess what? Our Harry Glass attended Littlehampton school with a certain Jem Falmer. And he doesn't seem to have an alibi for the night Robyn died.'

33. BRAMBLE

Present day, Two Cross Farm

Seed refuses to come downstairs.

Over the past forty-eight hours, she's barely left her office, instead keeping vigil in the window overlooking the quiet front gate, anticipating the threatened police visit, which so far hasn't arrived. Regine and I bring her trays of food and try to talk her down, but she's having none of it and will barely turn away from her view to speak with us. The room smells closed-in and stale, and I swear she hasn't washed in days.

'Honey, Fern's been asking for you,' Regine says when we go up to check on her after lunch. Her tray sits on the edge of her desk, food uneaten, water untouched.

'No, she hasn't,' Seed replies, without hesitation, her back to us. 'Fern barely remembers my name these days – or anyone's, for that matter.'

Regine gives me a resigned sidelong look, hugging thin arms about her stooped frame. 'OK, you got me. But I know she'd like to see you. She's gotten worse, honey. I don't think she's too long for this world.' It's not a lie; Fern's strength is declining rapidly.

At this, Seed turns to look over one shoulder, and in the gaunt lines of her cheeks it's suddenly horribly clear just how much weight she's lost in the past few weeks.

'What Regine says is true,' I tell her. 'Fern's fading quickly. She loves you very much, Seed, and you might want to pay her a visit before—'

'Before what?' Seed spits, spinning her chair to face us. 'Before she dies? I've been up here thinking about Fern these past few days, about the way she prepared me for this role, trained me for it, handed me the reins at thirty-three – about the way I had no choice in it. Does that sound like love?'

'But you were destined to be our custodian, Seed, even before you were born,' Regine says gently, taking a step towards her, raising her hands in defence when Seed's voice lifts to the rafters.

'Destiny has nothing to do with it! It's always about Fern, isn't it? Fern gets the casting vote in all matters! I didn't ask for this role – I didn't ask for *this*,' she says, gesturing towards the damaged side of her face, her hands trailing down her body. 'And I certainly didn't ask to be born into this damned house of deceit!'

I start physically at her outburst, for it is so out of character, so wounding, and I find myself reaching towards Regine for support. Regine's stiff fingers grasp mine.

'You're upset, Seed – it's natural,' I start to say, but she rounds on me savagely and my words fall away.

'Of course I'm upset!' she bellows, lunging to sweep her arm across the surface of the desk, sending pens and notebooks across the floorboards. 'Everything is falling apart, Bramble! Everything. Ever since—' She stares at me, but her words fail her.

I merely look on, open-mouthed.

'Ever since,' she continues, lowering her voice to an urgent whisper, her words spilling out, unchecked. '*Ever since the laundry room*. And it's not just that; I can't get Susan out of my head either. Susan, and the *baby*. What we did was so wrong, getting rid of that tiny creature, *disposing* of her, like she was nothing at all – and that's all down to Fern! That was under *her* instruction, under her *orders*! You say Fern loves me – what kind of love is that?' Seed is ranting now, and neither Regine nor I seem to have the ability to interrupt her, to douse her flames. 'None of us wanted to give up that child,' she continues, tears now flowing freely, '*especially* after what happened to Susan. And we tried to persuade Fern to change her mind, but you remember, don't you? She *wouldn't* have it. She wouldn't allow it . . .' Seed's voice trails now, growing softer. 'Fern wrote the Code. Fern decided how and when to follow it. And Fern had the power to overrule a democratic vote. We were supposed to be *for* women, not *against* them. Tell me, how does it serve women to wrench them from their children, and keep them apart?'

With unfading clarity, I recall Fern's words from that night all those years ago. *If Susan and this child are found on our property, we are all complicit. Kathy more than any one of us – Susan died under her care. To not act now would blow apart everything we have striven for over the past twenty years. It would put women out on the street; it would break up our family. Just think about it for a moment or two; ask yourself, even if you evaded arrest, how would you fare out there? The child must go.* My instinct at the time had told me it was wrong, but my selfish fear of losing our community had won out. I remember the stricken expression on Kathy's face, Kathy who had begged to take Susan to a hospital a week earlier, when the baby was already overdue. Kathy, who never really got over that loss.

Now, Regine and I have no reply. There is no answer we can give; no words we can offer in defence of our dying founder. Seed looks away, her hands protectively rearranging the scarves that cover her head, her eyelids closing slowly as though attempting to restore her inner calm. With a graceful hand motion she appears to dismiss us and returns to her window view, but, instantly, something in her demeanour shifts and she presses her palms to the glass. Regine and I step closer, both, I think, expecting to see a large police entourage waiting at the gate. But instead there is a small trio standing on the other side of the iron bars, where the rope pull is now swinging as the sound of the bell rings out across the lawns.

'Who can they be?' Regine asks.

'Whoever they are,' Seed replies calmly, her focus still firmly on the little group, 'you're to let them in. Let them in, Bramble, and welcome them, and tell them they may stay.'

'But, you can't—' Regine starts to object.

'You are to tell them they may stay,' Seed repeats, coldly sounding out each syllable as she turns from the window, arresting us both with the strength of her glare. 'Go!' she growls when neither of us moves.

Regine hurries ahead of me, already calling down the stairs, instructing the sisters to let the newcomers in.

'Will you come down too?' I ask when I'm halfway out of the door, feeling all at once terrified of what Seed might do next, to herself, or even others. I've never before seen her like this, never before feared her in this way.

She nods slowly, and, framed against the window by a halo of dancing dust motes, her hard expression relaxes and she nods. 'I'm fine, Bramble, really. I just need twenty minutes to take a shower, to freshen up.'

'Who do you think they are?' I ask, a last question.

She gazes at me gently, like a mother appraising a child. 'They're a sign,' she replies, simply. 'And maybe, just maybe, they're a second chance.'

34. CELINE

Present day

After they'd finished speaking with Dave Aston in the car yesterday afternoon, Celine and Una returned to the house and found Pip and the girls, and many of their things, gone.

Celine was at first concerned, as they'd not parted on the best of terms, but after a brief scout of the kitchen Una found Pip had left a note explaining that she'd returned home for a day or two, to take advantage of the fact that Stefan was away for a few nights on business.

I've given it a lot of thought, the note read, *and I've decided I'm going to file for divorce. I need a bit of time to sort through some paperwork at home, while he's away.*

This was the best news Celine had heard in weeks. That, and the fact that the police seemed to have snared a real live suspect for Vanessa's murder, something that even now she is having trouble truly believing. She keeps returning to that conversation she had with Harry Glass in the garden, feeling a chill dread when she thinks of the interest he's shown in Pip over the past couple of weeks. When they'd seen Pip's note, Celine had texted with an update about Harry being questioned, but Pip has yet to reply, and Celine wonders if she's still smarting about the cross words they'd shared.

This morning, Celine is sitting across the kitchen worktop from Una in her pyjamas, thinking about Harry Glass. 'He certainly had me fooled,' she says now. All night long, she's thought of little else besides the fact that the police have linked Harry the gardener with Jem Falmer – and with the discovery of Susan Green's body. 'Looked like butter wouldn't melt.'

'Who, Stefan?' Una replies, misunderstanding. 'Pip won't have an easy time getting him out of that house.' She pours Celine a coffee and pushes it across the worktop. 'He's grown accustomed to living rent-free, and he won't take it well.'

Celine doesn't bother correcting Una, as her mind is diverted back to her youngest sister. These *men*, she thinks – all these men taking advantage of all these women. Celine is better off on her own, making her own decisions, pulling her own strings. The single life has worked out just fine for Una, hasn't it? Who ever said you needed a man in your life to make you whole? Delilah, that's who.

'River Terrace is legally Pip's now, which means her husband will have a legitimate claim on half of it. I deal with cases like this *all* the time,' Celine says, feeling a shudder of guilt at having left her boss in the lurch for so long. 'Why the hell couldn't she have sorted this out before Mum died?'

'Bad timing. Stefan hadn't knocked her down the steps in front of her children before Delilah died.'

Celine tuts irritably. 'That *bad timing* has probably cost Pip and her girls half a million pounds.'

'Yes, but don't forget she'll have her share of the proceeds from this place too. She'll be able to buy Stefan out if she has to, if he insists on claiming half. She's got choices, Celine, that's the most important thing, isn't it? Pip isn't trapped now. She doesn't have to rely on him for money any more.' Una catches the toast as it pops up. 'You know, she's even started talking about going back to work once Olive starts school. I think being here with you, Celine – she's finding her strength again.'

A pair of Beebee's tiny shoes lie kicked off by the back door, one straight, the other upside down. Celine recalls the moment the girls came to say goodnight to her and Una the evening before last, when Beebee took Celine's face between her dimpled toddler hands and kissed her on the nose, telling her not to let the 'bed bubs' bite. It's become a nightly ritual for Celine to kiss Beebee's Lady-Dog and Olive's Spider-Boo goodnight too, and she's begun to feel a ferocious wave of love towards those girls, an overwhelming desire to sweep them up; to pull them close to her and never let them go. 'I hope you're right,' she murmurs.

'I know it sounds morbid, but in many ways I think your mother's death has released her.' Una sweeps a cloth over the crumb-scattered worktop. 'Now Pip just needs to know we're behind her. We don't want her losing confidence and buckling. In my experience, controlling men rarely change – Stefan's likely to try to sweet-talk her, convince her it was a one-off. We need to keep her on track.'

Celine taps out another message to Pip: *Proud of you, sis. Keep us posted on when you're getting back here and send love to the girls xxx*

After breakfast, she has a quick shower and heads off in the car, while Una stays behind, waiting for an update from Dave Aston. The tense wait is getting too much for Celine, so she decides to drive around Arundel while she thinks about the case, and after a time she finds herself passing the castle walls, and parking in the road next to Swanbourne Lake, where Susan

Green's body was found in 1995. She leaves her car on the country road beyond the red entrance gates and continues on foot, to walk around the perimeter of the lake, where a dozen or more white-painted pleasure boats sway in the water alongside the bank, each of them named: *Basil*, *Sweet Lady*, *Oops A Daisy*, *Mim*. Was one of these wooden dinghies Susan's final resting place? Or one much like it? What was her boat's name? Surely the police would have removed the boat from service, to crawl over it in forensic detail before eventually having it decommissioned and destroyed. No one could want to take a pleasure trip in it after what had happened.

It's still early in the day, and not yet high season, and so the walkers are few, far outnumbered by the waterfowl that make this nature reserve their home. Swans and their cygnets cut through the glassy water in perfect formation, as Muscovy ducks preen themselves in the shallows where the lake runs to gravel. All around, little pathways and trails lead off into the woods, alive with birdsong and dappled with spring sunlight. Halfway around the lake, Celine takes a seat on a wooden bench and looks back across the water, taking in the surroundings, the café and woods to one side, more benches and footpaths to the other. So, Harry Glass had been the young groundskeeper here when he discovered Susan Green, her blood-soaked body cold and lifeless, just hours after she'd given birth. From what they can tell from the police records, it was believed she'd made it on foot to the Poor Clares convent at Crossbush, where she'd abandoned her baby on their doorstep before heading here to die. What unearthly show of strength or despair had allowed her to do that? To walk, still bleeding, all those miles, with a child no doubt swaddled close, only to hand it over and turn back into the darkness, alone. Childless. Did Susan really row out into the water alone, or was she put there? Celine's mind races over the possibilities. Was Harry Glass not just some innocent bystander but instead somehow involved in Susan's death, or at least the depositing of her body? And was Jem Falmer there too, Harry's old school friend – an accomplice in murder?

A gaggle of water birds congregates nearby, delicate creatures, black with little white heads, efficiently moving about as they peck for insects. Celine takes her phone from her pocket and types 'Poor Clares' into Google maps, and discovers that the convent is just six minutes away by car.

With renewed purpose, she marches back along the lake's edge, mentally going over the many confusing threads of this case. If Harry Glass is their man, it means Seed and all the other Two Cross women are out of the frame. And yet, Seed is definitely hiding something, Celine is sure. Bramble too. The dead women's tattoos say something, but, arguably, that something might just be a marker of the fact they were all residents at Two Cross Farm at some point. But the location of the bodies, the placing of them so carefully and near to water, can't be ignored. Vanessa on Brighton pier; Robyn at the River Arun; Susan, here, on Swanbourne Lake. It certainly feels like a compelling argument that this is the work of one man – or two.

When she pulls up on the drive outside the convent, Celine doesn't waste any time; she heads straight for the large front door of the imposing building, yanking the hanging bell rope and sending it ringing out across the grounds. She takes a long breath, telling herself to slow down, to keep her impatience at bay. It never wins her friends.

The middle-aged woman who answers the door introduces herself as Sister Joanna. 'How may I help you?'

'I'm Celine Murphy,' she replies, extending a businesslike hand. 'I'm here about a woman called Susan Green. She abandoned a baby on this doorstep in 1995 and I was wondering if there is anyone here who would remember that night, or know anything about it?'

When the nun frowns a little, Celine expands.

'I've been working with the police,' she explains, 'trying to help them with a more recent crime they believe could be related. Do you know anything about the baby at all?'

Sister Joanna raises her eyebrows in a surprised, guileless expression. 'We *all* know about the baby. It's one of those events that has gone down in Poor Clares' folklore. I wasn't here at the time, but Sisters Angelique and Maria will almost certainly be able to help you; I've heard them talk of it many times. Would you like to wait while I fetch them?'

Inside, Celine sits on the wooden bench of the vestibule, taking in the quiet hush as she waits in taut anticipation. The peace of the place is somehow embedded in the very fabric of its panelled walls and cool stone floors. It reminds her in no small way of Two Cross Farm. Here she is, not two miles from that place, in another wholly female sphere, a matriarchal community where peace reigns. Is it always this way, or do these women have their own kind of battles too, just as men do, just as men and women together do? She wonders what it is that ignites all the rage in the world; what it is that makes people want to control, to dominate, to overcome and rule. People like Stefan. Like Jem Falmer. Like Harry Glass, if the police's suspicions are to be believed. Because here, and at Two Cross Farm, when you strip everything of material value away, when there is nothing left to own or acquire, what need is there to reign over anything?

Soft voices beyond the corridor alert Celine to the approach of more women, and when Sister Joanna returns she has two elderly nuns with her, both of them in their eighties. Despite their equally slight physiques, they move with the dignity of elephants.

'Sister Angelique and Sister Maria – this is Celine Murphy.' Sister Joanna gestures towards a room just off the front entrance, and the three of them sit beside the unlit fireplace in a cluster of old armchairs, while Joanna fetches tea.

'I understand you want to know about the baby?' Sister Maria says. She brings her hands together, touching the underside of her chin with steepled fingers. 'The Baby in the Blankets, we call her. She was a beautiful little mite. We had her for two nights and one day.'

'You seem to remember it – her – very clearly,' Celine says.

Sister Angelique spreads her hands expansively. 'We've only ever had a single child over the years since I've been here – I arrived in 1985, from Somerset, where I'd known of a few. In past decades there were many more, when unwed mothers would go to untold lengths to avoid the shame. But since the 1980s it's been a very rare phenomenon. They keep them these days.'

Both women bob their heads sadly.

'Do you have children?' Angelique asks.

'No,' Celine answers. Daylight cuts through, slicing a bright shaft the length of the room, coming to land on an elevated statue of the Virgin Mary. It's been carefully placed there, Celine thinks, to receive this midday light as the sun moves around the building.

The door eases open and Sister Joanna backs in, balancing a tray of tea things which she slides on to a wooden sideboard. She pours four cups and joins them, perching on the edge of the remaining chair. 'You said the mother's name was Susan Green?' she asks. 'Sister Angelique, did you ever know who the child belonged to?'

'Not for certain,' she replies. 'Though, some years later, a local told me that a woman had been discovered dead that same night, and that the police eventually concluded they were connected. Is that the case?'

'Yes,' Celine replies. 'We believe so.'

'And why the interest now? It's years since—'

'Twenty-five years,' Celine says. 'And I can't really tell you why the police are looking into it, just that they feel the details of this may help them with a couple of later crimes they're still investigating.'

The sisters don't press the point, and merely nod, accepting.

Thinking it might make her appear more credible, Celine takes a notebook and pen from her bag, and adopts a poised-to-write stance. 'Would you mind telling me about that night? It was December 1995.'

'It was a cold winter that year,' Maria says. 'I remember that very clearly, and we were grateful that the child was brought to us – not left out somewhere, to be found.'

Celine inclines her head encouragingly.

'After prayers, we retire early here,' Angelique explains. 'So, when the front bell rang out, past midnight, it woke the entire household. It was most irregular, of course, with us being out here, somewhat remote – and we certainly weren't expecting any visitors. Moments later we were all out in the corridors – on the landing – wondering what on earth it could be. It unsettles one, doesn't it, the unexpected? The unanticipated phone call or knock at the door – we're programmed to fear the worst at that time of night.'

Celine instantly recalls her own response when the call about Delilah had come at 12.05am that night three weeks ago, rousing her from a deep, dreamless sleep. She'd felt instantly nauseous as she'd reached for the phone, certain it could only be her sister calling so late. *Celine, it's me*, Pip had whispered, shock-voiced, robotic. *Mum's gone*, she'd said. *It was the sleeping pills, they think.*

'It can only be bad news,' Celine agrees now, as she realises a response is expected.

'Sister Jennifer took control,' Maria says. 'She instructed us all to repair here, to the Holy Mother's room.' She motions towards the sunlit figurine. 'And, once we were assembled, she and Sister Angelique answered the door.'

'You were right there?' Celine asks Angelique. 'When the baby was found?'

'Yes.'

'Did you catch a glimpse of the mother at all? Or was she already gone?'

Angelique smiles, remembering, the warm lines of her face furrowing deeper. 'The child wasn't just left – she was handed over. Her guardian was right there, still holding the baby when we opened the front door.'

Celine can barely believe what she's hearing. 'Susan Green?'

'No. No, it definitely wasn't Susan Green.'

'How can you be sure? Did you speak with her? What did she say to make you think she wasn't the mother?'

Sisters Angelique and Maria exchange an affectionate glance.

'A few of us had drifted into the vestibule at the sound of the infant's crying,' Maria says. 'I could see the stranger beyond the doorway, beyond the sisters, but not the detail. I don't know if this person wouldn't or couldn't speak, but they didn't utter a word, just stood back in the shadows holding out that child like an offering.'

Celine looks down at her notepad, wanting to write it down, but too mesmerised by the details she's hearing to do so. 'What was she wearing?'

'A full-length dress or tunic, not unlike a habit. A hooded coat – and a scarf pulled high so that not much more than eyes and a nose were visible.'

'She really didn't want to be identified, did she?' Celine says. 'But I still don't understand how you were so sure that this woman wasn't Susan Green.'

'Because,' Angelique replies with that customary smile, 'she was a *he*.'

For a moment Celine is too stunned to answer. 'How could you tell?'

'From the hands. When I took the baby, I caught a close look at those hands – they were large, strong and elegant. Like a pianist's, you know?'

Maria is nodding in agreement. 'Definitely a man. He handed the baby to Angelique, and backed away, stumbling a little – heartbroken, I thought. Then he sprinted out into the darkness, and, as I watched, there was no doubt in my mind that this was a young man.'

'The father?' Celine asks.

'We can only speculate,' Angelique replies. 'But that seemed to be the general consensus.'

Sister Joanna has remained silent throughout. Celine looks at her now and there's something in her calm expression which reminds her of Seed, and she feels an overwhelming need to see her again, to look into her eyes and ask her what it is that she knows. What does she really know about Susan? About Vanessa? About Robyn?

As Celine returns to the car, her mind is a jumble. Could that man on the doorstep of the Poor Clares convent have been Harry Glass? Was it possible that he had been involved with Susan Green, a woman many years older than him at the time, a woman supposedly living in celibacy, confined far from the distractions of men within the safety of Two Cross Farm? Sitting at the wheel, she types a message to Una: *Police should test Harry Glass DNA against Robyn's – possible father?*

She receives Una's reply immediately: *They're already on it.*

They're close, Celine can't help hoping it – so close to bringing all these connections together. And yet – and yet, still some of the answers feel infuriatingly out of reach. Thoughts racing, she pulls out on to the main road and speeds towards Una and home. She thinks of the nuns' description of those large, elegant hands, and recalls the feel of Harry Glass's hand in hers when they met; it was rough, calloused from years of manual labour. But back then, as a twenty-year-old, could his hands have been described as elegant? Perhaps. And what of Jem Falmer – he's the same age as Harry? Could it instead have been he who delivered that baby to the convent, having abandoned her dead or dying mother at the lake? Or was it really feasible that the two men had worked together, one of them at the door while the other drove from the lake?

As Celine swings her camper van on to the unmade road towards Belle France, she visualises the dining room at Two Cross Farm, her mind's eye scanning the great table, stopping at each of the place settings, scrutinising the women in turn. She's outside of herself again, disconnected enough to access the minutiae of this remembered scene, to almost smell the aroma of the food, to soak up the tense, fascinated atmosphere of the room. The bowls of food steam as they're handed from one sister to the next, hand to hand, fingertips brushing, small physical connections being made. She sees Bramble passing a plate of potatoes to Una; Una to Seed; Seed to Celine. Their skin connects too; she feels that clench of electricity deep in the core of her, and it transports her forward to the moment when Seed clasped her strong hands around Celine's, holding her back before she fled through the waiting press pack. There's something there, some clear answer just at the edges of Celine's thoughts—

Without thinking, her right foot engages the brake, bouncing the van to a jerky halt directly outside Two Cross Farm. Through the bars of the iron gates, the grounds to the left and rear of the property are illuminated warmly in the late afternoon sunlight, and Celine finds herself mesmerised by the sight of two small girls, chasing each other around the windmill folly to the far left of the garden. Their high, excited laughter lifts on the spring air and Celine knows she's not imagining this: the two children are Olive and Beebee.

When Celine slams to a racing halt on the gravel outside Belle France, she is in such a state of panic that for a moment she can only stare at Una as she appears in the doorway, her expression open and unknowing.

'She lied!' Celine spills out of the car in her rush to reach Una, to tell her everything, to get to her girls.

'Who are you talking about?' Una asks, unmoving.

'Pip! Pip lied. She isn't back at her place at all – she's with Seed! She's at Two Cross Farm, and she's got the girls with her. Don't ask me why, but I don't think they're safe, Una. We have to get them out of there!'

Barefoot, Una jogs down the front steps, reaching for Celine's hand, but she's batted away. 'OK, baby,' she says, raising her palms to show she's not the threat. 'Calm, OK? Let me get my shoes on, and we'll go down there now. But listen, Pip and the girls are in no danger. The police have more or less discounted Seed and the other women as suspects – they've called off the search warrant. It's only a matter of time before they formally charge Harry Glass, and track Falmer down.' She holds on to Celine's shoulders, attempting to anchor her. 'Are you listening, Celine? Aston thinks he's found those women's killers – *Vanessa's* killers.'

'OK, Una, I get it!' Celine yells, shaking her hands from her shoulders. 'That's good! That's great! But Vanessa's death is in the past, and *right now* I'm worried about Pip! Something's not right about Two Cross Farm, about Seed. I don't know exactly what it is she's hiding, but I truly believe she – or any one of those commune women – could be a danger to Pip and the girls. You heard her say she'd rather burn the place down than let the authorities inside. I believe her; I think she really meant it. What if she works out that Pip is connected to us? What might she do? *We've got to get them out of there!'*

Una fixes her with a stern gaze. 'I want you to slow it right down, Celine. Let's go inside and talk about this before we go rushing in there. You need to tell me exactly what you're worried about. And then we'll make a plan.'

35. BRAMBLE

Present day, Two Cross Farm

It is the arrival of our unexpected visitors that ultimately draws our leader out of her room, and, desperate to restore equilibrium, Regine and I accept that they may stay a night or two.

There's no denying that it breaks the Code of Conduct, allowing children inside, but the little girls are charming and the mother is desperate and in true need of shelter. More to the point, Seed appears transformed by their presence, and I pray that they might in some way help us get her through this, help bring her back to full strength once more. The young woman, Pip, is in her late twenties or early thirties, although it's hard to tell as she is so petite, the darkly blooming bruises on her face making her look more vulnerable than perhaps she'd otherwise appear. Where has she come from, to be so far off the main road with nothing but the clothes she stands up in? When we ask her to surrender her phone, she does so without argument, and when we enquire who inflicted her injuries she makes eyes towards the children and the subject is dropped.

It's mid-afternoon and, as the girls run along the hallway, the oldest, Olive, stops to sniff the air at the threshold to the kitchen, joy crossing her flawless little face. 'I smell biscuits!' she announces, and the toddler claps her hands.

I stoop to their level, confidential, my stomach turning over as memories of little Seed rush in at me. 'Honey and oat biscuits,' I whisper, indicating towards the open door of the kitchen. 'Shall we see if we can find you one? I think Oregon will be taking them out of the oven any minute now!'

The mother, Pip, reaches out to touch me on the shoulder, mouthing a thank-you before she heads off to the gardens with Seed, and it's a wonderful thing to feel useful, to be diverted by these two small angels. In the kitchen, the girls are given glasses of milk and warm biscuits, before Oregon puts them to work making shapes from some pieces of pastry left over from the pies she's made for tonight's supper. I leave them sitting at the workbench in the sunlight, their sweet laughter fading behind me as I make my way out to the lawn to join Seed and the mother.

'Ah, Bramble,' Seed says, holding out a hand. 'Pip here says she has relatives in Bournemouth. Didn't you used to holiday there as a child?'

I nod, remembering the golden beach days of my mother's younger years, she in a floral sundress and oversized hat, me in a knitted swimsuit, pouring water from a bucket and watching the sand shift. I see my father in the distance, dressed as though for work, in brown suit and polished shoes, his thinning hair parted archly, not joining in, but watching. Always watching.

'And where did you say you've come from?' I ask, noticing the way her gaze drops whenever we navigate close to the cause of her distress.

'I – I've come from London,' she says, and I wonder how economical she's being with the truth. 'That's where our family home is – where my husband is now.' She looks beyond me, back towards the house. 'Olive and Beebee – are they all right? I don't like to leave them for too long, not since—'

And there it is again, that coy downward glance with her glossy lashes. Is she to be trusted? But then all at once she breaks down, pressing fingers to her mouth as she sheds heavy tears.

Seed's hand springs out, almost making contact with the young woman, before she loses confidence and her arm drops to her side. There is something in Seed's broken expression that terrifies me, and I push the thought away in my rush to comfort the girl, never having been able to tolerate witnessing another human cry.

'Oh, come now!' I say, and I slip my arm beneath the young woman's and we walk, the three of us, past the allotments and wood store, round through the orchard at the back of the house. The sisters we pass try to conceal their interest, nodding genially and saving their chatter for when we are out of earshot. There's always great curiosity when a new resident arrives, particularly one who comes unannounced, unvetted and uninterviewed. Of course, she won't be allowed to stay for more than a day or two; Regine, the old stickler, will see to that. But for now Pip is welcome, and I mentally make lists of instructions to hand out over tea. As our tour of the grounds comes to a close, the bell sounds out, and, all around, sisters lay down their tools and head for the dining room. In a burst of joyous laughter, Beebee and Olive come tearing out through the French doors, and there is a holiday feel in the air, and my beachside memories and their tinkling shouts and cries merge in my mind, sweet and sour.

At the table, Seed asks the sisters to shuffle around a little to make room for our guests, and she explains that today is a special day, because, on a visit to the Elders' dorm this afternoon, she found Fern well enough to join us for tea in the dining room. Among our number, words of gratitude are shared, but this joy is lost on our dear old founder, who sits in her assigned seat at the opposite end of the table, her posture a little slumped as she casts docile eyes about without understanding. We give thanks for the gifts we have received.

'Sisters,' Seed says. 'Firstly, let me apologise for my absence over these past two days. The loss of our sister Robyn hit me hard, and I needed time to reflect and repair. These have been the most troubling of times, for every one of us here at Two Cross Farm. But I believe our fortunes are about to turn again, for providence has sent us Pip and Olive and Beebee.'

I glance over at Regine, who is suddenly pale-faced, shocked into silence – as am I. I want to shout out, *no!* I want to save Seed from herself, for she's surely taking leave of her senses, making reckless decisions that will affect every one of us. Whether it's intentional or not, Seed does not look in my direction at all, but instead gestures towards the tiny family, like Jesus casting his hands over the loaves and fish, and it occurs to me that now, for the first time in many weeks, every place setting, every cross, is occupied.

A new thought appears to cross Seed's face, and she asks, 'Pip, tell me, how old are you?'

Pip raises her eyebrows, surprised by the personal question, I think. 'I'm thirty-three,' she replies, and Seed smiles, widely and brightly, like a child presented with a longed-for gift.

'And *we* are thirty-three once more,' she says. 'We are at full strength, my sisters, and together we will flourish!'

Regine and I lock eyes again, and when I turn back to Seed the euphoria in her open expression sends terror to the very core of me. With a jolt, I recall a dreadful time when I'd seen that expression once before.

It was almost thirty years ago, right before she threw herself into the flames.

36. CELINE

Present day

After an hour's surveillance, hiding out in the riverside hedge at the back of Two Cross Farm, Una gives the nod, and Celine drops down at the side of the large greenhouse, careful to stay in the shadows.

She's still twitchy, Celine knows, having left countless messages on Aston's phone, knowing that he's unlikely to respond for a while, tied up as he is interrogating Harry Glass.

'You know we're breaking the law, trespassing like this,' Una whispers beside Celine, passing her the small binoculars. 'Dave Aston will never ask me to help out again.'

Celine raises the binoculars and trains her vision on the rear windows to the commune's main living room, where the curtains are only partially drawn. Through the open French doors, Celine can see the fire is lit, despite the mild evening, and they know Seed and Pip are in that room, because they've already spotted them entering with a tea tray before vanishing from view behind the curtain panel. As far as they can tell, the two women are alone, the lights of the upstairs landing having gone on some time ago. Where are Olive and Beebee now? Have they already put them to bed, or are they in the living room too, out of view behind those pulled drapes?

'Aston will understand,' Celine hisses. 'This is an emergency. We couldn't just sit by and do nothing, Una. Pip and the girls could be in danger. If I'm right about Seed—'

Una brings a finger to her lips. Edging around the greenhouse now, past compost mounds half-shrouded in moonlight, Celine feels a tug on her arm as Una cautions her once again to go slow, not to rush in.

'We don't want to blow it now,' she whispers. 'With any luck Dave will have picked up my message – and, if he has, he'll be on his way. Just hold back a minute, OK?'

Celine snatches her arm away, fear making her prickly. 'You've already made me wait long enough!' It's taking everything in her power not to break into a run and just launch herself through the crack in the door, to wrestle Pip and the girls out of that place for good. Yes, Aston has Harry Glass at the station; yes, it looks as though Vanessa's killer has been found. But that's not what's at stake here. If Seed is as unhinged as Celine believes she could be, they may all be in danger – not just Pip and the girls but every woman under that roof. 'It's gone ten,' she says, trying to keep her voice level, her focus fixed on the back of the house. 'You know they all turn in at nine o'clock. We should rush them now! Take them by surprise!'

'What about Olive and Beebee?' Una says. 'If they're in another room, any aggression on our part could put them at risk. I say we try to reason with Seed, explain that we're here because we care about Pip – not because we fear *her*. This is supposed to be a peaceful community – no one's going to make this easy for us if we use force, Celine.'

Celine breathes deeply, as she tries to rein in her fear and rage. 'OK, we'll do it your way. But we do it *now*.'

Once again, Una checks her mobile phone, and, finding no new messages, she finally concedes. 'Right. We're gonna stay in the shadows. See the log store at the end of the path? On my word, sprint to the far side of it. We'll be able to make it across the lawn in one hit from there. So long as no one's watching from the upstairs windows, they shouldn't see us in the dark.'

Celine follows her instructions to the letter, and moments later they're directly outside the living room, edging their way along the wall until they reach the spot where the drawn curtains run out and the French doors open on to a clear view of this small portion of the path, lit up by the interior lights. They stand, side-by-side, their backs against the living room windows, silently assessing, waiting for the right moment to make their presence known.

'What do you feel about the place so far?' they hear Seed ask. 'I think you could bring a lot to our community. We have plenty of women here who would benefit from your skills; you'd be making a difference to people's lives, young and old.'

'I don't know. I haven't practised my physiotherapy for a while. I'm really rusty,' Pip replies. 'I haven't worked for five or six years.'

'But can you imagine yourself here?' Seed asks.

There's a short pause before Pip's voice drifts towards them. 'I can. I love how you and the women organise yourselves in terms of labour and hierarchy. Also that the group has you as a mentor, but not a dictator.'

'Don't get me wrong,' Seed replies, a smile in her sonorous voice. 'There are rules, Pip. We have a very firm Code of Conduct here, and of course if you decide to stay it would be on the understanding that you subscribe to that Code.'

'Of course.'

'You'll be leaving a lot behind. We don't get to come and go here – that's how we maintain our equality. No one woman has privilege over the next; no one gets to keep more from their old life than another. It's a fresh start, and it's the bedrock of who we are. Are you ready to embrace all of the rules? Because, if you're not, that's OK. You and your daughters will just pack up in the morning and head on your way, in peace, and we'll open the vacancy to the next woman on our waiting list.'

Oh, she's good, Celine thinks. *Smooth.* More concerning is that Pip sounds deadly serious – could she really be considering Two Cross Farm as an option, or is she simply playing the game?

'What about the girls?' Pip asks, her voice small.

There's a delay in Seed's answer, and the sound of movement in the room, of the fire grate rattling and another log being dropped on with a crackle.

'I've spoken with my fellow sisters,' she says. 'And we have decided, in this rarest of occasions, to embrace you all. Your unexpected arrival marks our return to thirty-three at a time when we are desperate for stability. I believe the presence of children will focus our sisters, and give us renewed hope.'

'But the rules—' Pip starts to say, her voice growing shaky with emotion.

'When I say embrace you all, I mean you will be giving your daughters up to become the children of all. Here, you can't "own" your children in the way of the outside world. Here they will have thirty-one mothers. If they stay, you would have to surrender your special status. Or you can leave them with someone outside.'

For a moment, all Celine can hear is the hiss and snap of the fire and her own shallow breathing.

'I don't know if I could give them up like that,' Pip replies. She hesitates before continuing. 'My sister is too busy. They love their aunt, but I couldn't ask her to take them. She's already helped to bring up one set of girls – she won't want to take on another. It wouldn't be right to ask her.'

The words hit Celine like a physical pain, and, afraid, she turns to look at Una. Does Pip mean that? Is she really thinking about this, or is she just reeling Seed in? Cautiously, Celine inches along until she can see a small slice of detail through a gap in the drapes. Pip is sitting beside Seed on the sofa, the only light in the room cast from the full flames of the fire. On the coffee table before them is the tea tray, but they're drinking liquor from small glass tumblers, their contents glistening warmly in the glow. The scene is cosy, and yet, Celine senses, taut with danger.

Pip is gazing into the flames with an expression of deep sadness. 'The girls need *me*.'

Seed lays a hand on her forearm. 'And they would still have you. But these women need you too,' she says. 'You could work wonders here, Pip. And just think: no more pleasing others; no more fear, or responsibility, or oppression. No more wondering what mood your husband will be in each night; no more trickery around money and possessions and rights. Here we only exist for the community, for each other. You want that kind of equality, don't you? Here, you – the three of you – could have it all. You could shed your material shackles, and, at the same time, have everything.'

Una nudges Celine, holding up her mobile phone to show her the text that has just come in from Dave Aston:

Tried calling you but straight to ansaphone. Need to know – in residents book did you spot the name SANDY? Call me straight back? Also have new breakthrough from forensics – we WILL be searching 2XF first thing tomorrow. Call me back! D.

A second later, he follows with:

PS Harry Glass released – insufficient evidence to keep him.

'What the hell . . .?' Celine mouths.

'Shit,' Una whispers, keying in a swift reply. *What about Falmer?*

Dave: *Still no sign of him.*

Una stares at the screen for a moment, before signing off: *Can't speak now. At 2XF. Will call soon to explain.*

Through the glass they see Pip knock back her drink. On the mantelpiece, an earthenware jug is filled with garden flowers, its shadow thrown large against the wall by the flickering light of an old-fashioned oil lamp, giving the room the feel of another age. Seed takes the empty glass from her, placing it on the low table as Pip's expression crumples and she brings shaking hands to her face. Without hesitation, Seed draws her close, cradling her head against her shoulder, caressing her hair. It's a strangely intimate, almost maternal scene, the two women lit up only by the light of the flickering flames in the grate.

A swift reply from Dave appears.

GET OUT NOW. We've matched an original fingerprint from Vanessa's 2005 records to SEED.

But when Una holds it up to show Celine she can barely take in the information, so fixed is she on her youngest sister and that strange woman beyond the glass doors.

'You know you're safe here?' Seed says. 'You and the girls.'

Just as Celine decides she cannot hold back for a moment longer, there's a creak from the inner doorway and Bramble appears.

'Seed!' she remonstrates, looking at her watch. 'Why are you both still up?'

In one burst, Celine and Una push through the French doors, and Seed springs back, away from Pip who glares at them in wet-eyed surprise.

'Get over here, Pip,' Celine commands. When Pip shakes her head, Celine strides across the room, grabbing her sister by the wrist and dragging her to standing. 'Now!' she yells. 'Where are the girls?'

'They're asleep in Bramble's room – they're only a few doors away, down the hall.' Pip shakes her wrist free and stands reluctantly at her sister's shoulder.

Seed is rising too, backing away, a cornered expression in her eyes. 'What do you want?' she asks, her fingers fumbling for the fire poker at the hearthside, which she raises in threat.

'Seed, no,' Bramble says, stepping towards her. '*No*. You know that's not the answer.'

'I thought this was a peaceful community?' Una says, calmly. 'Seed, you don't want things to end like this, do you?'

'What do you mean, "end"?' Bramble asks, and this time it is she who looks fearful.

'Please,' Seed implores, lowering the poker, sinking into the fireside chair, apparently exhausted. '*Please* just leave us alone.'

Celine takes a step forward, closing the gap between the women in the room, as Una hangs back by the doors with Pip. Shadows rise and fall with the increased movement of the fire, the spring breeze through the open doors feeding its flames. 'Pip is my sister,' she says, addressing Seed, and it is clear from the confused tilt of her head that she had no idea. 'Just like Vanessa was.'

'Bramble?' Seed says, looking suddenly young and vulnerable – no longer the imposing creature she had seemed on that first sighting barely two weeks ago, as she confidently addressed the press crowd outside Two Cross Farm. She's weeping now, tears streaking her cheeks, causing her scars to glisten white in the half-light. 'Make them leave, Bramble. Please.'

There's another creak in the doorway, and they all turn to see little Olive standing there in her crumpled knickers and vest, rubbing her eye sleepily with one fist, her careworn cuddly spider held limply in the other.

'Take Olive and get her and Beebee ready to leave,' Una directs Bramble, stopping Pip from reaching for her child. 'She doesn't need to hear this,' she says with a shake of her head.

Celine is focused on Seed beside the fireplace, whose spirit seems so fractured, all hope apparently gone.

'*Now*, please!' Una demands when Bramble hesitates. The old woman blinks and nods, before leading the little girl from the room on hurried feet.

For a second no one speaks, as Celine studies Seed, wondering how the police force could have got this so wrong for such a long time. If she has correctly understood the meaning of Dave Aston's text, he surely believes that Vanessa's killer is *here*; that the person who took their beloved sister from them is Seed.

Unable to contain her rage for a moment longer, Celine lunges forward. 'You murdered our sister!' she yells as Una blocks her passage, her pleas for caution falling on deaf ears. When Seed doesn't respond to the accusation, Celine's anger rises further still and without thought she shunts Una aside so that she's looming over the woman, demanding the truth. 'You killed Vanessa! Won't you even deny it?'

Seed appears unable to speak.

'Step away, Celine,' Una hisses, but Celine is lost to her rage.

'And what about Susan? You know something about her death too, Seed, I'm certain of it!' she shouts louder still, prodding

Seed's shoulder with the tips of her fingers, desperate for some kind of reaction.

Seed, once so dignified, now appears diminished in her fireside chair. The flames flicker brightly, making strange shapes of her shadowed face, and she lowers her gaze with an expression of – what? Shame? Guilt?

'Did you kill Robyn too? And those other women – the other Founding Sisters? Where are they now? What have you done with them?'

As Celine leans in closer still, Una hooks a hand under her armpit, forcibly yanking her away. 'Celine! This isn't helping.'

She takes a staggering step backwards, only now remembering that Pip is with them, and she casts about the dimly lit room to see her sitting on the floor beside the sofa, her knees pulled tight beneath her chin. It's what she used to do when she was little, Celine recalls in a hot flash of emotion, whenever she'd wake in the night and find Mum still gone. She's scared, and Celine realises with remorse that it is she who is scaring her.

'Why won't you just tell us what you did to Vanessa?' Celine demands wearily, sounding out the words slowly, regaining her calm. 'Your fingerprints have been found on her clothing, Seed – and we know you were one of the last people to see her alive. Have you nothing to say?'

It's as though the lights have just come on again behind Seed's eyes, because suddenly she cries out in frustration, striking herself in the head with a closed fist, again and again. Pip flinches in shock, covering her face, releasing a low, horrified groan.

'I didn't kill Vanessa!' Seed protests as she allows her hands to fall to her lap. 'How could I have killed Vanessa? She was my friend; my dearest, kindest friend. I could *never* have hurt her.'

Celine steps back, to perch at the edge of the sofa, resting a hand on Pip's shoulder and silently blinking across at Seed in confusion and sorrow.

'Then who did kill her, Seed?' Una asks, taking the facing seat beside the fireplace.

Seed nods her head once, as though some great decision has been reached.

'I need Bramble,' she says softly. 'There's too much to tell on my own.' She lowers her head again, appearing to study her large, graceful hands.

And it's then that Celine remembers the words of Sister Angelique, and her description of the young man who left that newborn baby on the night of Susan's death. *'I caught a close look at those hands,'* she'd said, ' *– they were large, strong and elegant. Like a pianist's . . .'*

All at once, Celine's fight is extinguished. 'Oh, Seed,' she says, as so much of the puzzle – so much of what's been troubling her – slots into place. 'It really is time you told us the truth, Bramble or no Bramble. You need to tell us everything.'

37. BRAMBLE

Present day, Two Cross Farm

Beebee is still sleeping, and without complaint little Olive clambers back into bed beside her, drifting straight off again as I pack their belongings.

The light from the corridor streaks in over the wooden boards, and I move around the room quietly, feeling sick at the thought of what Seed is saying to those women in there, of how much she's giving away. The two angels sleep on, still too young to understand the complications of the adult world, and I envy them this short moment of innocence in their lifetime. Sitting gently on the edge of the bed, I note how roundly inexpressive children's faces are in slumber, as though sleep has the power to erase any concerns they may carry in their waking hours. I wonder how long it will be before they're immune to the protection of their youth; how long before their parents' damaged relationship takes its toll, or they fall prey to some sick man's version of love and family. They're safer here, surely, in the company of women who will only care for and nurture them.

Where the toddler is fair like her mother, little Olive resembles her aunts. With her dark curls and fine arching brows, she's just like that woman, Celine, who stands in our living room now, making accusations and threats; and she's like Vanessa too, Seed's beloved friend whom we lost all those years ago. Seed's voice drifts along the corridor, and I know she is setting our secrets free, unleashing them with God knows what outcome. I let my memories roam around the half-lit corners of the bedroom, for it was here Vanessa slept on the night that man broke in and stole her away, almost a year since she'd first joined us and helped to bring our Seed back to life.

Within a month or two of Vanessa's arrival, she and Seed, still six years yet from being made custodian, had developed a friendship so deep and strong, you might imagine they had known each other their entire lives. There was something about that girl, something so open and refreshing and funny and true, and when Seed persuaded Fern to let Vanessa have the ground-floor bedroom next to hers they became inseparable, often breaking the bedtime curfew to sit up late laughing and chatting into the night. I'd never had a friendship like it myself, and I, like my fellow Founding Sisters, was happy to turn a blind eye to such small rule-breaks in the face of Seed's happiness. It was not only Seed whose spirit was revived by Vanessa, but the rest of us too. Yes, we had got the old Seed back, but Vanessa was a joy in her own right, happy and grateful to be here, so hard-working and generous that her application for the marking ceremony was unanimously accepted after six months, so certain were we all that she was here to stay. It seemed she cared not one jot about Seed's scars or differences, and for a while life was good again.

As I grow older and more cynical, it seems to me that the way of the world is that all good things must die. Because, less than a year after Seed's fortunes had taken a positive turn, that man – that *devil* – came into our lives, on a still, cool night in March. In my solitary upstairs bedroom – I had not yet moved to the ground floor – I woke from a deep sleep, to the jarring sound of a man's voice downstairs, of heavy boots rampaging through the hallway, as he threw open doors and roared Vanessa's name. Breathlessly, I dressed, before rushing on to the landing in my slippers, where Kathy and Regine were busy urging the other women to return to their dorms. Our community was under attack, and from this monster's cries it was clear that Vanessa was his target.

'What about Fern?' Regine whispered as we started down the stairs. 'Her room is down there too. Kathy and I will go to her; you check on Seed and Vanessa.'

Downstairs in the milky moonlit corridor, all was at once still and quiet. Behind me, with a fierce snap of her fingers, Kathy directed two or three gawping women to retreat back up to their rooms, and within seconds the hallway was clear again.

'Shouldn't we call the police?' I whispered as we reached the bottom step, my heart hammering against my ribcage, cold sweat prickling at the back of my neck.

'Absolutely not!' came Fern's hissed reply as she stepped out of the shadows to join us, a large kitchen knife in her hand.

The man's voice had ceased less than a minute earlier, and now we stood in the darkness, four Founding Sisters, tuning in to the sounds of the house, waiting to make our move. Our silent attention was fixed on the closed door of the far bedroom – Seed's room – and we began to approach on soft feet, Fern at the front, her knife poised ready to strike. Vanessa's door, the next one along, stood open, the room empty.

'Where is she?' Kathy asked, terror in her voice, her hand grasping for mine. '*Where is Vanessa?*'

With a bellow, that man came bursting out of Seed's room, dragging Vanessa screaming by her hair, at first unaware of our presence. At a glance we could see Seed lying on the wooden boards of her bedroom, her face a bloody pulp, but she was moving, attempting to get up.

Our leader, Fern, still strong and fearless at fifty-nine, rushed at the man, plunging the knife hard towards his shoulder blade, but he'd seen her, and he dodged sufficiently to only suffer a grazing wound. With his one free arm he knocked the knife from Fern's hand, swiping her jaw with a fierce backhand and sending her reeling. As we rushed to her aid, he – Jem Falmer, we would later learn – hoisted Vanessa to her feet and shook her like a rag doll, punctuating his words.

'Bitches,' he spat. 'Come near me again and I'll kill you. I fucking swear I will.' When it was clear we weren't moving, he dragged Vanessa, half dazed, out towards the living room and the French doors beyond, her bare feet scraping over the boards as she fought with the little strength she had left. 'Think you can just leave me, do you, Ness?' he snarled into her hair as he wrestled her out through the doors. 'Think you can make a mug out of me?'

As Fern retrieved the knife, Kathy helped Seed to her feet, and Regine hurried back along the corridor to see off another cluster of women who'd started tiptoeing down the stairs.

'Get back to your rooms!' she instructed in a tone not to be argued with. 'We have this covered! Away, all of you!'

From my position, I could see through the glass at the back of the house, to where Falmer was now hauling Vanessa across the starlit lawn. Helplessly I turned to look at Seed, her cropped head uncovered, her absence of daytime attire rendering her exposed, vulnerable. Like a woman emerging from a trance, her blood-streaked vision cleared and her expression altered, and with a war cry she raced past us, intent on pursuing Vanessa's attacker. Without hesitation we followed, all of us terrified of what Seed might do to protect her friend, and of the harm she might come to.

At the far end of the gardens, by the greenhouse, Falmer had Vanessa pinned to the damp grass, his stocky grip hard on her neck as he landed blow after blow on her pale, slack face.

'Didn't you get my message, bitches?' he roared, turning his head in our direction. 'I told you to stay out of our business.'

Across the lawn Seed sprinted, her nightshirt billowing, thin, muscular arms pumping with fury, as she launched herself at that crouching man. With a thud, the pair tumbled clear of the girl, Falmer's attentions now firmly on Seed.

Regine was at the back door, standing guard, ensuring the scene was witnessed by none other than the Founding Sisters, while Kathy knelt beside Vanessa, turning her on her side, attempting to get her breathing again. I, God help me, stood useless, too paralysed to act, softly murmuring what could only be described as a prayer. I scanned the area for Fern, who seemed to have vanished into nowhere.

Falmer was now standing over Seed, who lay in a crumpled heap on the grass, the sharp angles of her ribs protruding unguarded beneath her thin white nightgown.

'What the hell are you?' Falmer sneered as he took in her appearance fully. Dispassionately, he kicked her hard in the side, like a child testing a dead animal for life, and turned to us in disgust. 'What sick kind of place is this?'

To my shock, Vanessa was now sitting up, both of her eyes swollen shut, her head turned blindly towards the sound of Falmer's voice. 'Seed?' she called out, and then, again, in panic, 'Seed! Jem, if you've hurt her—' she started to say, and that was all it took. With a roar, Falmer was upon her again, pummelling her face, punctuating his vile words with his fists, squeezing the last drops of life from her throat.

And that was when Fern reappeared, our wise guardian, stealthily striding across the dewy grass with the garden spade held against her shoulder like a rifle. As Seed staggered to her feet, the atmosphere shifted from terror to inevitability. Even Falmer felt it, I think, because for a fraction of a second he paused, tilting his jaw a little, sensing the change. But it didn't save him, because our sister, that leader of women, swung the spade high in the night air, and brought it down hard, felling the beast with a single solid strike to the side of his head. The man dropped from his prey in a wounded slump, and our sister stood square, breathing raggedly, knuckles gripped white around the spade handle, distraught eyes on Vanessa.

Beneath the stars, we five gathered around that poor, darling girl on the damp lawn, but we knew that our sister's brave action had come just seconds too late. Vanessa was already dead.

Along the hall, the low thrum of voices continues, and desperately I try to work out what to do next; how to help Seed. It's only a matter of time before those women join the dots, and then it will be too late to do anything other than give ourselves up. I think of old Fern sleeping in the room next door, as oblivious to the drama as these two sleeping babes at my side. I think of Fern and Regine, and Seed, and me, the four remaining Founding Sisters, and I think of everything we have achieved in the past forty-four years, and everything we have concealed, and celebrated, and lied about, and overcome. When the police find out the truth about Robyn, we will lose it all. Not just our lives here at Two Cross Farm, but our liberty. How would we fare in prison, Regine at her age; me at mine? Would they really send an eighty-four-year-old away? The thought of my darling

Seed incarcerated alongside the worst of all mankind makes me lightheaded with fear, and I think I would do anything rather than see her face that unjust punishment. There is so much I am unsure of, and so much to fear. But one thing I am certain of is that our secrets are about to be uncovered – all of them – and I urgently need to act.

I lean over the bed and kiss my sleeping girls on the tops of their heads. 'You wait here, little ones,' I whisper, careful not to wake them as I tuck their blanket beneath their chins. 'I'll be back to check on you in a little while.'

38. CELINE

Present day

Seed trails off, the pain of retelling this tragic story etched on her face.

'She died here? Vanessa died here?' Celine finds her fingers are laced with Pip's, as both sisters silently weep for their lost sibling.

'We tried everything to get her breathing again,' Seed says, softly, 'but she was gone. There was nothing we could do for her.'

'You could have called an ambulance. You could have called the police,' Una says, leaning across from her seat beside the fire. She touches Seed's knee with a light hand. 'Why didn't you call the police straight away?'

'We – Fern wouldn't hear of it. We had so much to lose, if the police had started looking into everything else – if they'd learnt about Susan and the child – about *me*. We might have lost the trust of our women altogether. It could have meant the end of the community, the end of Two Cross Farm. Where would all those women in need go then? We couldn't do that to them.

We had to stand strong.' She glances around the room, her gaze resting momentarily on the wall of black and white photographs. Rising, she crosses the room and reaches for one particular portrait, hung high; one which Celine recognises instantly as Vanessa. Seed unhooks it from the wall and passes it to Celine and Pip. It captures everything of their beloved sister, the spark in her expression caught as though the photograph contains her very essence.

'So you just dumped her, at Brighton pier?' Pip whispers.

'*No*. That wasn't how it was. We were devastated; *I* was devastated. You have to believe me. Vanessa was my closest friend, my dearest sister.'

'She was *our* sister,' Pip corrects her, but her tone lacks any punch.

'I know,' Seed replies, bowing her head. 'Fern was all for giving her a burial here, before the other women woke and discovered what had happened, but Vanessa had told me all about you two, and I fought Fern. I refused to go along with it. So, we compromised, and we took Vanessa to Brighton in the dead of night, leaving her at the pier where she'd be quickly found. I swear, it was to spare you, her real sisters, the pain of not knowing where she'd gone.'

Celine recognises the truth of Seed's words; *not* knowing where Vanessa had been all these years would surely have caused them so much more agony than the certainty that she was dead.

'And Jem Falmer?' Una asks. 'Where did he go?'

Seed glances towards the French doors and the darkness beyond. 'The blow to his head killed him. He's buried in the garden.'

There's a pause, while Celine follows the direction of Seed's eyes, coming to rest on the two large compost mounds they'd passed earlier. 'But that's not possible, Seed,' Celine says. 'He sent us a note to warn us off, just this week. He's right here in Arundel!'

Seed shakes her head, apology in her expression. 'It was Bramble who put that through your door, Celine. It was part of a note he'd sent us a day or two before that night he broke in, warning us to give Vanessa up – we'd kept it in the safe upstairs all these years, I don't know why. We hoped your police contacts would be diverted by the handwriting, and it looks as though they were. We thought, if you believed you were under threat – well, we just wanted you to leave us alone.'

And Celine and Una *had* believed they were under threat; in their hope and desperation, they'd fallen for it completely.

'Jem's dead,' Celine says, more to herself than anyone else, as she tries to suppress her shock. 'Fern really killed him, Seed?'

But Seed's attention is lost to the flames again, and there's no drawing her on the subject of Jem's death.

Across the room, Una, Pip and Celine gaze at one another in stunned silence. They've done it. Finally, they know what happened to Vanessa. It should be enough for Celine, and she knows they should give up while they're ahead – pack up the girls, get the hell out of here and leave the rest of this to Dave Aston and his team to sort out. But she can't leave it, and neither, it seems, can Una.

'OK, so, we know Susan died in childbirth,' she says as Seed reaches for another log, dropping it on to the fire. 'But what about her daughter, Robyn Siegle?'

Seed snaps into focus at the mention of Robyn's name.

'You *know* that Robyn was Susan's daughter?' she whispers. 'No one knows about that.'

'Well, we do,' Celine replies, her tone more gentle now. 'We also know she was left as a newborn at the Poor Clares convent – and I'm pretty sure it was you who took her there.'

Seed's eyes dart briefly to meet hers; an admission.

'If Jem Falmer was buried in your garden fifteen years ago,' Celine goes on, 'he certainly couldn't have killed Robyn Siegle a fortnight ago. So, who did? Was it Harry Glass? Did Harry Glass murder Robyn?'

Seed's expression morphs into confusion. 'I've never even heard of Harry Glass.'

39. BRAMBLE

Present day, Two Cross Farm

We can't stay here now.

As I pass into the hallway I can hear Seed in the living room, pouring all our secrets out, and when I hear Robyn's name spoken I push on towards the stairs and hurry up to Regine's bedroom on the first floor.

'Regine?' I whisper, entering unannounced, flipping on the light switch as I close the door behind me. She wakes with a start, cursing me noisily and shielding her eyes from the overhead bulb. 'Regine,' I repeat. 'We have to get Fern out of here.'

She drops her arm and gingerly eases her feet to the floor, scowling deeply. 'Whaddaya mean, "out of here"?' she asks, wincing, already reaching for her clothes. 'What's happenin'?'

'They're back. They're down there – Celine and Una – and they've got Seed talking. That girl, Pip, she's their sister – she's Celine and Vanessa's sister.'

'Jeez,' Regine whistles, her movements speeding up now.

'Regine, Seed's telling them everything! They know how Vanessa died, they know that Falmer is buried in the back garden – and, right now, they're hearing all about Robyn.'

'*All* about Robyn?' she asks, gravely. She hobbles over to her dresser and runs a brush through her long grey hair, allowing me to take over when her stiff knuckles struggle.

'*All of it*. They know Susan was Robyn's mother; and I'm fairly certain they're about to find out the rest.' I fasten a band at the end of Regine's plait and drop the thick braid over her shoulder.

She turns then, and lays her hands on me, clasping my forearms and steadying me with her sharp, intelligent gaze. 'You were right to wake me, honey,' she says, and I'm strangely taken aback by her affectionate tone. 'Once they know about Robyn, we're done for. Fern is done for. It's the end.'

I reach into my apron pocket and draw out the keys to the truck, pressing them into her hand. 'You go and get Fern,' I tell her, my fingers already on the door, my words coming fast. 'I need to fetch a few things from the office – and then I'll get Seed. We'll see you out there. Get the engine started.' I hesitate a moment. 'Do you think she'll come?' I ask.

Regine smiles sadly. 'She's reached the end of the line, Bren. If Seed has given herself up, we're just gonna have to let her go.'

There's nothing more to say, and in heavy silence I leave Regine, stopping in Seed's office to gather up the Last Will envelopes of the Founding Sisters, before returning downstairs. My soul feels weighed down. I pause in the darkness between my bedroom and the room where Seed sits talking beside the fire, and, when I hear the next words she speaks, I know Regine is right, that we have to set her adrift.

'We killed her,' she tells them, and her tone is at once forlorn and distant.

40. BRAMBLE

Two weeks ago, Two Cross Farm

None of us had meant harm to that poor girl, Robyn, and if Seed had been truthful with us – told us what Robyn really meant to her from the start – perhaps this could all have been avoided. Perhaps she could have been spared. But on that day, Robyn's final day, no one was quite themselves. I was exhausted, Seed was entirely distracted by Robyn's planned departure, and Fern's confusion was at an all-time high. Everything at Two Cross Farm seemed to be running out of sequence, out of order. The previous night, Fern had kept me and Regine up in the early hours, thrashing about in her old office, rambling about new number connections she had made in her sleep and creating illegible lists of instructions she wanted us to follow. She'd convinced herself that the number 33 was intrinsically linked with 666, the number of the beast, of the apocalypse, of *men*. She was raving. Over and over again, she demanded to see Dr Kathy, and I knew it was no good telling her that Kathy had been dead ten years now, because Fern's mind was no longer in the here and now – it was stuck somewhere in 1976, and there was no bringing her back.

The atmosphere between Seed and young Robyn had been strained all week long, but she wouldn't tell me why, and the more I badgered her about it that morning, the more she withdrew. That same afternoon, I asked Seed to meet me in the basement laundry room, below the main house, so we could talk in private while the other women took their tea. At last, she admitted that she was in turmoil about Robyn's plans to leave, and when she denied that their relationship was anything more than platonic I knew she was keeping something back from me.

'Seed,' I said, 'you put Robyn forward for the marking ceremony just a month after arriving here; that's unheard of. Why? What's so very special about this girl?'

I intended to reassure her, to tell her this was just a crush, a brief infatuation that she'd soon forget. But then Robyn herself appeared at the top of the stone steps, descending into the steamy room, suitcase in hand, calling Seed's name over the rumbling din of the washing machines.

As the girl approached, Seed clutched at my wrist and whispered to me, 'I'm sorry, Bramble. I will tell you everything, I promise.'

'Robyn,' Seed pleaded as the girl drew closer. 'Please hear me out, won't you? You don't have to go straight away – just stay and hear what I have to say?'

Robyn looked awkwardly from Seed to me, embarrassed, I could tell, at Seed's pleading tone.

'You came looking for answers about your parents,' Seed said, taking a step closer, 'and I've been selfish and cowardly with the truth. I haven't been honest with you, and I regret it. I – I don't really know where to begin.' She brought her hands

308

to her mouth, as though searching for a way to stop the words from tumbling out.

I was confused; who were these parents she spoke of? In the three months that Robyn had been here, I had been aware of the uncommon closeness she shared with Seed, and I'd sensed a secret between them but this – what on earth could it mean?

'Seed?' I ventured, my fear rising. 'What are you talking about? I know nothing of this.'

'Bramble, Robyn came to Two Cross Farm to find out more about her birth mother,' Seed said, extending a hand which the girl would not accept. 'She wanted to know more about Susan.'

This was Susan's child? Was it possible? *This* was the baby Fern had sent to the convent twenty-five years ago, on the night we'd lost our dear sister? How could she have found us, when we had left no clue to the baby's history, no note or explanation? And why had Seed concealed Robyn's true identity; the purpose of her visit?'

'I knew I was an abandoned baby,' Robyn explained. 'My adoption papers said I'd been left with the Poor Clares convent, but there was no record of a mother.'

'So how . . .?' I asked, unable to form the full sentence.

'It actually didn't take much to work it out,' Robyn said, 'because when I went through the local newspapers I found a report on a young woman found dead around the exact same time. Eventually, I tracked down her death certificate in public records, and – well, with her death ruled as post-partum trauma, it all fit.'

I glanced at Seed, who stood beside me, eyes downcast. I was shocked and hurt to think that she no longer confided in me as she once had, when I had so willingly given my life to her care. Fern always said that Seed had the blessing of thirty-two mothers, but really I was the one who had *truly* embraced that role, who had picked Seed up each time she fell, sung her to sleep when the night fears crept in. The realisation that she no longer needed me had been a long time coming, but standing there in the clammy heat of the laundry room, hearing all this from Robyn instead of Seed – well, I'd never felt loneliness quite like it.

'Why didn't you say anything?' I asked Robyn. 'Why all the secrecy?'

'Seed told me it was best not to. She didn't think you'd approve,' Robyn said, apologetically. 'Listen, Seed, I'm so grateful for everything you've done for me, for all you've been able to tell me about Susan,' she went on, 'but I've explained to you, it's time for me to leave now. If it's true that you really don't know the identity of my father, there's nothing more for me here. I need to get back to my own family and forget about chasing the past.'

What would Fern make of this – or Regine – if they knew that Susan's daughter had returned to us, to find out her truth? I didn't know whether to be glad she was leaving, or curious, or afraid . . .

'Robyn,' I said, 'I hope you won't make trouble for us, now you know about your mother. I hope we will be allowed to continue in peace?'

She nodded briskly and moved to pick up her bag, but Seed held on to her sleeve, not letting her go, and I felt the atmosphere in the basement room tilt. Suddenly it felt as though everything was at risk, for if Susan was Robyn's mother, then Seed—

'I have to tell her, Bramble!' Seed cried out, firing a terrified glance in my direction.

All I could do was stand on and watch.

Her voice shook as she spoke, and she hung on to that girl's sleeve as though her life depended on it. 'I'm not what I seem,' she began. 'I've been lying to you – to everyone for that matter – and I can't do it any more. Bramble,' she whispered low, turning to me, 'I have to tell her! I have to tell Robyn the truth!'

'What truth?' Robyn demanded, snatching her arm away. 'Tell me *what* truth, Seed?'

'That I'm not just some woman who took pity on you. That I haven't been selflessly helping you find out about Susan. I'm a liar! And I'm a fraud, Robyn! I'm your – your . . .' But here she ran out of words, never before having uttered them to a living soul, never having let them take on life.

In a wave of understanding, I knew this was my moment; this was my chance to support Seed, to demonstrate my unconditional love and support of her, and I stepped forward to speak. 'Robyn,' I said, drawing on some unknown strength. 'Seed was not born a woman, not in the sense that you will understand.'

A stunned silence ballooned in the steamy air between us, and I felt the shame pouring off Seed in waves.

'Seed was born male, by conventional standards, at least. Robyn, I know this will be a shock to you, but she and Susan were very much in love when you were conceived – and I can attest that neither of them wanted to give you away.' When the girl didn't respond, I told her, 'If indeed you are Susan's daughter, then Seed is your father.'

I'll never forget the blank expression on Robyn's heart-shaped face, as the implications of this truth fell into place. The truth that Seed had deceived her; the truth that Seed was her father. That Seed was a man.

Long moments passed, as Robyn looked from me to Seed, to the bag in her hand, to the foot of the stairs and her way back home – away from this madness.

Seed must have seen those thoughts passing over the girl's face too, because with no warning she reached out in panic, making a grab for Robyn's bag, trying to grapple it from her hands. 'Please don't go, Robyn – not yet,' she begged. 'Not when I've only just found you!'

As though a light had come on, Robyn's expression shifted from disbelief to confusion, before she grew suddenly hysterical. 'You're lying!' she cried out. 'No one in their right mind would string someone along like that – you've got to be lying, both of you!'

Sobbing herself by this point, Seed reached for her again, to comfort her I'm sure, but Robyn scratched at her arm as she wrestled herself free, before turning to run up the stone steps with Seed in her wake.

'How can I stay now?' Robyn gasped as together they came to a halt on the top step. 'How can I stay when you've deceived me like this? All those months I wrote to you, when you could have told me, could have broken it to me before I even got here. You said my father was a local man, that only Susan knew his name. But here you are, claiming he – he is *you*?'

'Please calm down,' Seed pleaded, bringing her hands together as though in prayer. 'Just give me a chance. Please don't just write me off—'

Robyn pulled back in anger. 'What am I meant to think, Seed? Is this just some kind of sick game to you? This is a women's refuge, for pity's sake. It's not just me you've lied to. You're tricking *everyone*. It's not right! You know I have to tell them, don't you? These women have to know who you really are.'

In that moment, all I knew was we couldn't let Robyn go, couldn't risk the damage her revelations would wreak, and I too made to ascend the stairs, but was halted at the sight of Fern, who seemed to appear beside them from nowhere.

'He-devil,' she muttered, coming between the pair and aiming a curved finger at Seed. She pulled a bemused face, not unkind, and for a moment she looked like no more than a child. 'What's up with yer skin, boy?' she asked.

Startled and upset, Seed batted her hand away, and with a shriek Fern flinched, staggering backwards to collide with Robyn. And, in one smooth, slow-motion journey, Robyn tumbled from top step to bottom and landed at my feet with an unearthly crack.

For long seconds, everything stood still, the only sound that of the laundry drums rumbling against the basement walls, drowning out the everyday goings-on of the house above. I thought perhaps I was dreaming, that this was some terrible nightmare, but that thought was short-lived, because the next thing I heard was the guttural cry of Seed, as she raced down, and bent, shrouded in steam, over the lifeless body of her daughter.

'She took her from me once before,' Seed groaned, her anguished face meeting mine before she turned to look back up the steps to where Fern stood on the floor above, gazing down in confusion. 'And, like a coward, I did nothing. And now—' Seed fell against me, slumping into my arms '—she's taken her again.'

There was nothing I could do for Seed but hold her, stroke her desolate brow, and wait for Regine to come and take Fern back to her room.

'We'll sort it out, Seed,' I told her. 'Trust me, my darling. We always find a way.'

And may God strike me down for admitting it, but my enduring thought was this: our secret is safe. *Seed's* secret is safe, and life will go on.

Now, in the midnight quiet of my bedroom, I pull on my coat and shoes and look down at the two little creatures asleep on the bed, and my heart cracks a little. They didn't ask to be born into a world so broken, and I fear for them out there, in that man's world, with only their tiny, vulnerable mother to protect them. Is she capable? Is she up to the task? How wonderful it would be, I consider in these few seconds of clear, plain thought, to take them with me, to keep them near.

I would have made a good mother, I think, in another life. I scoop up Beebee's little beanie dog and place it on the bed beside my bag. She'd be lost without that, I know.

41. CELINE

Present day, Two Cross Farm

A small, unconscious part of Celine knows what's coming even before Seed starts to unwind the scarves of her turban, letting them fall away to reveal a close-cropped head, further disfigured by burn scars. Seed's expression is one of resignation, and even when Pip gasps in disbelief she doesn't falter. With light fingers, Seed unravels her neck scarf, shrugging off her knitted poncho, so that she's standing there in a sleeveless vest, revealing the lean, muscular neck and shoulders of a man.

'It had to end eventually,' she says, her voice low and mournful. 'The police know, don't they, Una? They're coming for me?'

There is shock all around. Una, who has been furtively messaging Aston, now stands beside the French doors, hands thrust deep in her jacket pockets, apparently lost for words.

'They are,' Celine replies, transfixed by the figure before her, who has transformed before them in the space of seconds. How could she have missed it, when now it seems so plain to see?

'It's just a matter of minutes. But, yes, they're coming. Right now, they believe you killed those women, Seed, but this is your chance to put them straight. Just tell them exactly what you've told us: that Falmer murdered Vanessa. That Robyn's death was a terrible accident.'

Celine reflects on her early impressions of Seed, when she'd first seen her standing, graceful and commanding, on that podium outside the gates of Two Cross Farm. She was lean and elegant, tall for a woman, sure, and perhaps not conventionally 'feminine', but Celine hadn't suspected this at all. She'd seen what she wanted to see: a confident leader, a fearless protector of women. And really, is that not what Seed is? If what she says is true, Seed fought almost to the death to save Vanessa, and Celine has witnessed herself the lengths to which she has gone to maintain the sanctity of this community, to keep these women sheltered as she, and Fern before her, had vowed to. Does she see herself as female or male? Does it matter? Watching her sitting there in the firelight, stripped of her turban and scarves, Celine feels profound compassion towards Seed the human being.

She glances at Una, who gives a small jerk of her head to suggest they ought to leave. But Celine's not ready.

'Seed, how did you convince all these women that you were one of them, for so many years?' Celine is embarrassed by her question the moment it is out, but it needs asking. It's what everyone in this room wants to know; what the police will want to know.

Seed smiles gently, making it easy on her. 'I'd been raised taking care to cover my differences, since the youngest age, and I find people don't stare too long when your face is damaged in the way mine is.'

It's true, Celine thinks. She was conscious of it herself on that first visit, of wanting to look more closely at Seed, but fearing she might seem rude.

'And in the early years,' Seed continued, 'my life never *felt* like deception. I was raised in an all-women community. It was all I'd ever known.' She hesitates a moment, glancing at the hallway door, perhaps wondering how the older woman, Bramble, will feel about these revelations. 'I didn't meet a single man until I was seventeen years old, when I started helping with the market business in town. I'd been raised as a female, I was in all but my obvious differences a female, and for a large part of my childhood I never had much cause to question it. In all my forty-three years, with the exception of Vanessa, only the Founding Sisters ever knew the full truth, although I am sure there have been a few who suspected there was something unusual about me.' She pauses a moment, her gaze falling on Pip, who is now rising to her feet at Una's subtle prompting. Seed gestures towards her facial scars. 'I was fourteen when I had my – my "accident". My skin was damaged so badly that when I reached puberty I never grew facial hair the way a normal man would. Kathy, our doctor, and Fern, both came to the conclusion that my instability at that time was due to my "differences", to a "biological glitch" they said they could help me with. They started me on some conventional medication, which Kathy had somehow managed to obtain, and for a while I took it. Long enough to start developing some female characteristics and to arrest the deepening of my voice.'

'They gave you *hormones*?' I ask, astounded at the recklessness of these women.

'Yes, but I soon began to doubt it was good for me, and I stopped taking the medication.' Seed pauses again, looking at each of them in turn, clearly wanting them to understand who she really is, how she'd arrived here, through no design of her own.

Una moves closer, and leans against the arm of the sofa. 'How could they do that to a child?'

317

'They thought they were doing the right thing,' Seed says, 'I do believe that. And they thought it was the medication that had levelled me out and made me happy again, but really it was Susan who'd changed everything for the better, once we'd been allowed to share a room.' She lowers her eyes, and it is painful to witness the shame she clearly feels.

'But wasn't she much older than you?' Celine asks.

'She was, but it didn't matter to us. Susan was hardly more than a child herself when she came here, and so I was her first love too. Initially it really was just friendship, but over time our relationship developed into something more – by the time she fell pregnant I was eighteen, and she was thirty-five.'

There is a pause as they take in the huge implications of Seed's admission: Robyn really was her daughter.

'And you and Vanessa? Were you in love too?' Pip asks.

Seed's eyes glisten as she gazes back at the three women assembled before her, and Celine suspects that she has, for most of her life, lived with great regrets. 'I *loved* her,' Seed replies, with feeling. 'After Susan, I'd never dared to hope I might find a true friend again, and then I did, in Vanessa. But I promise you, it was only ever friendship. She meant so much to me and I miss her every day . . .' Her words trail off with the pain of remembering. She reaches beneath the neckline of her vest and removes a pendant, unhooking it over her head and passing it to Celine with care.

'The evil eye?' Celine murmurs, turning the blue glass nugget over in her hands, recalling Georgie's description of the gift she'd sent from Greece. 'This was Vanessa's?'

'I was only looking after it for her,' Seed replies. 'It's yours now.'

For a moment there's nothing but the sound of the fire, and it is as though Seed has forgotten they're there altogether, so lost is she in her memories. Faint voices trail in through the French doors and the four women turn in that direction, seeing the back lawn lit up by the lights of a vehicle turning at the front gate.

'That'll be DI Aston,' Una says calmly, and Seed nods, rising to her full height, acceptance in her expression.

But when the women step out on to the back path it's not a police car they see, but the community truck, engine idling at the front gate, bright headlamps flooding the driveway. There is a woman already at the wheel, and, as Celine squints to make out if there's anyone else inside, Bramble appears at the rear passenger door, helping a small person into their seat.

'The girls!' Pip screams. 'She's taking the girls!'

She breaks into a run, with Una and Celine following close behind, but it is Seed who takes the lead, sprinting like an athlete over grass and gravel, with that idling truck in her sights.

'No!' she cries into the night, gaining on them fast. '*No*, Bramble!'

Bramble is at the entrance now, struggling to release the lock, and when the gate springs open the driver accelerates at speed – stopping only at the bone-smashing sound of crumpling metal, as Seed's body is thrown to the path.

'Mummy! Where are you going?'

This furious shout comes from Olive, not in the truck as they had feared, but standing at the side of the house, hand in hand with little Beebee, a baffled look on her sleepy face. The passenger gazing out from the back of the truck is not a child, but an old woman.

Fern.

As the flashing blue glow of approaching squad cars lights up the woodland path, Celine knows it's finally all over.

42. CELINE

Two weeks later, Arundel

Sitting on the riverside bench behind Delilah's Arundel home, Celine gazes out over the shimmering water and feels at peace for the first time in weeks.

The champagne is slipping down easily; it's an expensive bottle, carefully selected this morning from Mum's cellar. Celine will only have one glass, so Pip shares the last of it with Una, and together they raise a toast to Delilah, the perpetually absent mother. After the coroner had officially released her body, the cremation and small service had gone ahead today as planned, finally drawing a line under that phase in the Murphy women's lives. Now it's just them, and Celine feels that perhaps these people are all she really needs in her life. A little way along the river path, Olive and Beebee are occupied poking sticks into the bulrushes, giggling at the ducklings that bob and scoot across the water's surface, and once again Celine is struck by her love for them, these curious little girls with so much living ahead.

'I always said those tablets would finish Delilah off,' Pip says, giving the girls a wave. 'She used to knock 'em back like sweets. She was bound to get the dose wrong some day or other.'

'Don't be too harsh on her,' Una replies, patting Pip's leg. 'Your mum wasn't an easy woman, but she had her own demons to deal with. I'm afraid she got used to leaning on the pills to help her through.'

Celine smiles sadly. 'So, tell us again, Una. When Vanessa called to stay with Mum that last time, she wasn't here?'

'Apparently not. According to Harry Glass, he was working on the garden the day your sister called at the house, saying she'd arranged with your mum to visit for a few nights. But when Harry explained that Delilah was away with her boyfriend in Italy Vanessa got quite upset. She told him to forget it, and headed straight off to Two Cross Farm, where she was due a few days later.'

'And the link between Harry Glass and Jem Falmer turned out to be meaningless after all?' Pip says.

'Yep, pure coincidence,' Una replies. 'Both men were local, and they'd attended the same school, but they were never friends, and Harry hadn't seen or heard of Jem since they'd left.'

'I thought you didn't believe in coincidences?' Celine smiles.

Una laughs. 'Well, we can all get it wrong from time to time, can't we?'

For a while Celine sits quietly, her mind travelling the short distance along this very path, to Two Cross Farm. She thinks of the police digging up the compost mounds beside the greenhouse, of the bodies buried there not five years apart: that of Jem Falmer, and of Kathy Hawks, the community doctor, who the forensic team confirmed died of heart failure. And she thinks of Fern, their original leader and the artist behind those magnificent photographs that adorn the walls of Two Cross Farm. She'd seen the self-portrait of Fern among them, taken back in 1976, when she was a strong young American with a bold gaze; with a look that suggested she could take on the world and win.

Only two days ago, Dave Aston had called to tell them the news that seventy-four-year-old Fern had been taken directly to hospital after the events of that final night, critically ill with pneumonia, and that she had passed away in her sleep. Celine is glad that she will escape trial for the killing of Jem Falmer; in fact, she wishes she'd lived just a little longer so that she might shake her by the hand. Whoever Fern Bellamy was, Celine is certain her original vision for her women's community came from a place of goodness.

'Do you think Alex will face charges?' Celine asks Una now. 'Is there a case to bring?'

Alex. It's the name Seed has chosen since deciding to reshape his world as a man, now that he's free of the constraints of his old life at Two Cross Farm. In choosing his own name, he wanted something simple, ungendered, unconnected to his past life and the person he used to be.

'Honestly, I couldn't say,' Una replies. 'The circumstances of his birth are still tying the authorities in knots: he doesn't legally exist, never having been registered as being born, and his role in the various crimes within the walls of Two Cross Farm was as a witness at worst. Dave Aston says he's never come across a case like it in all his years of policing – and I can say the same.'

Pip sighs. 'Dave says that Bramble and Regine are giving nothing away either. Apparently their versions of events have been synchronised down to the tiniest of details – you know they were allowed to return home to Two Cross Farm after just a day of questioning? You'd think they'd be charging them for concealing bodies – Jem's and that Kathy woman, their doctor – at the very least.'

'They had letters,' Una replies. 'A sort of final will filed by every one of the Founding Sisters, except Susan, giving instructions to be followed in the event of their deaths. Apparently, Kathy asked to be buried there, which, while not legal, might serve to get them off the hook to some extent. They're both claiming ignorance of pretty much everything else.'

'Where do you think they were planning to go that night, when they tried to escape in the truck?' Celine asks.

'I don't think they had a plan,' Una replies. 'I think they just realised everything was about to come crashing down around them – and I think they wanted to protect Fern from the repercussions of that fall-out. Poor old thing; she didn't have a clue what was going on at the end.'

Rising from the bench, Celine signals to her nieces with outstretched arms and they run to her, wrapping themselves around her waist with customary enthusiasm.

'Are you going?' Olive asks, her face creasing crossly.

'Only for a while. Don't forget, we'll have all the time in the world when you come down to stay with me in Bournemouth next week.'

Olive nods earnestly. 'It's going to be fun, isn't it, Mummy?'

Pip smiles. 'It's going to be *so* much fun, girls. But Auntie Ceecee had better watch out, hadn't she? Because if we like it too much we might not want to leave.'

Celine disentangles herself from Olive and Beebee and picks up her coat and car keys, hugging Pip and Una in turn. 'I'll see you back at the house in a few hours,' she says, and leaves them looking out over the river. As she reaches the back gate to Belle France, Una calls after her.

'Say hello to Alex for me, will you? Tell him I hope he's on the mend.'

Celine simply gives a thumbs-up and heads towards her camper van.

43. CELINE

Alex is sitting in the upright armchair of his private room at St Richard's Hospital, dressed in a flamboyant Paisley dressing gown and eating from his lap tray, his attention transfixed by the wall-mounted television.

One leg, encased in plaster, is propped up on a plastic foot-stool, a single signature scrawled along its shaft: Celine's scrawl. For a few moments she remains in the corridor, just out of view, watching through the glass window and taking in the difference in Alex, not just in his appearance but in the expression lines of his face. This is only the second visit she's made since the night of the revelations, but, in the short time that has passed, she's witnessed the transformation in him. He's smiling at something on the television, and it occurs to Celine that this stay in hospital may well be providing him with some of his first direct experiences of cultural media in his forty-three-year-old life. As Celine enters the room, Alex looks up and smiles, immediately reaching for the remote control and switching the

324

box off, graciously accepting the flowers and chocolates she's brought with her.

'I didn't know what to get you—' Celine starts to say, but Alex drops the gifts on the bed and extends his hand to draw her near.

'It was your mother's funeral today,' he says softly, as Celine perches on the side of the mattress. 'How was it? How did Pip cope – and you for that matter? These things are so difficult, especially when relationships are other than straightforward.'

Celine sighs, again experiencing that strange sensation that Seed – or rather, Alex – knows her intimately. 'It was fairly weird,' she admits. 'We all cried – well, not Olive and Beebee, of course – but the rest of us, me, Pip and Una, were in floods. Until this horrible moment when the automatic curtain around the coffin got stuck, making this awful grinding noise, and we got a fit of the giggles. The vicar didn't know where to look; it was terrible, really. Thank God there wasn't much of an audience. Delilah would have been mortified.'

Alex covers his smile and pats her hand, and his silence is good-humoured and well-placed.

'So, how about you?' Celine asks, shifting the conversation. 'It's been a fortnight since your accident, but I'm guessing you've still got a lot of things to work out? I don't just mean your injuries. I mean, you must have a lot of things to resolve. Have any of the sisters been to visit you?'

He shakes his head. 'I wrote and told Bramble not to. With the police, and the ongoing investigation – well, I don't want to make things worse for them. My lawyer said it's best if we distance ourselves for the time being, until everything is settled, because we're still not sure if the police plan to charge me with conspiring to pervert the course of justice.' He retrieves a counselling information leaflet from his bedside table, and hands it to Celine. 'They've assigned a social worker to me, you know?

Off the record, she's advised me to answer "no comment" on all counts, whether it's an official interview or not.'

'Sounds like good advice to me,' Celine replies. She reaches into her rucksack and pulls out a charity shop bag, handing it to Alex. 'And how's the leg? I managed to pick up a couple of pairs of jeans while I was in town – I thought you might want something a little bit less, um, *tunicky* for when you get out of here.'

Alex unwraps the jeans and holds them up, a pleased smile forming on his face. 'They're perfect,' he says, eyes filling with tears. 'You're a true friend, Celine.'

Celine feels her face flushing, and she knows she is pleased to hear Alex's words, that she wants them to be friends – that she doesn't want this to end here. 'How are you feeling, since the news about Fern, Alex? You must be deeply upset to lose her; you'd known her since you were tiny.'

A single tear spills over and trails down Alex's face. 'I'm fine, really. I just wish I could be there for my fellow sisters, to comfort them in it. Bramble and Regine in particular.' He hesitates a moment, before asking, 'Celine, do you know how the police worked out the truth about me in the end? Do you know what tipped them off?'

She nods. 'It was a former sister from Two Cross Farm, a woman called Sandy. Do you remember that name?'

Alex appears to think for a moment. 'Vaguely, though we had so many women pass through our doors over the years.'

'Well, she remembered you. DI Aston said she'd read some of those recent news articles, the ones accusing you of being a cult leader, and she came forward to make a statement claiming she'd met you as a child.'

Alex listens, rapt.

'She claimed there had been some incident with spilled inks in the art studio, which prompted her to strip you out of your dirty

326

clothes, revealing that you weren't the little girl the Founding Sisters presented you as, but, rather, a boy. Apparently, when this Sandy woman threatened to tell the others, she was forcibly ejected from the community. At first, DI Aston wasn't sure if Sandy was just some crank – but when a second caller came through just hours later, making similar claims – saying she'd caught sight of you undressing for the shower – Dave couldn't ignore it.'

Alex nods, taking it all in. 'Fern had this rule: *banishment is final* – the kind of threat Sandy was making wouldn't have gone down well at all. Fern was fiercely protective of all the women in the community, but especially of me.'

Celine stares at his face a moment or two, and marvels at the dramatic difference in Alex's appearance now that he's free of his scarves and robes, the shroud of Seed having been stripped away. 'Alex, the police can't find any record of you. None whatsoever. No birth certificate, no passport, no National Insurance number, no previous address.'

He stares back at her as though she's missed some great big piece of the puzzle. 'Well, they wouldn't,' he replies, as though it's obvious.

'So, when did you first arrive at Two Cross Farm?' she asks. 'You said you were brought up there, but I'm confused, I suppose, because I've seen the Code of Conduct, and it's very clear on the rules about children.'

Alex nods slowly. 'I arrived in 1977, some months after Two Cross Farm first opened its doors to women in need. Fern had a clear vision that there must be six Founding Sisters, and, of those, the sixth would be an infant – "unsullied by the world", she said – a future leader of women. I was that sixth sister.'

'That bit I understand,' Celine replies, 'but why adopt *you* – a male – when it was a sister they wanted?'

Alex blinks back at her. 'They didn't adopt me, Celine. I was born at Two Cross Farm.'

Celine is shocked into silence.

'Celine?' Alex says. 'Don't you see? Fern was my mother. At least, she was the one who gave birth to me. She didn't know it then, but she was already pregnant at the very first meeting the five ever had – before Two Cross Farm even opened its doors.'

'Did the other sisters know this?'

'The Founding Sisters all knew, eventually, and a few of the early residents who came and went at the start. But for the others who came later I was simply already there. They had no cause to suspect I was Fern's, because it was Bramble and the others who raised me, really.'

'Fern rejected you?'

'Not exactly,' Alex replies, his creased brow showing his struggle to find the right words. 'But it was one of the Codes: *All who dwell here must first shed their limpets.* Fern brought me into the world, but she handed me over to the community from the outset. At Two Cross Farm, I was everyone's child. And no one's.'

'And your father?' Celine asks after a pause.

Alex shakes his head. 'Not a clue. No one knows, and, from what little Bramble has shared with me, that included Fern. Apparently, he was just some guy she met at her exhibition in London, right before they set up the commune. It was a brief encounter, and she never saw him again.'

Just like her own story, Celine thinks. A brief encounter; a fleeting collision of bodies and DNA, and here she and Alex are, alive in the world. Exhaustion washes over her, and she flops back against the pillows of the bed, allowing Alex's fingers to lace gently with hers. They sit like that for long minutes, she laid out on the bed like a woman struck, he upright and dignified in

328

his hospital chair, the quiet between them like some unspoken communion. They've both been robbed of so much; they've both missed out on great chunks of childhood and normality, and Celine wonders for the very first time if there might possibly be, other than Pip, this one other person who feels the world something like she does.

'You know, when this is all over, Alex, I'd like you to come and visit me in Bournemouth for a while. I mean it. Will you come? Promise me you won't just leave here and be alone?'

She feels the increasing pressure of Alex's hand in hers, and, when she turns her head in his direction to see the peace in his smiling face, she knows his answer is yes.

44. BRAMBLE

Present day, Two Cross Farm

Regine massages chamomile oil into her arthritic knuckles, and waits for me on the office sofa as I finish off my call to DI Aston.

'As you know, following your statement, the coroner has confirmed that Robyn Siegle's broken neck is entirely consistent with an accidental fall,' he says. 'Seed – or rather, Alex – has provided a separate statement which appears to corroborate your version of events. I just want to confirm that you still maintain that Fern Bellamy acted alone in moving Robyn's body to the riverside, and that no other person was involved?'

'That's right,' I reply, picking up a framed photograph of the vibrant young Fern that now sits on the desk before me, and recalling how frail she already was by the time Robyn died. She couldn't have moved a kitten by then. 'She acted alone, detective. No one else had any knowledge of it.'

'And Vanessa Murphy. We're satisfied that she was murdered by Jem Falmer in 2005, but again, the removal of her body – you're saying that was Fern too?'

'It was. Her alone.'

It gives me no pleasure to sully Fern's name in this way, but Regine and I stand shoulder to shoulder in our bid to protect the living; to protect the current and future community at Two Cross Farm.

'Hmm,' he says, and, while I hear in his tone that he's not at all convinced, he's a good man, and has already hinted that it's in nobody's interest to chase after those of us on the sidelines of these more serious crimes. We'll just have to wait and see how the Crown Prosecution Service chooses to proceed with the charge of failure to report a crime, but our legal advisor tells me there are loopholes we can take advantage of.

'I've been going over your formal statements,' DI Aston continues, 'and you're still willing to stand up in a court of law and testify that it was Fern who landed the fatal blow against Jem Falmer? You and Regine are both prepared to name Fern?'

'We are,' I reply. 'We both want this whole thing cleared up as soon as possible, for everyone's sake. It's what happened, detective, and we have nothing to hide.'

As I return the phone to its cradle, I'm transported to that final moment in our moonlit garden in 2005, when Seed staggered to her feet and took the spade from Fern's hands, her expression shifting to rage as that monster squeezed the life from Vanessa's throat. I can see the scene today as clearly as then; I feel the gentle swoop of our barn owl as it soared overhead, and I hear the whoosh of that spade as Seed swung it, powerful and wide, felling Falmer with a dense and final thud. Seed had collapsed again then, from her own injuries, and, when she finally came round, Fern managed to convince her it was *she* who'd killed Jem, that Seed was confused about the order of events and had merely witnessed it. Once Falmer's body was disposed of, that night had never been spoken of again. When it came down to it,

Fern had acted as any good mother would: she had done what she could to take away her child's pain.

I gaze at Fern's photograph for a few moments longer, and, as though she is reading my mind, Regine claps her hands to snap me back. 'Don't beat yourself up, honey. We don't call 'em lies if they serve to protect. If it was me who kicked the bucket, you'd have my blessing to pin anything on me. You'd do the same, Bramble, wouldn't ya?'

And I know, without hesitation, that I would. I'd do anything for my fellow sisters. Even for Regine, the mouthy old dame.

'Good,' she says, waving a dismissive hand towards the file on the desk in front of me. 'Let's move on. It's what Fern would have wanted.'

The folder before me is labelled 'Letters of Application', and I open it up, pushing my spectacles up my nose. 'We have a few vacancies to fill if we're to get back up to thirty-three,' I say, taking a letter from the top.

Regine nods sagely. 'We'd better get on with it, then.'

And of course, she's right. There's women's work to be done.

ACKNOWLEDGEMENTS

My latest novel is a story concerned with the significance of numbers, and the power and spirit of women. And so, it seems fitting, in the year that I turn fifty, that I extend thanks to every one of the wise women who have helped to shape my life so far. I won't name individuals for fear of omitting others, but I'm confident you know who you are. You are my friends, family, team-mates and cheerleaders; you are near and far; you are recent and long ago. We have laughed together, cried together, stayed up late deciphering the world together. You've influenced my choices and encouraged my endeavours, and you are, every one of you, a blessing. Power to you all, sisters. Love to you all.

Read on for a sample from
Beautiful Liars by Isabel Ashdown...

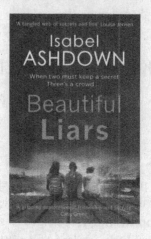

A Death

It wasn't my fault. I can see that now, through adult eyes and with the hindsight of rational thinking. Of course, for many years I wondered if I'd misremembered the details of that day, the true events having changed shape beneath the various and consoling accounts of my parents, of the emergency officers, of the witnesses on the rocky path below. I recall certain snatches so sharply – like the way the mountain rescue man's beard grew more ginger towards the middle of his face, and his soft tone when he said, 'Hello, mate,' offering me a solid hand to shake. Hello, mate. I never forgot that. But there are other things I can't remember at all, such as what we'd been doing in the week leading up to the accident, or where we'd been staying, or where we went directly afterwards. How interesting it is, the way the mind works, the way it recalibrates difficult experiences, bestowing upon them a storybook quality so that we might shut the pages when it suits us and place them safely on the highest shelf. I was just seven, and so naturally I followed the lead of my mother and father, torn as they were between despair for their lost child and protection of the one who still remained: the one left standing on the misty mountain ledge of Kinder Scout, looking down.

I can see the scene now, if I allow my thoughts to return to that remote place in my memory. I watch myself as though from a great distance: small and plump, black hair slicked against my forehead by the damp drizzle of the high mountain air. And there are my parents, dressed head-to-toe in their identical hiking gear : Mum, thin and earnest, startle-eyed ; and Dad, confused, his finger pushing his spectacles up his florid nose as he interprets my gesture and breaks into a heavy-footed run. Their alarmed expressions are frozen in time. There is horror as they register that I now stand alone, no younger child to be seen; that I'm pointing towards the precipitous edge, my eyes squinting hard as I try to shed tears. There are no other walkers on this stretch of path, no one to say what really happened when my brother departed the cliff edge, but the sharp cries of distress from the winding path far below suggest that there are witnesses to his arrival further down.

It wasn't your fault, it wasn't your fault, it wasn't your fault.

This was the refrain of my slow-eyed mother in the weeks that followed, while she tried her best to absolve me, to put one foot in front of the other, to grasp at some semblance of normality. 'It wasn't your fault,' she'd tell me at night-time as she tucked the duvet snugly around my shoulders, our eyes never straying to the now-empty bed inhabiting the nook on the opposite side of my tiny childhood room. 'It was just a terrible accident.' But, as I look back now, I think perhaps I can hear the grain of uncertainty in her tone, the little tremor betraying the questions she will never voice. *Did you do it, sweetheart? Did you push my baby from the path? Was it just an accident? Was it?*

And, if I could speak with my mother now, what would I say in return? If I track further back into that same memory, to just a few seconds earlier, the truth is there for me alone to see. Now at the cliff edge I see two children. They're not identical in size and stature, but they're both dressed in bright blue anoraks to match their parents, the smaller with his hood tightly fastened beneath a chubby chin, the bigger one, hood down, oblivious to the sting of the icy rain. 'Mine!' the smaller one says, unsuccessfully snatching at a sherbet lemon held loosely between the older child's dripping fingers. This goes on for a while, and on reflection I think that perhaps the sweet *did* belong to the younger child, because eventually it is snatched away and I recall the sense that it wasn't mine to covet in the first place. But that is not the point, because it wasn't the taking of the sweet that was so wrong but the boastful, taunting manner of it. '*No !* ' is the cry I hear, and I know it comes from me because even now I feel the rage rear up inside me as that hooded child makes a great pouting show of shedding the wrapper and popping the yellow lozenge into its selfish hole of a mouth, its bragging form swaying in a small victory dance at the slippery cliff edge. The tremor of my cry is still vibrating in my ears as I bring the weight of my balled fist into the soft dough of that child's cheek and see the sherbet lemon shoot from between rosy lips like a bullet. '*No!*' I shout again, and this time the sound seems to come from far, far away. Seconds later, he's gone, and I know he's plummeting, falling past the heather-cloaked rocks and

336

snaggly outcrops that make up this great mountainous piece of land. I know it is a death drop; I know it is a long way down. I can't say I remember pushing him – but neither can I remember *not* pushing him.

So, you see, I'm not to blame at all. From what I recall of that other child – my brother – he was a snatcher, a tittletattle, a cry-baby, a provoker. Even if I did do it, there's not a person on earth who would think I was culpable.

I was *seven*, for God's sake.

CREDITS

Trapeze would like to thank everyone at Orion who worked on the publication of *33 Women*.

Agent
Kate Shaw

Editor
Phoebe Morgan
Sam Eades

Copy-editor
Linda McQueen

Proofreader
Linda Joyce

Editorial Management
Sarah Fortune
Charlie Panayiotou
Jane Hughes
Alice Davis
Claire Boyle

Audio
Paul Stark
Amber Bates

Contracts
Anne Goddard
Paul Bulos
Jake Alderson

Design
Debbie Holmes
Lucie Stericker
Joanna Ridley
Nick May
Clare Sivell
Helen Ewing

Finance
Jennifer Muchan

Jasdip Nandra
Rabale Mustafa
Elizabeth Beaumont
Sue Baker
Tom Costello

Marketing
Lucy Cameron

Production
Claire Keep
Fiona McIntosh

Publicity
Alex Layt

Sales
Laura Fletcher
Victoria Laws
Esther Waters
Lucy Brem
Frances Doyle
Ben Goddard
Georgina Cutler
Jack Hallam
Ellie Kyrke-Smith
Inês Figuiera
Barbara Ronan
Andrew Hally
Dominic Smith

Deborah Deyong
Lauren Buck
Maggy Park
Linda McGregor
Sinead White
Jemimah James
Rachel Jones
Jack Dennison
Nigel Andrews
Ian Williamson
Julia Benson
Declan Kyle
Robert Mackenzie
Sinead White
Imogen Clarke
Megan Smith
Charlotte Clay
Rebecca Cobbold

Operations
Jo Jacobs
Sharon Willis
Lisa Pryde

Rights
Susan Howe
Richard King
Krystyna Kujawinska
Jessica Purdue
Louise Henderson

Help us make the next generation of readers

We – both author and publisher – hope you enjoyed this book.
We believe that you can become a reader at any time in your life,
but we'd love your help to give the next generation a head start.

Did you know that 9 per cent of children don't have a book of
their own in their home, rising to 13 per cent in disadvantaged
families*? We'd like to try to change that by asking you to
consider the role you could play in helping to build readers
of the future.

We'd love you to think of sharing, borrowing, reading, buying
or talking about a book with a child in your life and spreading
the love of reading. We want to make sure the next generation
continue to have access to books, wherever they come from.

And if you would like to consider donating to charities
that help fund literacy projects, find out more at
www.literacytrust.org.uk and **www.booktrust.org.uk**.

THANK YOU

*As reported by the National Literacy Trust